Exterminators

When Dreams Become Reality
Thank you for all the support!

Chapter One – Files

Carl rubbed his hands together and placed them on the files named "Case 224". He felt a knot begin to twist in his stomach as if he was about to get some bad news from his doctor. His eyes darted from side to side waiting for someone. He gritted his teeth together getting weary of waiting for the woman he had an appointment with.

Carl looked around this empty, small house he was so used to. It was built over fifteen years ago. It was chipped all around; the walls looked old and moldy. Even the chairs, the newest things in the place, creaked already. It had an ugly brownish paint over the original black color. The house still had the new paint smell even though it was done over three years ago. For a joke every month one of his friends would buy an air freshener with the paint smell to annoy Carl. Carl then would slash the tires of whoever did that. Well into his thirties, Carl would never let someone get the upper hand on him. Even in a prank.

The sun's ray glared through the open windows. However, not a single gust of wind came through. The room stayed quiet and humid. It had been a few years since Carl had gotten back to his work and he began to miss it. The room he could live without, the work he couldn't. He bit his lip and began tapping his foot getting annoyed. He checked his watch, 5:45 it read. "Where the hell is she?" he muttered under his breath. As he spoke he heard the door creak open.

Carl's head rose as he studied his old friend's face. She had a stern look on her, almost as if she was mad that he was early. He smiled at her and rose from his chair. "Ross, it's always nice to see you," he said respectfully.

She went over to him, keeping her blank face on. Once close enough she smiled and hugged him tightly. "You big ass, don't ever leave like that again," she said with her voice cracking. For a second he thought he heard her let out a small cry but she stepped back, wiped her face, and stood looking at him. "Well you haven't changed much. Then again you never looked that good in the first place," she said with a wink.

"Yeah, you don't look too bad yourself now days," he replied, grinning back at her. As they sat down Carl felt as if the weight of the world was finally lifted off his shoulders. "Sorry about the leave but I needed some time. Now that I'm back I'd really like to help though." She nodded for him to continue. "So I read over the files you gave me. Out of the thirty I picked these four." He passed the four folders out of the pile to Ross.

She picked up the first one and studied the name on the top. It spelled out *Nick Rambo.*

"I'd really love to just stay in one place for more than four months," Nick thought as he pushed a few strands of his jet black hair out of his eyes. He shifted the box from the back of the truck onto the ground and took a breather. He looked up to the orange sky, wondering if this was the final resting stop; his mind drifting back to his last home.

It wasn't as if New York was far from Washington but it was a pain to move every few months. Nick had finally met some great friends in Washington and had begun to really settle in. Then by the fourth month his dad was able to move his operation to New York, with a nice pay raise. Nick just wanted the chance to settle down in one place.

"Come on…what can you possibly be looking at?" his father screamed from the car and Nick quickly looked back down at his father. "Well?" his father asked impatiently. His father was a strict man, but that didn't mean he didn't care about his only son. He wasn't the best father in the world by a long shot but he provided for his son the best he could while being a single parent. He stayed healthy and fit to ensure Nick would have his father around for a long time. Nick's father also tried his best to juggle his construction business, watching the occasional football or baseball games with Nick and also keeping his Washington construction division up to par. It was a hectic life but one he got used to very quickly.

"Sorry pops," said Nick as he quickly picked up the box from the street and began walking over to the new house. They had just moved to Brooklyn, since his Dad's company reopened like they said they would back in 2009 and his dad was welcomed back. Though he had just barely gotten use to Washington, Nick figured he could adapt to the change here rather quickly. The city-like mentality seems to be similar in every place from California to Florida, Washington and now New York. Nick grew up knowing that he would probably only be around a few months. No reason to ever get too attached to people.

After several minutes of moving the boxes inside the house, both men sat on the porch. His dad patted him on the back and gave him a smile. "I'm proud of you son. You're strong like your father." His father gave a little muscle motion with his arm. "You even got your fathers good looks." Nick let out a small laugh and his father laughed with him. "I know you hate to move, but we have to. I hate leaving and going to a whole new place too but if we want money we have to make sacrifices," his father said looking up and closing his eyes. "You know your mother was just like you."

Nick groaned and looked away.

"She'd just sit and pout all day. Like it was the worst thing in the world. I don't love moving either but it's like a fresh start. No one knows you here. No one has a pre-judgmental attitude towards you. So it can be a lot of fun." He nudged his son. "Come on now, your mom wouldn't want to see you like this." He smiled at Nick, nudging him again.

Nick didn't like hearing about his mother so he quickly jumped up to his feet. "Listen, it's late. I'm a bit tired from driving. I'm going to go lie down," Nick said and before his father could respond, he ran into the house. His father shook his head and looked back towards the sky, wondering what to do.

Carl sat there quietly as Ross read the file on Nick. After a few minutes she looked up to Carl almost confused. "The boy moves every few months. Is it wise to bring him into the organization if he does so?" she asked.

"Point taken, but I know for a fact this company's work will be here for a minimal of five years. Meaning, even if he moves after that, the boy would be able to make his own living here." Carl seemed to have satisfied her as she nodded and placed the file to the side.

"You know I'm just here to check over these files. In the end it's ultimately up to you," she told him. Carl nodded as she began to pick up the next file.

"It's true it may be up to me. However, I'd like to hear some advice from my best friend. I mean you are still the one I trust the most with my ideas," he replied smiling. She opened the next file up. The name on it was *Marshall Roman.*

"Stop being an idiot and pass the ball!" Marshall screamed out. He was running over to his little brother who kept on laughing while holding the green ball. His brother ran down the alley, laughing the whole way. Marshall followed him until his hat got caught in a clothing line and flipped off. His brown hair came down and some of it covered his eyes. He growled as he snatched up his hat, fixed his hair, and placed it back on his head. "Need to get a haircut," he muttered under his breath as he slowly walked down the alley towards his brother.

Marshall finally reached his brother, who was still laughing, and pulled him close. He grabbed the ball and pushed his brother into the side of the building. Marshall's brother went to push him back but Marshall moved out of the way and his brother almost tripped. "Come on! It was my ball first," yelled Matt but Marshall just kept walking now, slapping the ball in the air. Matt was six years younger than his brother. He had just turned eleven and got the ball as a gift for his birthday. Marshall loved to steal his gifts just to annoy him.

"I don't care, just shut up," shouted Marshall. For a second

Marshall thought his brother was going to cry but instead yelled and cursed at his brother while running back towards home. Marshall just kept smacking the little ball in the air and catching it. He watched as his brother ran across the street and busted into their house screaming. He smiled, thinking back to when he was Matt's age. How much he was just like his brother at that age.

After slowly walking to his house he entered and threw the ball on the counter. He walked into his bedroom and slammed his door. Closing his eyes he let himself fall onto his bed backwards. He hadn't been feeling well lately and knew tomorrow wasn't going to help. Moaning as he rolled over and grabbed his T.V. remote he switched it on.

Despite feeling sick he was kind of happy school was starting in two days. It's not that he was nerd or geek but he just wanted to go back and be with his friends. Most had jobs while others were on vacation. He spent his whole summer with his younger brother playing video games or sports. He heard a knock on the door and screamed, "Yeah!?" Then his mother entered. She was well into her thirties but she looked like she was in her 20's with her beautiful blue eyes and brownish hair.

"Honey, dinner is ready," she said and he turned over to look at her. "Come on, you don't even eat with us anymore."

"Sorry I'm not in the mood. I still don't feel well." His mother was about to protest but he spoke first. "Just leave, okay!?" She left quickly. He groaned and put his head back the way it was to watch his T.V. program. It's not that he didn't like sitting at the table with his family but he felt tired. Boredom was taking over and he couldn't wait much longer to get back to school.

"Seems like this one is a very anxious one. From what they can bring up he tries to impress a lot of people with his big mouth. I'm sure he'll get along with the rest of the kids." Ross looked to Carl who nodded.

"It's true the boy has a way of showing everyone he's boss

but isn't that what we need? An ambitious kid who doesn't mind sticking up for himself every once in a while?" he said with a small grin. She shook her head with a smile and began to pick up the next file.

"You have a knack for picking up the tough ones don't you?" She looked down at the next file. It read, *Fred Parrish.*

"Yeah, you could go to hell too!" yelled Fred through the headset he wore. He clicked the buttons in quick sequences attacking whoever was against him in the game. He groaned, yelled, cursed, and slammed his fist into the couch when he was mad. "Get it! Get it! Go now!" he roared into the Mic.

"Yeah, that's what I'm talking about!" he shouted as the results of his game came up. "I'm just too good for this game! All right guys, I got to go, later," he said and took off his headset. His phone rang so he picked it up. "Yes, I know…eight? Yeah that's fine. I'll be there," he said then hung up the phone. He zipped up his black hoodie. He wore as much black as possible. In school kids teased him and such, calling him a Goth. Although the Goth group in his school wasn't large he still tried to fit in. He felt like a loner, so he stuck to dressing like one. Somehow, even without the approval of everyone, he felt proud to stand out.

He went into the kitchen and grabbed a soda then went back to watch some T.V. After a few moments of watching another reality show, he grabbed his phone, dialing in his friend's number.

"Hello, is John there?"

"Yes, hold please."

After a few seconds of Fred picking his nose his friend came on.

"Yeah?"

"Yo, John! Whatcha doing today?"

"Going to work later, why?"

"I don't know; thought we could chill, guess not."

"Nah man sorry, maybe tomorrow. Plus school starts Monday so we could chill after."

"Just got to remind me of school huh?'

"Yeah well, you know."

They both laughed and his friend continued to talk.

"Well, I got to go and get ready for work. I'll call you when I get home."   "All right, later."

"Later."

He snapped his phone shut and threw himself on his bed looking right at the empty white ceiling. He hated school and now in less than three days he would be going back to it. He turned back to the T.V. and began watching more reality shows with the hope of forgetting his own reality. After a while he fell asleep, dreaming of ways to win in his video games.

There sat the last boy in the files, named Peter. He sat at his computer, typing away at the keyboard. Skinny he was, weighing barely 120 pounds. He had bushy brown hair and dark black eyes. He was in most of the science fairs, winning ninety percent of the time. He was, as they call it at school, a part of the "Geek squad" or "Nerdy Losers", either one was just as bad. He always found it funny though. Seeing as he hung out with no one at school.

He didn't care much about it though; as long as he passed he knew he had a better life coming than the ones who couldn't even conjure up a C grade average. He always strives to be the best. He quickly rubbed his hair and began typing on the keyboard even quicker. After a short while, he stopped and got up from his desk trudging into the kitchen to grab a soda.

Once back in his room he sat back down and began to read a new book he got from his mother. He was a quiet kid, no friends, yet that's the way he wanted it, but never had a girlfriend of any sort. He stayed at home most of the time. He was content spending his time on the computer or watching T.V. or even working on his projects. He wore regular clothes; normal blue tee-shirt and normal jeans for which kids also made fun of him.

He heard a sound on his computer and quickly closed his book. Looking directly at his twenty-two inch screen, he smiled and began to type fast as he could, writing all sorts of messages.

Then he jumped as his door slammed open and a little girl walked in, his sister, Karin.

"Hey, Mom said dinners in a few minutes," she said with no emotion whatsoever then she slammed the door closed. He frowned and shook his head in disapproval.

"I gotta get a lock," he muttered to himself as he turned back to his computer typing away. After a few minutes of typing he left his room and sat down next to his mother, father, and little sister.

A few minutes into eating some of his macaroni, his mother began to speak. "Well, you two are going back to school on Monday, right?" Both nodded and she smiled. "Good! Peter, you will take your sister to school, right?" She asked nicely. It was more like a command though.

"What, why?" He asked surprised. He didn't really care though. It was just another thing to do.

"Cause your mother said so!" His father roared. Already slightly buzzed from the drink he was having.

"Fine," Peter said without another fight. He didn't want to start anything with his father tonight. Most nights he kept to himself while his father became drunk and yelled at his mother. He felt no sympathy for her. He actually felt nothing for either one. He detached himself from the world around him. He just wanted to get by and nothing more.

"Is that them?" the woman sitting down asked. She was looking at the four boys and their profiles. "What makes you say they can do the job?" she inquired looking up, no hope in her brown eyes.

"I see them as different. Obviously reading about them you can agree to that. They each have their own weaknesses; however, together they may make one of the strongest units out there. They can cover each other's weakness and use their strengths together. I believe that those four will do the jobs we give them," said Carl. "Please Ross. I need this chance. I can fix the mistakes I did last time."

Ross raised her hand. "Stop. I don't need you going back to that again. You said you cleared your head. You said you were ready to handle a new unit. I can't have you bringing up past mistakes if you plan on handling these four boys' lives." She stopped for a moment. "Carl, are you sure you're ready?" she asked, sadness ringing in her voice.

"Yeah. I'm ready. I won't let you down. I won't let these boys down. I'll be there for each of them. I know I can do this. So, just give me this chance." Carl stood up. "I know it's scary to trust someone who ran from his past. Who hasn't always been there, being the protector I was supposed to be. The one who failed to finish what he was supposed to finish. I stand here today though to prove I can do this. I can raise these boys to be the warriors this organization needs." He watched her, hoping to see a glimmer of hope in her eyes.

Ross stood up. She watched Carl, his face filled with conviction. "Don't let me down. I know you can do this. I believe in you. I give you permission to bring them in. Just..." she stopped and looked out the window. The sun was almost completely gone. The darkness began to fill the room. "Please keep a close eye on them. They are now your responsibility." She smiled at him. "All right, enough business talk I gotta get back down there. Good luck friend, train those kids to their fullest potential.

She walked to the closet, opened it, and walked inside. A bright light came from the closet and Carl listened as the sounds of the tubes began to go off. Just a few moments later the light disappeared and Carl was left alone in the dark room. He placed his hands on the files. "This is it. My chance to make things right." He smiled at the names. The Exterminators were finally chosen.

Chapter 2 – The Letter

"All right Nick I'm off. Got to keep an eye on the new guys at the apartment. Knowing them they'll build a bathroom in the living room," Nick's father joked. He was searching for his car keys again. Nick rolled his eyes as he picked up the newspaper revealing the keys. "Hey Nick, you've seen my keys?"

"Heads up," Nick called out and threw the keys towards his father. His father caught them with ease. His old baseball training came in handy. He nodded for thanks as he quickly took out his wallet and threw a twenty on the table. "Food for later." He ran out the door before Nick could even respond.

Nick got up and grabbed the twenty lifting it to the light. After checking to make sure it was real he shoved the money into his pocket, resuming his breakfast. The door rang and he looked towards it with no emotion. "I bet anything he forgot his underwear," Nick muttered while walking to the door. He opened it and saw no one. Just a gust of wind hitting him while some kids were on the street playing. He closed it, thinking it was a prank. As he began to turn away he caught a glimpse of a letter on the floor.

He snatched it up, went inside, and sat down. He stared at it in confusion. The mail already came earlier today. He knew it wasn't from his friends for two reasons; they didn't know where he lived yet and they would never take the time to sit down to write a letter. It was addressed to him though. He quickly tore it open. Getting intrigued by what it could be or whom it was from. His excitement was short-lived as he studied this typed note.

Good Morning, young Nick Rambo.

This message is both an invitation as well as directions on how to get to your new destination if you choose to accept. You should arrive at the place around five PM. Please do not be later than five fifteen. This message was sent by me, Carl, and I choose to give you this because it can be a new future for you. It's quite simple. You should come, but if you choose not to. that is fine. You will soon forget about this, in that case.

You will report to the corner of 73rd Street and 3rd Avenue. On this corner you shall see a little white house. Stand at the entrance of the house 'till you are introduced to three other boys. Have a good day, sir. This message is no longer needed.

Nick shook his head trying to understand the meaning of the letter. "Damn stalkers," he told himself as he threw the letter onto the desk. Before it made contact with anything it blew into a little fire and fell to the ground in ashes. Nick slowly moved towards it, tilting his head, not sure of what to think. He backed away again and went for his shoes. At first he dismissed the letter for some crazy stalker guy. However, the letter just blew up into ash right after he finished reading it. He wasn't about to miss out on whoever or whatever sent him the letter.

"Whoa," yelped Peter as the letter was destroyed. He looked at the ashes and touched them. It wasn't hot at all. It was just ashes of the letter lying there, cold.

He jumped as the phone ringer went off. He hurried towards his living room where the phone was. "Hello," he answered quickly. He felt on edge after receiving the odd letter.

"Honey, are you okay?" a soft voice came through the phone. It was his mother who now sounded worried.

"Yeah, I'm fine." He thought about telling her the events that just occurred, but he decided against it. She would just ask again later anyway.

"Have you been running around the house again thinking you're a super hero?" Peter almost hung up the phone at the insult from his mother. She gave a couple of chuckles. "I'm only kidding around. I'll be home in time for dinner, so don't spoil your appetite!"

"No problem, Mom. I don't like to eat much anyway." He looked at the ashes wanting to find out about this place he read on the letter.

"Yeah, well, you should. Your body fat is below requirements for your age and height." Peter glanced at his arms. He never had a problem with his body till his mom brought it up. He really didn't care much though. Just like everything else in his life it was just another thing.

"Okay Mom, I have to go now," he replied trying to speed up the conversation. "Love you, bye," he said quickly and received the same answer from his mother before hanging up.

The clock showed 3:45. "*If I leave in a few minutes, I can probably be there with plenty of time left. Scope out the place. See who else was going to show up,*" Peter thought to himself. He hurried to his room to grab his sneakers, ready for the mystery to unfold.

Marshall was lacing his shoes when his brother came in and jumped onto the end of his bed. "Matt, I'm busy, so go play with your Barbie doll or something." Matt punched his brother in the arm as a response but didn't budge from the bed. "Seriously - leave. If you don't I'll pound your face in."

"I'm not a girl and I don't play with Barbie Dolls! So why did you say I play with them, butt wiper!" Matt liked to call his brother names even if they weren't always the right way. Marshall liked it when he did. It gave him more reasons to punch his little brother. Marshall grabbed Matt and threw him to the floor. He then proceeded to push his foot into Matt's back so he couldn't move. "I give! I give," Matt shouted, trying his best to get out from under the mighty older brother's Foot of Doom.

"If you give in then be quiet! I have to get going now. So you stay here and I'll be back in about an hour, okay?" Matt just moaned at the question. Marshall let go of his brother and stood up straight. He proceeded to open his bedroom door slowly before exiting the room. "Just do me this one favor and stay here. Don't go outside. Don't run over to the next house and scare the dog. Just sit in this house till I get back," he said before shutting the door closed.

A cold gust of wind hit him. Marshall let the coldness flow through his body. It felt different. It wasn't too cold, just enough to provoke Marshall to walk at a faster pace. He passed by a bunch of stores, but it was Sunday so most of them were closed. Kids were at home getting ready for a new school year while parents were returning home early to help them. It was another dreaded school year for the kid with a C minus grade average. "If the school caught on fire it wouldn't be the worst thing in the world," he said smiling as he walked even faster to get to the destination on the letter.

He stopped as he looked down the street. He saw no one but the big empty road ahead of him. "Whoa…spooky," he said to himself as he put on his normal grin. He walked down the block to see the others mentioned in the letter but no one was there. The letter said there would be three others. Marshall gave a quick glance back and forth but saw no one. "No freaking way am I first. I'm never first. I don't even want to be first. I look like an idiot, don't I?" he shouted as he looked to the ground.

He rested on the steps of the house and waited for the other guests to arrive. He wasted time by looking at his cell phone and text messaging his friends, which weren't really his friends outside of school. In school they seemed to be friendly enough; talking about video games, girls, and sports. Outside of school was a different story. No one ever called to hang out with him or play a game or two of football. Nothing. It was like he only existed to them inside of school.

After a few short minutes, Marshall became bored and stood up again. He kept looking up and down the blocks. He began to get irritated. "What the hell!? I knew this was a stupid idea." He focused on the house but the windows were too dark to see anything. He shrugged. "Waste of my life," he muttered as he turned away from the house. Before he could take another step someone was in front of him.

"What are you doing here?"

After getting the weird letter, Fred decided to go on this crazy hoax. He started walking towards his destination. From what he read, it could only be a joke, but he still didn't get the whole burning paper thing out of his mind. He thought about telling the cops but then what proof would he have? The ashes could have been from anything. Not to mention that they were now ashes, what good would they be in an investigation? Finger prints would be impossible to gather from them. The whole idea made Fred feel uneasy but as long as there would be three others joining him it wouldn't be so bad... At least that's the thought he tried to console himself with until he realized that there might not be three other people there. He was just going off what the letter said. "This is how kids get abducted, isn't it?" he mumbled to himself.

He took a break to get a soda. After finishing it, he continued on his walk. It had been one long day, and since school started tomorrow he wasn't really up to this whole joke. School was one of the most annoying things to Fred. Ever since he started high school kids have treated him like he was a freak. Even before changing his style of clothing to a more Gothic look. He just wanted to fit in, but no one wanted to be friends with the chubby guy who plays video games and has never even been kissed.

He rubbed his eyes and looked forward, walking until he reached the block the address the letter stated. He slowly made his way down the block. He still wanted to be cautious just in case someone wanted to jump out and kidnap him. He also felt out of breath. Which was largely due to being out of shape. He was almost at the house now and saw someone standing near it.

Fred stopped and immediately noticed who it was. Marshall took a step towards Fred and spoke. "Why the hell are you here?" Marshall and Fred use to be the best of friends. Hanging out after school; having sleep overs when they were kids. They played video games all the time together and told each other their secrets. Then in 8th grade things changed. Marshall wanted to hang out less and less with Fred. Fred confronted him about it and it led to a huge fight. Things were never the same after that.

"I'm here on business. Why are you here?" asked Marshall. He almost seemed kind of annoyed Fred was even there. Marshall and Fred couldn't stand each other. They trusted each other even less.

"I'm here because of business as well," replied Fred as he walked right past Marshall towards the house. Marshall took a look at his old friend and spat at the ground. Marshall was getting ready to leave before, but now he had to stay. Seeing his old friend sparked some heated emotion he had never let go of. Once both of them reached the steps, Nick came up from behind, wiping his sweaty forehead.

"So, you're the other people the letter mentioned, I'm guessing?" Nick spoke and the boys nodded. "Well, this is weird, isn't it? Especially seeing as I just moved here. I didn't even know someone knew me from here." Marshall looked at him and laughed. "Is something funny?" asked Nick who was clueless as to why Marshall was laughing at what he said.

"Oh nothing, just watch out here," replied Marshall, who was trying to act tough. Fred rolled his eyes and walked towards Nick. He put his hand out for a handshake and Nick smiled as he obliged.

"Hey guys wait for me," shouted Peter, who was only across the street now. "You're the other people that are supposed to be here?" he asked once he made it across the street.

Marshall wiped his face and shook his head in disgust. "Do you see anyone else here? That means we're the ones that are supposed to be here. Get with the program kid." Marshall tried his best to show who was in charge here.

"Sorry, I was just…," Peter began but Marshall just shoved him to shut up. Nick stepped in the way and pushed Marshall back, almost causing a trip.

"What's your problem," yelled Marshall, now back in his stance to fight. "Why you getting all up in my business over some geeky little kid," Marshall shouted in Nick's face. Marshall wasn't the strongest kid on the block but he got into enough fights in his life to know how to handle a situation. If you stand tall, and the person you are fighting is scared, they will back down. Marshall was riding on that scenario. If not, he was willing to get into a scrap.

Nick stood there for a moment. He wasn't sure what to make of Marshall just yet. He then backed up a little. He made sure eye contact was always there though. "Don't tempt me to kick your ass, kid," Nick emphasized on the kid part. "I know you think you're some big tough guy. That's fine. Picking on a guy who can't defend himself against some bully? That's pretty low on your part." This made Marshall's face turn red.

"How dare you. I outta kick your…" His voice was lost as the door flung open. Carl was standing in the doorway. The boys all turned their attention to the one who wrote their letters.

"Ah, a wild bunch of kids, eh? Just what I was hoping for," he said as a big smile swept across his face. This was the start of something new. The boys all glanced at each other as they were trying to decide what this mysterious man was doing here.

Chapter Three – Tools

Nick sat down first, with the others following his lead. After everyone was seated, Carl looked to each boy, nodding. He was reading their faces and body language. To Carl this was the interview for his new unit. "We all got a letter," said Nick. Carl nodded, acknowledging the words. Nick looked to the other boys thinking of this as some type of joke. Maybe this was a prank to pull on the new guy in town. None of them had a smirk though. They looked even more confused than him.

"Yes, you did. All of you did and then soon after you finished reading it, they were terminated. That is correct, yes?" Carl asked and each boy nodded. "Good, well this is a big day for you. This can be the very beginning of changing your life forever. You'll be working under me. A work force that most people won't believe is possible. I promise you that what I show you here will be amazing. If you choose to accept it, that is." The boys didn't seem to understand any of what was spoken. Marshall let out a few chuckles, which made a very unpleasant Carl show himself. "Is there something you need, Mr. Roman?" The voice was sharp like a sword.

Marshall stopped the laughing. It was replaced with a grin. "Listen dude, your silly expectations about doing work for you is crazy. We don't even know what it is. Not to mention I don't even know who you are. However, I'd like to know the real reason you called us in here," replied Marshall, but all Carl did was made sure eye contact was there. "Also, I would like to know why these guys are here. Why am I here? Who are you? Last thing is what was that letter thing, and how was it destroyed?" Marshall's questions finally came to a halt. The boys looked to Marshall and then to Carl who had a wide smile on his face.

"That's enough from you, young one." Carl's voice was harsh. He didn't want to come across as a mean guy. However, he had to make sure they understood he was in charge. "When you speak to me you will treat me with respect. Do you understand? Some of your questions should be answered though. I will start with what you will be called. Exterminators are now your code names. They are the title you will be given." All four boys looked at each other and then back at Carl. "You will learn of what that is in good time. Next thing Marshall asked was why you three are here." Carl looked at the remaining three boys. "Well, to put it quite simply, you will all be partners." The boys looked to each other, disbelief on all there faces. None of them could see themselves working with the others. "A Unit" He finished.

No one liked the idea of being partners with each other. Especially since some held on to old feuds. Marshall especially didn't like it since he seemed to have a problem will all three but Carl spoke before he had a chance to retaliate. "My name is Carl and I will be your commander or general, whichever you would like to call me. In our terms, I would be your supervisor. The label that is given to us is titled "Bora" which means leader, teacher, or commander." Peter's eyes widen. It almost sounded like he was thrown into some fantasy world. He usually lacked emotion but he felt somewhat excited about what he was hearing. The other boys were still more confused and cautious. "Once you read the guide the information I'm giving you will make far more sense." Each boy looked towards the wall of the house to see four silver cases. The cases made the scene look like some top secret military secret. The boys wanted to all get up and look at them but waited until they were commanded. "You may go retrieve one of the cases. Please do not open until instructed."

Each boy stood up and slowly made their way to the wall. They all took a look at the cases. After realizing that all of them were the same, each boy grabbed one; right away noticing how light the cases were. Whatever was inside wasn't very big. After sitting down again with their cases in front of them Carl began to speak, "Please open your cases to find three items inside." Each opened their cases to reveal the three very items Carl just mentioned. The most noticeable one was an item that looked very similar to a handle or hilt of a sword. Its black covering over the dark gnarled wood made it seem very comfortable and easy to grasp. The bottom had rings attached with a small crystal on the end, which was protected by a see-through shield of some sort. "That is the first and most important equipment you will receive today. It's called a Rod and this will be your main weapon in fighting."

"A Rod? I can see the resemblance, but sir...," Peter said while tilting his head. He was trying to finish the question but was too absorbed in studying the new item he had just received to focus his thoughts. After a moment Peter looked back up to finish the question but saw all the boys were now looking at him. He hesitated before finishing. "You said these are weapons. This look like a piece of wood with a crystal attached to it. I mean even you said it's just a rod." The boys gave a slight chuckle, and even Carl let one slip.

"A name given long ago, young one. The power is unimaginable, uncontrollable even, if you don't know how to use them correctly." The boys all took a look at their new weapon again. "To make sense to you boys, they are tools that can transform into anything you want." At first the boys looked at the object, speechless. Then Marshall once again came out laughing; the other boys started asking questions.

"A sword?" asked Peter.

"A gun?" asked Nick.

"Money?" asked Fred.

"Are you guys serious!? You believe this crap?" Marshall didn't believe a word coming out of Carl's mouth. Carl was not offended by the words, he just smiled and nodded.

"Why do you always have to get so worked up?" Nick asked.

"'Cause I can. You got a problem with that?"

"I'm starting to have one." Marshall didn't like the tone Nick was responding in.

"I just want to know if this really can become money. 'Cause I sure as hell can use some right about now," Fred interrupted.

"Well, not money, but yes a gun or a sword is very possible," Carl responded. Marshall just shook his head and laughed. Though not as loud spoken as Marshall, the boys were agreeing more with his point of view. That is when Carl came in telling them the downside of the object, "You may only change the object once a night to whatever you desire."

"Once a night? Well, why's that?" Fred asked, puzzled. The way the Rod worked was beginning to intrigue all the boys except Marshall who sat there laughing at the weapon. He eventually flung it on to the table and looked outside the window. Despite trying to act as if he didn't care, he was still listening closely.

"I will cover that later. First let's take a look at what else you got in those cases," Carl spoke mysteriously so the boys listened. They each picked up the next object, which was a dark black belt. "The belt which you hold now, and I have all your sizes so don't worry, will go with your other object." They all then looked to the little black device with three colors on it. Red, green and white which were the only three buttons on it. It also had a small screen where words would pop up. "As you can see, there are three buttons. Red is to turn on Stealth mode, while green is to stop it. White is one of the most important ones. After each mission, when you eliminate the species, press the white button to tell the station you've completed your hunt. Soon after, a crew will come by, so be patient. They will clean up the mess with their equipment and take care of anyone injured. This is very important so please listen very carefully." Carl finished and the boys nodded, as they understood. Marshall just threw the device onto the table without a care.

"So basically a beeper. Thanks 1999," Marshall joked.

"You may call them beepers. Let me assure you though that they are far beyond just that. They are one of the most important tools you can have on a mission." Carl stopped for a few seconds to take a few breaths and get some questions in before continuing.

The boys all took a second to check this new equipment. Understanding most of it was simple but what to use them for was still a mystery. "So what do we use them for in the end result, though?" inquired Fred, who was messing around with the Rod.

"Ah well that brings me to the next subject. Why are you called Exterminators and why did I just give you all these tools? This may be hard to understand but what you will be hunting are beasts. Some are very well known beasts such as dragons and Cyclops. Then there will be others, which you won't know, such as Rockus, or Ruks for that matter. We titled all these monsters under the code name "Unknowns". They are very real, just not in our realm. It may sound strange but these beasts can break though. How you ask? Because some are strong enough to break through the realm of the living. It's also because we have enemies who want to bring these creatures to our world. Believing they can create a new world or tame these monsters. I will assure you, these animals are very dangerous. A mission's dead line is the day you get it and it must be completed in that day. Otherwise, we will send out an elite hunter, otherwise known as a Protector. I don't take excuses and neither does this place so I advise you to do what you're told." The words sunk into the boys' heads.

"So, in other words, this is really a game of life and death?" asked Peter. Carl answered with a nod, which made Peter slightly excited. He liked reading about this stuff. Now he might actually be apart of it.

"This isn't a game. That's one of the most important things to learn from today. You won't come back if you die. There is no restart button. No, this is real life. Meaning you can get hurt and if not careful end up dead." The boys began to think twice about the deal. "I am not saying it's helpless to fight at your level, though. The book that is also inside the case will help you. It's a guide and it will show you great strategies to beat the Unknowns you will encounter. It's years of killing these things that those plans are made from. So you have the best hunters writing those. You'll be fine if you study them and hunt the monsters carefully."

Marshall got up, brushed himself down, grabbed his case,

and walked to the door. "I'm leaving. Thanks for the souvenirs, but this stuff is bull anyway. I don't have time for this. I got school in the morning. This fantasy stuff can wait for another day." Despite not believing, Marshall still took the case. The door slammed, making Peter jump back into reality. His mind lost in the thought process of creating weapons to kill Unknowns. Peter noticed Marshall was gone and felt relief flush over him. Carl on the other hand was angry.

"Don't worry about him. When he needs help he'll come to me," said Fred, getting Carl's attention. "He always does, even though we aren't friends anymore. Well, continue. Any more information we need? Like how we'll be getting these missions? 'Cause I don't even have a cell phone yet." Fred changed the subject quick. Carl looked towards Fred and smiled.

"Right, good question. Always wear the Beeper, which will then give you a mission. It's not a simple message you will see. Instead the message will be shown to you. In good time you'll come to understand what that means," Carl said, the boys now paying close attention. "Once the Unknown is found you will get a message, trust me you'll know when the message is there. Once given the mission you will have until the end of that day to complete it. After that our Protectors will be sent out to hunt the monster. You could get the mission anytime on any day. I suggest you read your books so that you find all the information you will need about the things you'll go up against." The boys all looked at the book, analyzing a few pages then turning back to Carl.

Carl took a look at his watch again and began to speak "I'm sorry, but I must go. If anything comes up I will mail you like I did today or send you a message through the Beepers. Please remember to wear it tomorrow since that is when your jobs could begin. I have faith in you all…even Marshall. Have a good day now," said Carl as he got up from his seat and walked to the closet door. He opened it, gave everyone a smile and a wave goodbye, then closed it.

"Well…that was new," said Nick, looking at the three new things in front of him. Fred began to put away the items so Nick followed. Peter was already packed, but kept out the book. They all got up after gathering their stuff in their cases and left the house. It was getting dark out when they began their way home.

"Guys, this is crazy," said Fred with a confused look. "I mean I've seen plenty of movies and cartoons about aliens…" Before he could continue Peter interrupted him by pointing out that they are monsters, not aliens. "Okay, monsters, creatures, aliens, whatever! These things, whatever they are, I thought can never really be out there," ended Fred. Nick nodded in agreement but Peter disagreed.

"I must say, I believed some of what was spoken. The thing I don't understand is, why us kids? I mean, why not adults?"

"Maybe because adults would try to get these guys arrested for thinking this is ludicrous," Fred said.

"I see that. Still it seems weird to pick up a bunch of seventeen year old kids to try and take on these so-called monsters. I mean, this sounds like a really dangerous job. I'm kind of freaked out," Nick responded.

"Do you think any of it's real?" Fred asked.

"I don't really know. If it isn't, that was a pretty awesome set up for a prank," he said laughing.

"Guy seems cool. A bit weird though." Fred said about Carl.

"Yeah, gives off that teacher vibe. We didn't even start school yet and I felt like I was in a classroom."

"A dirty small room counts as a classroom now?"

"Well I did say "felt like" and not was one," Nick said pushing Fred jokingly.

"Well guys, this is my way," Peter said pointing towards the left side. "I'm going to read some of this book. Maybe you all should too. We can try to get some answers. I'll see you at school. Bye," Peter said and walked away. The others waved and began to walk again.

"Man, it's like living in a video game. If this stuff is really going to happen, then I bet we're going to have a lot of fights," said Fred smiling and Nick agreed. It was a bit scary, but they found it to be more exciting. "Imagine what we will be fighting."

"Dragons!"

"Cyclops!"

"Big Foot!"

"Unicorns!"

"Unicorns?"

"Yeah, the thing with the horns and wings."

"I know what it is."

"Then why'd you ask?"

"I'm just saying...why unicorns?" Nick asked with a laugh.

"Dude, whatever! I'm just imagining what we'll be seeing. Fighting. Killing. It's crazy!" Fred felt his blood rushing. He was getting more and more excited by the moment.

"We don't really have to imagine," answered Nick as he stopped at the corner. "It's all in the book. Well, I gotta go this way, so I'll just see you in school. It'll be my first day but I'm pretty good with directions." Fred nodded.

"Later," Nick called as he began to run off with his silver case in hand. Fred waved goodbye and then started his way home.

Chapter Four – School

Nick slowly rose up, stretched, and went for his dresser. After throwing on some clothes he made his way into his bathroom to wash his face. He had started to grow a mustache, which was beginning to show. A slight beard began to grow along with it. He thought about learning how to shave correctly as he examined his reflection. Then he spiked up his hair and brushed his teeth. After checking himself in the mirror he pushed his hair back down deciding he hated the spiky hair look now that he was older. Nick did his daily routine, sliding down the stairs banister like he did in his old house. Making his way to his kitchen he saw some doughnuts and scooped one up. "Doughnuts? Do you want to get heart disease?" His father was very picky when it came to food. Nick had snuck a box of doughnuts into the shopping cart the other day when Nick went with his father to do the food shopping. A little treat for him. His father agreed to it only because he could use the left over doughnuts to feed the birds outside.

"Of course, Father. I forgot how unhealthy I am. With me weighing a total of hundred and forty pounds and all. I'm going be the new fat kid on the block." Nick rolled his eyes as he put down the jelly filled doughnut. He and his father bickered about small things. It was how they bonded. Nick always remained respectful though. He put the doughnut down and grabbed his book bag. "Well, this is my first day at school, wish me luck." His dad waved goodbye as Nick shut the door behind him.

The weather outside was beautiful. Nick wanted to run towards the beach instead of school. This year though, he wanted to do better since last year he flunked most of his classes. Not to mention the big brawls at school didn't help. Somehow he always ended up in a fight every so often. It wasn't that he wanted to start them, he just found himself finishing them. The wind rushed into him, a breeze so powerful it chased away any drowsiness he had left. Still, once the wind died down the humidity fell over him like a thick blanket. He wasn't enjoying the new change of weather in New York City.

He stopped to tie his shoe and when getting up, saw Fred walking down the block across from him. He was so excited to see a familiar face he went dashing across the street. A car stopped short and beeped at Nick, yelling and cursing at him from the driver's seat. "Sorry! Sorry! My bad," Nick called back as he walked onto the sidewalk. Fred looked at him, smiling. "Dude...I don't know if you noticed but everyone is kind of mean around here," Nick said smiling back.

"Yeah. I wouldn't advise running across the street without looking."

"Well maybe he should look to see who's coming across the street. What if I was an animal or a deer?"

"A deer is an animal."

"Okay what if I was a dog or a deer?" Nick asked laughing. "Better?"

"Just watch it around here. No one has patience." Fred replied as he patted Nick on the back. They shook hands in the way teenagers do and began walking to school while talking. School schedules came up and Fred checked over Nick's. "Hey we even got four classes together. Only difference I could spot on here would be science and lunch. That means I won't be chilling with you first period. Science is an annoyance but mandatory subject in this school, so we'll talk more in math." Before leaving, another handshake occurred and both boys went their opposite ways.

The school was huge with almost three thousand students to fill the rumbling halls. It wasn't too dirty, surprisingly, but it still had too many kids for the size of the building. "Could use another paint job," muttered Nick to himself as he pushed through the halls to make it to class. He finally pulled out from the ruckus and into the front of his classroom door. He looked into the class to see only half of it full before making his way over to the right where a few seats remained free next to the window. He made himself comfortable and closed his eyes to feel a few cool breezes that blew through.

He heard a few more kids entering but none were coming to sit close to him, so he kept his eyes closed. He was thinking of back home when the classes weren't much bigger than twenty kids. The class here was only half full and Nick remembered seeing twenty kids already. With at least thirty five plus students, Nick was ready to just skate by the class and keep his mouth shut. He didn't want to start any trouble at the new school.

While enjoying the cool wind that hit his face he heard someone finding a seat next to him. He opened his eyes to reveal one of the most beautiful girls he had ever seen. Her jet black hair went right down to her shoulders. Her lips were the perfect size. Not too small but not too big. Her eyes were light blue; her skin had a light complexion but still a slight tan to it. She had on colorful purple pants and a Beatles shirt, almost no makeup to be found. She wiped her head to get the sweat off and then looked to her side and smiled.

Nick felt himself turning red, and it wasn't cause of the heat. The girl next to him introduced herself with sweetness in her tone. "Hey. My name is Kelly and yours?" Nick smiled back as she waited for the answer. After a few seconds she asked again. "Are you okay, you look a little red?" Nick snapped out of it and sat up straight.

"Oh yeah. Umm.... My name's Nick. Uhhh nice pen." She tilted her head. *"Nice pen? What in the world am I saying. NICE PEN!?"* Nick felt his face turning even redder.

She smiled then shook her head. "Well, okay...I'm going to just turn around now. Nice meeting you, Nick the pen identifier." She winked before turning her head towards the front of the classroom. He felt like running out of the classroom and slamming his head into a locker. He just met his first girl since he moved to New York City and the best he could come up with is "nice pen". *"I am such a geek,"* he thought to himself.

"Umm, what I meant was," Nick began to speak but the classroom was too loud for her to hear. At least over thirty kids were in the classroom now, a lot of them speaking loudly about

28

their summer vacation.

"I see we both like science huh?" Nick turned to see Peter sitting behind him. "I didn't know you liked it that much. Advance biology can be pretty tough," he said with a smile. Nick noticed that the smile was too big for Peter's face, making him look odd.

"Yeah, I absolutely love science. So much in fact that they threw me in whatever class they had available and I somehow got this. Did I mention I love "ADVANCE" science?" Nick was getting annoyed. He took a quick glance at Kelly but she was deep into texting someone on her phone.

"Hey, do I detect a little bit of attitude?" Peter asked.

"Sorry, it's just this girl here -" he gave a quick thumbs up towards Kelly. "is super cute. My grand opening line with her was that she had a nice pen." Nick almost laughed at what he said. He probably would have if it wasn't for the fact he wanted to cry at the same time.

"Kelleh," he asked, pronouncing her name odd.

"Yeah, don't call her that."

"Why? It's what I've called her since we were five. Hey Kelleh, how was your summer?" Peter asked loudly. Kelly turned around and waved at Peter.

"Hey Pete! Summer was good. I mostly stayed at home and worked on my art. Nothing too fancy this summer. How 'bout you? Did any schooling during the summer?"

"Eh a little bit. I focused mostly on creating my own website. I'm trying to launch it sometime next year. It's basically a site to help formulate math problems a lot easier for younger kids. Basically breaking it down into games so they can learn and have fun."

"Are you trying to scare her off!?" Nick roared in his head. He took a quick look towards Kelly, expecting her to be completely bored.

"That sounds awesome," she said, her hands flying in the air with excitement.

"What in the hell...," Nick was in shock.

"Oh, by the way, this is Nick. He's new here. I think he just moved."

"Oh yeah-" Kelly looked towards Nick. "-the pen expert. He's a bit of an odd one. Pete you pick the strangest friends."

"What friends? He's probably my first."

"HEY! What about me," she exclaimed. She made her face look annoyed, even though she was just teasing.

"Well, of course! I meant guy friends. You know what you're always saying. "Pete go out and-" he began to say but she jumped in.

"Do some bromancing! Yes! Glad to see it finally working." She looked at Nick. "If Pete is your friend, you have to be good people. So for now I'll accept you as the nice guy Pete is friends with. Even if you are odd. Pen expert," she said giggling and then turned back towards the front.

Nick turned to Peter. "Dude...what the hell? Somehow you're the guy who knows the really hot girls in this school? How is this possible?"

"Actually-" Peter began as the class door opened. The teacher was walking in. "-Kelly has been my friend for over ten years. She's like my sister. Talking to girls, as in girls to date, is almost impossible for me. Now that you're here maybe you can show me the way," Peter rushed with a smile spreading across his face. Nick felt the smiles were coming off forced or fake. Something odd about them.

"Yeah, well, we'll work on that," Nick answered before turning towards the classroom. He was still in shock about Peter knowing the cutest girl that he's seen in school so far.

Fred yawned as he entered his class. He knew a few kids and on the way to his seat gave them a quick handshake. He was still tired from playing games last night so he slouched in his seat, closing his eyes. He began to dream about being a hero with all different kinds of powers. About mysterious monsters jumping at him while he slapped them away with a huge sword. He imagined dragons flying over him while he summoned his own dragons to fight. He imagined shooting lighting out of his hands while screaming he was a powerful overlord. Right as he was about to get into another fight with a dragon he felt a strong clap on the back of his shoulder. Fred opened his eyes and grabbed the slapping hand. He took a look to the person who did it only to see Marshall standing over him with a grin on his face. "Hey buddy," he said sarcastically as he pulled his hand back. "What did that weird dude finish saying last night?"

"Why do you care? You never care about anything. Always too busy trying to show off. How about you just leave me alone this year," Fred replied and Marshall just shrugged. Fred turned around, making sure there was no way he could see Marshall who would only make him madder.

A short man entered the class room. He had huge glasses and a small hat which looked to fit his head perfectly. He was of Asian descent. As he reached the desk in front of the class, he smiled to the students and waved. "Good morning boys and girls." The voice was funny making almost everyone laugh. "I am Mr. Wang." Marshall rolled his eyes. Fred saw this and prepared himself for the insults sure to fly out of his old friend's mouth.

"Yo, Mr. Wang can I leave," called Marshall. All the students looked towards him. Mr. Wang looked confused and then smiled. "Well, do you understand me? I'd love to leave!" Marshall was beginning to get restless. "I don't think you even speak enough English to pass me. Do you know what the letter 'A' means?" Some of the kids laughed. Others took it offensively as a racist comment.

"Ah I'm sorry… Marshall is it?" Marshall nodded. "Well, I'm sorry Marshall but you will not be able to leave. You must treat your elders with respect." Marshall let out a huge laugh. "What is this laughter from you for?" Mr. Wang's face was turning red now with anger.

"Listen dude, I gotta go to the bathroom. Now can I please go or do I have to keep on looking at your ugly face turning multiple colors." The insult got to Mr. Wang as he smashed his ruler on the desk. The entire class jumped as soon as the ruler made contact with the wooden desk, including Marshall.

"I'm sorry but you may not speak like that. Let me make this clear young man. Insults are created to hide behind one's own shame. You think you are funny, young one, but in reality you aren't. Racist comments will also not be tolerated here!" Mr. Wang was turning back to his regular self, his pale face returning. Everyone was quiet now waiting until their new teacher spoke. "Oh and Marshall..." Marshall looked back towards Mr. Wang. "I may not know the meaning for the letter 'A', as you say, but I sure know how an 'F' would look in your grades. Would you like one of those?" The class now laughed at Marshall instead.

"Now see, that was just sad, when will you grow up?" asked Fred quickly and quietly. Fred used to care about Marshall. He used to be his best friend. Now days Marshall just did whatever he wanted in class. Always trying to show off and gain some attention.

"Hop off." The slang words were used a lot by Marshall so it didn't come alien to Fred. Marshall raised his voice and was about to curse at Fred when Mr. Wang yelled again. He informed Marshall he was on the verge of getting kicked out of class. The remainder of class went quietly.

Nick sat down at an empty lunch table and put his head down. He enjoyed new things, but the school was far too large for his taste. He didn't like most of the kids and the one girl he began talking with probably wouldn't talk to him again because his opening line was one of the worst in the history of first liners. "Yo! You okay?" The voice was the slick tone of the one and only Marshall. Nick yawned while lifting his head to see Marshall sitting down on the opposite side of the table. "Bad day homie?" he asked while grabbing an apple off his tray.

Nick sat up and shrugged, feeling too tired to explain much. "Well, not really, just the classes here are even more boring than the ones back home," Nick answered and Marshall nodded.

"Well that's life in this school. I see we have some hard ass teachers this year too. When will they learn this crap doesn't mean a thing?" spat Marshall, taking a bite out of his apple. This time Nick answered with a nod. "Well, that's life I guess. So what's your deal? Why did you stay yesterday," asked Marshall holding his apple out in the air while Nick put his head back down. The pain was striking the front of his head from the migraine forming.

"Well, did he say any more stuff we need to be "WORRIED" about," Marshall pressed on, making sure he put emphases on the word worried. This time though, Marshall did have some curiosity in his voice. Nick closed his eyes for a second to get at least a little rest but soon was asked the same question. He opened his eyes and looked back up.

"He said what was in the case, and then how to use it. You were there for that. He said we have some other things to do but I'm too tired to remember any of it," Nick finally answered. He put his head back down to get some shut eye. "Also, he told us to wear the small beeper-looking thing on us always," mumbled Nick through his shirt where he had his face buried.

Nick remembered days when he would sit at home with his parents and try to decide what to do in the summer. His father sometimes was able to get whole weeks off because both his parents worked and had enough money. One summer day they decided to go to the park and spend the whole day there. Nick had so much fun playing soccer with his dad then cards with his mom. The memory brought back happiness, something he felt was missing for a while now.

"That little thing that looks like it's from the 90's? Man, I left that at home." Marshall took another bite of his apple before continuing. "Why do you have it?" Nick tried to ignore him. He wanted to remember the good days. "Hey dude, why you believing all this stuff anyway!?" Marshall raised his voice as he threw his apple to the side.

"What if it's true? All of it?. Then, yeah, it could come in handy. I mean it can happen, can't it? And if it does then what will you do with no weapon to protect yourself with?" challenged Nick. Marshall found that amusing. Nick really didn't want to keep going with the conversation but Marshall insisted.

"Come on man, this can't be true 'cause it sounds too fake. Monsters? Like vampires and dragons? All of it is bull. Just sit back and chill. We got the girls. We're in our final year of High School. You got to start over here so forget all this silly stuff. Enjoy this life, not some fantasy some crazy dude was babbling about." Nick wanted to, but he was already having a bad time in the real world. He almost wished these monsters would show up so he could take out some of his aggravation on something.

"Well, I get what you mean and all but I still have this feeling…just what if?" asked Nick. Marshall just shrugged. The conversation came to an end and they sat there just looking around. Marshall talked some more about a few hot girls he found in his class. After a few minutes of listening to Marshall carry on with the single-sided conversation, the bell rang. The boys said their goodbyes and went their separate ways.

Nick and Fred were walking together when Fred stopped right at the front of their class. "I'll be back in a few, I have to see someone," Fred said abruptly and went past the classroom. Nick walked into the class and sat down closer to the back. He then felt a tap on his shoulder, which made him get madder. He wasn't in the mood for anyone else to annoy him. Another irritating person like Marshall talking in his ear wasn't on his agenda. He looked up to see the beautiful Kelly sitting down in the seat next to him.

"Hey Pen Identifier - you're in this class too. That's pretty cool. You know, in case I need to know which pen to use and all," she said with a smile. Nick smiled back. He looked into her bright blue eyes. He felt like touching her soft-looking skin; wanting to guide his hand across her cheek and kiss her beautiful lips.

"Yeah. Well, you can never be too careful with pens. There are blue ones, black ones, red ones." He picked up his orange pen. "Even the odd colors like this. So, yes. I will be your guide for using the right pens that are cool!" A grin swept across Kelly's face.

"Awesome. I was afraid. I heard about terrorist using these pens to attack people while they sleep. I'm sure if that's the case you'll let me know, right?" she asked, sounding so innocent.

"Don't worry Kelly, I'll be your protector," he answered with a pound to his chest. She let out a huge laugh. Little did she know Nick meant it seriously, as well. He already felt the connection with this young lady.

Nick got home around five o'clock. He threw his book bag to the side and flung himself on his bed. He let his eyes rest for a few moments trying to recover from the busy school atmosphere. He already felt a friendly bond with Fred and Peter. Fred seemed to be the average guy you hung out with every once in a while, but somehow he came off very trust worthy. Nick really valued that in a person. Peter was more of the odd type but still seemed to have interest in being friends with Nick. Nick was just glad to have met them both.

Then Kelly slipped into Nick's mind. He rolled over and looked up at his ceiling. He couldn't stop thinking about her beautiful smile. He raised his hand to the ceiling and imagined touching her soft-looking skin. Imagining her right in front of him while he brushed his hand through her hair. He wanted to be close to her when he barely knew her. He didn't know if it was weird but he honestly didn't care. Lust took over him and he gladly accepted it.

He dropped his hand after a moment and it hit the beeper. He looked down his side to see his beeper attached to his hip. "Well, guess no mission..." he said almost expecting it to suddenly show him something. Even though he didn't expect anything, he couldn't help but feel disappointed.

Chapter Five – So It Begins

"Come on, Nick, wake up," yelled his father from below. He tried covering his ears but his alarm clock went off a moment later. He went to shut it off, but rolled too far and received a face plant from the wooden floor. *"Loving New York City so far,"* was all Nick could think of while lying on the floor. After much debate on whether it was even worth getting up from the floor he forced himself to stand. He grabbed a new set of clothes for school and hit the bathroom.

"Goddamn it! This thing is freaking useless!" He grabbed the beeper off the counter, ready to fling it. He was looking in the mirror and watched his anger build up. He took a deep breath as he snapped the beeper back onto his belt. He leaned over and looked into the sink. "Just be calm. Not everything works out." He wasn't having a tough time with the move. He just couldn't get use to the environment, and kept having old memories creep back into his mind; his hope was for the missions to create a diversion so that he wouldn't keep getting these thoughts. After washing his face, he got dressed and left the bathroom ready to face the day.

He rode down the banister again and leapt off the bottom, almost tripping. He went through his living room, taking a few mints from a glass container before entering the kitchen. As he sat down he popped one in his mouth. "You know that's no substitute for brushing your teeth," his father told him disapprovingly after finishing his bagel.

"Oh trust me pops, I know. I know since you tell me about eight times a day. My teeth are white, I brush them at night and that's good enough." Nick liked to have an advantage of the arguments against his father. His father however, gave him a look that told Nick keep his mouth shut.

"Don't talk to me like that, you know better now."

"I'm sorry pops," Nick responded, finishing off his mint.

His father finished the last bagel and threw his dish into the sink. He flung on his jacket and picked up his tool case. A long day lay ahead of him. The new building would take at least ten hours a day for a long while. "I'll see you tonight for dinner." With that, his father left while Nick sat there popping another mint in his mouth before heading to school.

"I'm leaving," Peter said but his father stopped him at the door.

"You didn't bring home any homework last night," his father stated, annoyed. It was a rare occasion his father wasn't drunk yet.

"I finished it at school. Plus most classes don't give homework on the first day back to school." Peter wouldn't look up at his father. This person, his father, demanded too much in life. At first Peter thought it was just because he cared. Lately though, Peter felt his father just wanted to torment him because Peter did so well. If someone is smarter than you, chances are they will be jealous of you and will want to find ways to make that person feel stupid.

"Yeah, just remember to keep up with that. Trust me you don't want to miss an assignment. If I find out you're lying... Oh boy." He pushed Peter into the door as he walked into the kitchen. As of late Peter's father had become violent. Never beating him but always pushing and shoving. But Peter felt he never did anything bad enough to be pushed or shoved around.

Nick was walking towards school, only a block away. He couldn't stop thinking about life before the whole incident. His mom dying suddenly changed too much. It put both him and his father on edge far too often. They would bicker about the smallest thing. He just wanted to go back to the days when he'd come home, see his mom, and get the best cooked dinners. Then his father would go outside and play a few games of catch with him before heading to bed.

As Nick walked up the stairs towards his classroom, head

hanging low, he felt a strong force on his shoulder before he was smashed into the staircase violently. He forced his eyes wide open to see the attacker. A kid by the name of Ryan stood there. He was big. Not so much fat just really well built. Everyone knew him because he was a star player on the football team. He was shaved completely, broad shoulders, and over six feet tall. "Hey kid, why didn't you move out of my way sooner?"

Nick was about to get up swinging but he calmed himself down. He didn't need to get into anymore altercations in his life. Especially since they had just moved to New York City. He shrugged it off, saying sorry as he stood up. He could hear the kids around him muttering under their breath to each other, some of the girls and guys laughing. He rolled his eyes every time someone pointed to him. Ryan just gave him a stern look as Nick began walking away to his class.

"Peter, is everyone here just huge a-holes? Cause it's starting to feel that way," Nick asked as he arrived in his seat. Peter looked up from reading his book and nodded.

"Yeah. Just about. By the way I read a lot more of that guide Carl gave us. These creatures are scary. I mean some have their whole body built out of rock. Others have the ability to fly. You have to read some of this stuff. It's crazy," Peter told Nick excitedly.

"I really don't wanna hear about it today."

"Did you read the guide at all?"

"No. Like I said..."

"You really should. In case we get called on a mission."

"Whatever dude. Just...whatever." Nick was getting frustrated now. He started giving up on the actual idea these missions and creatures were even real.

"Hey!" Nick spotted Kelly walking towards him waving. He waved back. She sat down quickly. Nick felt the urge to push the desk out of the way and grab her. Pick her up, kiss her, and more. "Hey pen expert, you can stop staring down there." Nick didn't even notice he was staring at her breasts. He quickly looked to her blue eyes. He was about to say sorry but she spoke first.

38

"I'm kidding. You looked zoned out. Are you okay though? Pete, your friend isn't adjusting too well here, huh?"

"He's an odd one," Peter replied chuckling.

Nick gave a helpless look. "Sorry, I'm just tired. It's been tough adjusting to the new area. Not to mention fights with the old man."

Peter quickly looked up at Nick. "Your father?" Peter could feel the need to speak about his abusive relationship with his father to someone that can finally relate to him. Peter shut off all emotional connection, but if someone could finally relate to him. Maybe he had some hope, after-all.

"Yeah, it's been weird getting used to the fact we don't have my mother anymore. Even months later. Not to mention his hours at work are just killing him. So we get into the smallest arguments," Nick responded shrugging.

Peter let his shoulders fall. Nick couldn't relate to his problems after all. There was no one he could speak to about his issues with his father. His mom was scared and fragile, not willing to stand up to her husband. His little sister wasn't getting abused so why would she speak to him about it. Peter slumped back into his chair. "Oh, that's unfortunate."

"Yeah, but it's cool. He's still the coolest old man around," Nick said laughing. Kelly laughed along with him. Peter gave a slight laugh as well. Not able to get the picture of his father standing over him, angry, out of his mind.

"Yeah, so I think I finally agree with you. I don't think these monsters are even real. It was kind of stupid to believe it," Nick confessed to Marshall. Marshall let the grin say "I told you so". Nick continued. "I kind of always thought it was dumb. Still, I had hoped it would be kind of real, ya know? Especially so we could of done something other than focus on this school."

"Eh, it's not that bad. You just gotta sit and skate by. Do well enough and it'll be over before you know it," Marshall responded. He ate the rest of his chips.

"It's pretty bad. It's boring for the most part. Kids here are just straight up bullies. I'm trying to talk to people but most are annoyed when I ask them how they're doing. The rest come off as idiots."

"Hey, better not be talking about me."

"Why would I be talking you if I thought you were an idiot?"

"Fair point."

"You do come off as an idiot though at times."

"You wanna see an idiot," Marshall growled, looking at Nick, annoyed.

"That doesn't even make sense. Are you trying to say you're going to show me how tough you are by being an idiot?"

"I...yo, man, shut the hell up before I punch you."

"Please do so. Maybe it'll make this day much more exciting," Nick challenged, laughing. Marshall cracked a smile.

"You can be a real jerk sometimes, you know that," Marshall said trying to impersonate a sweet, honest, little girl voice. "I'ma tell on you!" Nick laughed at the impression.

"Marshall can be a cool guy. Lately, though, he's been trying to show off. Try to show he's always the big tough guy in everything. I don't really know why either," Fred said as he walked with Nick towards their classroom. They both made it in and sat down. Kelly was already there taking out her school supplies for class.

"Heads up guys. Our first test is next Friday," She said seriously. Nick wanted to hear her talk more so he didn't respond right away. She looked up, catching his eyes, they both felt a connection. Sometimes a weird feeling that made them seem so close. Nick looked away first, feeling his cheeks turn red again.

"Thanks for the heads up," he answered sheepishly. He still couldn't get over how cute she was. Every time he saw her he wanted to touch her. She kept getting ready for class while he took out his notebook.

Fred leaned over. "Kelly is awesome. If you get with her

that'd be great. She's funny and cute. Just so you know, she never really dates. Well, no one that I know of. We've been going to the same schools for a few years and I've never seen her with a guy. So, she might swing the other way, ya know?"

Nick swung around. Really quietly, but with panic in his voice, he asked, "Are you serious!?"

"No."

"I hate you." Nick looked towards Kelly one more time before turning to the front of his class.

The bell rang and the classed flushed out. Kelly said goodbye with a wave and walked towards a group of girls. Fred shoved Nick playfully. "Man, she definitely wants you. She used to be kind of okay looking but now..." Fred made the shape of a really skinny girl with a big butt using his hands. "Now, she's so fine. You better get with her," Fred said, elbowing his friend.

Nick pushed Fred outside the school building. "Shut up. I'ma ask her out real soon. Just watch."

"Hey man, that's all I'm saying. Don't let it slip away. She's worth it!" Nick nodded to that.

Both began walking towards their houses together while discussing classes. "Yeah, I hate Spanish. What are we really going to need it for anyway?" Nick asked Fred who just shrugged for response. "Man, I'm getting so tired of talking about school and I just started. I almost wished those missions were real." Fred stopped at the last comment. Nick turned to look at his friend who was now just standing there. "What?"

"I don't know. I see something. Something isn't right. My head is pound-" Fred grabbed his head and began slowly rubbing it. The throbbing suddenly turned to a sharp pain. He winced at it as he slowly sunk to the ground. Nick began to walk back towards his friend to check on him. He looked around to see if he could call anyone for help but no one was out on the street.

Nick bent down, trying to check if his friend was okay. "You sure you're doing okay man?" Now, Nick began to worry, as his friend would occasionally let out small moans. "You don't look too good man." Nick's voice began to trail off while Fred mumbling to himself.

Fred opened his eyes as the pain began to subside. The pain was almost completely gone and he stood back up. Nick just stood there puzzled, looking at his friend. "Yeah, I'm fine. It's just that..." Fred looked straight ahead while speaking. He saw a huge stone in front of him. "What is that?" Fred whispered looking scared. Nick looked to the side but he saw nothing.

"You sure you're okay? There isn't anything there," Nick said worriedly. His friend, who was almost about to collapse a few moments ago, was now staring at nothing.

"No, dude its right here." Fred walked up to the stone in front of him. It had an engraving on it. On it displayed an address that was only twenty minutes from his current location. "You don't see this?" Fred asked as he pointed towards the huge rock.

"Dude, I think you're going insane on me," Nick answered as he shook his head. "Trust me when I say there is nothing in front of you." Nick walked towards Fred.

"No, man it's right here." Fred turned back around to the rock. He memorized the location and smiled, thinking this might actually be his first mission. Then he heard a loud hard swipe as something tore into the rock. A rip appeared over the location where he was just reading. He jumped back at the sound and almost fell over. The rock shook and crumbled into pieces. Fred felt a small sharp pain in his head. He winced as he grabbed his head. Once he opened his eyes again the rock was gone.

"You sure you're okay? I think maybe we should go to the hospital." Nick patted his friends back.

"No. It's a mission. Nick, I got a mission," he told his friend, sounding both worried and excited.

Chapter Six – The Alleyway

"A mission?" Nick looked surprised.

"Yeah, a mission."

"Like...like a mission to hunt down monsters?"

"Like a mission to hunt down monsters."

"Like a mission to hunt down "real" monsters?"

"Dude, I just saw a huge rock with engravings giving an address. Then it shattered into pieces. I think this is as real as it gets." Fred sat on the curb trying to relax.

"Everything…," he began and took a second to gather himself. His body felt weird as the air began to flow in through his nose and out his mouth. He could still feel some of the pain in his head. He saw everything kind of shift. Everything looked the same, except for the huge rock, but it felt different. As if he wasn't truly in the same place as Nick. He didn't know any other way to describe it but the feeling of being in two different realities at once. "Everything looked the same but nothing was the same. I felt such a heavy pressure. To be honest, it scared the heck out of me." He let out a huge sigh. "Yet, I gotta admit. It was pretty cool."

Nick listened to every word his friend said. He spoke after a few moments of silence. "I just don't know if I believe there are monsters. I mean it's monsters. It can't be. There's no such thing as monsters."

"It felt real. I felt like I was pushed into something... I can't describe it."

"I dunno man."

"I'm telling you man it's real!" Fred was yelling now.

"I believe you." Nick put his hands up to calm Fred down. "I'm just saying it's still hard to digest the fact that these...monsters...can be real. I'm not saying you're wrong or lying. I'm saying it's hard to believe in general."

Fred understood but he still began to get agitated. "I'm serious man. I know it sounds crazy but what just happened to me proves it." Fred looked to the ground. "I mean if rocks can suddenly appear and give directions and then shatter I'm sure there are weirder things out there." He looked up at Nick.

Nick didn't know what to do now, standing there just as confused. "I don't know what happened. I didn't see a rock or anything. If you told anyone else they'd think you were a nut-job!" Nick made sure the message got through and it did, loud enough so the people across the street could hear. "I mean come on man. I've only known you a bit but you gotta admit it's crazy. Plus, how do I know you aren't just messing with me right now?"

"I get that you don't want to believe it but it's real. I'm scared out of my mind and need your help. You have to believe me!" Fred looked towards his friend. Nick watched him but then shook his head.

Nick started pacing back and forth for a moment before speaking. "Okay, say I believe this crazy stuff. What do we do now? Go to the address?" Nick seemed to be coming around which relieved Fred.

"Well the rock told me to go to 60th Street and Third. It's not far from my house. It's a twenty minute walk, maybe, from here. It wrote the address, after I read it though it sounded like something scratched it. Like a huge claw or something slammed its paw into the rock and shattered it," Fred told Nick.

"Well I just moved here but this doesn't sound right. I mean people are walking on these streets at all hours. How can no one see these things? These Unknowns!?" Nick now sounded distraught, his attitude changing every few seconds. Frustration was building up in him and he wasn't sure why. Fred took some offense to the aggressive attitude Nick was giving but was too busy thinking about the possibilities of there being real monsters in the world he lived in.

"An alternative realm." That's all Fred had to say. Nick just watched as his friend pondered. "Remember the book we got from Carl. I only read a few chapters but they mentioned these "monsters", Unknowns, come from the realm of the others. Some type of realm that connects our world...universe...whatever, to another. I didn't read deep into details. Where's Peter when you need him?" Fred got up and looked around.

"I didn't read any of it yet but this sounds just crazy man. I'ma head home and read some, maybe get an idea of what we're dealing with. Let me go check on a few things. Not to mention I left that Rod thingy at my house. So I can't even do anything against these "monsters" anyway." Nick backed away from Fred. "I'll call you up in a bit."

"Wait, you aren't coming with me?" Fred said, sounded worried. His voice almost broke up but he stood waiting for an answer from his new friend. Nick turned around, eyes looking down to the ground, and stood only a few feet away.

"Let me go read more about this. Once I figure it out I'll call you up."

"I only have 'till tonight, remember? I don't have time to go and fool around. Are you helping me or not?"

"I'll call you..." Nick's voice trailed away as he walked towards his home. Fred stood there hurt, not sure if he was more upset at the fact Nick wasn't helping or that Nick didn't believe him.

Fred sat on his bed, trying to figure out a plan for tonight. He only had an hour or two before he had to head out and tackle whatever was at the address. With almost no training or counseling from Carl, he was worried. He tried reading more of the book that was given but it only made him uneasy. Details about monsters that can wrap their claws around your back and rip you apart scared him too much to continue. He figured the missions given to the new recruits were minor monsters that slipped through the realms. He focused on what weapon he could use to fight an Unknown. "A sword would be useful. Then again so would a gun. Then again it's a monster. What if it could eat bullets? What if it has wings, or spits out fire? This little thing is what's supposed to protect me?"

He held his Rod in his hand as he kept turning it side to side. The bottom crystal shined with a beautiful silver-white color.

His mother knocked on the door. "Come in," he called out. The door opened slowly. The rare occasion when his parents were home, his mom was too busy looking at her cell phone to even notice her son. She just handed him the house phone and walked back out. "Hello?"

"Hey, it's Nick. Are you still going tonight?" Nick's voice came through the line. Fred would have hung up but this was his last chance to have some backup. "I mean, you do know this is utterly impossible?" Nick's voice sounded stern, as if he didn't believe the words he was saying himself.

"I have to go. I don't have another choice! This could be a joke, but it wouldn't explain everything that has happened. Listen man, I know it sounds crazy but what if it's real? What if I don't stop whatever is out there? What if it hurts someone?" Fred began to feel some type of commitment to stopping these Unknowns. Even if he didn't fully believe they were out there yet.

"It's not real. It can't be real man. We watch all these movies, TV shows, read comics, but it's all make-believe. Monsters do not exist. You know it and so do I." Nick sounded like he was trying to convince himself more than Fred.

"I don't need this. Are you with me tonight or not?"

"I..."

"If you don't want to answer, fine. You know the address. I got to do this. I need to find out if these things really exist or not." Fred hung up the phone before Nick could respond, then tossed the phone to the side of his bed and got up. He attached the beeper to his belt and clipped the Rod to the other side. He took one last look around his room. "Well, it was nice knowing you room. You always did smell kind of funky. That could have been me. Goodbye sweet Xbox, I will miss you," he jokingly said before climbing out of his window.

Nick threw his phone to the side of his bed. "What an idiot?" he barked. He sat down at his computer and began typing away. "How can he believe this stuff? Monsters do not exist. This stupid book-," he said as he picked up the heavy book given to him by Carl. "-is all nonsense." He looked through the names of the monsters. Most of them sounded old and made up, which made sense seeing as this so called organization he was working under created the names. They can literally make up whatever name they saw fit for these beasts. The way they described some of them though made Nick worry. Some had the power to lift a human and tear him into pieces. Some could use fire or electricity as weapons. He even saw one that had his whole body made up of stone.

He let the book slide out of his hands and turned on the TV trying to get his mind off the Unknowns. He wanted to forget everything and just worry about school and his own personal problems. Monsters were great in fairy tales but in real life, when school, girls, and family problems were happening all at once - monsters were the last thing needing to be added to the list.

He sat back watching a comedy, hoping to forget about all the monster talk. However, Fred and the Unknowns kept flaring up in the back of his mind no matter how loud the TV got.

Fred began to walk towards the address that was given to him. He ignored the fact it was already around nine o'clock and his mom would probably find out that he snuck out. She was rarely home and even when she was she was so busy she might as well not have been home. He brushed off the fact that she'd get mad and tried to focus on the mission.

"Damn it," he muttered under his breath as he began to walk quicker through the heated night. The wind was paper thin as it barely brushed his reddish cheeks "Why does this stuff always happen to me?" He wondered why he was the first to get a mission. Why hadn't Nick or even Marshall gotten one yet? Why was he the chosen one - the chubby guy who did nothing but play video games and eat? Fred felt that he lacked all the luck he needed tonight.

Fred grabbed his beeper and looked at the small black device. "He said red or green to start?" As he tried to remember, a couple that was strolling close together began to walk up the block. Fred decided to go with the red button, which made his body heat up. A small spasm hit his head again and he doubled over. Once the pain subsided he looked back up. He grabbed every body part to make sure nothing was wrong or missing. His body temperature quickly returned to normal. He took a look at his hands, still visible to him. "I thought I was supposed to enter the other realm. What the...." he said, and then saw the couple who was walking his way earlier. The girl bumped into Fred.

Fred stepped back as the girl almost fell. The guy took a look to where Fred was as he answered. "Hey, I'm sorry I didn't see her," Fred tried to explain but the guy just helped his girlfriend back to her feet.

"Something is there," she screamed as she ran past where Fred was standing. Her boyfriend took a look in front of him and when seeing nothing, he shrugged and chased after her. Fred just watched as they ran. She could feel him there but they couldn't see him. Visible to Fred, but invisible to the rest of the world.

"Cool." A grin spread appeared on his face.

Nick tossed around a bean bag, which he loved to do. He kept throwing it from hand to hand while watching a basketball game. Occasionally he would look to the side at his Rod but never too long, as he didn't want to miss any part of the game. Once the game went into break he took another look over, this time deciding to pick it up.

He stood now with the Rod in his hand thinking about what he was about to do. "I mean, all I have to do is concentrate right?" he said before glancing around his room. He then spotted a Batman action figure from when he was a kid holding a spear of some sort. "That's it," he shouted and closed his eyes.

Slowly, he let everything in his mind go blank. He blocked out the sound of the game and focused only on the spear. Once getting the spear into his mind he began willing the Rod to change. After a few seconds of straining, Nick let out a breath. Then the Rod shined so bright the whole room lit up. Nick almost let go but he was afraid it would break. He covered his eyes with his free hand as the light shined so bright the windows lit up.

Once finished it became the very thing he imagined. The staff was long and thin. The greenish bottom matched with the blackish middle and the steel white top. A extra hook coming out of the tip. The pole seemed to fit his grip perfectly; the staff was neither cold nor hot. It was almost four feet tall. Nick felt scared, excited, nervous, and surprised all at once.

He twirled it around. It went in perfect motion with his hand. He almost dropped it but grabbed it with his other hand and swung it. It knocked over his alarm clock which smashed on the floor. He jumped back. "Damn. That cost twenty dollars." He laughed. He took a long hard look at the spear. "If this can actually be real then..." he started and looked towards his bedroom door. He knew his father wouldn't be home till well after eleven. Another late night at work. "It's time to take out a few monsters."

Fred reached his destination, still playing around with being invisible. He saw a guy pull over on the road before he got to the address. He slammed his hands on the hood of the car. The guy inside jumped and hit his head on the roof while Fred got a good laugh. "If I'm invisible, then will this thing see me?" he wondered as he reached the exact street the Unknown would show itself on. *"Of course it will. It's in this realm isn't it? It's not in our realm. Otherwise people would have seen these things too."*

The night was beautiful. The moon was up and the whole sky looked bright. Fred walked around the front yard of the first house on the street he was supposed to be on. He looked around but it was empty. A bunch of parked cars along the side walk. A broken mail box on the forth house a little farther down the street. A screaming household across from him. A flickering green light on the end of the street. Yet not a monster in sight.

"Did I read the address wrong? No way. I looked at it like four times. This is the place. It has to be," he thought to himself while looking around some more. He went into the back yards of the houses. He saw one or two pools but again, everything was empty. He began to get annoyed. "They want me to go hunting but there's nothing to actually hunt," shouting as he knew no one could hear him.

He looked back towards the alleyway entrance that leads to the backyard. He began making his way there when he caught a motion. It was quick and blended in with the darkness from the alleyway. "Who's there?", but no answer came from the pitch darkness. "Listen, come out. I got an army of people to hunt you down. It's best you just come out now and give up!" he shouted into the alleyway. *"Do monsters even speak English? Do they even speak?"* Thoughts flushed through his mind as he kept his eyes on the light-less alleyway in front of him.

"I will not be the one who is hunted tonight," a deep voice boomed from the blackness in the alleyway. Fred jumped back scared, almost tripping over himself. He looked hard into the darkness but didn't see anything. He tried to make a shape out of the voice but nothing came to mind. He took a step forward, feeling sweat fall down his cheek.

"I said I got an army coming. You really should just give up now before they get here!" Fred put his hands on the Rod. Still not sure how it worked but he was already thinking of a gun to use as protection against the masked voice.

"Bring the army," said the voice. Its eyes opened bright yellow. "More for me to hunt," it said before it started to scratch the side of the house. Fred took another step back. Not sure what to expect once the Unknown crawled out of the alleyway.

Chapter Seven – Scream

The creature laid in wait for Fred to make the first move. Fred slowly crept to the side of the backyard, trying to figure a way out of the situation. Running through the house, even when invisible, wasn't the best idea. However, jumping across the neighbor's fence to get into the next yard would leave him exposed for a moment. Fred still wasn't even sure what the Unknown was.

The clawing across the house came to a halt and Fred relaxed for a moment. "Are you afraid?" the voice hissed from the darkness. Its yellow eyes were shining bright against the darkness it hid in.

"No, but you should be." Fred said as he tried to edge away from it some more. He decided jumping the fence to the next yard was his best option.

"I should be?" Fred could hear movement finally. "Boy, you look like you're ready to die of fright. Do I scare you?"

Fred's back hit the fence. "What are you?"

"Do you really want to know?"

Fred turned around as quick as he could, grabbed the top of the fence, and hoisted himself up. With every ounce of strength he had in his arms he pulled himself over, kicked off the fence, and landed on the other side. He fell directly on his left shoulder and felt a surge of pain course through it. He quickly pushed himself up, feeling a sharp pain spanning along his entire left side. Ignoring it and stumbling backwards, he kept looking at the fence he just jumped over.

He could hear footsteps from the other side. Strange, loud claps were hitting the grass. Almost horse-like, but heavier. It was getting closer but moving at a slow pace. Fred proceeded to walk backwards, keeping his eye on the fence. "Just you wait, help is on the way," He said, words fumbling out of his mouth. He couldn't cover being scared any longer.

"Death comes for us all," the voice came from right behind the fence. The shadow of the creature was coming through the cracks of the fence. Fred could hear it breathing heavily. "The question I always ask my prey is this. Are you more afraid of the hunt or the actual dying part?" Its claws started playing alongside the fence. Fred stood there, too scared to move. "My favorite part? It's finding out which one it is." It began to laugh.

"I can't believe I made a freaking spear!" Nick was twirling the spear as he made his way outside his house. He slowly walked down the street studying his new weapon. *"I've never actually used a spear in my life. I don't even know how to use this thing as a weapon."* He couldn't help but laugh at himself. He saw the streets were mostly empty but wanted to make sure he wouldn't be seen, so he checked his beeper and hit the red button. His body became hot real fast, he felt a spasm in his head, and then it was all over. Nick wasn't ready for it so he took a moment and sat down.

"Ouch," he moaned, as he rubbed his temples. The pain was gone but the sudden spasm caught him off guard. Unlike Fred, he hadn't felt it before with the instructions for the hunt. This was something completely new to him.

"Man, I was such an idiot before." He thought about the way he had treated Fred. "How could I let him do this all by himself? What kind of friend am I? To just let him go off in the night fighting God knows what." He looked at his spear. "But I really didn't believe it. I didn't think this was real." He stood up and began the walk towards his destination.

Fred turned around again and ran down the empty alleyway. There was complete lack of light as he ran through it. He heard a shattering sound behind him but he didn't dare look back as he ran as fast as his chubby legs could take him. "Yes run. I love the sound of fear!" it roared as he pulled through the alleyway at last.

He got to the end of the front yard before turning back. He peered into the dark alleyway in which he just ran through but saw nothing. The beast was playing games with him.

"I don't know what the hell you are or what you want but..." Fred actually didn't know what to say. The creature hadn't shown itself yet. He had no clue what he was even talking to. He grabbed for his Rod and snapped it off his belt. He began to concentrate, trying to create something to fight the beast. He felt his body getting tighter as he thought about a gun. His bones felt stained, his eyes held tightly shut, and then a huge light shined through the night. He opened his eyes a moment later and in his hands he held a gun. Even with this powerful weapon in his hands he still felt weak. "I got a gun. You better not come out here!"

"A gun? What's that going to do against me? Do you know what a person with wolf's blood is called? There are many names for us. Tales about us since the beginning of time. I am a god amongst my species. Why you ask?" the voice asked, coming from in front of him. He held the gun towards the alleyway but saw no shadows or shapes. "Because I am more advanced than a simple wolf." The voice now came from above. He raised his gun to the roofs of the homes. "I hunt better than any human can imagine." He aimed towards the third building to the left. He heard the voice come from there but he saw nothing. He tried to aim as steady as he could but his hands kept shaking. "I want nothing more than to kill you. However, I need you." Its voice coming from below. He aimed his gun to the grass below his feet, backing up. "Do not fear me, for I am the bringer of new life." The voice came from behind. He turned just as the beast struck.

"I know I'm not in the best shape, but come on." Nick came to a halt around five blocks away. He felt too tired for only walking a couple of blocks. Something was draining his energy. His body began to feel tight all around. *"Could it be the spear? Carl didn't mention anything about this."* He let out a huge sigh but kept moving. "I gotta get to Fred and ask him about this."

Fred jumped back but the beast was too quick. It slashed him right below the neck, across the chest causing him to stumble backwards and trip. He quickly recovered and scrambled away while aiming the gun at the beast. He could feel a burning sensation on his chest. While he knew that he was struck, he didn't want to see how bad it was. He just felt the blood tickling down his stomach. The beast looked up, it's deadly yellow eyes staring at him.

"You sure move fast for a fat kid," the Unknown said, laughing at its own joke. Its face was covered with scars and ripped skin looking mostly human, though huge missing chucks of flesh were gone. The whole chest was covered with fur as was the rest of its body. It had pitch black looking fur. It wore no clothes, only concealed behind its massive fur. Its claws were at least four inches long, with each fingernail sharp and deadly. The combination made for a lethal hybrid of human and beast. "No matter, you won't be able to escape me again." The creature made its way off the roof of the car. The hideous yellow eyes focused on Fred.

"What the hell are you!?" He kept his gun aimed at the beast while moving backwards. He wanted so badly to scream for help. He was scared out of his mind. Who would help him though? Who would believe him? No one else can see this realm. This realm where this beast stood, waiting to finish off its pathetic prey.

"What am I? I told you already."

"You said you aren't a wolf or a man. So are you both? A werewolf?" He wasn't sure what to do. He was trying to buy time while thinking of what to do next.

"Werewolf? I believe you watch too many movies, boy. I said I am a god. I am no wolf. I am no human. I am both but neither," it replied as it took a step closer. "Yes, fear me, young one." It took another step closer. He was ready to pull the trigger. "I am something far beyond both. You will know the true meaning of being hunted," it growled heavily as it was ready to strike again. A massive chunk of its skin was missing where its teeth were located, making the razor sharpness show even more. It was both repulsive and menacing at the same time.

Only a block away now Nick felt tired. He kneeled over for a moment taking a breath. "What the hell kind of trick is this? Yeah, make whatever you want out of this Rod thingy," he said, mimicking Carl's voice. "Just remember that it might exhaust you to the point of death! Thanks, Carl!"

Nick looked up into the sky just as a nice breeze hit him. He let the cold air give him a boost as he wiped the sweat off of his forehead. "Almost there." He slowly walked towards the end of the block before he had to turn down the street Fred was supposed to be on.

Fred shot right at the beast. It didn't bother to move, it just took the bullet in the chest. Fred felt a surge of energy through his arm, then his muscled cramped and he almost dropped the gun. If it wasn't for the fact he was scared he probably would have fallen to the ground. He could feel the energy from his body getting ripped away.

The beast looked up at him and smiled. "Honestly, I was wondering if you were going shoot that thing or just hold it all day." It stepped forward, letting the blood from the bullet wound seep down.

"Get back!" Fred shot again. This bullet hit the beast right in the stomach. It let out a growl as it folded over. Fred moved back again, and could feel almost all his energy leaving his body. His muscles were getting tighter, his eyes becoming heavy and his arms were becoming weak.

"You don't even know your own weakness." The creature walked forward now. Fred went to shoot again but his energy was almost completely gone. He dropped the gun on the ground and fell to his knees. "The saddest part about killing is watching the prey give up. In a few months from now it would have been more fun hunting you." The beast stood over Fred, whose eyes could hardly stay open. "Prey is still prey though," it said as it launched its open mouth and clamped down tightly on Fred's shoulder. Fred's eyes opened as wide as they could. He let out a horrible scream that echoed for blocks. It was a scream so loud that if he was in the realm of humanity every person on the block would be outside now.

He wasn't in the realm of humanity, though. He was in the realm of these monsters; these creatures that could easily kill him at any moment. He felt something burn his shoulders. It was worse than the terrible burning of being bit. It felt like something was ripping into his shoulder. He let out another cry, screaming for help. No one could hear him. No one but Nick, who stood only twenty feet away, but was too scared to help his dying friend.

Chapter Eight – Lifeless

Nick had no words to say once reaching the site. He saw the wolf hybrid stand over its pray with howls of excitement. Blood dripping down from its mouth. *"It can't be,"* was the first thought to enter Nick's head. His friend was laying there, motionless, blood sprayed all over the grass of the yard.

Nick took a step forward as the monstrous creature had not noticed him yet. He studied the Unknown, hunched over, teeth sharp, and claws even sharper. Its yellow eyes were staring down at Fred. It stumbled backwards for a second like it had been hit with a surge of electricity. Nick didn't let the moment of weakness slip away as he flung himself forward with the spear in front. The creature only turned half way around, receiving the tip of the spear through its side. This time, the beast howled in pain.

Blood appearing almost instantaneously to the attack. The spear had made a deep impact, blood dripping down the length of it. The tip was deep inside its body. Nick withdrew the spear and took a step back. The beast took a step closer but fell to one knee, holding its side while blood squeezed through its claws. Nick knew it was in pain, and he was ready to build upon that.

Nick drew his spear back, readying for another strike. The monster let out a small cry, as though begging for pity, sounding like a dog. "Shut up you bastard!" shouted Nick, ready to put the spear in the monster. The creature's eyes lit back up, as it rolled to the side just when the spear came down. As the tip hit the dirt the beast jumped forward, with claws ready to strike. If it wasn't for the pain the beast would have torn through Nick with ease. The wound however, stopped it from doing a full lunge and it was only able to rip through the front of Nick's shirt.

Nick jumped back, pulling the spear with him, readying himself for another attack. The creature rose and held its bloody wound. Once looking at the damage. it howled at Nick, "You...common...bug..." Its breath was coming heavy. The wound was bad, and it was losing energy at a quick rate. Not wasting any more time, it came at Nick once again.

Nick lunged with his spear but with no training his grip was off. The monster knocked both the spear and Nick's hand away as it came closer. Nick threw his left hand forward for a punch but to no avail, the beast's face felt like it was made of stone. Grabbing Nick's left arm it dug the razor sharp claws into him. It let out a howl of excitement as Nick roared with pain.

Nick let the spear slip backwards through his right hand till the tip wasn't far from his hand. He tightened his grip and shoved the tip of the spear right into the stomach of the beast as it held him. Those yellow eyes widen, flickering, and Nick could see behind the yellow eyes it had red ones. The beast let go of Nick and held its new wound. Blood was gushing out of this one at an alarming rate.

Nick took the few seconds he had to back step a few feet. He didn't want to retreat, but at the way his energy was leaving his body there wasn't much more he could do. His vision slowly began to become fuzzy. He stopped a few feet away from his friend lying on the ground. "Fred," he cried out. He saw the massive amount of blood. He felt he was already too late.

The beast growled at Nick. Its pain was very apparent, but so was the fact it wanted to rip Nick into pieces. "Yeah, big boy, I'm not going anywhere. I will kill you!" Nick pointed the spear at the beast, this time holding it with both hands. The beast roared into the night sky.

"This wasn't the plan," it shrieked at Nick. Nick stood there quietly; spear in hand ready for defense. "Why did you show up? Who are you?"

"The person who's gonna kill you."

"Kill me?"

"I'm sorry; did I hit you over the head or something? Can't hear me? I said I'm the one who's gonna kill you." Nick felt the adrenaline building inside of him. He could feel he was getting weaker the longer he held on to the spear. He fought against his body, commanding it to hold out just a little longer.

"Why does every kid in this town talk back to me like this? You should bow down before a god like me!" Now it was standing back on its feet. Nick could see that it was losing balance, with its eyes flickering, and body covered with blood.

"Bow down?" Nick pointed the spear towards the Unknowns' face. "Sorry, but I was taught to never bow down to things lesser than me." He glanced at his friend lying on the ground. He could feel the anger building up in him. "Especially something who preys on the weak!"

"Ah, but hunting is the fun part of life, no?"

"No, hunting the ones who are a challenge," Nick began as he stepped forward, tightening his grip on the spear. "That's the only real fun in a hunt"

"I think I found my challenge then." The beast smiled. The huge ugly face twisted, showing the disgusting teeth through the empty patches of skin. It stepped forward, and Nick stepped backwards.

"It's almost dead. Keep back, strike from afar. Keep hitting it till it can't stand anymore. Keep it at a safe distance. You've been through worse. Stay with me, body." Nick could feel his body was getting tighter, his breathing became heavier. He wanted to just fall down and sleep but he wasn't about to give in. Not after he saw his friend assaulted so viciously. He would stand until he could stand no more.

The beast came flying forward. Nick moved to the side. The wounds made the creature move clumsily. It stumbled, almost falling to the ground. Nick took advantage and took another stab. The tip of the spear hit the right leg of the beast. It howled but Nick kept up the attack. He withdrew the spear, circled behind the beast and struck again. This time the tip pierced through the upper back of the giant wolf. It screamed it agony but Nick ignored it and went to for another stab. The creature turned quickly, swiping at the spear, knocking it to the side. Nick backed away and he could feel the energy seeping away. He felt so weak that he almost fell right there. The beast got back up but fell again. Nick kept moving back, almost tripping multiple times. The beast tried to get back to its feet but just fell forward again. Nick kept stumbling backwards until he leaned against the mailbox in the yard. He held it tightly to keep himself up. The beast crawled closer, crying and growling every inch as it got closer.

Nick felt a hand rest on his shoulder. "I got it," Peter said smiling. He walked forward and pointed a huge black gun at the beast's head. Without flinching, he pulled the trigger; the bullet drove straight through the large head. It didn't howl. No more growling escaped from the jagged teeth. It just laid as motionless and silent as Fred was. Peter trotted back to Nick, grabbing his right hand. He felt the energy slip away too but he kept his composure up.

"Where did you come from?" Nick was so tired. He could barely stay on his feet.

"Carl called. He told me something was wrong and to meet him at this spot. I was closer than he was so I made my way here before him. He said to be careful, something was interfering with the mission. I think he meant this thing." He nodded towards the Unknown lying on the grass, dead.

"What the hell? Why did they send Fred to do this by himself? This thing nearly killed both of us. I'm pretty sure Fred is..." he let his voice trail off. He pushed himself from the mailbox, almost falling face first, and slowly trudged towards Fred. Peter ran up to Nick and put his arm around him, helping him walk.

"I don't think they did. This creature isn't supposed to be hunted by us. It's far too strong. Actually, from reading the book these things aren't even supposed to be hunted alone. They are fierce predators waiting to hunt multiple preys. How you survived this long is beyond me." Peter let Nick go as they both stood over Fred.

"It wouldn't shut up. Gave you time to get here and save us." Nick looked at his friend and bent down. He saw the wound, blood still coming out. Dark red and purple bite marks.
Strange, Nick thought. He then looked up at Peter. "How far is Carl?"

"He said he was only twenty minutes away about fifteen minutes ago. He should be here any minute."

"Ah, good. 'Cause I don't think I can stay... awake." Nick let his eyes shut. He let go of all the tightness in his body and fell forward. He couldn't hold on any longer. He let himself drift away.

Chapter Nine – The Station

Nick felt his body shake. He slowly opened his eyes to feel a slight breeze of air pass over him. His mouth felt dry, as if he'd been sleeping with his mouth open all night. As he slowly regained his senses he could hear chatter to his left. He saw Peter standing above him. "You okay?" Peter asked. Nick winced as he tried to stand. He still didn't fully recover all his stamina from the fight.

He sat up slowly, feeling like he was hit by a bus. He wasn't in any condition to move quickly so he took his time. He took a look to his other side and saw Carl and two other people standing there. He couldn't hear from this distance but Carl looked annoyed. The other two shook their heads. One was of Asian descent. The other was African American. "Yeah, I'm okay," Nick muttered. "What's up with those guys? Where's Fred?"

"They took him back to a place they call *"The Station"* but I'm not sure what that is." Peter watched as Nick slowly rose. He went to help his friend but Nick put his hand up. He wanted to do it on his own. To show he still had some strength and dignity left.

"Well, let's go find out what exactly that is then," Nick said as he made his way towards the group. Peter followed close behind. The injuries Nick suffered weren't horrible but he felt his body aching beyond anything he had experienced in the past. It was like he was lifting weights for the last five hours or went on a million mile march. His legs felt like noodles, his arms were weak, and his head was pounding. Yet he kept moving forward, needing to know what had happened to Fred.

As the boys approached Carl looked towards them. "Glad to see you're standing again," Carl said smiling. Nick nodded. "This is Jin and Tyson." He pointed towards the two men next to him.

Jin extended his hand. "Hi, nice to meet you both." The boys took their turns to shake his hand then Tyson's. "I'm sorry about your friend."

"Is he okay?" Nick felt his face flush white. He feared the worst about Fred when he thought back to seeing him lying on the ground before he went unconscious.

"Two people took him back to the Station. His wound is severe but they have hope. They were able to stop the bleeding using a seal. Still, he bled a lot before they got to him," Carl informed Nick. He looked angry while saying it, like he was blaming himself. The guilt was all over his face.

"I want to see him," Nick said. His voice cracked from his dry mouth. Jin passed him a water bottle. Nick took a sip, letting the cool liquid slide down his throat. He coughed but it felt great to not feel the rough, hard, dry feeling. He took more deep gulps.

"We can go." Carl turned around to look at the scene. "Let's head to the house. We still don't exist in this realm just yet. I know you're feeling some extra pressure but we don't wanna be seen. Especially you Nick, with all the blood smeared on your shirt." Carl began walking down the block, Jin and Tyson at his side.

As they walked, Nick kept pace with Peter. Both walked a few feet behind the adults. Nick felt his legs give out every so often, but he kept moving. After he checked to make sure his friend was okay he'd finally let his body rest. Nick wanted to focus on seeing Fred but something in the back of his head kept pounding at him. He had no choice but to open his mouth. "Peter," he started. Peter looked over at him. "Listen, thank you for before."

"No need to thank me again. I was just helping out," Peter said. "Just glad I got there in time."

Nick looked at his new friend. He wasn't sure how to word what was on his mind. He needed to get it out in the open though. "I do thank you. Without you, I'd probably be dead right now. Just... something I need to ask you."

"What's that?"

"When you came up to me, you said you had this, walked up to that creature, and shot it. Like, right in the face. Without even flinching, really. Like you've done it all before. I thought you just started this."

Peter looked at Nick confused. "Well, I never have but I saw you were hurt. So I did my job."

"But you killed it without even stopping for a moment. Like it came really natural for you. Have you've shot anything before?"

"No."

"So, how did you do that with such ease?"

"It was a monster."

"Yeah, but he was lying on the ground. He wasn't going to be able to do much. He was dying. You had no problem going up to his face and blasting it. I mean, I thank you for that. I'm just a little worried it was too easy for you," Nick rushed. He wanted to make it clear he wasn't judging his friend harshly but he needed to know the truth. Peter looked as though he was annoyed. Nick looked closer though, maybe it wasn't Peter getting annoyed. It was more than that; Peter was perfectly calm.

"It," Peter stated.

"It?"

"It's an 'IT', not a 'he'. It was a monster. It tried to kill you. It almost killed Fred. I did my job. Why didn't you do yours? Maybe Fred wouldn't be in critical condition if you did your job." Peter was now in a defensive position. Nick looked at Peter, almost not sure how to continue. Peter made sure to keep looking back at Nick, waiting for his answer, pressuring him. After a moment Nick looked down.

"I know it was a monster. I don't mean to judge you. It just scared me that you were able to kill it so easily and I didn't."

"It was just that. A monster. Not a he or she. A hideous monster."

"I know but I'm starting to wonder if that would have even mattered." Nick looked back at Peter. Now Peter's eyes were darting from side to side, anger flared in his face. Nick went too far, Peter was angry.

"I don't want to talk about this anymore." Peter began

walking quicker, leaving Nick behind. Nick felt the guilt building up inside. He hadn't meant to offend Peter but he also needed to know what was going through his new partner's head. He had to fight alongside Peter one day, but how can you fight alongside someone you can't fully trust?

They arrived back at the house. Carl let the two other men go into the house first before heading in with the boys. He looked back at his students; half of his unit. "I'm going to find out what went wrong. None of you were supposed to be on a mission this soon. We didn't go over the safety procedures. Most of you never even used your Rod in battle. Most of you don't even know my number to call me in emergencies. Our "Callers" never even sensed this beast. Something went very wrong and I promise I'll find out what it was," Carl said determinedly. The boys looked at their mentor, not sure how to react. Carl was an honest man. He wanted to hide nothing from any of his students. This was important, a life-or-death situation. This wasn't a game, people got hurt. "I'm sorry."

"I wanna know what happened," Nick began. He looked at Peter who looked away. "However, it's more important to find out how Fred is right now. Let's go." Nick began limping towards the old house. Carl looked at Peter who nodded. They followed Nick into the house.

"This is going to be strange, but do not fear, you'll be okay," Carl said. He walked to the closet and fully opened it. Inside were four tubes. They were made of glass and swirled around an elevator-type machine. "We take this down to the Station."

"Down?" Nick felt his stomach knot. Unlike most people he wasn't afraid of heights. He just wasn't a fan of being underground though.

"Yes. Don't worry it'll take only a few minutes. Once you reach the bottom level you'll be at the Station, the area where our local Exterminators meet up as well. It's also where the bulk of our operation is. We keep it out of the public's view just so we can operate peacefully while protecting the population. So just jump in and hold on." Carl touched the glass; it lit up blue and opened up. He entered the tube and turned around. "See you two down there." The glass closed and the tube shot down quickly.

"Yeah, that seems safe," Nick said jokingly. Peter didn't laugh or look at him. Just stepped forward and touched the glass. It opened up quickly. "Listen Peter, I'm sorry." Peter ignored him. He went inside the tube, the glass shut, and down he went.

"Damn it. Why do I always open my mouth too soon," Nick muttered as he went up to the glass. He tapped it. The glass opened, inviting Nick to step inside. "Oh, this is some scary stuff. This can't be safe." He slowly stepped inside. Once fully inside the glass shut and the elevator began to light up some. "Uhhh, go down?" It didn't move. "Move please?" It still stood still. "What the heck? They didn't say anything and you just shot them all the way do-" He began right before the tube shot down. It went at a speed Nick wasn't ready for and he could feel himself tipping over. Smacking his head hard against the glass he held on tightly for dear life. The pressure of the speed was hard to adjust to but after a moment Nick was able to stabilize himself on the ground. He slowly rose and felt the pressure starting to lessen up. "It's slowing," he said under his breath as the elevator began to move at a far slower speed. After a moment it made a ping sound and the glass doors opened. He quickly scrambled out and fell to his knees again.

"Are you all right?" Carl stood a few feet away.

"I never...ever...want...to...do...that...again," Nick said, running out of breath. He wasn't tired but still scared out of his mind. He much rather fight another wolf-type hybrid monster than go back in the tube.

Carl laughed, so big that even Peter backed up. "I needed that. Thanks." Carl walked up to Nick and held his hand out. "Up you go." He pulled Nick to his feet. "Let's go check on Fred," he said smiling. Nick nodded and then began walking down the hallway, with Peter following.

Everything was white. The ceiling, the walls, even the

floor was white. All giving off a marble look, with reflections coming off the walls. Nick could see himself in the wall and waved. Peter did the same, trying to understand how a whole station can be put underground. As they walked through the hallway they began to wonder if there were any rooms. There were signs on the wall every couple of steps but no door. The end of the hallway had two huge doors, but they were ways off. "Hey, do you guys actually have rooms here?" Nick placed his hand on the wall while walking. He could feel the cold from the wall tingle up his fingertips.

"We've passed a bunch of them. You just aren't use to rooms like this. Here's the medic room." Carl stopped. Nick and Peter stopped alongside him watching their mentor stand there, looking at the empty white wall. Carl placed his hand on the wall and let it rest below the sign that spelled out "Medic's Station: Intense Care". After a few moments the wall came to life and slid open. Carl stepped inside and the boys followed. As they walked in they could see over twenty beds in a long hall. Again, almost everything in the room was white.

"How's he doing?" Carl asked.

A woman who was filling out his paper work looked up. "We've sealed the wound for the most part. He lost a lot of blood but the healers were able to fix most of the damage. We've given him a blood transfusion as well. So for now, he's in stable condition. Whatever attacked him did a real number on him though."

"Thanks, Cindy," he smiled and she nodded. As she left the room the door closed behind her. Carl looked at his student, his soldier, wounded on the table. He grasped the edge of the bed. He wanted to shout, wanted to scream, wanted to punch something. He let his anger flare, his eyes shut tight, trying to picture the beast digging it's teeth into Fred. The way this poor boy must have been scared beyond belief. Scared and crying, wondering why no one was coming to his aid.

"Hey Fred," Nick said walking up to his friend on the bed. Carl opened his eyes and watched Nick looking down at his friend. "I'm sorry for leaving you out there by yourself. You must have been so scared." He placed his hand on his friend's chest. "I won't ever leave you alone to fight these things. You counted on me and I let you down. It'll never happen again. You see we're a crew. A unit. We fight together from now on. Me, you," he began as he looked back at Peter. "Peter here, and even that idiot Marshall." Peter laughed, Carl let a chuckle out. "So please forgive me. I promise it won't happen again man."

Fred opened his eyes and smiled. "I'm not dead, ya know. No need to be so dramatic," he said, smiling. Nick jumped back. Carl let go of the bed, smiling. "I was scared as heck though. Carl, what in the world was that thing?"

Carl looked at his unit looking back at him. "Well, it was a hybrid of a human and wolf. I guess you can call it a werewolf from other fantasy material. I just labeled it as a wolf hybrid." Fred was about to speak but Carl continued. "No, you cannot transform into one from being bit. That's just nonsense. These things are born that way. Though these creatures are still very rare. Their species are so small now days that they never really dare attack or head into our realm. They usually keep to themselves and stay in their world. Not to mention-" he began. He wasn't sure how much he should reveal but the kids watched him, eagerly awaiting more information. "Our "Callers" never even felt its presence. Which is odd, 'cause they should have when he came breaking through our realm."

"What are Callers?"

Peter answered for Carl. "They are the beings that sense Unknowns passing over to the other realms. They can sense when something is making their way into our realm. They are almost always right which makes this an odd case." Carl looked at Peter, surprised.

"How much did you read in that guide?"

"Around half-way through now. I like to be prepared."

"Yeah, no kidding. Well, Peter explained it very well. Callers are meant to pick up on these things passing into our world, or our realm. Which is why I don't understand how they didn't pick up on this one."

"Unless it was already here," Fred said weakly from the bed. They all looked at him. "Hey, give the broken guy some credit. I'm hurt, not dead."

"We'll have to investigate some more but for now let's let Fred get some rest," Carl said. He looked at his student. "I'm sorry. I will find out what happened."

"I know you will," Fred replied, nodding.

"Get better soon man. Call me when you're out of this place," Nick said smiling and walked out the room with Carl.

"Feel better. Let me know if you need anything. I put my phone number into your cell phone along with Nick's and Carl's as well. I also took down Marshall's and spread it around between us. Just in case we need backup we'll be there next time." Fred nodded. Peter pattered his friend's unharmed shoulder and smiled. "We'll find out what happened and fix it. Count on us."

Peter walked out of the room and the door slid closed. "He looks like he'll be okay. That's a relief," Nick said, feeling completely drained. "I think it's time I head home. My dad's going to kill me."

"Yeah, it's one thirty... and we both have school tomorrow. We probably should get home. Hopefully my dad is too drunk to even remember I was out all night," Peter said with a dry laugh. He began walking towards the tubes.

"Goodnight Carl!" Nick waved goodbye and went to catch up with Peter.

"Goodnight..." Carl let his voice drift. Something was very wrong. If the Callers didn't pick up on the creature, something was interfering with the realm's balance. Someone was out there and Carl had a good idea of who that might be. He shook his head and walked back to his office, piecing together the clues he had.

Chapter Ten – Rock On

"Nick, wake up!" It was so loud Nick flew out of his bed. He flipped over, fell to the ground, and waited there until he could feel the rest of his body react. He got home well past two the night before. His dad was waiting for him, giving him a big lecture about how late it was, yelling that it wasn't safe in this city, and that if he ever did it again he'd be grounded for months. Nick was so tired he only heard parts of it, but it mostly came down to the fact that Nick was out past eleven o'clock on a school night.

Nick grabbed the dresser and pulled. He rose like a zombie from a grave. He still felt sore but far better after sleeping it off. While it was only a few hours of sleep it gave him enough energy to get to school. He slowly made his way into the bathroom to get changed for school. He kept viewing the scenes in his head from the night before while changing.

While kids were getting ready to go to bed last night he was fighting a hybrid wolf, which nearly killed his friend, and almost ripped his own head off. Its vicious eyes told Nick that if the Unknown was at full strength it would of easily ripped him to shreds. Nick remembered how hard his heart was pounding as he made advancements towards the creature. Every time he stabbed the beast he focused on getting away again. Taking his time to slowly kill it, but scared at any moment he, himself would be killed. He made it through the fight thanks to Peter. He couldn't help but think if he had taken a misstep and would have been slaughtered by the beast. He tried pushing the thoughts to back of his mind as he grabbed his beeper and started to head out of his room.

Nick's father was giving him the eye the whole time he sat at the table eating. It was to show just how mad he really was. Nick grabbed a bagel and began eating it. "Hi...sunshine?" Nick tried to joke around. His father kept silent. "I'm sorry about last night," Nick said. "It won't happen again."

"You're damn right it won't!" His father didn't divert his

eyes. "If you are ever out that late again without my permission you will be grounded for so long, you'll never see the outside of this house again! Do you understand?"

"I got it pops."

"Do you? 'Cause I'm pretty sure you want to come back with some smart-ass remark. I can see it in your eyes."

"Dad, I said I'm sorry. I don't know what else you want from me."

"I want my son not to be hurt or killed out there. You looked like crap when you got home. You won't tell me what happened, fine, but I won't accept you getting into fights at one in the morning. No, not in this house," Nick's father said getting up and putting his dish in the sink. "I lost someone too close to me already. I won't lose you, too." Nick's father said before grabbing his keys and leaving the house, slamming the door behind him.

Nick studied the bagel as he thought about his mother. He missed her so much. The memories resurfacing were always painful. He tried to keep those away. He refused to let it bring him down again. He held her memories in his mind but every time he thought about her it hurt again. He threw the bagel out and went to school, hoping it would distract him enough.

"You look dead," Kelly said as she watched Nick at his desk. He had his face buried into his arms, trying to block out the world. He wanted to sleep, he still felt crappy from the fight the night before.

"I'm fine. Just not feeling all too well." He mumbled under his arms.

"Well, maybe you should head home then. You look like you're about to pass out and die right here."

Nick raised his head. "I'm fine, I promise."

"Okay, whatever you say." She turned back around.

"Great, be mean to the only girl who's talking to you. Great job Nick, anyone else you wanna piss off?" He let his head rest on his arms. Peter walked in and sat behind him. *"I got to make this right but what do I say?"* Nick turned around in his

desk.

"It's fine. You don't have to apologize. I understand why you were concerned, and I thank you for that. I promise I'm not crazy or anything. I was diagnosed with sociopathic tendencies. Sometimes I don't feel things, one being remorse. I-" He was trying to think how to explain it better. "Sometimes I don't understand why people act a certain way they do. I lack some emotions at times. It makes me odd. Maybe you don't want to be friends with me for that, and I understand." Peter always felt embarrassed about his condition. Sometimes people cried at certain points in movies or TV shows while he just sat there trying to figure out why. Other times people got angry, while he simply just felt nothing. Other times he felt angry, sad, or happy. He wasn't sure why these emotions were on and off but he lived with them this way for his whole life. He learned to accept them, even if no one else would.

"I just need to know when we work together you have my back. I don't care if you're happy or sad. I just need to know if an Unknown is attacking me, you'll jump in and help." Peter felt a new feeling as Nick spoke. He felt...wanted. "We all got issues. I don't like elevators. Fred obviously loves food a bit too much. You don't have emotions and Marshall is an idiot. So, we all have issues? Our plan should always come back to working together. We're a unit now. So as long as you have my back, you will always be a friend in my eyes." Nick finished.

Peter would usually feel empty yet somehow, in this moment, he felt something he never did before. No one ever wanted to be his friend. Most people were decent enough to him, and said hi. Kelly was the one person who always made him feel something. Not love or lust, but a bond. She was like a sister and he respected her in that way. He felt like he had to protect her, probably because she always protected him. For his mother he felt love, or maybe it was just the fact she was his mother that he felt that. He wasn't sure if he really loved her. He thought nothing of his father. Sometimes he felt himself becoming angry; meaning he probably hated his father. He felt disconnected with the world thanks to the way he was brought up. Yet, at this current moment he felt something completely new. Something that made him feel... happy. A joyful emotion that overcame his entire body. He smiled, and for once it wasn't forced. "Thanks Nick. I'll always have your back." Nick grinned and turned back around.

Peter sat there, unable to get rid of the smile that was plastered across his face. He could get used to this feeling.

Marshall ran up to Nick at lunch and sat down. "Dude. Dude. DUDE!" Marshall kept shaking Nick Nick pushed him off and looked at him like he was crazy. "Dude, I saw something crazy. Dude, it was like a freaking rock or something popped up while I was taking a piss. It nearly scared the piss out of me."

"No pun intended," Nick pointed out, chuckling.

"Huh?"

Nick sighed. "Nothing, keep going."

"So, I saw this rock show up right. I walked up to it and it showed an address. It then crumbled to pieces. It was crazy!" Marshall was so excited he was shouting. Luckily the lunch room was so loud no one could hear him.

"Fred saw that too. Carl wanted to talk more about how to deal with these missions and begin training but it seems these missions are just popping up. This is bad man, Fred almost died." Marshall stopped fooling around. He looked at Nick, worried now.

"What? What the hell happened? When did this happen?"

"You didn't hear about last night?"

"Hear about what?"

"Fred fought a monster. The thing almost killed him. I fought it too, I almost died. Luckily Pete came in time and shot it," Nick finished. Marshall's jaw was hanging open, shocked. Nick figured Peter or Carl would have told Marshall about the events. Nick only just realized that they were probably busy with their own personal problems. No one bothered to text or call Marshall about the events.

"This is..." Marshall began. He looked down at the table; trying to grasp the fact his friend was almost killed. "Fred's okay though, right? It wasn't too serious, right?" Marshall couldn't control his emotion in his voice. He sounded worried and scared at the same time.

"Yeah, he'll be okay. Sorry no one told you. I figured someone would have gotten to you but I guess we've all been busy trying to figure this all out."

Marshall waved his hand. "It's okay. As long as he's okay. Well damn, these creatures must be pretty wicked."

"Wicked? Are you British now?"

"Wicked isn't British!"

"Yeah, it is."

"All right fine, these beasts must be pretty nasty." Marshall said rolling his eyes. Nick laughed and patted him on the back. "Listen man, I'm kind of freaked out. I think maybe we should team up."

"Yeah, figured you'd say that. I'll meet you after school outside. I'll text Peter to meet us there," Nick said, Marshall felt relieved. Working as a real unit this time. Nick didn't want any more friends hurt. This time, together, they'd take down these creatures without any more casualties.

Nick sat in his last class writing down some ideas for his weapons. If the Rod could really become anything, he was all for trying different combinations. It wasn't limited to just real-life weapons. He tried thinking of magical things. Fire or ice hands. Make his whole body filled with spikes. He started to wish he actually read the guide that he was given, so he had some ideas of what the more advanced Exterminators used.

He took a look back and saw Fred's empty desk. He felt relieved to see his friend awake in the bed last night, but he still felt guilty. He was always so willing to try and help people. Why did he hesitate with Fred? Why didn't he go with him last night, even if he didn't believe in the monsters? He finally settled on the answer that he was just scared. He had no real excuse for not helping out a friend.

"Where's Fred?" Kelly sat down. Nick looked to her, took a quick look back to the empty desk, then back to her.

"He wasn't feeling well. He should be back soon."

"Oh well, that's good. As long as it isn't serious," She said. She looked at Nick oddly.

"Ummm hi?"

"Sorry, I just have this feeling you're dealing with a lot."

"That's a pretty good guess." He felt his heart pound faster. The more she talked to him, the bigger the connection felt.

"What's up? Are you still trying to get used to the city?"

"Yeah, and the deadly creatures that come with it," he thought. "Yeah it's been a bit tough. I lost-" He wanted to speak more about it but decided to skip over the fact he struggled to deal with the loss of his mother. "I just can't get used to this place too well. I miss my old friends and all that." It wasn't a complete lie. He did miss his old friends.

"Well, you'll just have to make new friends. This city is huge, and hectic, but I'm sure you'll find a good group of people. Fred's a nice enough guy, Pete's awesome, so you'll be fine."

"Yeah, I just need to find a girlfriend now," he said jokingly. He felt his heart wanting to break through his chest. His throat became extremely dry. He could feel his face heating up. "I mean, not that I'm asking you out. I'm just saying I need to find a girl. Who wants to be a friend? Like a close friend. Like a-" He looked at her while she just smiled. "Okay, I'ma shut up now."

"You're the strangest kid I've ever met," she said giggling. He frowned.

"Kid?"

"Sorry, *man.*"

"Now, you're just being mean," he said grinning.

"Well, are you going ask for my number?" She had her phone in her hand ready for his number. He quickly put his hand into his pocket, trying to retrieve his phone. "You didn't even prepare? Oh, you sure do know how to make a girl feel special," she teased in a terrible southern accent.

He pulled his phone out too fast, almost dropping it when he got it out of his pocket. "Okay, ready," he said ready to dial. He tried to conceal his excitement but he couldn't. The very idea of being on a date with a girl like Kelly made him so excited he was about jump out of his skin.

They exchanged phone numbers and put their phones away. Kelly turned around to get ready for class. "Don't lose it now. I'll be waiting. Remember its Friday so if I don't get a call by Sunday I'll be losing somebody's number." Nick couldn't see her face but could imagine a smile was on it.

"You said we'd be going through training first. Marshall got a calling, an address a few minutes away from school. He's never been in combat, he's pretty scared," Nick said on the phone. Marshall was sitting down on the side of the road while Nick was talking to Carl.

"I'm not scared!" Marshall threw a pebble at Nick.

"It should be fine. The signals on this one are weak. It shouldn't be very strong. If you could take down a hybrid wolf you'll have no problem handling whatever it is. Just be cautious. Also, keep Marshall from doing anything stupid," Carl finished.

"You're on speaker ya know," Marshall said annoyed.

"All right, we'll call if anything goes bad. I told Peter to meet us there but no response from him."

"He might have forgotten his phone. Just be careful out there. Work together as a team and you'll have no problem. Tell Marshall how to use his Rod. Be on alert and always looking for a striking moment. I have faith you'll do fine. A cleanup crew will arrive soon after you kill the beast so don't worry. Call me later with the details. We'll begin training as soon as I get back into town," Carl said his goodbye and Nick hung up.

"All right, we ready to do this or what!?" Marshall was up on his feet.

"We're ready. Let's head into their realm. Hit the red button on your beeper," Nick instructed as he hit the button on his own beeper. He then looked to his side and began to panic.

Marshall hit the button as well, entering the new realm for the first time. Once in it he shivered. "What the hell was that? My whole body felt like it was on fire. That was...well that was pretty awesome actually," he laughed.

"We've got a problem."

"What kind of problem?"

"My Rod. I left it at home."

"Yeah, that's gonna be a problem."

"Listen kid, just give us the cell phone and any money you have," Ryan said. The big bully of the school was now targeting Peter.

"I don't have a cell phone. Just leave me alone." Peter tried walking past Ryan but his two friends blocked the way. "Listen, I don't want any trouble. I just want to get to my friends, please." Peter never resorted to violence. He had been bullied most of his life. Due to his small frame the bullies took advantage of him. He wasn't sure how he'd fare in a fight but as of late he was getting more anxious to find out. He'd just killed a beast with tremendous power the night before. He was sure he could handle all three boys. If only he was able to use his Rod. He read multiple times in the guide that the use of the Rod for personal use against innocents would result in termination. As in ending one's life for a crime they committed.

"Friends? Like you have any," roared Ryan as he pushed Peter back. Peter almost tripped over his own legs but managed to grab hold of the bar to his side just in time. He watched as Ryan's friends moved closer.

"I really rather avoid this altercation. I just want to go. Please, leave me alone." He could feel his phone vibrating. He was either getting a call or text. He wanted to find out what it was but with the three standing in front of him he didn't want to show them he had the phone on him. "I have only three dollars. If that's all you need then I could give that to you." He was trying to figure a way out of this without getting into a fight.

"Three dollars? What kind of kid only has three dollars?"

"Well, you're asking for money. So that means you don't even have three dollars." Peter knew the second he finished speaking it was a mistake. He winced at his own words.

"Thank you. You just gave me a real reason to beat your face in," Ryan said smiling. He began to advance with his two friends following.

They were only a block away from their destination. "I can't believe you forgot your Rod."

"*I* can't believe I forgot my Rod."

"I can't believe you forgot your Rod. Like for real."

"Yeah, I get it Marshall. I forgot my Rod and you can't believe it. Neither can I. Now all our hopes of victory rest on your shoulders. So listen to me when I say how to use the Rod," Nick finished speaking. Marshall looked at him then smiled. He grabbed the Rod out of his hand and twirled it around. "This is serious; we have no clue what we're facing."

Marshall stopped twirling the Rod and nodded. "I got it man. No more joking around. What should I transform this thing in to anyway?"

"I don't know yet. I'd wait to see what we're up against." Nick turned the corner and stopped. "Okay this is the address. Whatever we're supposed to hunt should be around here." He slowly walked forward, checking for any sign of an Unknown. The block looked deserted for the most part. No people were walking down the old abandoned looking block. There were a couple of older cars but besides that the street was empty.

"Maybe the address is wrong?" Marshall surveyed the area but to no avail.

"You're the one that saw the address. What did it say?"

Marshall looked up at the street sign. "No, this is the right address. This is really odd." Marshall began walking forward. Nick went to shout out to slow down but it was so quiet Nick decided to just walk along side Marshall. They began checking under the cars, and looking inside the alleyways between the houses. Their search came to a stop when they almost reached the other end of the block. "Okay, what the hell? Where are these monsters?"

"It would just be one Unknown," Nick replied. He looked back. "It's strange though. We should have see-" He began but then heard a weird growl from the middle of the road. They both darted into the streets and saw a creature slamming its head into the concrete. It was small, no bigger than three feet. Its body looked to be made of rock, rugged, and colored very white. Nick noticed right away it didn't have eyes Instead its nose was double the size of a regular one. "It must sense things by smell." Nick said pointing to the beast's huge nose.

"Oh, well, then you're in big trouble."

"This is serious."

"Okay, serious face on!" Marshall moved forward. Nick grabbed him by the shirt and pulled him back. "What's the deal man? Let's go kill that little thing. My dogs' bigger than that."

"We don't know how strong it is. It could turn into a huge hulking monster the second it goes into fighting stance. We have to be careful. Not to mention only you have a Rod. Meaning all our hopes are pinned on you." Nick took another look at the creature. It stopped hitting its head and began sniffing the air.

"Listen dude, we won't find out just standing here. Let's go kick this things ass!" Marshall pushed Nick off and began walking forward. Nick trailed behind, cautious every step. Marshall held the Rod tight and looked at the beast as it turned left to right, looking for something. "Hey, little ugly rock-looking monster." It heard Marshall and quickly turned. It sniffed the air. "Yeah, now you hear me. I'm an Exterminator. I was sent to kill you. Can you kindly just stand there while I do that?"

The creature stepped backwards. Then its front temple grew a large horn over a foot long. Its whole body began to tremble and pieces of its rock skin chipped making its body more ragged. Its whole body filled with sharp rock piercings, going into a defensive-type body mode. It began to growl at the boys.

Marshall and Nick stepped back. "It grew a horn? Talk about growing pains. This was a very bad idea!" Marshall screamed as the creature began to charge at them.

Chapter Eleven – Hard Case

Marshall jumped on top of one of the cars. Nick did the same across the street from him. Before Marshall could fully turn around to face the creature it smashed its face into the front of the car. Marshall slipped and smacked his left hand on the roof. He was about to fall off but he grabbed the other end of the roof with his right hand, catching his balance. Letting a few curse words slip out as he hung on.

The beast backed away from the car. It growled and shook its head. It was in a fury, wanting to smash everything that was in front of it. "This thing is crazy! It's like a miniature bull!" Marshall was shouting, positioning himself on top of the car.

Nick stood on top of the car row looking around the area. The block was still empty. *"Good, don't need any innocents getting hurt."* He looked to Marshall trying to regain his posture. "Hey, we gotta stop this thing. Grab your Rod, we're gonna have to use a weapon that's strong enough to break rock...or stone. I guess rock. I don't know what this thing is but make something really really strong."

Marshall nodded. He looked around the roof of the car. "Uh, we've got a problem."

"Of course we do!"

"Dropped the Rod. I didn't even notice I did," Marshall said, with a slight laugh. "This is bad."

"Yeah, real bad. Find it. I'll think of something in the meantime." The beast growled right before shoving its head into the car again. Marshall tipped over but was able to keep most of his balance. The car's whole left side was broken in. The front door barely hanging on.

"Please hurry up with that plan," Marshall cried out.

Ryan's first friend grabbed Peter by the shoulder. He tried backing up but Ryan's other friend was already grabbing his left shoulder. They threw him against a pole while Ryan slowly walked forward. Peter felt nothing. He just focused on his cell phone. *"Is it a mission? Is it Nick? Fred? Carl? I need to find out as soon as possible."* Peter's mind kept jumping places. What kind of situations his new found teammates could be in.

"You really are a weirdo, kid. Pay attention when someone's about to beat you senseless," Ryan said smiling. He pulled his hand back and Peter braced himself. He's been hit before, a lot, so he knew how it felt. Still, nothing prepares you for the first strike. It came hard, right across Peter's face, and he almost immediately fell to the ground. He let the pain sink in.

"It wouldn't be Carl. It has to be Nick or Fred. Fred wouldn't be in danger though so he wouldn't call more than once or twice. The phone vibrated four or five times. Meaning text messages and not calls. So it must mean-" Peter's thought process was interrupted by Ryan kicking him in his side. He rolled over, holding it. *"But if it's Nick could this mean he's alone in the hunt? Fighting whatever is coming to our realm? Did he let Marshall tag along?"*

"Hey freak, you gonna defend yourself or just lay there?" Ryan was standing above Peter. Peter watched the bully but didn't move. He was trying to adjust to the situation. He might not have felt too many emotions but he felt pain. He let go of his side and slowly got up. "You're taking too long," Ryan said. With that he let another fist hit. This time connecting with Peter's cheek. He stumbled to the side, then fell. "Come on, fight back!"

"I found it!" Marshall pointed to the Rod on the back end of the car. "It must have rolled over when I got on top of the car," He said. Then another crash, the front door fell off. It growled. Not because it was hurt but because it was getting fired up. "Okay, do you have a plan now? This thing is getting really pissed!"

Nick jumped off the car. He slowly made his way to the

front of the car. He grabbed a few pebbles and began launching them at the creature. At first the rock Unknown didn't notice. It just kept shaking its head, getting ready to smash into Marshall's car again. Nick then grabbed a bunch of pebbles and threw them all at once. It rained on the creature making it turn around, fast. Nick sprinted the opposite way as the beast began to give into the chase.

"Brilliant idea!" Marshall hopped off the car. He grabbed his Rod. "Now what do I do?"

"Are you kidding me!?" Nick threw himself to his left. The creature missed but kept going. Once in motion it wasn't about to stop. It hit the light post, its horn ripping right through the metal. Nick crawled away before launching himself back up. "Seriously dude, concentrate on a weapon. Anything. Something that can stop a rock-made creature. Something really, really strong." The beast ripped itself away from the pole. It turned again and began chasing towards the sprinting Nick. "Think fast, this thing is really going to kill me!"

Marshall held on to the Rod. He tried thinking of something. Something powerful. Something massive. *"A tank,"* he thought. He concentrated, trying to block out all sounds. After a few moments he let out a sigh. "This isn't working."

"Are you serious!?" Nick jumped on the back of an old truck. He launched himself in right as it slammed into the back of the truck, the horn completely destroying the license plate and nearly going through the back of the truck where Nick was laying. "Do you know the meaning of concentrate!?"

"Maybe I should let that thing stick its horn right up your-"

"Listen man, think of something fast," Nick interrupted as the beast backed his body off the truck. "Think of some way to stop this thing 'cause it's going to kill me at this rate." Nick backed up and reached for the top of the roof, pushing himself on top of it. It was very small and he could only put half his body on top. Legs dangling off the back end.

Marshall closed his eyes. *"Something strong. I need a*

body. A steel body. Yeah, make me invincible!" The Rod began to light up. Its shine got the attention of the beast. Nick looked over, covering his eyes, trying to see what Marshall was making. The Unknown growled and went charging at the light.

"Marshall! Watch out! The thing is coming right for you!" Nick shouted. The beast was in full charge just a few yards away from the light. "Marshall!" Nick shouted. He slid off the top and landed heavily on his feet. He hadn't fully recovered from the night before. He felt his body weaken for a moment. He glanced up quickly.

Marshall threw his hand out; open palmed, and grabbed the horn. He did it with such ease, lifting the creature up by it, and flung it across the street into the damaged car he was once hiding on. Nick looked at Marshall, watching as this metallic looking material was riding up to Marshall's right elbow. Marshall's whole arm was nearly encased in a steel looking armor. "Let's see who hits harder now," Marshall said grinning.

"I think he's had enough," one of Ryan's friends held Ryan back. Peter's face was a bloody mess. Punched four or five times, open wounds showing on his cheeks. "We don't want him calling the police or anything."

"I'll say when he's had enough." Ryan replied, pushing away his friend. He lifted Peter. "You've had enough freak?"

"How do I act? Don't act mad. Act upset. Like you want to cry. It hurts, so act it." Peter frowned. He felt pain but didn't know how to fake being sad. So he bit his lip and shut his eyes. "Please, I can't take anymore."

"That's more like it. Now give me those three dollars." Ryan ordered, tightening his grip on Peter's shoulder.

Peter handed him the money. "Now will you let me go?" Peter was eager to be released. He needed to find out who was trying to contact him. It was the only thing on his mind.

"Depends. Maybe I should beat you more so next time you keep that mouth of yours shut."

Peter felt something. It was building up throughout the whole altercation, but now it was starting to reach its boiling point. "I really need to go." His words were short. He felt anger. He was becoming livid. These three boys were stopping him from getting where he needed to go. He was done not feeling anything. He closed off his feelings too many times at home to let these three do the same to him. "I won't call the police. I won't tell anyone. Just let me go and I promise I'll never talk back to you again." Peter held his fist tightly. He wasn't sure how well he could do in a fist fight but he was getting close to the point where he was going to find out.

"All right, good call." Ryan let go. Peter could feel his anger subsiding quickly. "Get out of here freak." Ryan walked back towards his friends, who laughed like they were on cue to.

Once Peter was far away from the group of boys he turned a corner. He pulled out his phone and saw a slew of text messages. Most of them citing that Marshall and Nick were heading to a certain location. He then read the message that pointed out the location. Peter put the phone away and began running towards that location. He felt the same feeling he felt when Nick talked to him earlier today. The feeling of being wanted. It made him smile.

The beast was back on its feet. It shifted to the side, trying to sniff out its prey. Marshall watched it closely, letting his new metallic right hand hang in front of him. The weight of the hand was nothing. Still, he felt his energy drain slowly. He took a quick glance behind him to see Nick walking forward. "I think I'm getting the hang of this Rod thing. Just look at my hand. Pretty awesome, huh?"

"It's very awesome, but be quick." Nick leaned against a car a few yards away. "Using the Rod as a weapon drains your energy. Soon you're gonna feel yourself getting weaker. Kill this thing before that happens." Nick felt dizzy. He didn't fully recover on top of little sleep. Not a good combination.

"I got it," Marshall began walking forward, tightening his

right hand into a fist. The beast caught the scent of Marshall and charged. Marshall whirled his whole arm around and struck the beast right in the side of the face. The horn caught the tip of Marshall's shirt and tore it. It slammed to the side and moaned. "I bet it didn't see that coming. Get it? 'Cause it doesn't have eyes."

"Yeah, I got it," Nick answered rolling his eyes.

"Whatever. Trying to lighten the mood here." Marshall took a step closer to the beast. It slowly got back on all fours, but was badly damaged from the hit. One whole side of the face looked cracked, black liquid coming out of it. "I think this thing is leaking."

"It's dying. Finish it off."

Marshall looked at the beast. Watching it try to recover from being hurt. "It doesn't look evil."

"It doesn't matter!" Nick pushed himself away from the car. "These things are trying to kill us. Fred was almost bitten to death. I was almost clawed to death. Don't let it take advantage of you. Kill it quick!"

"But-" Marshall began but the beast was charging. Marshall threw his hand back but he knew it was too late. Instead he dodged to the right. The horn went through his left hand. Marshall could feel the force of the creature as it pulled him down. It dragged him a few feet, his hand still stuck on the horn, while Marshall screamed in agony.

Nick ran towards him. He grabbed Marshall's hand and quickly pulled it off the horn. Blood fell over the beast's face, making it growl at the new smell. It could smell someone else was close. Nick began to drag his friend to safety when the beast turned. It was ready to charge again.

"That son of a-" Marshall said, holding his bloody hand. He got up and stumbled forward. The beast let out a huge growl. Ready to strike as hard as it could. Marshall turned to meet the creature. "You wanna play like that. Fine!" Marshall walked forward.

"Marshall, your hand!"

"I'm fine." Marshall winced. He never felt such pain

before. However, he felt his blood boil. He wanted to finish this creature off by himself. "I've been in worse fights than this," he lied.

Nick backed up to the car and watched. "Careful. You miss again and we're probably dead."

The beast charged. This time Marshall already had his hand pushed back. He threw it forward, this time making direct contact with the horn. It was a loud clash, then the horn broke off and Marshall's fist went flying into the temple of the creature. It roared in pain as it was swung backwards. It was laying on its back, moaning and crying. Marshall fell to one knee. He could feel the energy in his body leaving quickly.

"You did it," Nick said. He was almost in disbelief his friend was even still standing. The wound on his left hand looked horrible, blood dripping from it.

"Yeah, well ya know. I always get the last swing in." Marshall got up and walked to the creature. He laid his bloody hand on its belly. He could feel it was soft; rising up and down. The creature had no fight left in it. "I guess this is where it ends."

"Ends? This is just the beginning," Nick answered. Marshall looked at his friend then back at the fallen creature.

"I guess," he said before lifting his arm and striking the beast in the stomach, eliminating it.

Chapter Twelve – Monsters

Jin walked up to the dead Unknown and bent down. He turned it over and shook his head. "I see you took care of this little one." Marshall and Nick stood watching as the other two Exterminators behind Jin picked up the creature and walked away. "Great job. Without training, you guys are doing really well." Jin offered his hand to Marshall. "My name is Jin, nice to meet you."

"Doing really well without training, huh?" Marshall denied the handshake. Jin tilted his head while retreating his hand. "Are we doing well enough where one of our friends is in intensive care, not even able to get to class? Are we doing that well without our training?"

"Hey, Marshall chill man."

"Nah, why didn't Fred get any training before his mission? Why didn't we get any training before this? Why are we fighting these things? I got questions and I want some damn answers!" Marshall slammed his foot on the ground. Jin took a moment before responding.

"I get that you're upset," Jin began speaking softly. "I know you want answers. I really shouldn't be the one giving them, though. We'll talk to Carl. He should be back to the Station in an hour. I think he'll do better with those questions than me."

"He better. Just 'cause you don't ask questions on why you do what you do doesn't mean I won't." Marshall pushed past Jin and began walking towards the house above the station.

"He's a nice one isn't he?" Jin looked towards Marshall.

"He's forceful but," Nick started then looked at Jin. "He's got a point. He's got questions. Hell, we've all got questions. I think it's time to answer some of them." Nick began to follow behind Marshall with Jin coming along shortly after.

Fred looked to his side. All he saw was white. He looked to the ground. More white. He looked up, all white. "What is this?" He looked all around, everything is white. He was trapped in some white room and couldn't escape. He felt locked down. A prisoner.

"This is our area. Our safe zone. No one can touch us from here." A voice was so close, yet Fred saw nothing. He quickly looked in all direction but couldn't identify where the voice was coming from. "Do not be afraid. This is your new home. Here we could be calm. We can relax. There is no fighting. There is no death. This is the place you ought to stay. It'll keep you safe."

"Who are you?"

"Well, I'm you of course."

"What? What the heck do you mean you are me? That can't be. I'm me, you're just some voice!" Fred barked. He was getting frustrated, not being able to find the exit or the voice in the room.

"This is your home. Why do you fight it?"

"This isn't my room. Trust me, it's never this clean."

"This is where you belong. Take a rest here and I'll take care of your problems. Trust me young one, this is where you want to be."

Fred could feel his body wanting to fight whatever was talking to him. Yet the words it spoke sounded so nice, so humble. To simply lie down and forget all about his problems. Something most people would gladly accept. "Sorry, I can't do that. I got to get better so I can fight with my friends."

"Better? You are better. You aren't hurt."

"Listen wannabe me, you should check up on me more often. I was just in a huge attack, with the thing nearly killing me. I mean us," Fred spoke, almost laughing. "Am I really talking to some voice? Either I've finally gone insane or this is a dream. Can I realize I'm dreaming in my own dream?"

"And if it is a dream?"

"Then I guess I gotta wait till I wake up to find out."

"Wouldn't you rather just stay here? Let all the darkness out while you rest here? Rest young one. Rest."

"It sounds tempting, my weird inner self, but I can't do that. I have people who count on me to help them. If you're really me then you would understand that." Fred smiled as he spoke. He could feel the tug on his body loosen up. He could feel himself becoming lighter.

"Fine, it isn't time just yet. Go, explore, live, but be cautious. Things are coming. Things you aren't ready for. When you feel tired you come back here and rest. Understood?" Fred nodded. "Good. All right...off you go!" Just like that Fred woke up, sweat dripping down his head. He could still feel the slight presence of the white room. After sitting up for a minute or two he could feel all the pain and suffering go away. It was almost like a complete sweep of terrible memories.

Nick was the last to make it down to the Station. This time he was able to walk out on his feet. He still had shaky legs though. "I really dislike elevators. Did I ever mention that?"

"That was awesome," Marshall said, throwing his hands in the air.

"I'm not a huge fan of it myself, Nick. Still, the more you come down here the quicker you'll get used to it." Jin looked towards the end of the hall. "Let's go see Fred and then we'll go talk to Carl.

"Sounds good to me." Nick and Marshall followed.

It was the first time for Marshall. He touched the walls as they went down the white hallway. Marshall liked the white slick look, making the whole place look futuristic. "This place is awesome looking," Marshall grinned.

"It's something else," Nick muttered. The place was very plain for Nick; he wasn't amazed by any of it.

"It's a place of calm. Every time I walk these halls I feel relieved. Like all the problems of the world don't exist when I walk down here. It's calm, peaceful, and relaxing." Jin smiled. He let the walls relax him. The white walls, no colors, made his mind rest. He could take in all his problems and just let them fly away.

They reached the medical room. Jin placed his hand on the door and moments later it opened. Fred turned his head to see Jin,

90

Marshall, and Nick walk in. "Hey guys, nice to see you're all still alive," he joked.

"Dude, how much does it suck?" Marshall sat at the edge of the bed Fred was laying on.

"Huh?"

"How much does it suck that you got your butt so badly whooped on your first mission!?" Marshall said slamming his hand down on Fred's leg while laughing. Fred just shook his head.

"You could of left this guy up there, ya know," Fred told Nick and Jin.

"Yeah, but then he would just cry for an hour of how we treated him unfairly," Nick laughed.

"Plus, I didn't want him to get into any trouble," Jin added.

"Ya know, I'm sitting right here," Marshall finished.

"We just came from a hunt. We were able to take down another monster." Nick pointed to Marshall with his thumb. "This guy came through big time somehow. He not only stopped it from killing us both, he actually killed it."

"No way," Fred said waving his hand away.

"Yeah man. I didn't get my butt kicked. I went in there to do some ass-kicking and that's what I did. I made my hand into a metal arm and slammed the creature so hard with my fist it couldn't even move. I was a total badass." Marshall raised his right hand in victory.

"Uhhh Marshall," Fred said.

"Yeah?"

"Your left hand. It's kind of bleeding."

Marshall took a look. The hole wasn't huge but big enough to keep the blood coming. The horn only caught his hand, didn't go down too far. "Dang. Yeah, can I get someone to look at that?" Marshall looked towards Jin who nodded.

"I'll go get our healers. Sit here," Jin said moving towards the door.

"Let me tell you all about the hunt. So we were going down this block. This guy forgot his Rod. Awesome help on his part," Marshall said sarcastically. Nick just rolled his eyes and

Fred laughed. Marshall continued the story.

Peter arrived at the place but no one was there. He went into the other realm but just saw blood left over from Marshall's wound. He went over and stood near it. Looking at it, he noticed it wasn't a lot but it meant the other boys were hurt. Meaning they would have gone back to the Station. He went back into the human realm and began making his way towards the Station.

He cleaned his face, noticing some blood was still on it. The beating from Ryan wasn't terrible, but he left enough damage on Peter's face to make it noticeable. He wiped away as much as he could, not wanting to be questioned about it.

He felt new emotions as he began walking. At first it was the feeling of being wanted. He enjoyed that feeling, a feeling he never really had before. This other feeling he was getting now was betrayal. He felt them leaving was wrong. Then again he felt it was his fault for getting stuck in the altercation with Ryan. If he got here sooner maybe none of the boys would be bleeding. It was a small amount of blood so he hoped for the best. He then thought of Ryan. Making sure Ryan would pay when he saw him again. Anger began to fill his body, and this time Peter was feeding off of it.

A small creature came in. Its face was squished in with an ugly blue tint to the skin. Three small eyes were forming a triangle shape at the top. Its hands were large; fingers puffed up and looked jelly-like. Nick backed away from the creature as it entered the room. It looked to the boys and then back to Jin. "Which one needs to be healed?"

Jin pointed to Marshall. "His hand has a hole in it. If you could fix him up that would be great." The creature nodded.

"Uh, no. That's a damn monster!" Marshall was on his feet now. "You didn't tell me the same creatures we hunt are the things that cure us." He felt angry.

"Listen, healers are here to help. Not every creature we encounter is bad. How do you think we know when the creatures are crossing into our realm? We have Callers. They can read signals, tell us when something is trying to break though. These Healers are here to heal. They help us and in exchange we try to keep out the vicious creatures who keep trying to get in to this realm. There's no need to be scared of her. She's quite harmless; all she can do is heal." Jin smiled at the Healer. "Not to mention she's saved all of our lives more than once here. She's part of the organization."

Marshall still felt hesitant. Nick walked forward and stopped in front of the Healer. "The way I see it, you're part of us. Even after just two fights I can see we can use all the help we can get. Especially when it's someone to help us when we get injured. If you're helping us, saving us, then I gladly accept you as part of the team." Nick held out his hand for a handshake. The Healer smiled and shook the hand.

"I'm glad to help you all," she answered with a smile.

"Fine. If you take my hand off though, I got another. And trust me. This hand can do some damage." Marshall held his left hand out. The Healer grabbed it and began rubbing it. It began to speak a language none of the boys could understand. She then placed her left hand over his hand and Marshall could feel something attaching to his skin. He could feel his wound inside closing, just as the skin actually closed up over it. It burned but at the same time it felt amazing. Like he was gaining back something he lost.

After a moment the Healer let go of his hand. He took a look at it, turning it over to check for the wound. It was completely healed. No scars or damage present on it. It was like he was never wounded from the beginning. The Healer on the other hand had a hole on her hand now. A moment later it began to close up, though it was a slower process then Marshall's healing. "Wait, why do you have my wound? I mean my old wound."

"We healers can transfer the damage to other people. We Healers heal far quicker than your species. So we transfer your wounds to us and let us heal our own bodies. It's easy enough and keeps you guys alive. We don't die nearly as easily as all of you." She said laughing, a weird hollow laugh.

"Right. Well, that's not freaky," Marshall said looking at his hand. "But thanks." She nodded in acknowledgment. "Now I got some questions for Carl."

Peter walked off the elevator and towards Carl's office. He's been there before and remembered it was only three doors down from the elevator. In front of his office he stood, trying to figure out what he wanted to ask. He wanted to know a few things but most of all he wanted to know how he was supposed to defend himself against regular people when he couldn't use his weapons. He placed his hand on the door and it opened up.

Carl threw his bag on the floor and looked at Peter. "Oh, hey, come in." He said waving his student in. As he fixed up his desk he continued speaking. "Sorry, been out of town. How are you doing, Peter?" He moved a few things off his desk to the garbage pail and sat down. "Sit, no need to stand there." Carl motioned towards one of the three chairs in front of his desk.

Peter sat down and took a quick look around the office. Like the entire Station it was mostly all white. However, there was a picture on the desk Peter couldn't keep his eyes off. It was of Carl with four young boys, even younger then Peter himself. They all were waving at the picture while the much younger Carl in the picture was laughing. Peter went to grab the picture when Carl snatched it and brought it close to him. "That's...let's not talk about that." Carl placed the picture in his drawer.

"Okay." Peter didn't understand why Carl was scared to talk about the picture but he didn't care much about it. "Did my friends come here?" Peter let the word friends linger a bit longer then he wanted. It felt odd for him to say it. He never had friends in his entire life. He never felt feelings like this.

"I haven't seen the others, not yet. I think they might be here soon though. I told them to come visit once they finished the mission." Carl noticed the cuts on Peter's face. They weren't going to leave any scars but Carl still felt the urge to ask. Peter spoke up first.

"Well the mission is done already. I was just at the scene."

"Oh, well then they should be here," As soon as Carl finished his sentence the door opened. Marshall, Nick, and Jin walked into the office. Jin leaned himself against the wall while Marshall and Nick sat in the other two seats. "Nice to see you boys. Sorry, I was out of town. We have other units out there trying to build up. I was sent to check in on one, they lost someone recently and it's my job to check up and see how they are dealing with it." Carl explained his situation.

"That's all fine and dandy but we have problems here. If you haven't noticed Fred in there nearly died. Today we got chased by some rock creature, I'ma call it Rockies for short, and almost ripped my damn hand off. So, sorry if I'm a little pissed that you aren't paying attention to us, but I'm a little pissed!" Marshall watched as Carl took it all in. Carl nodded and looked towards Nick.

"I'm sorry I haven't been there. You've been in two hunts now. Everyone else one. None of you had any training and it is my fault." Marshall calmed down some and leaned back into his seat. "First off, Fred's altercation was wrong. Something went horribly wrong and the weak signal the Callers got and sent was not the one that Fred fought. That hybrid beast was far above the level I'd ever send recruits out to fight. You guys don't even have proper training. That thing should have been able to tear all of you to pieces. I'm not sure why it didn't, but something wasn't right about the whole ordeal. Needless to say we are setting a full investigation into it and I assure you we will find out what happened. I swear on it."

"Fine," Marshall said. "I still have more questions though."

"I can answer some but not all. Some you must experience to understand."

"All right then just answer me this. Why are we killing

95

these things?" As Marshall spoke he remembered the creature he just killed. It was on its back, defenseless, beaten, and yet he had still killed it. He still threw his hand into the belly of the beast.

"These creatures, the Rockus that you just killed, would have rammed one of you. Chances are it would have killed you if it did." Carl pointed to Marshall's hand. "You said you were injured. Luckily it was just your hand and not your head."

"That doesn't explain why we killed it. Why didn't we bring it back here and cage it? Why not just send it back to their realm," Marshall questioned. Nick was also wondering why we didn't return them to the place they came from. If they can jump into our world, can we jump into theirs?

"These Unknowns aren't friendly. They come out of their realm looking for blood. As you all know, by now."

"Then why do you have some who are just floating around here on our side?" Marshall pointed behind him. "One just healed my hand. What if she came through the realm and we just bashed her face in. Then what?"

"The ones who come to help give advance notice that they are. I'm not saying all these creatures are bad. The monsters, Unknowns, the others, and whatever else you want to call them. They exist just like we do. Some want to harm while others want to help. The ones like our Healers aren't here to harm us. They see the threat of the other creatures and they choose to help instead. Chances are in their realm these creatures hunted them as well."

"So, we're basically using them."

"I never said that."

Marshall shifted in his seat. "It sure sounds like it."

"For someone who didn't care a few days ago," Carl said, standing up now. "You sure want to know a lot now."

"I'm just trying to piece this all together. Why we have to kill them is all I'm wondering. If you say they want us dead, then I guess I have no choice but to defend myself. Still, I'ma figure out why they all want to attack us one day. If I find out they are just scared..." Marshall let his voice trail off. Carl watched for a moment before coming around the desk.

"Training begins at the end of this week. You'll meet at the gym here after school on Friday. Take this weekend and most of the week to rest up. Spend time with your families, your friends, whomever. Once training starts things will change. I will be your Commander, Jin here will help out as well," They all took a look back at Jin. He waved. "I need you to understand that these missions are very serious. These hunts aren't a game. You guys get injured, you could easily die. I won't allow that to happen," Carl's face was stone cold. The boys all looked intensively at him. "I'll let Fred know before he leaves here today. I need you boys to understand something. What we do here is a dangerous task. We face creatures, Unknowns, that could easily kill us. We face them, beat them, almost die, and get no recognition. I know none of you are in this for rewards, but it's important to note no one will know about this. No one can know about this. If someone outside the organization knows they will either be terminated or forced to join and keep secrecy. It's living a double life from now on. If you want out now, let me know."

"You can't let them out now. It's too late," Jin spoke up.

"I can if I want. These are my recruits, no one else's. It is my choice. No one else's." Carl looked to his recruits. He saw Nick's face, struggling to decide what he should do. Marshall's face gave away his anger but he was already determined to fight. He was too hungry for information to back out now. Peter just watched, eyes empty. Carl knew Peter would stay; he had too much interest in the organization.

"I'm in," Marshall said.

"I am, too," Peter added.

"Dude, what happened to your face?" Marshall finally took a look at Peter's face. Peter looked to the side.

"I fell," he muttered.

"You fell?"

"Yeah, fell down some stairs."

"Well news for you, the stairs won."

"Back to the point at hand. Are you all in?" Carl asked loudly. Marshall stopped talking, and Peter looked up at Carl.

Nick took a second before looking up. He watched as his two teammates looked at him. He saw Carl looking at him, waiting for his answer. "Well I don't wanna be the lame one out. I'm in." Carl nodded and stood up.

"All right kids, get out of here. Be careful out there." All three boys stood up and began exiting the room. Nick lingered for a moment longer.

"Is everything okay, Nick?" Jin asked from Nick's side. Nick turned his head.

"Should I be nervous?"

"I'd be surprised if you weren't," Jin said.

"My life is never going to be the same, is it?" Nick watched for a response. Jin looked towards Carl, who looked back towards Nick. "Guess that's the only answer I needed," he said before walking out the door.

Chapter Thirteen – Bonds

Nick just got out of the shower. He was going through his clothes, trying to find something nice to wear. It had been four days since the fight with the Rockus. Nick felt fully recovered, and full of energy. He had asked Kelly out on a date the very same night he returned from the Station. She gladly accepted and they planned on meeting tonight, at six o'clock. It was already five and Nick couldn't find something he liked. "Come on! Why don't I have anything fancy!?" He looked through his closet searching for dressy clothes. He tried on a button down. *"You're not going to prom. Come on!"* He threw it off and tried on another shirt that was all white. It hung off baggy. He threw it off quickly. He shuffled through his clothes but found nothing. *"This is insane! I need to go shopping starting tomorrow."*

Nick's dad knocked at the door. "Pops, I'm really busy right now. I can't find a decent shirt in this pile of what I call clothes. I really need to go shopping."

"First off," Nick's dad came in holding a nice brown button down shirt, "Your clothes are fine. You're just worried about the date. Here," he said. He handed his son the shirt. Nick took it, studied it, and then put it on. He looked into the mirror. "Looking good kid. She'll love it."

"You think?"

"You're my son, of course."

"Thanks dad," he said smiling. He looked at his dad and smiled. "I really like this girl."

"Sounds like it," his father winked. He brushed off his son's shoulders before letting his hands rest there for a moment. As he looked at him he could feel a tug in his heart. A feeling of being proud, excited, scared, but most of all the feeling of his son being almost a grown man. "I'm very proud of you."

"Oh, don't get all mushy on me!" Nick laughed.

"I won't, I won't. Just have fun and live life. Go get this girl." He patted his son on the shoulder.

"Thanks again, pops. Later!" Nick called as he started walking quickly to the door.

"Oh and Nick," his dad said. Nick stopped and turned. "Don't you dare do anything that will make me ground you for the rest of your life! I don't care how old you are you'll be trapped here forever if you do something you'll regret. Trust me." Nick laughed and nodded. He walked out the door and was on his way to meet Kelly. Nicks' father smiled and sat on his bed. "My son..." his voice faded into the air. He couldn't help but picture Nick as a child. Holding him with his wife. They would tickle his belly and he'd laugh. He'd get angry over not having any food. He'd cry if they went too far from him. Now he was on a date with a girl. His father couldn't have felt prouder at this moment.

Peter was looking at the guide. It was basically a scrap book of Exterminators experiences with these hunts. He felt that most of the advice was obvious. Always keep alert, don't use too much energy consuming weapons, you can't hurt yourself with your own Rod. Peter had been alternating weapons on and off throughout the last few days. His weapons ranged from swords, guns, and his favorite - gloves. Not just regular gloves, but the glove he was able to create was a magical one. While using the glove he was able to summon elemental powers. Such as creating fire, water, or electricity. However, with the amount of energy it took to use it he had to rest a long while before trying it again. Not to mention the elements fell apart all too often. Fire breaking apart, water spilling everywhere, electricity frying his lamp. It was gonna take a lot of work to learn to control the different magical elements.

He liked the idea of being in control of a weapon. He never had violent tendencies but the fact that he can use weapons to defend himself now was amazing. Still, none of it could be used on problems at school. The bullies pushing him around were just the tip of the iceberg. It was his own father who he wanted to put a stop to. The way his father became more abusive over the past few years made Peter shut off any emotions he had. He concealed himself behind a blank statue of his former self. He hated that. That emotion he could feel trying to break though: hatred.

He jumped on to the computer to see if he could find anything about monsters. Every time he searched he just saw video games, TV, and movie monsters. Nothing to really point him in the direction of a community of Exterminators. The organization must have eyes everywhere, meaning finding anyone would be impossible unless in person. He wondered if anyone else at his school could be an Exterminator as well. He wouldn't put it past some people.

His cell phone went off and he jumped. Only time it ever went off is when his mom called. His mom was in the other room, asleep though. He grabbed it and looked at the caller ID. He picked it up. "Heya Kelleh!" He tried to sound louder than usual.

"Hey Pete! How's everything?" she asked. Pete couldn't see her but sensed something different in her voice.

"I'm fine. Are you okay?" He got off his bed. He felt something was wrong as he heard shuffling around on the phone.

"Oh yeah, I'm fine. I'm getting my shoes on and heading out. Listen, can I ask you a weird question?" Peter calmed down. She wasn't in danger.

"Shoot," he said going back to reading his guide.

"I'm going on a date with that Nick kid. I'm a little worried 'cause I don't know much about him. Can you be honest with me and just tell me he's a good guy or if he's a slime ball."

"This is strange. You've been on dates before but never asked me about them," he said, making his voice sound curious despite not really caring. He knew Nick wouldn't hurt Kelly, she wasn't in any danger.

"Well yeah, but I never dated someone you've known! I know you just met him but does he seem nice?"

"Yeah, he's nice." Peter turned the page to study a picture of a gigantic bear-type creature.

"Did he talk about me before?"

"He said you were really cute."

"Really?"

"Really."

"No way!"

"Yes way."

"Are you listening to me?" She sounded annoyed. Peter looked up from his guide.

"Yes. I'm sorry I didn't mean to ignore you. I'm just reading. Yes, he thinks you are cute. I'm sure you'll have a great time," he told her with a calm and soothing voice. He wanted to make Kelly feel comfortable.

"Thanks Pete, makes me feel better that he's not some total creep. Well, I'ma go meet him. Talk to you later, goodnight!" He responded the same and hung up. He felt a sense of happiness for his friend. He really enjoyed Kelly's happy attitude. He was also fond of his new friendship with Nick. Their being together would make them both happy. Peter wondered if that would make him happy as well. Having someone to be together with. He pondered the thought for a moment before looking back to the guide.

Nick stood at the movies entrance, pacing. He was nervous but excited. He couldn't wait to see Kelly, but he was scared to see her at the same time. He tried to calm himself down and just breathe in deeply. The nice cool night breeze blew through his clothes. It cooled him down before he got his clothes soaked from sweat.

He looked up at the movie theater sign. "What to see," he muttered as he looked at the names. Action movies galore with two romantic comedies on the menu. He chose one of the romantic comedies, the one that had the least horrible actors. He figured even if it's bad he could take the opportunity to glance at Kelly when she wasn't looking. Study what she thinks of certain parts of the movies, so he knew how to counteract later, when he went in for a kiss.

"Figured what movie we're gonna see?"

Nick jumped back, scared out of his mind. He stumbled backwards then laughed. "Okay, thanks for scaring me. We aren't seeing a horror movie now." She giggled. "I say we go to see one of the romantic comedies."

"Really?"

"I just figured you'd like that."

"What? I wanna see things blow up, people screaming, cool car chase scenes. I don't wanna see some boring romance movie." Nick laughed. He liked how open Kelly was about expressing her views.

"All right then let's go watch one." He grabbed her hand. Her face lit up, and she smiled. He held tighter, loving the way her hand felt.

"Plus, we can fill in that romance movie time later," she said winking. Her grip became tighter as well.

Marshall knocked on Fred's door. Fred had been home a few days, Marshall figured he'd check up on him. Marshall and Fred still haven't been on good terms. Still, he was one of his oldest friends. Even if they weren't friends like they used to be, he still cared about his health.

Fred opened the door. "Oh, hey," Fred said in surprise. He wasn't expecting to see Marshall, of all people. Marshall waved while he entered the house. It was clean to perfection. "Cleaners left about an hour ago. Daily routines."

"Parents in town?"

"Are they ever?"

"Good point," Marshall said sitting down. "I'm sorry for the other day."

"What happened the other day?" Fred joined him on the couch. His shoulder burned a bit every once in a while but besides that he was back in top shape. He sometimes couldn't believe the speedy recovery.

"I should have been there when you were fighting that wolf thing." Marshall kept his head down. "I've been thinking a lot lately. Why we don't talk like we used to. I think I just wanted to be noticed. I mean I wanted to be popular. I just never actually wanted to be popular, just the idea of being popular." Marshall began fumbling his own words. "Point is, I know I've been acting strange these past few years. I'm sorry about that." He looked up and pointed to Fred's shoulder. "Maybe if I wasn't acting like an idiot you wouldn't have that."

This was the first time in years Fred heard his old friend Marshall speak truthfully. He felt the connection of friendship he had years ago come right back into place. As if they never fought all those years ago. "No one is to blame. Nobody thought these creatures were real. I didn't, Nick didn't, Peter...well Peter might have. Still, no one thought they were really real. So I don't want you sitting there thinking it's entirely your fault."

"I'm just glad you're all right." Marshall lifted his head. "I mean who else am I going to make fun of for being chubby on the team."

"I will punch you. In the face. Really hard." Fred drew his hand back, Marshall moved to the side of the couch laughing. It felt like they were back to their old friendship. Like when they were kids playing together.

Marshall sat back up. Fred looked behind him at the empty kitchen. It was dark, lonely, isolated. "Hey Marshall," he said as Marshall looked at him. "Wanna play some video games for a while?"

Marshall glanced around the house. He saw the empty halls, kitchen, and bedrooms. He already felt alone and he didn't even live there. "Yeah, got anything new?" Fred smiled while he went looking for a game to play. He was glad he didn't have to spend another night alone with his own thoughts in a quiet house.

"That was about the most amazing thing I've ever seen!" Kelly threw her right hand up. "I mean whoa! Did you see that building fall over? The sound effects!? It was like I was right there." She was speaking so loud and fast that Nick just nodded to everything she was saying. His real attention was placed on her face. He wanted to kiss her lips. "Then when that guy came running off the bridge and slammed on to the boat. Whoa! What a movie!"

"Yeah, it was pretty awesome." Nick tried to pay attention to the movie as best he could. Normally an action movie for him is pretty easy to get through. Just sit, watch, laugh, and enjoy. However, next to Kelly, he just couldn't concentrate. He kept sneaking peeks over to her every few seconds. He couldn't control his need to want to talk to her. Be closer to her.

"Where to now?" She grabbed his hand.

"Wanna grab something to eat?" He pointed to the restaurants along the side of the road two blocks down.

"I could eat," she began. "You better not judge me though based on what I get. A girls gotta eat ya know!"

"I won't judge you," he said smiling back. "I think you're gorgeous. So whatever you eat is already what you've been eating. So keep eating it, 'cause you'll always be beautiful to me." The words just slipped out. He didn't prepare them at all but they came out so perfect.

She lit up and tightened the grip she had on his hand. "That was very sweet of you."

"Well, I'm a pretty sweet guy."

"Don't push it, you ain't that sweet to be conceited," she said laughing.

Carl threw some of his clothes in the dryer and hit the large blue button. He let the rumbling sound take over, letting his mind drift off as his clothes were drying. He was trying to imagine the kids he now had under his wing. Nick and his bravery. Marshall and his hard headed mentality. Peter and his smarts. Fred and his determination. All the boys lacked something, but together they could be unstoppable. He smiled as he pictured the group. Having new recruits back under his command felt good. First time in a long time he felt like a real Bora.

A Bora's job was always to raise Exterminators to be Protectors or Boras one day. They were there to train the Exterminators to be smarter, faster, and more powerful. They are to lead by example; showing these kids how to fight as a team and by themselves. He grew up the same way with three other fighters. Two of them were still on the hunts today. One was now a protector and the last one a Gada. He was very proud of his friends.

He closed his eyes, imaging Ross. Remembering the very first time he met them all at fourteen. She stood there smiling, waiting for the instructions by their Bora. She was a year older than him but so short, that by looking you'd think she was younger. He wanted to run over to her and sit next to her but kept his seat in the back of the group. He didn't want to make it obvious to anyone that he liked her. She eventually walked over after the instructions were over and asked if he wanted to walk together. To keep each other protected.

Carl opened his eyes. He felt his cheeks were wet. *"Crying again you old man? Come on now,"* He thought, laughing. He wiped his face and walked away from the dryer. He needed to get away from his memories. The memories that still haunted him today. The experiences that changed his life forever. For the good and for the bad.

"I only brought fifty dollars. You, of course, order about forty five dollars' worth," Nick said chuckling.

"First off it was only twenty dollars. Secondly, I'm hungry. Third, you're cheap." Now it was her turn to laugh.

"Fair points," he responded nodding. He took a sip of his drink. He was trying to figure out the next question. He knew he didn't want any awkward silences. So, he used his moment to drink while coming up with something that she would answer.

"Why'd you ask me out?"

Nick almost spat his drink out. "Well," he began, trying to clear his throat. "I just found you very pretty. You seem really laid back as well, which is great. Peter likes you, so you must be a good person. I asked you out because I wanted to get to know you." His answer couldn't have sounded better. It also couldn't be any truer

"Well, I'm glad you asked me out. Usually I get the creeps asking me out. I try to avoid them at all costs. Then, I get the older guys who can't find someone in their own age bracket. Like your thirty, guy, please get away from me!" She used her hands to show what she meant, her face giving a disgust look.

Nick laughed at her. "Well I'm not a creep. I'm only seventeen. I also would like to note that I'm not from here. So that puts me on the "I'm not super mean" list right?" She giggled and nodded. "I also just wanted to ask you out 'cause I haven't met anyone I liked here yet. You seem to be the only girl I'm really attracted too. If I came off rash about asking you out, I'm sorry. I just really hate being alone."

She smiled at him. She leaned over the table and held his hand. "I think it's very sweet that you asked me out. I understand about not wanting to be alone. I understand that, all too well. So don't worry about it being weird or anything. I'm super glad you asked me out," she told him with a bigger smile. Her teeth showed through this smile and Nick took a second to also register that. Her teeth were perfectly white. He wanted to run to the bathroom to make sure his teeth held up.

"So, what's your favorite thing to do around here?"

"Yeah, that's all. If I get any more information I'll let you know. All right. Okay. Bye," Jin said hanging up the phone. He let out a sigh and got up from the bench in the park. He felt the sudden weight of the world on his shoulders. All he wanted to do was run away for a few days and forget about everything. His girlfriend wanted to move in. His father is dying slowly in the hospital. His trainer has been missing in action for two weeks now. He was also still waiting for his promotion. He began to wonder if anything could go right.

He was walking down the block when he saw two kids running towards him. They weren't much older than seven or eight and they were playing tag. The one boy in the lead was outrunning the other at a good speed. Eventually, the one in the front would lose energy, whereas the slower one took his time keeping up but never using up too much of his energy. Jin knew how to study the signs of how someone is using their body from a massive amount of training. He saw the one behind jogging at a nice steady pace, whereas the one in front was running frantically with his arms up in the air. As they passed Jin, the small one looked up with a big smile. They dashed past him without even slowing down.

Jin felt the need to escape. To rip away from all the chains that kept him in this place. He wanted to be free like the kids chasing each other. Run around without a care in the world. That isn't the life of an Exterminator though, and Jin is an Exterminator. He questioned if he wanted to be one anymore.

Nick walked down the block, trying to think of things to say. Kelly held his hand the entire time they were walking back home. He felt the need to speak but he also liked the feeling of walking and studying the world they lived in. The lights were bright at night. The houses on every block looked old but antique-like. The streets were filled with cars passing by. Nick took it all in, finally accepting the new area he lived in.

"Do you like it here so far?" Nick diverted his attention back to Kelly.

"I do. It's growing on me, anyway. Certain people here are making it worthwhile," he said, a warm smile on his face.

"You know, you really are a sweet talker," she said, pushing him with her shoulder. He laughed and pushed back gently. She giggled as she went to the side and back. He pulled her in just then, arching her back and putting his face to hers. He could sense she wanted more. So, he put his lips on hers, a little sloppy at first with his lips going over both hers. On the second kiss it felt perfect. Their lips touching each other like they were meant to, the connection he felt with her grew. He felt like he wanted her more than ever, even though he'd never been closer to her than where he was right now. Another kiss and then he pulled her back up. She stood there for a moment, putting her finger on her lips. "Well then, that was something."

"Sorry, I didn't mean to-"

"Didn't mean to do what I've been waiting for you to do?" She giggled. "Sometimes men are so thick."

"I really like you," he told her earnestly. He needed her to know.

"I really like you too." He was relieved to hear those words. She felt the same connection he did. She looked directly into his eyes. Her heart was pounding, she could feel that certain feeling you get when you first meet someone and you know they're gonna be special in your life somehow.

"Does this mean we're dating?" He sounded hopeful.

She shook her head. "I don't just kiss someone I don't plan on dating."

"Okay, sorry, just making sure."

"Stop being so sorry all the time. You're a lot better at being a pen expert than a dating one, huh?" She laughed out loud. He laughed alongside her. Nick hadn't felt this happy in a long time. He couldn't stop smiling at her the whole way back home.

Chapter Fourteen – Silver

"Do you not see what they are doing?" Fred looked around the empty white room. He was back in this isolated room he began to hate so much. He walked away from where the voice came from but it followed. "Why not become something different? Better?"

He stopped after seeing nothing but white walls. He touched the walls but they didn't open like the ones in the Station, even if they looked nearly identical. He tried punching the wall but it did nothing. "You know, I really hate my mind."

"Do not fear, we will become one. This room will become your salvation," the voice boomed. Fred waved his hands in a "leave me alone motion", but the voice continued. "You must relax. Let me take you to a place you can finally live your life. Somewhere you can let all the pain you stored up disappear."

Fred let the words sink into him. Letting all his frustration drift away would be ideal. He had a hard time coping with the fact his parents were never around. He already disliked school despite it just starting. He still couldn't control his weight issues. Letting all these stressful matters float away so he could rest sure sounded nice. "Listen self, is it cool I call you self? I just can't drift away. I got responsibilities. Things I gotta do. So, if you'd kindly shut up and let me do those things that'd be great."

"I am here when you need to rest."

"Okay, thanks."

"I will always be with you. Do not fear."

"Thanks self, you can shut up now."

"Do not let the pressure build. Let me help."

Fred turned around and screamed. "I get it! Now leave me the heck alo-" and before he could finish he sat up in his bed, sweat dripping down his face. He let out a long breath, he felt his shoulder burn. He felt his head banging as his heart was finally slowing down. "What's happening to me?" He buried his face between the bed sheets.

Nick never felt so good in his life. He was sitting at the table eating his breakfast. His dad walked downstairs and slapped his son on the back. "How's my son feeling after that date? Did it go well?" His father poured some cereal for himself and sat down. He took a bite and looked up at his grinning son.

"Better than that pops," he began. "I kissed her. Not just a regular kiss either. Was like one of those movie scenes. I arched her back, I leaned forward, and bam!" He kissed his own hand to show his father. "It was amazing. She loved it!"

His father laughed. "That's great. I knew you would get my moves. That's almost the same exact thing I did to your mother."

"No way."

"Yes. Well except for the fact that when I arched her I tripped, she fell to the ground with me following." Nick slammed the table from laughing so hard. "Hey, don't laugh! I don't think I've ever been so red in my life."

"Pops," he began but had to catch his breath. He was still laughing. "That is the greatest thing I've ever heard. How can you drop someone after trying to do the most romantic thing ever? That's awesome but so sad." Nick broke out in another loud laugh. His father just shook his head, smiling.

"Well, I'm glad it went well. Are you taking her on another date?" His father finished off his cereal.

"Yeah. We plan on going out sometime this week after school. I think we're gonna try to catch another movie or head to Manhattan and do some sightseeing. Either way I'm excited. She's an awesome girl," Nick replied. He then took the last bite of his breakfast and got up. "Well I gotta meet up with some friends. I'll see you tonight."

"Friends? Well that was quick."

"Well, ya know pops, I do get my awesome personality from someone." He grinned. His dad smiled back and he ran out the door. His father looked down at the table and smiled. His son was growing up so fast he almost forgot to spend time with him. He looked around the house. It was getting lonely already.

"Dude, I'm talking mega hot. Not just "She's all right", nah, she was so hot I think I almost died from the heat of her hotness. Ya know?" Marshall sat on the steps of the house talking to Peter. Peter stood there looking down the block waiting for the others to arrive. He came earlier, figuring he might run into Jin or Carl. He wasn't expecting Marshall to be waiting at the house early. "Yo dude, who you think is hot in your classes?"

"I don't find anyone in my class that I'm attracted to." It was true. Peter found certain girls to be very appealing in looks but none in his class.

"You gay?"

"No, I am not a homosexual."

"I know you're a human. I'm asking if you're gay."

Peter looked down at Marshall. "Homosexual means gay. The word you're thinking of is homo-sapiens." Marshall looked at him confused as Peter told him the difference. "It's two different things."

"I knew that."

"Clearly, you didn't."

"Listen bro," Marshall started. Peter looked away from Marshall, eagerly waiting for anyone else to show up. "I know the difference. I just got them confused for a second. So if you aren't gay, then why aren't you attracted to girls?"

"I am attracted to girls. I'm not attracted to any girl in my classes. That's all." Peter could feel the same feeling he was getting when Ryan and his friends beat him up. It was anger, but not against Marshall. This time it was because no one else was showing up. He wanted to get to training, not discuss girls.

"All right, I feel ya. We got some ugly girls in our classes. Besides mega hottie, I'm not really interested in much either." Marshall laid his head on his arms. "Whatcha think we're gonna be training with?"

This caught Peter's attention. "My guess would be other Exterminators. What better way to test our skills than to spar with the strongest hunters out there?"

"What's the point of fighting each other?"

Peter was confused. "What do you mean? How can we judge our skills without facing the strongest predators out there? Humans. We are above any other animal for hunting skills when we use them correctly."

"Yeah, but we aren't facing humans on the field." Marshall pointed to the nothingness on the roads. "We're facing monsters that use claws, breathe fire, and try to ram us to death. Humans don't fight like that. So, why wouldn't we fight monsters?" Peter was taken aback. He didn't expect Marshall to come up with a good point. He was almost unsure how to answer.

"Fair points. At the same time, humans are the safer bet. We know when to stop and not kill our prey as well. In training that would make the most sense." Peter saw two figures coming down the block.

"I feel ya. I just think it makes more sense if these creatures we fight are our testing ground." Marshall got up when he saw the two people coming down the block. "Either way, let's work on our teamwork, right?" Marshall put his knuckles up in the air, waiting for Peter to hit them back with his.

"What's this?" Peter asked bluntly.

"Pound it man. It means we're in this together." Marshall smiled. Peter wasn't sure why but he smiled back. Maybe he was just so use to mimicking others expressions, or maybe he actually felt happy. He pounded back.

Fred and Nick walked up to the two other boys. They all exchanged handshakes. The bond of friendship was starting to grow the more they all hung out together. Nick told them about his date. "She's pretty amazing though. We're gonna try to go out again this week."

"That's awesome dude!" Marshall slapped Nick on the shoulder.

"I'm glad you've taken a liking to Kelly. She's a great person, please take care of her." Nick nodded to Peter. He understood Peter cared about Kelly in the way a brother does a sister.

"Well, I say we head down there and see what's on the dinner plate," Marshall said jabbing his thumb behind him towards the house.

"Dinner Plate?" Fred tilted his head.

"Yea," Marshall responded.

"Why a dinner plate?" Nick asked.

"Cause we're about to serve whatever we are facing. Get it?"

"Wouldn't we be the ones getting served then? Because we'd be the ones losing," Nick pointed out. Fred laughed. Peter followed. Marshall waved his hands.

"You guys just don't get it. Let's go whoop some ass!" Marshall began walking up the stairs, the others following close behind.

"Carl said the gym is straight ahead. All the way down. We can't miss it 'cause we can't go past it," Nick informed them as he re-read the text he got from Carl that morning. The boys followed closely together, still weary of the Station. The white walls gave them a soothing feeling while they walked through the halls, but also very isolated.

"Anyone read any of the guide yet? It's kind of like a scrap book," Fred asked while they walked down the long hall.

"I read some. It's pretty cool but feels like just a bunch of notes put together." Nick pointed out. Fred agreed.

"I didn't read any of it," Marshall added.

"Surprise, surprise," Fred responded and they all laughed.

"The guide helps learn the weaknesses and strengths of the Unknowns the Exterminators have met. It's helpful in that sense. I do agree, it could have used better structure but it's something to read to help us prepare." Peter looked to the boys, seeing if he could read their faces. He was quite good at finding certain emotions.

"I agree Pete. I've been messing around with certain

114

weapons at night to get an idea." Nick tapped his Rod. "I've been practicing with the spear but I really like the feel of the sword. I did almost cut myself but the Rod simply turned back to its base form when the blade touched my skin. I thought that was kind of cool. Though it did scare me that I almost chopped myself in half," Nick said, half laughing.

"The elemental blaster." Marshall stated. They all looked at him shocked. "It's the only thing I read from the guide. I wanted to try a new weapon today. I think I'll try that."

"Maybe you should start with the elemental gloves. The blaster takes an immense amount of energy. The gloves are a lot easier to control." Peter didn't understand why he cared. Yet, he felt like he wanted to protect even Marshall. He didn't want to see any of his new teammates get hurt.

"I got it man. Don't worry. I use to run track, I got plenty of stamina!"

"You never ran track." Fred laughed.

"I did so chubby. You can't run so you never saw me out there."

Fred pulled his shirt out to make sure his stomach wasn't outlining it. "You went to track three days then quit. Remember?"

"Yeah, well those three days I was like the best in class. So, whatever!" Marshall got to the huge silver doors. They were the only different colored doors in the whole white hallway. "Well, this is it right? Who's ready?

"Ready," all three of the boys answered in unison. Marshall pushed forward and they entered the new area.

"Whoa," was the first thing Nick muttered. The gym was huge, the size of a football field. They all took a step inside to see the brownish looking stadium that stood before them. It was an empty place yet it looked like there were barracks set up throughout the field. Places to jump over and hide behind. There were pillars on the side of the gym, laid out across the entire place. Nick stepped forward and a huge echo came from his steps. The others walked forward, heading to the center of the field.

"This place is crazy big," Marshall said looking around. He

was stunned how big the gym was.

"Least it's not gray," Fred muttered. Nick chuckled.

"This is perfect. It's the type of training ground one hopes for," Peter said stopping in the center of the gym. He twirled around, letting the essence of the gym enter him. He could sense many years of training that were done here. Many Exterminators before him fought hard to prove their skills. He was about to do the same.

"Glad you boys could get here in time." Carl was walking towards them. They all took a look at their unit leader as he wore a very definitive brown vest over his button down shirt. The boys were used to seeing Carl in dressed-looking clothes, almost business-like. The new look was strange for them.

"Nice clothes, you look like a tourist from Florida," Nick joked.

Carl ignored the comment. "Today, we will be doing some training. It's to focus on teamwork. A lot of times you boys will head out on missions alone. So I do advise you to figure out your own unique strengths and weaknesses. Work to improve those. However, teamwork can be very important. Today you will face off against a creature that is cunning, quick, and brutal. It's trained and part of our team but it will still act as if it isn't. It'll attack and keep you down, though it won't fatally injure any of you. I want you to work together to figure out how to beat this Unknown." Carl walked behind the boys while speaking. He had his hands behind his back, a smile across his face.

"Any tips on fighting it?" Nick was curious. If it was an Unknown it could be anything.

"That's the fun part. That's the part that makes training so interesting. For you not to know the enemy and still conquer the fight." Carl turned around to face the boys. He put both his arms out pointing to the gym. "You have this entire gym. It's empty save a few barracks and pillars. Use those to your advantage though. Strategies. Do not just attack head on. This beast will be too powerful for any of you to take one on one. You don't know how to hunt something like it well enough. So fight together." Carl

116

turned back around. Heading for another door on the opposite side of the gym.

Nick watched closely as Carl made his way towards the door. "Anyone got a plan?"

"We beat it till it can't fight," Marshall said loudly.

"That's not a plan." Fred moved back. He sensed something terrible. What was behind the door scared him. "Guys, not feeling too well."

Peter looked back at Fred. "Stay focused. Together we can defeat it."

The door opened and a paw entered the doorway. Its silver fur started at the tip of its leg all the way up to its massive head. The wolf came walking through the door, bigger than anything the boys were imaging. It was easily ten feet tall, its massive body weighing more than all four boys combined. It had eyes of crystal blue. The teeth were sharp, making them the perfect tool for tearing things into pieces.

Carl patted the creature on the head as it bowed and nuzzled it's nose on Carl's face. "This is Silver. He's only a year old, but don't let his age fool you. He's one of the most powerful allies we have." Carl continued to pet the huge wolf.

"It's one of them though!" Marshall roared. "You said they are all creatures bent on killing us!" Marshall felt like he had been lied too. Stories about these creatures kept changing so frequently.

"True. Most come into this world ready to attack us. However, Silver was born in our realm. His mother was one of our allies and made her pact with us before the second war. Very few creatures want to join us against their fellow creatures. They rather be left alone but some see their own kind being used. Used to destroy, and they hate it. So they join our cause. Unfortunately, it comes down to hunting these monsters. But the alternative is to let them fully cross over and kill innocents. No one wants that." Carl stopped petting Silver. He howled at the excitement of fighting.

Marshall didn't fully accept the answer. He wanted to know more about the entire situation of coming through the realms. Nick watched as Fred cowered behind one of the Barracks. His

117

breathing was heavy, sweat forming on his forehead. "Hey Fred, you okay?"

Fred shook his head. He felt his whole body sweating. He felt his heart pounding. He felt his shoulder burning. "I can't...it reminds me of the wolf hybrid. I can't fight that thing," he said almost crying. Nick grabbed his shoulders. Fred jumped and pushed away his hands. He could feel the burning pain grow in his shoulder. He grabbed it like he was grabbing for dear life. "It hurts!"

Carl couldn't see behind the barrack. He had no clue when he told Silver to go. "Silver, take them down. Make sure to show them how brutal Unknowns can be." Silver howled even louder, before stalking his way towards the group.

"We need a plan now." Peter stepped back. Looking at the now panicking Fred. "What are you guys doing?"

"Fred isn't doing well," Nick said. "He's scared of that thing. It reminds him of the first creature we killed."

"We don't have time for that." Marshall put his hand on the barrack that Fred and Nick were hiding behind. He had his back to them, watching as the wolf slowly made his way towards them. "This thing is getting ready to attack. If we don't go on the offensive soon it's gonna get us."

"He has a point," Peter agreed, now watching the Unknown observing the gym. Trying to find an opportunity to slip away and strike.

The wolf stopped looking around and dashed. Silver's speed was almost unmatched. "It's heading right for us! This thing is fast!" Marshall grabbed his Rod, Peter did the same. The brute was only a few yards away from them when he ran to the right. His speed was so quick it took both boys by surprise as they jumped back. The wolf flew towards the pillar, then back around, coming full speed. Silver was building up momentum.

Peter focused on his Rod. He created the elemental gloves he'd been training with the past few nights. Marshall watched as the black glove molded onto Peter's arm. Once armed, Peter concentrated. He knew the words. "Fire" he muttered and the flame grew in the palm of his hand. He grabbed it like a baseball, forming it into a ball shape with his fingers and flinging it. The ball of fire was small and Silver easily dodged it to his side. The ball of fire blew up giving off a small little explosion of flames. The wolf still came at full speed.

"Good try," Marshall said as he ran towards the wolf. "Let's see how you deal with this." Marshall concentrated for just a split second, and his arm slowly became the metallic arm he was getting used to it. The second it was completed he threw his arm forward, it made full contact to the wolf's face, knocking it to the left. Silver's momentum was so strong though it made Marshall slip to his side and roll over a few times. The speed at which both were running was a sudden clash that knocked both of them back.

"Well, that hurt me more than I thought it would," Marshall said coughing, pulling himself up. Silver was already on his feet again. The beast shook his head, brushing away the hit he'd just suffered. "I think I'm more hurt than this thing," Marshall joked.

"Nick, we need help," Peter said looking at them both again. "Silver is strong. We can't beat him by ourselves."

Nick studied Fred. He could see no matter how much talking he did Fred just wouldn't listen. "All right. Fred stay here and lay low. We're right here." Nick got up and walked next to Peter. "All right, let's do this." Nick grabbed his Rod and formed it into a spear. "I'm going to head over to Marshall and use defensive maneuvers while he strikes offensively. You focus on support. Throw those elements whenever you see an opening." Nick's plan seemed simple enough. Peter nodded; he could feel some of his energy leaving him after the last attack.

Nick darted towards Marshall. Marshall slowly rose to his feet. Silver was already on him though. Before Marshall could throw up his fist the beast pushed him down with his left paw. He slammed Marshall to the ground, Marshall gasped for air. Nick did a 360 turn and twirled the spear's side towards Silver. Silver was already expecting it and jumped back. The spear missed completely. Nick now stood over Marshall, spear in hand. "Get up.

This thing isn't playing around."

Marshall grabbed his chest, coughing. "Ya think? Damn thing almost crushed my chest." He rose up slowly. The wolf slowly walked around the boys, trying to pick which prey he would strike at next.

Fred fell to his knees. He couldn't hear anything. He just felt weak. He felt his heart pounding, he felt his shoulder burning. It felt like it was going to rip open and something wanted out. A beast that wanted to fight more than anything. *"Join me in the room. I can take away the pain. You won't be scared anymore,"* he could hear himself think. He felt his thoughts, as if they were another persons'. Like someone was talking to him. He shook his head. He had to focus, had to help his friends. Yet he sat there, unable to move an inch.

Nick swung the spear again; the beast slammed his paw down on it. Silver speed and aim were perfect, it launched itself at Nick. Marshall threw his fist forward, the wolf moved just slightly to right, dodging the fist completely. Marshall's face was now side to side with the beast. Silver slammed his head into Marshall's, knocking him over. He then swung his paw sideways into Nick. Nick let go of the pinned spear and flew to his side, slamming down hard. Silver howled in victory, but it was short-lived. A ball of fire flew into the beast's side, knocking it to the side and leaving smoke drifting into the air from his fur. Silver sent out a small cry of pain. Peter fell to his knees; the elemental attacks were beginning to take a toll on his body.

Marshall pushed himself back up again, this time a lot slower. He could feel his body's energy getting eaten away. He bit his lip and rose up. He wasn't about to back down just yet. Silver was already back on his feet, growling now. "Oh you gotta be kidding me. How strong is this thing?"

Nick slowly rose. His whole left shoulder was shooting up with sharp pain. "This isn't good. We're doing minimal damage and he's knocking the crap out of us. This isn't working," Nick said back on his feet. He walked over to his spear and picked it back up. The wolf was ready for another fight, darting his head back and forth between Marshall and Nick.

"Fred, snap out of it," Peter said as he got back to his feet. "Without you we might not win."

"I can't," Fred responded. He was scared.

"You have to help. What if this was a real fight. What if we were really in danger!?"

"I can't-" Fred began.

"Enough of this can't stuff! Push those thoughts out of your mind. Push all of your thoughts away. Wipe your mind clean. Let yourself be free," Peter spoke kindly. He knew being rash wouldn't solve anything. "Please Fred. Help us."

Fred tried to listen. He heard most of what Peter was saying. He could feel his body ease. *"Do not listen to him. You go out and fight and you'll die."* The thoughts came rushing back to him. He ignored them. He stood up, his shirt soaked from sweat. He looked at Silver, who was trying to eye which boy he wanted to attack. "What do you want me to do?" The voice came cracking out of Fred's mouth.

"Attack him head on. I'm support. I got maybe one more shot with this thing. I'm going to try something new, so keep in mind I might not be of any help. Get his back turned to me though. That will be my only chance to strike." Peter kept calm. He knew how to release his stress. He didn't let emotion cloud him. He didn't have many emotions for that to happen anyway.

Fred walked towards Silver. He wasn't sure what to create. What could hurt a beast of that size? Nothing. He remembered reading the guide though. Something came to mind. If he couldn't hurt the Unknown, he could keep it distracted. He placed his Rod next to his legs. "Zoran," he muttered. The image of boots came to mind. The Rod attached to both feet, forming around his shoes. It became two boots with lightning bolts engraved on the sides. Fred smiled and dashed.

He'd only been using this weapon for two days but he already got the hang of it. His speed was increased tenfold so he moved like he was flying. So light and free, Fred felt great. He dashed yards in seconds, and was already on Silver before he knew what was happening. Fred wasn't strong by any means but the extra boost of speed made his fist hitting the wolf more painful than expected. Silver moved back, shaking his head violently. Fred stood with both Marshall and Nick now. Ready to join the fight.

"I never seen a fat boy move so fast," Marshall joked.

"I swear I'm going to punch you right in the face when this is over," Fred responded.

"Now, let's do this. Fred move to the side, keep him distracted. I'ma try to strike, if I miss, you're up Marshall." Nick stepped forward. "GO!" They dispatched, following the plan.

Fred darted forward. Silver snapped at him but he already changed his course of direction before getting close enough and dashed to the right. Nick flung his spear forward; the beast expected it and dodged to the left. Marshall was already aiming for that spot and swung forward, the wolf met the fist head on. A crash and the wolf was able to push Marshall backwards despite the arm hitting it head on. Marshall fell backwards, tumbling over. The wolf then went to snap at Nick from the side but Nick already swung the spear. It nailed Silver on the side but didn't move the mighty beast. Silver growled as he went to snap again. This time Fred was already there. He jumped on top of the beast and grabbed hold of Silver's hair. Silver roared in anger. Nick swung back his spear again before striking. Silver saw it coming and knocked Nick down with his paw. The Unknown pressed hard, showing Nick he was defeated. Marshall was back up but Silver used his tail to whip him across the face. Marshall went tumbling down before even fully getting up. Fred kept punching Silver from up top. The pain was minimal. Silver growled and then rolled over. The pain Fred felt as the wolf rolled on him was almost unbearable. He let go of the beast and laid there, pain everywhere.

Then the blue ball hit the beast on his right lower leg. It blew up into an electricity field. Silver howled in pain. It went on for a few seconds and once done smoke was coming from the wolf. Silver looked like he was about to fall over. "Fall..." Peter whispered, letting his voice flee from his body. He felt his whole body shutting down. He felt weak, impossible to keep his body up much longer.

Silver didn't fall though. The beast shook his body off and turned to Peter. The Unknown began walking towards him. The other boys were lying on the ground. Most in so much pain they couldn't get up or lacked the energy to move. Peter kneeled, waiting for what he knew was coming. He didn't have any other energy to fight back. Silver came up to Peter's face and stared into his eyes. It then licked Peter's face. Peter didn't know how to react. He just sat there for a few moments in silence. Then he laughed before falling over, exhausted.

"That will conclude the training for today!" Carl walked towards the boys. "Boys this is just the beginning. As you can see it's gonna be tough. We'll be facing plenty of creatures far more deadly than Silver here. However, with Silver here the training will go quicker than expected. Together we'll make you into fighting machines. You did well." He walked over to Fred and helped him up. "You fought as a team." He helped Marshall to his feet. "You fought like you were fighting as a team forever." Silver nipped Peter's shirt to drag him to his feet. Peter patted the beast as he helped him up. "Best of all. You worked together as a team that I'm proud of. From today on I'll help you to become the strongest Exterminators in this organization." Carl smiled as he helped Nick up.

All boys looked beat up, tired, exhausted, but happy. They worked as a complete team for the first time. They felt the connection that they needed for these hunts. Now they had to harness this teamwork and sharpen their skills. It was time for the real hunts.

Chapter Fifteen – Halloween Dance

Weeks have passed by since school started. The boys all began their training in the beginning of September. In the past two weeks they had started heavy training; using thirty pound book-packs to weigh them down while they did laps in the gym. Every morning Fred and Marshall also did their additional three mile run before school. They did it four times a week, skipping between the days to rest. Four days during the week they all would head to the gym together and formulate new strategies. They learned how to use certain weapons together.

Nick would use his spear to keep the monsters at bay. The spear made him feel swift and agile. Peter would then use his elemental gloves to be on the offensive. He was learning to use the gloves and shape them into the perfect weapon. It was both fun and challenging for him. Marshall would work with Fred in ways to better suit their teamwork. Fred focused on using his Zoran weapon, which created boots to make him run at a far quicker speed than humanly possible. To him it was almost like gliding in air. While doing that Marshall would move in close and use his metallic fist to do some serious damage. He felt like he has a boulder for an arm.

They switched on and off, using different team work methods with each other to get better results. They trained so much that school became a second thought, even to Peter, who always obtained straight A's. By October they all got their progress reports. The boys mostly did C's with the exception of Peter who scored B's. Still, these were lower scores than expected.

Nick felt his relationship growing with Kelly in ways he had only hoped for. Any free time Nick had he spent with Kelly. After the first few dates they began to hang out around the house, in the parks, walk along the bay. Any ways they found to spend time together they took advantage of. They sometimes spent whole days together just walking around the city. Nick had never felt closer to anyone before in his life.

Peter focused solely on training. He read as much as he could from the guide but spent most of his time training his mind. He was able to form elemental balls much easier than he could month ago. He created them far quicker, they were more destructive on impact, but the true achievement was the fact he could throw over five now before feeling a real type of drain on him instead of just three. Carl promised the more stamina building, the more training, the more working out, all of it would increase the body's resistance. Upon increasing their stamina, the more they used the Rod the more it fuses with the body. This enabled them to become one with the weapon.

Fred kept up his daily routines in training. By the end of October he had dropped over two pants sizes and was working on the third. He was reaching the other boys' weight faster than any one could have expected. He began changing his eating habits, working out, as well as training. All of those factors had contributed into creating a much healthier Fred. He was still dealing with the voice in his head though. Some nights when he went to sleep he was back in the white room. However, he was able to block it out most of the time. If not, he suffered through it before coming back to reality.

Marshall kept working on using his fist. Upon hours and hours of training he was able to fuse the metallic arm up to his shoulder. He could feel it was becoming stronger. The more he trained and used the weapon, the more it filled his body with a powerful force. He envisioned his whole body one day being this unstoppable metallic body. He worked towards getting to his goal every single day.

"I killed that Rockus so easily last week. I'm kind of eager to fight something different," Fred said taking a bite of his banana. Nick looked to the side of the gym. He still hadn't gotten his first

125

mission. Fred got two more as did Peter, even Marshall got another one. Nick was still waiting to be called on his first mission.

"Yeah, I'm still waiting to fight anything," Nick said. Fred nodded in agreement., slapping his friend hard on the back.

"Don't worry buddy, soon you'll be one of us."

"I'm already one of you guys!" Nick spat.

"I'm kidding man. Listen, let's get out of here. I'm tired as heck and want to go home and play some video games. Wanna come?" Fred stood up and wiped the sweat off his face. They had both just finished training in the gym; a quick running spree and a warm up spar between the two. Fred felt great, he slapped his stomach. "Just about all gone."

Nick got up, wiping off his pants. "Yeah man, you're looking great. Keep it up!"

They both began walking out of the gym. Fred looked at Nick oddly. "Hey so, you coming over or what?" Nick forgot he already asked him that.

"I'm sorry, I'm out of it today. Nah man, I'ma head over to Kelly's house. Her mom is cooking dinner." Nick smiled at his friend. Fred smiled back, a bit forced.

"All right, no problem. Are you sure you're okay though?"

"Yeah, I'm fine."

"All right, just making sure." Fred was concerned about his friend. More so, he really wanted Nick to still come hang out. He wanted to make sure he himself was doing alright. The voice in his head was growing louder and louder each day.

Peter bit his lip as he conjured the ice crystal in his hand. He let it rest in his right hand where he had the glove on. He held it tightly and it started to become mushy. Peter then imagined the crystal becoming hard again, it almost instantly did. He was training his mind to imagine the shape of the elemental he held. He threw the ice crystal against the empty alleyway wall, shattering and freezing over a sizable portion of it. Peter's elements were growing

126

stronger by the day.

"I see you're always training aren't ya?" Jin walked down the alleyway.

"I have to. I need to become strong."

"You are strong."

"I need to be stronger then."

"Pushing yourself over your limit can be bad. Remember to take it easy every so often." Jin leaned against the wall behind Peter. Peter let his fingers rest; he could still feel the ice cold freezing over his fingertips in the palm of his hand.

"Thanks, but I think I can determine my own limits." Peter began to walk away.

"You want power, right?" Peter stopped. Jin had caught his full attention. "I can show you power. The kind of power you can gain."

Peter turned fully around to face Jin. "What can you show me?"

"This," Jin replied. He grabbed two rods and created two elemental gloves. He smacked his hands together and pulled them apart slowly, a large shard of ice formed between his hands. Once it was a foot long he grabbed it with his left hand. "Let me show you what happens when you harness real power." He slammed the large ice crystal against the wall. The entire wall began to freeze over, the ice crawling up the entire building. Peter stood back amazed at the area the ice was reaching. After a few seconds the ice stopped growing. It covered over twenty feet of the wall - enough to freeze two or three people over.

"That's amazing," Peter whispered in shock. He was used to this feeling but didn't feel it often. He touched the alleyway wall, it was ice cold. The area effected was beyond anything Peter had hoped to create with his own weapon. "I need that power."

"Why?"

"Why what?"

"Why do you need this power?" Jin walked up to Peter. He cocked his head to the left.

"I need it because-" Peter started but didn't know how to

finish. He wanted the power. It would give him something that he could use. He never thought why he actually needed it. He just knew he wanted it. "I need it to protect people."

"Is that really your reason? I find that a bit hard to believe," Jin said skeptically.

"Of course it's my reason. Why would I lie about that?" Peter tried to throw in a crying voice. He knew people felt bad whenever he did that.

Jin laughed and waved his hand. "Listen, I'm just asking a simple question. You want the power but you don't know what for. The only way to gain this power is to figure out the reason of why you want it. Once you do that, you'll gain the power. It's pretty simple really. It's like math." Jin walked past Peter. "Once you're ready to figure it out, come to me. We'll start figuring it out together."

Peter turned to watch Jin go. He never thought much about the young hunter besides the fact that he was Carl's friend. Maybe even another student of Carl's. He never cared to ask before. Now that he witnessed the hunter wielding such tremendous power, Peter was intrigued. He was amazing at math, but this wasn't a problem he could figure out on his own.

"Listen girl, let's just go to the dance tomorrow," Marshall said, leaning against a store shop. He was talking to a girl from his class. While her name wasn't something Marshall cared to remember, he still found her cute none-the-less. The Halloween dance was tomorrow night and he still hadn't found a girl to go with. "I'll even pick you up. I might even get us some dinner. Whatcha say?"

"I say you should get lost. I'd never go with you, anywhere." The sting in her voice hurt.

Marshall laughed it off. "Hey, I'm offering you a little slice of the Marshall pie. You don't take a scoop now you'll miss the best meal of the night." Marshall gave a wink. She gave him a throw up motion in return.

"I'd rather not go out at all, thank you very much. Everyone knows you're a slime ball. Just stay the heck away from me!" She stormed off; offended that he'd even ask her. She felt she was far above anything Marshall had to offer.

Marshall wasn't a ladies man. He never hit it big in that department. He never really cared though at rejection, he just got used to it. He shrugged and walked away from the shop. If she wasn't going to go with him he was probably going to end up trick-or-treating with his little brother. It was something better to do on Halloween instead of sitting around at home all night. Still, he much rather be with a hot chick at a dance than walking around with his little brother picking up candy.

The next day everybody at school was talking about the Halloween dance. Tonight was the night everyone dressed up in the craziest looking costumes they could find and come to a school dance with the best partner. Most girls were asked to go with someone weeks in advance. In the case of the four boys, Nick was the only one to have a date, so far. Marshall tried desperately but no one seemed interested. Fred didn't bother, since he still had a poor self-image of himself. Peter just didn't care. His sights were set on training. It was one out of four for the crew.

Marshall walked into the lunch room. He saw Nick sitting a few tables down from the door. He began walking in that direction but stopped two tables short, bent over the empty spot and looked towards Lucy. Lucy was the girl no one was friends with. She never talked to anyone; she drew most of the time, and ignored almost all school activities. She was the loner of the juniors. Marshall found that as a perfect choice. "Hey Lucy, mind if I sit down."

"I do," she said simply. Her blond bangs covering her eyes while she drew.

"You mind if I sit down?"

"That's what I said." She kept her eyes on the paper she was drawing on; completing the left hand of one of her characters.

"You know, I like the ones that are hard to get."

"I'm impossible to get."

"That's even hotter," he replied as he sat down next to her. She gave a quick glance towards him before returning her attention to drawing. "Listen, I'ma be honest. Can I be honest with you? No girl wants to go with me. I really don't care about this dance but I don't want to go trick-or-treating with my little brother and his annoying friends. So I'm asking you if you could do me this favor and go with me. I'll pick you up. I'll take you to dinner if you want. I'll get you home. I just want to go and have a good time. Whatcha say?" He rushed to get his words out and then sat anxiously awaiting her answer.

Lucy finished the other hand and looked up at Marshall. She looked at him oddly, not sure how to answer. Normally she would just ignore him until he went away since she had absolutely no interest in him. She really hated school activities. Yet somehow, she was intrigued by the way he asked her to go so out in the open. "Pick me up at six. Do not wear anything too gross or I will shut the door right in your face." She went back to her drawing.

"You got it!" He slapped the table in happiness. Then he stood up and walked away from the table, making his way towards Nick. He couldn't be happier. Finally he had found somebody to go with him to the dance! Not to mention no one really knew Lucy, he didn't even know Lucy, which meant he could talk with her plenty to find out more about her. He was excited.

"Hey, why do you have the dumbest smile on your face right now?" Nick asked, putting down his food. Marshall slid into his chair, his smile getting even bigger. "Okay, now you're freaking me out. Joker much?"

"I got someone to go out with me to the dance. It's gonna be awesome!" Marshall was so excited he sounded like a five year old getting a shiny new toy.

"Really? Who's the unlucky lady?"

"First, kiss my ass. Second, her name is Lucy," he said proudly, pointing behind him to Lucy drawing. "She's kind of a quiet one, but she's pretty cute."

"Well, good for you. Please try to be on your best behavior. You aren't too good around girls." Nick went back to eating his lunch.

"Thanks for the vote of confidence. Why are we friends again?"

"Probably 'cause you couldn't live without me," Nick mumbled.

"Oh, I'd somehow manage, trust me," Marshall retorted. He was beyond excited. So excited he ignored any insults Nick threw at him for the remainder of lurch.

Fred walked with Peter towards the Station. Marshall and Nick went to their homes, getting ready for the dance tonight with their dates. Fred didn't bother asking anyone. He didn't feel like getting rejected. Peter wanted to focus on learning new elements and work on creating stronger ones. "So how's the training with the elemental glove coming?" Fred looked at Peter.

"It's going well. I still can't create large impact strikes but I can use over seven summonses before I feel drained. My goal is to hit twelve by the end of November," Peter answered happily. If any true emotion was to come from Peter it was almost always in relation to his power with the Rod.

"That's great man! Keep at it. I'm sure you'll be able to do it. I'm trying to focus on using these boots, but also began training with the sword play. Nick and I were dueling the other day with 'em and it's pretty amazing how great they feel. It's like whenever we create a weapon they just fit us so well. They flow with our body motion, you ever noticed that?"

"I have. I think it's part of the Rod. The more we use it, the more it becomes infused with our body. The more it infuses with us, the more it becomes part of us and enables the weapons to work as an extension of our body. It's how we can use them so smoothly, it becomes a fluid motion with our body instead of just a weapon." Peter pointed to his Rod. "Soon they will be an extension of us the more we use them."

"As weird as that sounds, it probably is exactly that," Fred said laughing. "Hey, so why didn't you go to the dance? "

Peter shrugged. "I'm not interested in any of the girls in my classes."

Fred's eyes grew. "None?"

"Not really. Is that really hard to believe? Marshall gave me the same look." Peter was beginning to wonder if he stood out more than he wanted. He tried his best to understand other people's emotions and follow along. When it came to girls he just couldn't fit in. He hadn't found any girl in any of his classes attractive at all. He focused on his studies usually. At least until the training came along; now that took up all his thoughts. He felt there was no time to date a girl.

"It's just odd, I guess. I mean there are some cuties in all my classes. What's your type?"

"I don't have a type," Peter answered awkwardly.

"Everyone has a type." Fred waved his hands around. "Is it some weird thing? Like the ugly red heads or something?"

"No. I just don't find anybody attractive. I don't have a type. I don't care about hair color or skin color. I could care less if they are fat or skinny. I just don't find anyone I'm attracted to. I really don't see what the problem is," Peter grumbled. He didn't realize it came off a bit rough, as Fred looked surprised.

"Sorry, dude," Fred muttered.

"I took no offense. I'm sorry if I came off upset. I'm just not sure why I have to be attracted to someone in our classes. I find certain girls attractive - just none in our school."

"Well who do you find hot then?"

"Well… my psychiatrist is beautiful." Peter remembered her beautiful black hair reaching all the way down to her lower back. She had glasses and a smile most of the time. Pink lipstick was her favorite, so she always wore it. She had a very thin and tall frame, which Peter instantly found attractive. He also loved the fact she was extremely smart. More so she always spoke to him like he was an adult. Very respectful. He loved that about her.

"I didn't even know you had a psychiatrist." Fred was surprised. He'd been hanging out with the guys a lot the last few months. They mostly focused on training though and making plans during fights. He never really bothered to learn about Peter. He liked him well enough but they never teamed up alone. Now he was interested to learn more about this fellow Exterminator. "So she's hot, huh? Maybe you just like the older ladies. I can understand that." He playfully elbowed Peter. Peter smiled back, as he pushed him away.

Peter never talked about his psychiatrist. He never spoke about his problems to anyone. "I go to her 'cause sometimes I feel...different. I don't know why I am the way I am at times. Sometimes I feel it's my..." He wanted to speak more. He didn't know why he found it easy to talk to Fred about the problems that clouded his mind. He just felt the words come out so easy. "I think my father being the way he is has made me not feel emotions like normal people do. I don't know if I shut my emotions off or I never had them to begin with."

Fred listened to his friend speak, formulating his own opinion on it. Peter looked at him, then to the ground. He was wondering if he went too far into detail about his problems. He was about to speak up but Fred spoke first. "I can understand that." Peter looked back up at Fred. "My parents are never around. They provide for me, money-wise, but are never around to even be with me. Is that even parenting? I don't know. Sometimes I feel like I'm raising myself. I just want a normal family, yet I basically live in a house that's empty. I don't feel the love from my mom or dad, I don't know if they even love me, to be honest." Just like Peter, it was easy for Fred to spill his thoughts. He wasn't sure why it was so easy either, but he had to get it off his chest.

"I feel like the fact my mom never wanted me to stay out past four on school days growing up and my dad telling me to keep quiet, shut up, and stay in my room turned me into this. This kid with problems. I can't even understand people's emotions at times. It makes me feel weird, like maybe I just don't belong with people. With you guys..." Peter let his voice drift off as he felt the stress slowly leaving his body. The words he had kept in for so long were finally leaving. Finally they were getting away from him. He gladly let them evaporate into the air.

"You belong with us. You're part of the team, remember?" Fred placed his hand on Peter's shoulder. "Don't ever doubt that. We're in this together, and that's that. When things get rough, we work through it, together. You can't feel emotions sometimes? That's fine. We'll help you. Don't ever think you don't belong with us."

Peter felt a tug, almost as if someone ripped away a part of him. The part he hated the most. The part that kept him under a shield. A shield that made him what he is today. That part of him just got stripped away. He felt like someone cared, something he never felt before. He felt like someone cared about him, and wasn't afraid to tell him that they cared. He felt like he had an actual friend. "Thank you," was all Peter could finally say.

They reached the house. Fred smiled at his friend. "Never need to thank a friend. Let's go do some training." Fred walked up the steps. Peter took a look at Fred going up the stairs. He smiled, as he watched him walk to the door. He never had a real friend before. These guys were his unit. Now they were becoming his friends. He liked that. "You coming?" Fred looked back from the door. Peter nodded and began climbing the stairs.

"You look amazing!" Marshall exclaimed as Lucy opened the door. She was dressed up as a zombie bridesmaid. She had on a beautiful white dressed with zombie makeup. Chunks of whole skin were missing on her face. Marshall felt under dressed in just regular clothes with ripped holes through his shirt. He also had a fake rubber knife in on his left leg. "You're by far the hottest zombie I've ever seen."

"You look like an attack victim. You aren't very scary," Lucy said laughing. Marshall shrugged. "I like it though. It could be like I attacked you, and tried to stab you. We match up." She shut the door behind her.

They walked side by side, at first not saying anything as they went down the block. She wanted to say something but she was never good with conversations. She usually said something odd and it made people just look at her weird. She wasn't sure how to start a conversation.

"I think this dance is going to be cool." Marshall finally broke the silence. He wasn't really sure what to say after that. Lucy wanted to say something, instead she just nodded. "I mean I can't dance, but it'll be fun. I think. Can you dance?"

"Not really. I have two left feet."

"Yeah, me too!" He sounded too excited. He tried to hold it back but she saw the excitement and giggled. "Hey, no fair. You can't laugh at me. You have two left feet, remember?"

She put her hand over her mouth, trying to hold in the laugh. "It's just funny how excited you got at the fact we both have two left feet."

"Well, you kind of make me nervous."

"*I* make *you* nervous?"

"You do. I think you're cute." Marshall may not have been a ladies man, but he had no problem speaking his mind. He could always straight out tell someone what he was thinking. It was his gift and his curse.

Lucy smiled, her face turning bright red. She had boys ask her out before, boys even telling her she's cute, but never someone saying it so out in the open. Through text or online messaging is one thing, but to say it to her face is another. She felt happy, scared, nervous, and excited all at once. "You know what, I think tonight is going to be pretty great," she told him.

"Yeah?"

"Yeah."

"Well, I'll try to make it as memorable as possible," Marshall returned smiling. He slid his hand in hers. Her heart stopped for moment then she gripped his hand tighter. She could feel the heat of his hand and she loved it. She gave a quick glance over at him and he looked back. She smiled. Little did Marshall know he already made this night memorable for her.

Nick moved his body in such an odd way it made Kelly almost fall over laughing. Nick didn't know how to dance, but that didn't stop him from trying. Kelly found it to be the funniest thing she'd ever seen. She slapped her knee, she gasped for breath, and she even begged him to stop. Still Nick proceeded to shake like an epileptic patient having a seizure, throwing his hands in the air. The people around him gave him odd looks as they moved away.

"Please babe, just stop!" Kelly threw her hands in the air. She couldn't stop her laughing, though. The song ended a few moments later and Nick stopped moving.

"Hey, people just jealous of my awesome dance moves," he told her laughing. She shook her head, grabbing onto him. He loved it when she grabbed him and pulled herself closer. He gave her a long kiss; something he wanted to do over and over again then grabbed her shoulders and pulled her even closer. Kissing her even more, he felt the old lust feeling finally turning into love.

They began a slow dance, working with the music and each other. They let the sound of the room move their bodies in a graceful motion. They went back and forth, close to one another, lost in each other. The feelings they felt for each other grew with each step they took together. Nick had felt so lost as of late, but with Kelly he felt whole. He felt like he was finally someone.

The song came to an end, and they pulled away from each other. "Let's go get a drink," Nick said, while grabbing her hand. As they walked back to the table of drinks they ran into Marshall. He was talking to Lucy, both laughing loudly. "Hey man, how's it going?"

Marshall turned to Nick. He gave him a boy's handshake. "Great man, this is Lucy." She shook both Nick and Kelly's hands. "We just got here a few minutes ago, this place is jam packed."

"Yeah, no joke. We just got here about thirty minutes ago, and been dancing as much as possible." Kelly grabbed harder onto Nick. She was so pleased to be with him. "Well, we're going to grab a drink. See you on the dance floor." Kelly waved goodbye as they walked away.

Marshall grabbed Lucy's hand. "Let's get to dancing. We should at least try to dance," he said winking at her. She giggled back at him and they went to the center of the dance floor. The song was a fast paced one so they both broke into a frenzy of throwing their hands around and shaking their bodies. To everyone around them, they looked insane dancing, but they both were laughing the entire time together.

Nick and Kelly arrived near the refreshments. "I'd actually like some water," Kelly told Nick. Nick nodded and went to go grab a bottle. As he reached over the table he saw an odd statue standing behind the drinks. He leaned his head over the table and saw an address on it. Only seven blocks away from the school. His eyes got wide. He checked his watch; it was already getting close to eight o'clock. "A mission," he gasped.

Chapter 16 – Bullet

Nick wasn't sure how to handle the situation. He knew he had a mission, but he knew he couldn't just leave Kelly at the dance. He gazed at the rock once more, mentally taking note of the address. He stepped away from the table and back over to Kelly. She tapped his chest. "Hey, you okay? You look like you've seen a ghost."

Nick looked towards the dance floor. *"I should tell Marshall,"* he thought to himself. He then saw Marshall dancing like a crazy man with his equally crazy-looking date. *"I can't ruin that for him."* He turned back towards Kelly. "Yeah baby, I'm fine. Here's your drink." He could feel the sweat crawling down his face as he handed her the water bottle.

Nick had been waiting weeks for this. He still hadn't had his first mission. He fought with Peter, Marshall, and Fred multiple times on their missions taking down a couple of beasts in teams. He still never had a chance to actually fight on his own mission, though. Now that he got one he wished it could have been any other time but now.

Nick leaned over to Kelly and kissed her lips. "I'm really sorry but I have to go. I'll be back in a few minutes. I need to grab some air. Wait for me?" She stared at him confused. "I'm sorry about this," he said, sadness radiating from his voice.

"You look terrible. You're sweating like a man who just escaped prison," She said as she wiped his forehead. Her heart twisted as she felt a sudden grief and became worried for her boyfriend.

"I swear I'm okay baby. Let me go grab some air and I'll be right back, promise." He began strolling towards the exit.

"All right...I'll be waiting here." He could hear the sadness in her voice. It killed him to hear that. He'd do anything for her not to be upset, but he needed to complete his Objective. He never knew the consequences of not finishing a mission but he wasn't about to find out.

Nick quickly went to the side of the school. In this empty space he clicked the button on his beeper and went into the other realm. He wanted to complete this mission as quickly as possible. He ran towards the address that he had written down.

As he ran through the streets invisible to the normal world, he watched as kids were all around the area. Even three blocks away from the school they were hanging out near cars, on lawns outside the house, in garages. He ignored it, focusing on the mission. He grabbed his Rod and began focusing on a weapon. He'd been training with the spear a lot lately. However, he wanted to master his skills in sword play. He loved the way the sword danced with his body. He focused for a moment, imagining a black handled, silver tipped, three-foot sword. In a matter of seconds it formed in his hand. It gave him a sense of power to hold such a weapon every time he created it.

He arrived at the address. Locking around quickly, trying to spot the beast that passed through the realms. He saw a few kids walking down the block but, besides that, the street was completely empty. Nick jogged up the block looking side to side trying to find it. He wanted to be cautious but also wanted to hurry back to the dance.

As he reached the end of the block he heard a hiss. Turning quickly to his right he backed up on instinct. He checked under the last car on the street and found a pair of red eyes peering back at him. He held the sword close to his side, waiting for the creature to pop out. It hissed again from the darkness. Nick hadn't seen or heard this creature before.

As if it was on a timer, the beast darted out from under the car and flew towards Nick. Its whole body was black, eyes dark red, with teeth that were razor sharp, and claws coming out of its paws. It looked similar to a wolf but mixed with a fox in terms of body design. Nick brought his sword up as the thing leapt towards him. He wasn't ready for its speed as it tackled him before he could even raise the sword up.

The creature used its weight to push Nick down. He slammed on the ground, letting go of the sword. The Unknown dug its front paws into Nick's chest. It tore right through the shirt and into his upper body. As it dug right in, Nick let out a cry of pain, and blood began seeping out almost immediately. The white shirt he was wearing was slowly becoming entirely red. On reaction he kicked his two feet up, knees hitting the creature, as he flung it off him. The creature hit a truck heading down the street head on. Nick heard a crushing sound and a few yards away the truck swerved to the side and came to a full stop.

Nick got up, coughing. He grabbed his chest and could feel the blood. He took a glance downwards realizing he looked a lot worse than it actually was. He tried to ignore it but the pain soared through his chest with a burning sensation that he couldn't do anything about.

He surveyed the truck down the road that hit the Unknown. He could see a blood trail not far from the truck. He had been hoping the impact would have killed the beast. He slowly walked towards the truck, trying to brush away the pain. He could hear a few kids from down the block shouting. They heard the impact from the crash and were now making their way towards the truck. Nick heard another hiss. Now he had to kill this thing before anyone could get involved. The mission importance just jumped tenfold.

Fred sat in the gym after a four mile run. He was holding forty pound weights in his backpack determined to build up his strength. He wasn't going easy on his body anymore. He refused to ever be in another fight and badly hurt like he was in the first mission he was on. He wanted to become an important part of the team, and to do that he had to push himself beyond anything he imagined before. He kept at it, never giving up.

Peter on the other hand kept playing with the elements;

forming them into different shapes while trying to figure out how to use them as weapons besides just throwing them. He learned a few new tricks that made him better at close range as well as farther away. He just had to figure out how to combine his skills to make him the perfect fighter. His strength was to push himself to the point of perfecting an art. This however, was also his weakness in that there is the occasional art that cannot be perfected no matter how hard he tries.

Fred turned to Peter. "Feels good to work out sometimes. Gets that pent-up stress relieved. Ya know what I mean?"

"Agreed," Peter nodded.

"I do kind of wish I had gone to the dance now." Fred wondered how the dance was going. Wondered if he should have asked someone after all. Maybe it would have been fun. He never really danced but to hold a lady and let their bodies move in unison would have been pretty special. At least Fred imagined it would be since he had never had the chance.

Peter couldn't understand the need to go to a dance. He never liked to dance in the first place. The dress up part was also foreign to Peter. He'd never gone trick-or-treating or done anything special for Halloween. He couldn't understand the fascination of going out and getting dressed up for candy. He didn't want to seem like the odd one out again though. "Yeah, could have been fun."

"Yeah..." Fred thought about it. He wasn't sure what else to say. He felt Peter wouldn't understand the need of being near a girl. Peter seemed content at this moment in his life but Fred ached to have a girl to comfort him. He'd never been on a date, never held a girl, never kissed one. At this moment he wanted to so badly; to just try, if for no other reason than to try something new. He also wanted to be close to someone. Being in a lonely house all day made him crave for another human being.

"Have you ever dated a girl?" It was as if Peter could read Fred's mind. Fred looked back in shock.

"O-of course," he replied stuttering.

Peter read his body language and response. It was easy to

see he was lying. "I never have," he said figuring if he told the truth that Fred would follow suit.

"Really?"

"Yes. I've thought about it occasionally." Peter didn't have much time for dating in his life. He figured one day he'd find someone but spent most of his time studying and now training. Still, every so often he saw a couple walking and felt like he was missing that. That connection that he dearly wanted. If he were to gain it he'd be feel even more normal. Something he wanted to be so desperately.

"Okay I lied. I've never dated. It just feels weird. I mean I'm seventeen and I haven't dated. How sad is that?"

"Nothing sad about it. Just 'cause you take your time in life with certain things, like dating, doesn't make you sad." Peter walked over to Fred and sat near him. He pulled his knees up close to his chest. "I do want to find someone special though. I don't have many reasons other than to find out how it feels. I want to see if I can form a connection that others are always speaking about."

"Yeah, I understand that. I try to envision the same thing. I want to know how it feels. I think I want that more than the other stuff. I mean, don't get me wrong, I'd love to get down and dirty." Fred said laughing, pushing Peter. Peter laughed back, sincerely this time. "I just want to know how it is to have someone you can love. Know what I mean?"

"I do." Peter wondered what it meant to love every day. He felt like he couldn't even love his own mother. The person who gave birth to him. So, did that mean he could ever truly feel that feeling of love? He questioned it every single day.

"Man we sound like two sappy losers, don't we?"

"I don't think so."

Fred laughed, patting his friend on the back. "Yeah, you wouldn't. All right, I'ma run another lap then we can get out of here." Peter nodded and Fred got up. They both went back to their training.

Marshall let Lucy's head lay on his chest as they slow danced. He could feel her movements every step they took. He could feel the heat of her body fuse with his own. He laid his head on top of hers, feeling like he was becoming closer every step they took. It felt amazing. Marshall was glad he went to the dance after all. He was overjoyed that he asked Lucy to accompany him.

The song ended and they pulled away from each other. "You're a much better dancer than you give yourself credit for," Lucy said smiling at Marshall.

"Who would of guessed?" he grinned.

"Thank you," she said, looking around the dance room.

"For what?"

"For taking me here. With you. It's something I never expected to do. I-" she began then shook her head. Looking back into his eyes he could see her's were watery. As if she were about to cry. He wanted to pull her in closer, to make sure she never cried.

"I've never had a date that was this great. Thank you for coming with me." Her smile grew as did his. He felt a bond he never experienced before flourishing.

"Marshall," Kelly walked up to them both. "Nick said he was going out for some air. It's been over thirty minutes. I'm starting to worry."

Marshall looked at Kelly; he could see how nervous she was. "He just walked out in the middle of the dance? Was he sick?"

"I don't know. He looked nervous. Now I'm scared." she told him. He could sense the sadness in her voice.

"I'm sure he's fine." He grabbed Lucy and looked at her. "I'll be right back. I'ma go look for him and bring him back here. Dummy probably got lost around the block," he said laughing. A hollow laugh that neither of the girls bought.

"All right, please hurry back." Lucy never thought she would say something like that. Especially to someone like Marshall, no less.

143

"I will. Kelly, stay close to her. We'll be back in no time. You both owe us our last dance, remember that!" he called back as he walked through the crowd. He made his way outside as quickly as he could. Pushing through the vast amount of kids at the dance was harder than Marshall imagined it would be. He didn't want to push anyone or get into a fight.

He reached the door and pulled through. As he ran down the steps and was about to make a turn he bumped right into Ryan. Ryan, the school bully, who looked angry as hell. He turned around and grabbed Marshall by the tip of his shirt. "Hey, little Marshall. I've seen you hanging out with the nerds and freaks. You loser." He pushed Marshall hard into the ground. Marshall fell, but only because he was busy trying to figure out which way Nick went. Ryan towered over him. "Hey loser, get up."

Marshall looked past Ryan. He could see in the distance a truck's back lights shining red. He figured that must be the way Nick went. Nobody would stop in the middle of the road for nothing. "Listen dude, I don't got time for this." He rose and began to walk past Ryan. Ryan grabbed him again but Marshall quickly pushed his arm away. Ryan didn't expect the swiftness of the much smaller boy. Marshall then broke out in a run. Ryan took a few steps then stopped. The drinking caught up to him and he couldn't get very far without wanting to throw up. He watched as Marshall ran around the corner, cursing under his breath.

Nick held the sword tightly. He was searching under the truck where the hiss came from. He saw the blood smeared along where the truck was and underneath it, but no beast. He smashed his fist on the side of the truck. *"Where the hell is this thing?"* He heard the front of the truck open. "No," he muttered. He quickly made his way from the back of the truck but it was too late. The second the driver stepped out of the truck the creature leapt from the top of it. The poor man couldn't see or even hear what was attacking him. He was just knocked to the ground as the beast dug its claws into him. He cried out in pain as the beast took another swipe at

144

him on the ground.

Nick rushed forward, his sword tucked to his side. He roared trying to scare the beast but it was too busy with its prey. Nick took advantage of the distraction and charged forward. He was able to tackle the creature from behind, sword sliding right through its side. It viciously let out a howl of pain as they both fell to the side. Nick recovered quickly, drawing the sword out of the beast.

The beast bellowed in pain. He wrenched the sword back, ready to finish it off. The beast reacted and threw all four of its short legs forward. It jolted him backwards; he dropped the sword while flying a few feet back. He could feel his back crack on the concrete. It hurt his chest even more, the burning was reignited and he bit his lip to try and forget the pain.

The brute got back to its feet. It fumbled around, blood pouring from the wound hole on both sides. It still held strong, snarling, angry at its attacker. Nick let out a painful moan as he crawled back to his feet. He didn't have time to recover, as the beast pounced once again. He was back on top of Nick before he could reach for his sword. It went to dig the long claws back into Nick's chest, but he grabbed the beast's head and slammed it into the street while rolling over. The creature growled, he reached his other hand up to put it behind the beast's head and slammed it again. It yelped it pain. Nick did it again, the beast cried once more before sagging to the side. Nick rolled out from underneath the bloody monster. He wobbled his way up and then took a breather.

He saw the crowd of kids from down the block surrounding the truck driver. He was bleeding badly and one kid was trying to hold pressure on the wound. The other three were on their cell phones. Chances they were calling their parents or the police. Nick stepped forward; he had to get his Rod back. Being invisible it would be no problem.

He then heard the hiss again.

"Are you kidding me?" he muttered angrily. He turned back around to see the beast was on all four, its face pushed in slightly. Blood dripped from its long snout. "Do you not know how to die?" He moved to one side. The beast reacted and dashed to the other side before launching at him. Nick rolled to the opposite way, just in time, as the beast flew past him and smashed on to the sidewalk. It tumbled over but recovered quickly. Nick backed away. He could hear the ambulance sirens now.

"I can't go near the kids to get the Rod. This thing will follow me, it'll hurt them. My first mission is to protect the innocent. What to do?" Nick looked around for anything. The beast stepped forward, this time making sure it didn't leap the wrong way. It wanted its prey badly but it wasn't stupid enough to pull the same mistake. Nick moved backwards, slowly, trying to find something, anything, to use as a weapon.

The beast howled as it moved forward. He spotted a brick loose near the steps of a house. He quickly dashed for it. The beast growled again and rushed forward. Hot on his trail, it was only a few feet away. Nick came low to the ground, scooping up the brick, turning around and slamming the brick down. The beast took the brick to the side of its face. It flew to the side, a thud sounded as it hit the ground. Nick backed off, dropping the brick.

He let out a sharp breath; he could feel his chest burning even more. The movements must have made the wounds bleed out. He knew it wasn't horrible; the wounds were not too deep. They still hurt, causing him to wince in pain with every step he took towards his Rod. The ambulance must have been close because he heard the sirens even more loudly now. His vision was becoming blurry. Fatigue and loss of blood during the fight was expected but it was taking a toll on him more then he imagined. If he had his weapon it would have been a lot easier, but getting knocked down and thrown around took too much out of him.

The hiss returned.

Nick turned around in shock.

The beast was back on its feet. It looked confused. Nick was thinking the brick had damaged it badly. It's one eye barely opened. The other eye that was fully opened peered straight at Nick. "Are you freaking kidding me?"

146

The beast stepped forward. Nick stepped backwards. They were almost to the street now. He couldn't believe the beast was still able to stand. Its brain should have been damaged beyond repair. It should have been dead by all accounts. Yet it was stalking closer towards him.

As the beast was almost upon Nick it was hit by a bullet through the head. Its red eye gave one more look at Nick before the glow disappeared. It fell over, blood spilling out from every wound that it had. The beast laid still, finally dead.

Marshall stood there, gun aimed where the beast once stood. He let the firearm drop to his side and transform back to his Rod. "You okay?"

"Yeah, thanks." Nick leaned on a car. He could feel the pain in his chest grow. He survived another fight. Yet, barely.

Marshall came over, bending down near the beast. He moved it to the side, checking out its features. The bullet wound was right above the jawline. The beast was certainly dead. Marshall still felt pity every time he put a creature down. However, when his partners were in danger he did not question it. Shoot first, wonder why he had to shoot later.

"My Rod is over there," Nick told him pointing to the group of kids. The ambulance was now parked in front of where the truck was. The emergency crew was trying to get the stretcher ready to load the truck driver up. "Mind grabbing it for me? I need to rest."

"Yeah, no problem. Stay here." Nick watched Marshall make his way towards the crowd. Nick look to his beeper, clicking the "finish button" then waited. He could feel the nice cold air brush over him. It felt good on his burning wound. Another fight. Another kill. This was now Nick's life. He sat up and laid his head into his knees, wondering what Kelly would think of him tomorrow.

Chapter 17 – Lust & Love

Jin watched as his Bora and Carl began to approach him. He was finishing a warm up in the gym, using a blade for his main weapon. He tried all different combinations as of late. He loved using his blade as well as elemental gloves. Another favorite of his was taking the elemental powers and combining them with his gun. Instead of shooting bullets, it shot small electric bullets. It was less deadly than a bullet per se, but to trap or stop someone it was perfect. As an Exterminator, his missions changed. As he hunted other things, besides just the beasts, he had to learn to use all different types of strategies.

"Hello Ram, how are you?" Jin said as he stood back up. He could see his Bora, Ram, smiling.

"I'm good Jin. You've been away as of late. See this one taking up all your time." He elbowed Carl. Carl laughed, pushing back.

"Yeah, Carl's a great Bora. He's been teaching me some wonderful tips. Not that you don't, I just like to get a variety of skills."

"Plus, I'm nicer," Carl added in.

"Ah, always the modest type." Ram gave another hardy laugh, Carl and Jin joined in.

"So, you guys wanted to speak with me?"

Carl looked at Ram. Ram nodded. "Carl's students are advancing quite well. They've done really well on their last few missions. Taking down the Unknowns in only a matter of minutes. No casualties yet. Only one innocent was injured and last I heard he would be okay in a few weeks. We've been discussing the next step for them."

Jin looked quickly at Carl. "Are we talking Summoner hunting? This soon!?"

"No, a face-off training. They haven't even had trainings

with humans yet. We wouldn't send them on the hunts." Ram assured Jin. Jin calmed down, as the hunts against Summoners were too dangerous at this point. The war behind the scenes was getting worse.

"The reason Ram came today is to find out if you and Emily would try a face off against the boys," Carl said. Jin nodded.

"I don't see why not. Do you really think we need two facing off, though? I think I can handle them."

"Trust me when I say these boys have some sneaky tricks up their sleeve. They train like I've never seen kids train. Almost every single day, in and out of this gym. At this rate they'll become amazing Exterminators." Carl felt proud speaking of the boys. His unit was growing in multiple ways. From becoming stronger in body to mentally expanding in strength. In a few short weeks they had achieved what he hoped most trainees would achieve in months.

"Not to mention Emily complains you don't spend enough time with her," Ram added. "I love the girl but she's your girlfriend, not mine. I hear more complaining from her than I do from my own wife. It's not very fun, I can tell you that." Ram informed Jin, giving another laugh.

"All right, I'll call her up. Tell the boys to be ready by next week." Jin began walking towards the exit. "Oh and Ram..." he began.

"Yeah?"

"Soon I want a face-off against you. I have a few new tricks up my sleeve as well." Jin's grin was massive. So Ram responded with one of his own.

Nick's knuckles tapped on the door. He circled around the front of the house trying to come up with an excuse. Two nights ago he left his girlfriend at the dance. He was rushed to the Station, where his wounds were sealed. He could still feel a bit weak but was more worried of what he'd tell Kelly. He heard shuffling of feet behind the door way. *"Just stay calm. Look at her and tell her you're sorry. She'll understand."* The door swung open. "Baby!"

The door slammed in his face. It took a second for him to register it. "Baby, please." He could hear her body slouching against the other side. "Baby, I'm so sorry. I got really sick."

"Sick!?" She threw the door open. "Sick? Seriously? That's the best you could come up with!?" Her eyes were so wide he thought they might pop out of her head. Her nostrils flared up, she was breathing heavily.

"I'm being honest. Marshall had to get me home. I was throwing up everywhere, I felt like I was going to pass out." He tried pleading with her. The anguish she felt reflected on her face and was making him feel guilty.

"Listen, don't lie to me. I know you and Marshall just left suddenly. Lucy was even more upset than me. She finally trusted someone to take her somewhere and he bails half-way through. I almost felt sorry 'cause it was YOUR fault!" She pointed at him. "You not only ruined my night, but hers too. So don't lie to me. Where did you go?"

He hadn't realized he might have ruined Marshall's chances with Lucy. After they both got to the Station and Nick was getting healed up Marshall went home. He hadn't talked to him since the events with the Jackle, which they found out was the name of the Unknown they fought the night before. He felt even worse; the regret he had started to feel was building up.

"Well? Why did you leave?" She stood there waiting.

"Cause if I didn't a beast would of passed in to our realm. Then probably run around tearing off people's heads." "Cause I was sick-" he began then stopped. He felt horrible lying, but he couldn't tell her the truth. "Listen, I can't explain it. I know it sounds like an excuse but something terrible happened and I had to get home. I swear I didn't want to leave you."

"Well, you did," her voice slightly cracked as she responded. He could see her eyes becoming watery.

"It won't happen again."

"Says you. They always say that."

"I'm not them. I'm me. I'm Nick. I swear I won't do that to you again."

"I don't want to hear it," she said as she began to close the door.

"I love you."

The door stayed half-way open. She was looking to the side of her living room, not moving. He felt his heart pounding. A heavy rhythmic-based sound ringing in his ears. He wasn't sure why he said it. Could it be the guilt? Could it be the anxiety? The fact that he might lose her? These were the questions racing through his mind. The reason though didn't seem important enough; the point was he actually felt that way. He had to make sure she understood that.

"You..." she began. She opened the door again, facing him. "You what?" Her voice was very low. Almost impossible to hear.

"I love you," he said again, this time with more conviction in his voice.

"You love me?" her voice cracking again.

"I love you. I'm not them, I'm me. So don't shut the door again. Cause I need you." He stepped up to her, his hand pushing the door open wider. She now felt her heart pounding. She wanted to speak but no words came out. "I love you," he told her once more.

"I-" she began, eyes brimming with tears. "-I love you," she cried out and grabbed him close. He let her lips lie on his for what felt like a lifetime. He wanted to stay right where he stood forever. He held her close, feeling her every emotion during the kiss. The feeling of lust was gone, replaced by love. There was no better feeling in the entire world.

Marshall texted Lucy, but to no avail. She wouldn't respond no matter what he said. He wasn't sure why he was trying so hard. Most girls he liked he just moved through quickly. He liked them, eventually they hated him, and he moved on. This one was different though. She was the odd one. The one most people didn't care to notice. This made him want to get to know her even more. *I'm sorry about the other night. I'm a jerk.*

He waited after texting her again. He just wanted to hear back. He wanted to know she still had some interest in him. After a couple of minutes his phone lit up. He checked to see a message.

Just leave me alone.

He closed his eyes and rested his head on his pillow. *"Come on smooth talker, write something nice."* But he felt like no matter what he wrote she would just continue to ignore him. He didn't really know what to say, so he typed something different. *What if I told you I had a secret?*

He wasn't sure what he was doing. He knew very well he couldn't tell her he fought Unknowns. For one, she'd just call him crazy. On the other hand, she might be in danger if she knew. Still, he couldn't help but feel like she was owed the truth. *What type of secret?*

It was the first time she responded quickly. *It's top secret. I can only tell you in person.*

Lame. Try harder.

Seriously. I can't say it here. Meet me in the park near your house. I'll show you.

He laid his phone next to him. He gritted his teeth. What exactly could he show her? He couldn't bring her to the other realm. He couldn't show off the Rod. Would he tell her he was a demon hunter? Would she just laugh it off or would she report him? Would she scream and run away from him? Would she punch him and call him a liar? Too many questions were roaming around in his head. *Fine. Be there in fifteen minutes.*

He jumped off his bed, slipped his feet into his shoes, and ran out the door. He was ready to finally see her again. The feeling of being close to her again like when they danced together beckoned. He yearned for that feeling. *"What the hell am I going to show her?"* he thought. He still wasn't sure what to do about that problem.

Fred woke up in the white room. He began to feel a strong hatred for the place, yet it calmed him. It felt like all his troubles began to disappear in it. "All right it, speak to me. Tell me that you want to comfort me and love me," he joked out loud. The voice in the room tried to always sooth all his problems away.

"Why do you always distrust me?" the voice boomed. He jumped at how loud it was. Every time he entered the room he noticed the voice was getting closer.

"It's not that I distrust you, it's more of the fact that I'm inside my own head," he said as he did a 180 around the room. Looking for some type of clue as to why he was in his mind in the first place. "It's like you want to tell me something but you never do. What is it you want me to know, Self? Am I just going crazy?"

"I am trying to let you rest. You've been through so much. This is an area of rest, yet you do not want to."

"I can't. I have obligations I have committed to. Things I can't just back out of. People who count on me every single day. I can't just walk away from those things."

"See, you say you can't but you can. You can let these clinging issues fade away into nothing. Let me deal with them while you rest."

"Tempting..." he started. "like I said though, no thanks." Fred touched the wall. He could feel its coldness. He knocked against it. Hollow and frail. "Why this room, though? Why place me in here, Self? Are you trying to tell me something?"

"Do not hit the walls!" The voice was even louder, angrier. He backed away from the wall. "Now come, rest here," the voice soothed, returning to its calm tones.

"All right then. Do not touch walls. Got it." He wanted to touch it again though. He wanted to know why he was in this room. He slowly crept over to the wall. He awoke before he had a chance to do anything else. He got up from the couch, sweat dripping from his chin. Each time he came back from the room the sweats got worse, the pain in his shoulder felt like scorching lava. He wasn't sure what was happening, and because of that it scared him even more.

Marshall was in the park waiting. It wasn't warm anymore, and he hid his hands in his sweater pocket. He even let out a breath of cold air. He wondered how long till it became so cold it would be a pain to fight. Heat is one thing to battle in, cold is a whole other story. He just hoped the next creature he fought would be an easy target. He didn't want to fight something so dangerous in such cold temperatures.

"This better be good," Lucy said as she arrived from the side. She had a small little beanie hat on with a skull printed on it. Her leather jacket matched with a tiny little "V" symbol on the left pocket. She walked up closer to Marshall, but still kept a little distance. He could tell she was still upset with him. "I don't really know how to say it." He wasn't lying. The whole way over he tried to figure out what to tell her.

"Just spit it out."

"It sounds crazy."

"You left me at my first dance. You danced with me like you cared and then you left me there. So, unless you have some amazing excuse to why you did this, I don't want to hear it." She was getting anxious. She wanted nothing more than to storm out of the park, yet she was intrigued by the possible secret that he held. Something so serious he couldn't speak over the phone about it.

Yet, he stood there, still battling his mind on what to say. *"If I tell her, and they find out, then what? What if they go after her? Try to hurt her? Then it's all my fault."* He tried to figure it out as quickly as possible. Time was running short however, she was about to leave.

"This was a waste of my time," she barked as she began to

walk away.

"Wait," he begged.

"No," she said as she kept walking.

"I fight..." he began. She stopped walking but didn't turn around, waiting to hear the rest of the sentence before decided whether to walk away or stay. "I fight monsters," he finally said after a few moments.

"I hate you," she said as she continued to walk away.

"No! Wait! I just told you!" he screamed, chasing after her. He grabbed her arm, but she pushed him away.

"You leave me at the dance. I cry all night, because I thought MAYBE for once a guy cared. Maybe for once, someone in this hellhole we call a world cared enough to take me somewhere. It was so perfect, and you up and leave. Now days later you come to me and say you fight monsters. MONSTERS!? Is that really the best you could come up with?" she yelled. Her face was bright red from the cold and anger.

He stood there, clueless on what to say. Then it came to him. He was ready. "I nearly died once," he said as he put his left hand in the air. "A creature put his horn right in my palm." He pointed to the center of his hand. "It scared the crap out of me. I thought it was going to rip my arm off." He laughed. Yet it was a hollow laugh.

"What are you..." she began but he continued.

"Another time, my friend Fred, he's like my best friend from elementary, almost died. He got bit right on the shoulder." He pointed to his own shoulder. "I mean, I wasn't there but the stories themselves scared me."

"Marshall, sto-" again she tried to speak but he continued.

"The other night I was almost too late. Nick was facing this thing called a Jackle. It had these terrible red eyes that glowed. It tried ripping out his stomach. I saw it slowly crawl towards him, ready to end his life. I shot it in the head. I have pretty good aim," he laughed again, and again it was hollow. "I mean we're killing these things and nearly dying. It's like a made-up story. I mean who the hell would believe us right?" His eyes became watery. He could feel the tears building up. "I mean who the hell even cares? We do this and no one knows. We kill, and we aren't held responsible at all!"

She watched as tears flowed down his cheeks. She didn't know if she believed him or not. He seemed crazy, talking about monsters and killing, yet she couldn't help but feel the truth was spilling out of him.

"I go out every day, I train so much, and for what? To end another things' life? Is that what this is now? Is that what my life is?" He looked away. He could feel tears dripping off his cheeks. He was embarrassed she saw him like this, in a weak state. "I don't know what to do anymore. I'm scared that one day I'll go on one of these missions and not come back right. I'll lose an arm or a leg, maybe even die. Lucy, it scares the crap out of me." She looked at him as he looked back towards her. His eyes were bloodshot red. "I don't know what I'm doing anymore. The only thing I know is I'm sorry for what I did to you. I need you right now though, please."

He fell to his knees and grabbed her. He started crying loudly, louder than he ever had in his life. He felt all the suffering, pain, and frustration leaving his body. He held it together for the last two months, but he just couldn't keep it in any longer. He felt bad dumping it all on her, but he had no choice in the matter. She bent down and pushed his head back. She looked into his eyes. "It's okay, we'll figure it out together," she said quietly. He placed his head on her chest, crying some more.

Chapter 18 – Summoners

Nick pushed open the gym door. It was days after he had apologized to Kelly. She forgave him for leaving her at the dance and he spent the rest of the day talking to her about issues he was facing in his life. Such as dealing with school, the move, and living with his dad. He wanted to talk about his mother eventually but for now he kept that subject at a distance. She spoke more about her time in New York and telling him how she grew up trying her best to focus on school. They both spilled out the fact they were each other's first true lovers. They had both dated before but never loved another person so sincerely. It was something special, something only they shared together.

"Yo, yo, yo, whatup?" Marshall said while stretching on the floor. Peter and Fred looked up, giving small waves. Nick made his way towards the group, stretching out his own arms. He then heard the door open from the other end.

Jin walked through with a lady by his side. Carl was following from behind. "Yo, who's the chick?" Marshall asked.

"I don't know. All I was told is today we're doing some intense training." Nick answered.

"I figured eventually we'd face off against other people," Peter added. "Maybe we can learn more about these beasts and why they come through." This sparked interest amongst the unit. Since the beginning, they've been hurting Unknows. They never questioned why, with the exception of Marshall, who was curious by nature. But the desire to understand and know more was definitely evident. .

"Hey guys!" Jin said loudly, cheerful and excited. "Ready for some real training?" He placed the bag he was carrying on the floor. "It's been awhile since I trained against other Exterminators." He began stretching out.

"Hi, my name is Emily." The girl waved to the boys. "I'm

Jin's girlfriend, as he proudly announced," she said sarcastically. "I'll be the other person you'll face today in this training exercise." She also began to warm up.

"Okay, I have two questions," Marshall spoke up.

"Of course you do. Go on." Carl said, the other boys laughed.

"One, what type of training? Why are we facing each other? I thought we hunt monsters. Now we hunt each other? Also, my other question relates to Emily. Why don't we have a chick on our team?" This was a legitimate question only in Marshall's mind.

"Once the training is over today I'll discuss some things I chose to withdraw from conversations up until now. I'll tell you more about the Summoners." The boys were intrigued by the title alone. "We'll discuss that once you complete the training. Now-" Carl began walking away. "-good luck. Jin and Emily do not hold back."

"Never plan to." Jin grabbed two rods. He created an elemental glove with one, slammed the other rod into his leg, creating the same Zoran attachment that Fred was so used to creating. Emily smiled and formed an elemental blaster. Her whole left arm became a vacuum looking blaster. The tip of it had four claw-like metal pieces closing the opening hole. The weapon's rugged, rocky-looking body was intimidating. "We strongly recommend you moving," said Jin, grinning.

The boys departed, charging four different directions, trying to use the advantage of having more bodies on their team. Jin dashed towards Fred, knowing what weapon he'd go for. Fred was half-way towards his leg with his Rod before Jin was upon him. Before he could reach his leg Jin grabbed him by the shirt and swung him over as if he was a sack of potatoes. Fred came flying down on his back with a loud crunch, and he was out.

Emily's elemental blaster had opened up. The claws on the tip drew back and a blue light began to form inside the vacuum hole. Peter reacted to this by creating his elemental gloves. They formed in a moment, and he was already creating a fire-like

158

energy ball. Nick also was now darting towards Emily from behind. He formed a pole-arm in seconds, not creating a spear, afraid of hurting anyone with the tip. As he was only few feet away from his target, Emily turned and raised the gun just to the side of him. A quick blue lighting ball flew out of her blaster, slamming into the floor of the gym. It shattered into a big force wave, knocking Nick back a few yards, slamming his legs and arms down in a horrible crash before finally rolling him over.

Peter took the moment of fighting as an opportunity. He threw the ball like a baseball. It was heading straight for her. *"Let's see you counter that,"* he thought as it was only mere feet away. With the Zoran weapon, Jin was already behind her. He grabbed the ball of fire, squashed it, and it absorbed into the glove. "Thanks," Jin said, then formed his own ball and threw it. It landed only feet away from Peter. Peter knew what was coming next, he covered his face. An explosion went off and Peter flew to the side, smashing down harshly.

"Thanks, dear," Emily said smiling.

"You got it, babe," he responded.

Marshall came from the side. Both turned just in time. Marshall threw his fist forward, ready to make contact with Jin. Jin put his hand up and a blue bubble-type force field magically appeared. Marshall's fist made an incent on the invisible looking wall, but it couldn't reach close enough to Jin's face. Jin smiled and then clapped his hand. The pressure of the bubble wall blew, and Marshall was swung backwards.

All four boys laid on the floor, feeling defeated. All their training seemed to have gone to waste against the two experienced Exterminators. Jin gave his lover a quick kiss, both stating how good of a job they did. The boys moaned and groaned, trying to regain their footing.

"Better than expected. Two areas of attack, they both almost landed. It's too bad Jin is so well trained. Another Exterminator would have been in trouble." Carl slowly walked around the back end of the gym, studying the fight. He was looking for opportunities to improve his unit. Soon he'd be taking

159

them one on one, training them to keep up their advantages in fights. Their teamwork was better than most in such a short time, but not nearly perfect. Not yet. "Okay boys, get up. You can't be beaten so quickly."

Nick was the first up. He wiped his face, feeling his side - hot from the attack of the blaster. Its force of impact did more damage than he expected. Once the ball of energy hit the floor, it ignited, and blew him backwards. The attack of the blue lighting ball still had some effect on him. He could feel his left arm tingle, his shirt ripped a bit on the bottom left side. "Guys, we need to try that again."

"Again?" Jin asked, surprised.

"Again. Everyone!" Nick roared. The boys rose as if they were on call. They all grabbed their weapons, Fred finally able to create his Zoran boots. "Formation B." Under the code, the boys moved.

"Babe, be careful," Jin said smiling. The challenge was always welcomed.

Emily used her free hand and created a metallic hand very similar to Marshall's. "If he's hard hitting, so am I. We got this," She smiled back at him.

Marshall went close to Peter. "Do it," he said. Nick and Fred covered the boys.

"You coming or just gonna stand there?" Fred egged them on.

"Does he think we're kids?" Emily asked. Jin already launched himself forward. "Thanks for proving my point, hun," she said, raising her blaster hand towards the boys.

"Fred, go!" Nick shouted. Fred dashed to the side, out of the way from the oncoming Marshall. Jin was trying to decide if he should chase Marshall or go ahead with his previous attack plan. He figured Emily could handle Fred so he went with attacking the boys head on.

"It's set," Peter whispered to Nick. Nick nodded and launched forward.

Fred stopped to the side and flung himself forward. He was

heading right for Emily at high speed. She aimed at him, ready to fire when he got closer. He darted left to right, trying to throw off her aim.

Nick pounced, swinging his pole-arm forward. Jin easily dodged to the side, grabbed the pole-arm, pulled Nick forward, and elbowed him. Nick felt a horrible, piercing pain in his stomach, right before falling over. Jin let go of Nick's weapon and charged forward. Marshall twirled around, fist flying towards Jin. Jin put up another bubble to block Marshall's fist. His fist once again began to go through the bubble.

"You guys need to try something new," Jin said as he held up his elemental glove hand. The bubble was keeping up no matter how hard Marshall pushed.

"See, that's the thing about you older folks..." Marshall opened his palm; a ball of fire was now attached to the bubble. "-you always think you're so damn smart." Marshall hopped back. Jin didn't have time to react, the ball blew up. The fire destroyed the bubble completely, leaving Jin wide open. Marshall was already on his way towards him swinging. He threw his fist out front. Jin put his hands up in defense. There was a hard "crack" and Jin could feel his right arm blaring with pain. He gritted his teeth as he was pushed backwards. He almost tumbled over but managed to stand his ground. He separated his arms before he saw a blue ball drop near his feet. It rolled right below him. He threw up another bubble but it was too late. The blue explosion ripped his bubble into nothing, while it knocked him backwards.

Emily was ready to fire. She could feel her hand heating up. It was the price of using the blaster, it felt like your arm was on fire. Especially when you shot the blast. Fred kept dodging left to right, far faster than any human could do normally. She took a chance and aimed to the right. Fred was close enough now to leap, but he made the wrong choice. The elemental attack hit the floor right near him. Before he could dodge it, he was hit bad, slamming into the ground near Emily.

Nick, Jin, and Fred were all on the ground. Emily looked up at the last two standing. "Hope you have another move," she started, aiming the blaster at both boys. "Because your time seems to be up."

She shot the blast. Marshall started running to the side. Then changed direction and went flying towards the blast. He was going to meet the blue electrical blast head on. Emily screamed "Idiot, move!" and Carl tensed up. The blast head on would do serious damage. He couldn't risk his boys getting critically wounded.

Marshall matched the blast head on before anyone could react. He had his metal hand slamming into the blast, then within a second the ball of electricity blew up. Marshall could feel his entire arm going numb, but more so was his face catching sparks. It felt like a million pinches to his face. He yelled as he fell backwards. As he fell over, two balls of fire flew past him. Emily couldn't react in time and took both hits. One to the stomach, the next to the shoulder. Both blew up on impact, setting her clothes on fire. Carl was already on her within seconds, using elemental gloves to summon wind. The flames blew out in moments. She laid there, pain in both spots where she was hit.

Peter stood panting; he could feel almost all the energy in his body was gone. He grinned. "I say we deserve an explanation now." He laughed, as did the other three boys on the floor. Even Jin laughed with Emily.

"No denying that. You guys did way better than anticipated. When you get fixed up, we'll finally talk." Carl watched his boys slowly get back up. He saw the determination in their eyes, the fight that burned so bright. He felt they were growing into one of the strongest units he'd ever witness. He was proud, as a Bora, to watch over such talented fighters.

Fred sat down last. He could still feel the numbness in his body. The last blast that struck him felt bad enough to shake around his brain. "So, first thing we all want to know is what these Summoners are. Are they like Exterminators?" he asked as he rubbed his shoulders.

"Actually my first question is, when are we getting an Emily on our team?" The other boys rolled their eyes at Marshall. Carl chuckled. "I'm serious. I'm tired of fighting guys all the time here. Not to mention, she kind of kicked our butts pretty bad."

"Aw, thank you Marshall!" she said smiling.

"Sorry lady, I got a girl now." Marshall put up his hand.

"Good, cause if you didn't I was about to pound your face in," Jin added.

"Ah, the love. How joyful you are." Marshall gave Jin the thumbs up. Jin shook his head and looked away.

"Sir," Peter spoke up. Carl locked at his student. He found Peter one of the most interesting in the group. Simply because he seemed out of place in his age group, or so it seemed, to Carl after watching him from a distance. Carl wanted to make him feel comfortable around his unit.

"Yes, Peter?" Carl asked.

"I was wondering if you could tell us about those Summoners." Everybody now had their eye on Carl. Carl gave a quick glance at Jin and Emily. They both nodded.

Carl turned to his students. "As you know, we prevent these creatures, which we refer to as "Unknowns", from crossing into our world. However, they don't just make their way in through the realms barriers. They are summoned."

"So you're saying someone is bringing them over. This isn't just an act of a wild beast," Fred spoke up.

"Yes, these monsters are pulled into our world," Carl continued. "These people who break through the barriers and bring them in are called Summoners. They summon Unknowns from different realms and bring them here. They seem to believe they can create a world that consists of both us and the Unknowns. As you know, though, these beasts are almost always vicious. They are animals based on deadly instinct to attack. The realms are meant to keep species separated from their different worlds. The Summoners look to break that."

The unit sat together, discussing the new information. Carl let them take in the information. He watched as questions arose and they tried to answer each other. Like school children, they kept throwing words back and forth.

"So, we do have enemies besides these monsters."

"'Summoners is a cool nickname for them."

"We have to figure out how to fight these guys."

"I think the most important question now is, do we hunt humans as well?" The discussion stopped once Peter brought up the hunting of others. The boys looked at him then back at Carl, awaiting an answer.

"Yes," Carl responded shortly. It was a chilling response. The kids sat there, unsure of what to say. Up until now they hunted Unknowns and that was okay. Killing them was killing animal-like creatures, not humans. Now they had to hunt human beings like themselves. People with family and friends, just like them. They weren't sure they could do it.

"Where are they?" Peter asked.

"They are in hiding. They have an organization just like us, except they are spread out more. They aren't as organized as us. We fight to prevent Unknowns from entering our world and damaging it. They spend days focusing on ways to bend the barriers and let them through. We do hunt them. It is part of this job." The kids were muttering to each other. Carl waited, letting the kids take in all the information he had presented.

"I don't want to hunt people." Everyone looked at Marshall. "It's not right. We aren't killers."

"We've been killers," Peter spoke up.

"No, we've killed creatures. Not humans."

"Humans are creatures." Peter protested.

"You know what I mean! We are going to hunt people like you and me. What if they have a family like us? What if one of them is family!? No. I refuse to do it." Marshall got up from the group. He was about to walk out but Jin blocked his way.

"Sit down," Carl said softly. Marshall had his back turned to him, staring at Jin.

"Move," Marshall muttered. The anger was building in him, he curled his fingers.

"Marshall-" Carl began. "-take a seat. I don't expect you to hunt Summoners anytime soon. You just have to focus on the Unknowns and that's all. Now take a seat." Carl pointed to the empty spot Marshall was once sitting in.

"Don't ever block my way again," Marshall gritted his teeth as he spoke to Jin. He turned back around and sat down in his place. Jin moved back towards Emily.

"So, these Summoners, they let the beasts come through. Are they some type of cult or something?" Fred asked.

"They are led by one man who has the power to bend the realms. As long as he, and the Gada in our organization stand, the barriers can be traveled. They have imbedded in themselves a barrier-altering power. This power is granted down through the years of previous owners. The point is to pass it down to your follower. The one who deserves it the most will take the mantel. It's been said for years that this has happened, but doing so takes a heavy toll on your own body. So when they pass on the barrier power, chances are they won't be around much longer. The body will decay much quicker than expected, due to the huge energy lost that the body was once used to."

"It's basically a death sentence then," Nick countered. Carl nodded.

"What happens if they don't pass it down?" Peter wondered.

"If the body of the one who holds the barrier power passes away, there is no way to contain that power. Chances are the barriers with crash, cutting off the realm jumping. Meaning all the creatures summoned will be drawn back into their own realms. This hasn't been proven, though. The opposite could happen and it might open every single gate, letting every Unknown through, into our realm. We just never know, because they always pass on the barrier power." Carl watched as the boys listened. He could feel their concern that they may have jumped into something way bigger than they once expected.

"I don't mean to place fear into you boys, but this information is very important. I don't want you to be clueless on exactly what you're doing out there in the world. Every mission given is very crucial."

"Good vs. bad, it seems so cliché." Marshall laughed at his own words.

"Shut up man. This stuff is serious," Fred said peering down at the floor. He felt nervous, the voice in his head was speaking to him again. It was telling him that no matter what, he'll be safe in the room. The room where he could forget all these problems.

"So, our job is to hunt Unknowns but eventually take down the Summoners? I am intrigued to learn more about these Summoners. When do we hunt one? I'd like to join in the search for one." Peter lacked the nervous and scared feelings the other boys were suffering through.

"You're a damn robot." Marshall said shaking his head.

"No, I am eager to take down people trying to destroy our world. Sorry that you're too stupid to see that." The boys were shocked, they had never heard Peter down play one of them.

"Hey you little son of-" Marshall began. Carl held his hand up. The boys fell into silence.

"This is a war that's been going on for far to long. The good vs. evil, the concept that one side is in the right and one in the wrong is very old. It also comes down to prospective. We believe we are doing the right thing, while they also believe they are doing the right thing. Who's really doing the right thing, you ask? No one really knows at this point. However, we have a job and we stick by it. You joined to stop them. That is your job overall, the one you are on right now." Carl watched Peter. He could see Peter was unmoved by any of his speech. The boy was already 100 percent involved in the project to hunt the Summoners.

Marshall, however, was not convinced at all. He wasn't about to hunt any humans any time soon. Nick and Fred sat at their positions, trying to contemplate what to do. Nick felt that if push came to shove, if Summoners were as evil as Carl said, he could hunt them down. Fred, on the other hand, felt it was hard enough to kill the creatures. He did it because they attacked him. Could he do the same against other human beings? He doubted it.

"I know it's a lot to digest," Carl continued to speak. "I know some of you never want to harm another person." As he spoke he looked at Marshall. "I know it's hard to accept that this is part of the job. It's a scary thing to hurt another person. Trust me; it's never been easy for me no matter how long I've been doing it."

"Then why do it?" Marshall asked.

"Cause he has to," Peter answered.

"He doesn't have to. None of us have to do any of this," Fred sided with Marshall. Marshall looked at his old friend. He smiled, having a friend back him in this argument felt amazing.

"We do have to though," Nick stood up. He looked in Carl's eyes a few moments before turning to the rest of his teammates. "Listen, we needed to know this. What if we were on the field and some random Summoner came up to us and tried killing one of you?" Nick look towards Marshall, then to Fred, last to Peter.

"Then we'd kill him," Peter answered, no remorse in his voice.

"We'd talk to him first," Marshall grunted. "We aren't hit-men. We just don't kill without knowing why."

"What if the Summoner came up to you and tried to kill you?" Nick asked Marshall.

"Then I'd defend myself," he responded.

"What if he went after your family 'cause he saw your face. He knows who you are, knows where you live, and studies you. Then tries to kill your family. What would you do to stop him?" Nick said loudly. Carl watched as Nick took control of the group. He finally realized that Nick was the leader of this unit. They all had their voices and opinions, but none followed each other like when Nick demanded it.

"I'd kill them," Marshall muttered. A imagine of his brother and Lucy flashed in his head as he said it.

"You'd kill them, yeah. You know why? 'Cause they'd have

no problem ripping out your mom's throat. You understand? If they are willing to press barriers, break them, let deadly creatures in, then they are willing to mass murder people with ease. This is scary and I didn't join to kill humans, but Carl didn't lie. Killing is now our job. Humans might get in the way and we have to take care of them the same way we do the Unknowns. We are Exterminators." The boys fell silent. No one answered, yet they all understood. Their missions just got far more complicated.

Chapter 19 – Behind The Scenes

Marshall was leaning against the counter watching as Lucy looked through the guide. He felt his gut wanting to rip in half. He knew he wasn't supposed to tell anyone outside the organization about the Unknowns but he didn't know how else to keep her trust. She was about to walk away, probably forever he figured. So he did what he had to, to keep her around.

"This stuff..." she began as she turned the next page. "This is unbelievable."

"Tell me about it." He pushed himself off the counter and sat on the bed across from her. "It looks a lot cooler than it really is. These descriptions don't give the Unknowns the credit they deserve. These monsters are really repulsive most of the time. Always dangerous too."

"You must be so scared out there," she said, looking up at him.

He looked back, feeling her eyes reaching into him, trying to search the hidden feelings behind it all. He wanted to spill it all to her, but he kept those feelings in. "I am at times. I keep level-headed most of the time. I don't want to freak out on the field and put myself or anyone else in danger."

"You're so brave."

"Hey, it's not nice to make fun."

"I'm not," she said gently while placing her hand on his arm. "I'm very serious." She moved closer to him. "The things you do are unbelievable. You're like a superhero."

"A superhero?"

"Yeah, *my* superhero," she giggled.

"Does this superhero get an award?" He leaned in. He was close enough to her face now that he could feel her breath, could smell the cheery flavored gum she had.

"I think you do." She leaned the last few inches in, and

they kissed. Marshall felt all the problems that were on his mind drift away. For once he felt like he was just a normal kid and not some Exterminator hunting creatures. He gladly accepted that.

Peter walked into the gym. On a Sunday afternoon the boys rested usually. It was a nice day to relax for most of them. With no school and rarely a mission ever called upon on the weekend they used this day to recuperate. Peter used the empty gym to push himself further in training. He grabbed his Rod and focused on creating an elemental glove. He was determined to push himself, to make the magic in him grow to new levels. Try new spells.

He walked in a circle, flexing his fingers. He wanted to feel the magic growing in him. The elements had to become part of him. He formed a gust of wind in his hand. He began running forward. His next step in fighting was to keep concentration on the elements while moving. He kept a steady jog while juggling the wind element in his hand. The gust was making vicious sounds as he ran onward. He held tightly to the element trying to steer right now. The movements could not interfere with the elements. They had to become one move, they had to complement each other.

Jin came out of nowhere, a sledgehammer in his right hand. It was huge, brown, and coming from the side towards Peter. He didn't have a choice, he put his palm out and let go of the gust of wind. He was holding it for so long that once it exploded the wind shattered, knocking back not only Jin, but also himself. They both landed on their rears.

"Not bad, I figured I'd surprise you with that one. You sure thought quick on your feet." Jin got back up. Peter slowly rose with him. Jin noticed he hadn't had a surprise look on his face. Most people would have still been freaked out by the sneak attack. Yet, Peter seemed to have brushed it off completely.

"That was good. I needed something surprising. You know-" Peter shook his hand. "-it could easily happen on the field too."

"I like the way you think. You think of all the possibilities.

You remind me of someone." Jin smiled. He gripped tightly on the sledgehammer.

"Okay, let's go!" Peter sounded excited. The excitement was more surprising than the actual attack. Jin never recalled Peter being so excited.

Peter moved towards Jin instead of waiting back. He formed the fireball in his hand, readying his attack. Jin stepped back a foot, hammer swinging back. Jin flung the sledgehammer in front of him. Peter dodged the hammer in the last second by stopping, it nearly hit his stomach. Jin was already self-recovering, while he put his energy to swing the other way. Peter, however, struck first. Squashing the fire in his hand the entire elemental glove went ablaze. He threw his fist forward and hit Jin on the chest. The flames ignited on impact and Jin could feel the blazing flames burn his chest.

Jin dropped back a few steps and patted his chest. The flames weren't big enough to catch the entire shirt on fire but the burn marks were already implanted on his chest. Jin could feel the burning pain around the place of impact.

"Not bad," Jin praised Peter, smiling.

Peter hadn't realized the smile that was plastered over his own face. He could feel something. Excitement? Happiness? Joy? He wasn't really sure. He was sure though that he felt alive. Ready to keep going. "Thanks," he answered happily.

"All right, let's keep going. Show me what else you got," Jin said, tightening his grip on the hammer. Peter put his hand up to his chest before creating the next element and charging at his opponent.

Nick was running up and down the bars at the park. He was working out, giving his body a warm-up run. He ducked down behind one bar, back up, back down another bar, back up. He repeated the cycle over and over again, feeling his speed grow. To create speed, to enhance movement, to grow stamina, he pushed his body. He had to put everything he had into training; otherwise he'd be putting himself in danger in the fights against the Unknowns. He was injured almost every time he fought. He wanted to change that.

Fred was doing push-ups against the bench next to him while trying to balance his weight with one hand at times against it. It was getting close to December and he felt himself growing in ways he never could have imagined. The weight was so far down he felt like a new man. He was almost as fast as the boys on the field now, even without his Zoran. He trained just as hard as they did, yet still made sure to push himself further when he could. He wasn't sure why, they wouldn't judge him at all. Yet he felt he had an obligation to better himself.

Nick stopped after the last bar on set and looked towards his friend. "I fought a Rockus the other day by myself. I got a few scrapes but I was able to take it down with the spear. It's pretty hard to trick it though, that thing is just a beast. I had to wait till it was on me, dodge, let it roll over, and then strike it in the belly. I probably should have just created a damn rocket launcher," Nick said, laughing.

Fred stopped the push-ups and rested on the bench. "Funny you say that. I tried to create one. I shot a missile in the air the other night just to see. Dude, I think my body almost went into a coma. It takes so much energy to fire one. I will not be creating one again. Though the explosion looked sick," Fred added. Both boys laughed to that.

"Do you think-" Nick began, Fred looked up at him. "-we are doing the job we were meant to do?"

"Whatcha mean?"

"I mean sometimes I feel like this job isn't meant for us. Like we shouldn't have been chosen at all."

"I don't think we ever choose the jobs we are given. They just happen to fall in our laps," Fred replied. Nick looked at him, giving a nod in agreement, but he felt differently about it.

"I just feel this job is draining. Like, why can't we just be normal high school kids? Instead we're thrown into this world of Unknowns and Summoners. I mean, what the heck is all this?"

Fred took a second to ingest it all. He agreed. He wanted to live a normal life at times, too. Just sit back and enjoy the small things in life. He'd finally felt so great about his body he was getting ready to ask a girl out. His grades were horrible when usually they were average. He wanted to be at least average for college. He wanted to get a job, make some money, but there was no point in that. He had no free time He too felt like it would be nice to live a normal kid's life.

"I agree. Still, we can't just walk away now," Fred spoke up after a while.

"I know. It's just I feel like I'm always lying to my pops and girl. It's like all I want to do is tell them I'm trying to save the world. Instead, I go home beat up and they have no clue. I get yelled at by both for disappearing, showing up later, not spending enough time with either one. It's like this creates more problems than anything."

"Yeah, but if we didn't do this look at what could happen. That truck driver who was attacked is alive 'cause of us. He was a single parent and now his kid won't be alone in this world. She has a father that's still alive, and that's 'cause of us. That's 'cause of you." Fred pointed to Nick.

Nick hadn't thought of it that much. He went on missions because he was told to. Not even thinking of the aftermath of it all. He knew he was fighting to save people, yet never thought about the situations he was put in. When Unknowns make it to the other realm, they can still damage or hurt humans. Even worse, no one can see them to prevent them from hurting anyone. No one except the Exterminators that is.

"It's true. Yet, when we're in danger, who's there to save us?" Nick said, Fred was surprised. Not so much at the question but the fact he'd never thought about it. They stayed silent for a while each lost in thought.

"We save each other."

"Huh?"

"We save each other," Fred started speaking. "We are a team because we save each other. That's who protects us, each other. The whole point of being a team is to have each other's backs. We've been hanging out so much we feel we're just one person. Save us? Who needs to save us when we HAVE us? We are each other's backup. We just get so focused on being a group we forget that."

Nick surveyed the sky. He forgot he was part of the team sometimes. They fought and trained so much they felt like one complete force. Combined together as a whole new person. They each had one another for backup though. They had Jin, Carl, Ram, Emily and more Exterminators on their team. They just needed to be reminded.

"You're right. I hadn't thought of it that way."

"We can do anything together. So let's get back to training so we don't have to worry about needing back up." Fred got off the bench and got into a sit up position. "Another thirty minutes then I'm heading home." He began his sit up routine.

Nick grabbed the monkey bars and began pull ups. He wanted to better himself, become the most important aspect in the unit so they could count on him. He wasn't about to back down now. He pushed himself past the ten pull up mark before dropping down and going into squats.

Marshall laid in bed, Lucy was beside him with her head on his shoulder. "I want to just be here forever. Not have to go to school. Fight these monsters. Do anything crazy. I just want to lay here with you forever." He kept his eyes closed as he spoke to her. She nodded her head lightly agreeing.

"Things aren't going to change. You have to do what you have to do to get through life. It's what my mom always said."

"Yeah, but why can't we take the easy route sometimes. Why can't I just stay here with you and forget all my problems? I guess that's silly. Nothing in life is that easy."

She rolled over and kissed his closed lips. He opened his eyes to look at her. She was so beautiful he thought. The way she looked at him with her small eyes, the way she smiled at him, the way she held on to him. "Things can be easier with some help. I'm here to help," she said smiling.

He kissed her back. Held it for as long as possible. He wanted to feel close to her, to not feel like all the obligations in his life were real. That this was some type of dream and his real life was with her. "Dreams," he muttered.

She looked at him. "Dreams?"

"Dreams." He simply answered.

"You're a weirdo," she said smiling, then relaxed back in his arms.

"You're dating the weirdo."

Silence crept into the room. Marshall felt a weird sense of tension on his chest. "Are we dating now?" she asked.

"I thought we were."

"I thought we were too...I think." She was unsure. It caught him off guard.

"Do you not want to date?"

"It just feels weird when you say it. Like its official."

"Well, it's been almost a month. It feels kind of like it should be official."

"Yeah, I guess it does."

"Listen, if you don't want to date just tell me." Now he was getting annoyed. He could feel the anger building in him.

"I do!" She shot up, shouting. She seemed indifferent, not sure how to continue. He felt confused in the situation. Not sure how to respond. Feelings were getting mixed up in such a short time.

"Listen, I like you. I mean, I really like you. You have to tell me though if you don't feel the same. I don't need to be led down the road that leads nowhere." He showed a side she hadn't known before. He was serious about relationships. The joker turning into the more mature adult-type when it came to this.

"I do like you. I want to date you. I want to be with you." She rested her hands on his bare chest. "You've been there for me when no one else cared to be with me. I know it's only been a few weeks but I don't want you to go anywhere. I just get scared when it comes to relationships. I haven't had any strong connections with friends let alone a boyfriend." She crawled over to him, sitting on top of him. "I do want to date you, yes. For sure!" she said laughing. She was nervous yet excited.

She laid her head on his shoulder. He let out a breath of relief. He began to form feelings for her quickly. If she left now it might have crushed him. He didn't know if she was just passing through or growing to love him. Either way, he wasn't going to let her go this soon. He placed his arms around her and held her tightly. He wanted to hold her forever.

Carl returned back to his home. It was a single room apartment where he slept and ate. The rest of his time was spent in the Station or traveling around. He threw his keys to his car on the kitchen table. After grabbing a drink from the fridge he went over to his bed. He sat on it and looked at the empty display on the TV. *"So tired. Just rest."* He thought to himself but he never listened. His body was getting more tired the older he got. He wasn't able to do the things he did ten years ago with such ease.

He grabbed the TV remote and turned it on. The sound of the sports announcer filled the room, yet he wasn't listening to a word. The sound was just better than the silence. Better than letting the silence eat at him, bring up memories he hid so well in his busy life.

He grabbed his bottle of rum and took a sip. It burned. The same burn that attacked his soul every single day. He coughed after the rum went down then took a sip of his coke. He figured if he drank a regular drink with alcohol he wouldn't be considered an alcoholic. He knew how silly it sounded but it was a way to appease his mind. To try to find a balance to please and yet also trick himself.

He looked down at his hand and saw the scar. It started at his middle finger up to his shoulder. It was the biggest mistake he made. The mistake that lead to a war. The idea of forgiveness. Of letting things slide. It was almost completely out of his mind these

176

days. To trust was hard enough, to forgive was damn near impossible. He set barriers up in his mind so he could follow those rules. By nature he trusted many, but by betrayal he knew better. He clinched his fist, looked away from the scar, and closed his eyes as he laid back on his bed.

He could feel the drink doing work on his mind and body. It began making him feel loose again. It was the only reason he drank. To feel calm and loose instead of building up past memories. Yet, he knew the real reason was to forget. Nobody wants to admit that the past, that eventually the past will come for the present. The past makes you what you are today. Carl hated that so he drank to try and forget. Yet the demons spoke to him when he was drunk enough. There was no way to win in the internal mind wars.

Peter sat down, exhausted. He held his shirt out. The whole left side was ripped off. He laughed and smacked the floor. "That was freaking great!"

"You turn into a completely different guy in fights," Jin said seriously, sitting down next to him. "You become...happier. It's odd. I have never seen you so upbeat and happy." Peter shrugged, still smiling brightly.

"I feel alive when I'm in a fight. I feel like I can become stronger. I feel like..." he was trying to find words to continue. He felt so many things in the fight that he never felt before in his life. It was like his real-self came out.

"You feel like you can prove you're something." Peter looked up, surprised. "You feel like when you fight you have power that otherwise isn't ever shown. You feel like this is the real you. You feel like the power you hold is something no one can match. Yet you can never reveal this self because of the rules. You hold this power and yet no one can see. So you bottle the emotions up to the point where you don't feel, yet when you fight you can let those emotions run wild. Something like that?" Jin watched Peter for a response.

Peter couldn't respond though. He knew every word Jin just told him was how he felt. He bottled so much up inside that he didn't have anything to show on the outside. All the emotions he had hidden, all the awkward situations, thanks to his upbringing, all his hatred he couldn't spew was because he didn't have the power. He had the strength now though. He had the power to show off yet no one could see it except his unit. He wanted to show the world yet he knew he'd never be able to. He felt like this was the most unfair aspect of the entire organization.

"I think you're right," was all Peter could mutter.

"It's okay. I've felt the same way at times. Always growing up in situations I couldn't control. People helped me get to where I am now. They trained me to harness those feelings and use them. I think I've come a long way." Jin said, smiling.

"Can you show me how to let these emotions out?" Peter never asked for help. He couldn't help but to ask Jin anyway.

Jin watched him for a moment. Surprised that he'd even ask for support. Sociopaths usually kept almost all their emotions bottled up or lacked any, in the first place. However, the more interaction Peter got the easier it was for him to show those emotions. It seemed the only time he showed those emotions was in fights. The violent nature is what made Jin think twice. Yet, he felt he could keep him in check, if he'd be careful.

"I think I can help." Jin patted Peter on the back. "Let's head home for today and we'll work on it."

Peter got up alongside Jin. "All right, thank you." Peter said extremely sincerely. Yet Jin sometimes had to question if it was real or an act. He let the benefit of doubt take over.

Nick returned home late. Pushing the door open around 11 o'clock. He announced to the house he was home. His father popped his head out of the living room. "You almost didn't make it home for curfew."

"Sorry pops was just doing some exercise." Nick could feel every bone in his body ache. He'd been training so much lately he almost never gave himself a chance to rest. He was pushing his body to its limits. His muscles grew but what did it matter if he was always tired? He felt conflicted with how much he trained but he never wanted to be in danger in a fight again. So he pushed himself as far as his body let him go.

"I'm glad you're working out. It's great, especially at your age. Forming your body. Yet don't push yourself too far. It'll eventually backfire on you." His dad pointed out as he was going through his book. He was figuring out floor plan blueprints for one of his jobs.

"I know pops." Nick opened the fridge and grabbed a drink. He collapse in the seat next to his father. "Hey pops, I think we should go away somewhere this summer," Nick said suddenly. He felt like getting away from everything for a while would be nice.

His father looked up from his book. "Where were you thinking of going?"

"I dunno, maybe Pennsylvania? I just want to get away from the city for a while after school. I know you're busy though so..." he began but his father waved his hand dismissively.

"That's the thing about being the boss. You have managers under you that can handle it. I think that sounds amazing." His dad's smiled was too big for his face right now. Nick couldn't help but laugh and smile back. He felt great talking to his father one on one. To go somewhere away from all the training and fighting to spend quality time with family would be the best thing in the world.

"Thanks pops. I just figured it be nice to get away."

"I think so too. We can go fishing, do a little camping, just like old times."

"Yeah, like when we went there with mom and stuff," Nick's voice trailed off. He didn't like to mention his mom much, it brought up strong feelings.

"Yeah," his father answered quietly.

"She'd be proud of you."

His father looked up at his son. The words hit him hard

like a bag of concrete. He felt goose bumps throughout his entire body. He hadn't heard his son speak about his mother in months now. He wasn't sure how to answer.

"You've done nothing but taken care of me. You work so hard to support me. You raised me alone the last year and you've done a great job." He looked up at his father. He could feel his eyes becoming watery. He could feel his body using the last of the energy he had for the night. "So I think she'd be very proud of you. I'm proud of you."

His father didn't even notice the tears falling down his face. He felt his heart warming; the feeling of being told by your own son that he was proud of you was amazing. He stood up and grabbed his son, hugging him tightly. He let his tears drop and could feel his shoulder getting wet. Nick was crying along with him. "Sometimes I forget how old you're getting," his father said sniffling. He couldn't love his son any more than he did at this moment. He held him tightly letting the tears continue to flow.

Peter shut the door behind him. His drunken father was in the hallway, trying to get his shoes on. "Hey you little brat, where you've been?" he said laughing. Peter tried his best to ignore him as he walked past. His father got angry and reached for him.

He grabbed Peter by the collar and turned him around. "Don't you ever walk away from me," he spat all over Peter's face. Peter pushed his father's hand off and tried to walk away again. His father's temper flared up and he struck Peter in the face. The pain wasn't awful. Peter had suffered a lot worse in the past few months, yet it hurt so much. To be hit by your own father was disgusting. He already knew his father was capable of doing just that.

"I'm going to bed." Peter held his cheek as he walked away.

"Don't walk away from me, you brat!" He roared as he grabbed Peter again. Peter wanted to form his elemental glove and shoot a fireball into his father's mouth to shut him up so he couldn't speak. He had the power to do it. Instead, he let his father grab him, twirl him around, and slam his fist into his gut. From his training, Peter was already weak, so the punch hurt way worse than it would have normally. Peter fell to the ground wincing. He could feel the spit in his mouth dripping out.

"That's right, you little creep!" his father slurred as he slammed his leg into Peter's side. Peter slammed his back into the wall; he could feel the pain soaring up through his whole body. His father gave him another punch to the face. This time it hit his nose real hard. Peter instantly tasted the blood dripping from it. "You don't ever walk away from me when I'm speaking to you!" his father shouted.

His father opened the door and looked back. "Just lay there and think what you've done. You hurt my hand you little bastard. So just sit there and think about it." Then the door slammed behind him. Peter could hear him shouting as he went down the stairs.

Peter rolled to his side. He could feel his bloody nose dripping all over the floor. He felt the pain in his gut. There was a sharper pain coming from his side where the kick landed. He screamed in a rage he never knew he had. He yelled so loudly, both his mom and sister came out of their rooms. He slammed his fist on the floor, tears dripping from his eyes. He yelled and slammed his fist down repeatedly. His mother ran over but he pushed her away. His sister stayed in her doorway, too scared to come out of her room. He calmed down after a moment and just sat there. Pain resonated all over his body. Yet for the first time he felt a pain in his heart. He hadn't felt rage like this ever, and now it was awakened like a vengeful monster.

Chapter 20 – Merry Christmas

Nick pushed the doors open from school. "Free!" he shouted. Another month had past and it was snowing in the great NYC. School had just let out for winter vacation. The kids flooded out as if every second of freedom was precious. Nick turned around and saw Fred, Marshall, and Peter walking out behind him.

"Later bro," Marshall said giving another boy a fist pump before heading over to Nick. "Yo, whatsup my man."

"Not much, glad to be on vacation." Nick laughed. He'd have the next few weeks' school free to relax. He planned on taking this time to rest his body from training as well. The Callers hadn't called any of them on missions since the beginning of November. It was odd but the boys strangely liked it. All except for Peter.

"Any missions yet?" Peter asked, eagerness in his voice, as he approached the boys.

"Dude, just chill and enjoy some free time." Marshall chipped in.

"I want to hunt. Not sit around and do nothing."

"What you need is to get a girl."

Peter waved dismissively at Marshall and glanced at the kids leaving the school. Fred was the last to catch up to the group. He pulled his pants up again as they sagged down. He hadn't had a chance to pick up new clothes since the weight loss started. He was now an entire four sizes down and feeling amazing. His clothes just kept sliding off of him though.

"What's everyone's plan for Christmas?" Fred asked.

"My dad and I are going to Kelly's house to eat," Nick answered, watching the snow fall on him. It felt great to have that slight cold touch on his face and then melt away.

"Nothing," replied Peter in a monotone response. He wanted a fight more than celebrating a holiday he cared less about.

"Well, unlike Mr. Grumpy over here, I think I'll have a nice Christmas dinner. Lucy and I will probably go out and eat somewhere," Marshall finished.

"Hey, Pete would you like to come over for dinner? I'm not doing anything," Fred asked. He was trying to keep the desperation out of his voice. He was used to spending dinner alone for most holidays, yet he wanted to be close to some type of family this Christmas. The boys had become the closest thing to family that he had, as of late.

"Fine. If any of you get a mission though I want to know." Peter walked away from the group. He was so set on fighting he lost sight of anything else. He kept his head low and walked towards his home. The same home where his father beat him down to the ground a month ago. The same home where he built up an emotion called rage. The same home he couldn't stand to be in.

"Well don't know what that loser's problem is but why don't you come with us?" Marshall asked Fred.

"I'm not going to be a third wheel. No, thanks," Fred chuckled. Sadness could be heard if he spoke any louder.

"Dude, come on. You're one of my best friends. Come. Plus you kicked my butt in Halo the other night. So come on I owe you a dinner. Lucy will be okay with it."

"I just told Peter he could come."

"Loser will get over it. He's been all serious lately anyway."

"He's always been serious," Nick pointed out.

"Exactly! So he won't care. Just come with us. It'll be fun." Marshall sounded excited. He hadn't had a chance to hang out with anyone and with Lucy. He wanted to show her off to them. Not because he wanted to prove anything, just to show her off because he enjoyed her company and wanted to share it.

"All right, I guess. I'll text Peter and let him know. Thanks," Fred said and then began walking the other way. "I'ma head home, I'll see you in a few days." He waved goodbye while walking down the block.

"I'm going to Lucy's so I'll hit you up later man." Marshall gave Nick a handshake and was on his way. Nick turned towards his house and began walking. The holiday season was about to begin and already so many plans were in the air.

Jin sat down in Carl's office and rested his legs on top of Carl's desk. Carl gave him a look, one that would scare off most people, and he immediately put his feet back on the floor. "So the kids are doing real well. I'm worried about Peter though. He seems...different."

"I noticed," Carl muttered as he was looking through files.

Jin waited for more but nothing came out of Carl's mouth. "So-" he began waiting for Carl to say something. "-do we just ignore it? He seems really down as of late, more than he usually is. Something isn't right."

"I know. I just don't have time to investigate right now."

"Investigate?" Jin sounded annoyed.

"Yeah, I can't just drop this stuff. Activity with the Unknowns has been odd. The Callers haven't been as active as usual. Something isn't right."

"I get that. You're student is phasing out though. Did you see those marks on his face awhile back? He looked like he'd been in a fight with a Jackle." Carl ignored him. "Listen Carl, I don't mean to intervene..."

"Then stay out of it!" Carl slammed his fist on the desk. "I can't do everything, and your nagging isn't helping." Carl was infuriated, his face bright red. All the anger he'd been holding in was taking effect. Just on the wrong person.

"Whoa, calm down," Jin said, putting up his hands. "I'm just suggesting we figure out what's wrong with him. No need to jump down my throat."

"Just back off. I'm trying to get this stuff fixed, they lost four Exterminators last month in Florida, and everything is falling apart. I can't focus on problems my students are going through

184

every minute. They have to learn to grow up and take care of themselves."

"How can they grow up if they have no guidance!?" Jin was now shouting back. Carl felt like leaping over the desk and grasping his friend by his collar. "You sit here doing all this work for other people, do your own damn work! You're falling into a deep dark spot again. I can smell the drinks on your breath."

Carl fist curled up. "That's none of your business."

"It is my business when you put these kids' lives on the line. If you don't like what I'm saying do something about it!" Jin stood up, flinging back the chair as he did. "I'm sick and tired of watching you wallow in the past while trying to stick your nose in other people's work just to keep yourself preoccupied. They've been here over three months and you haven't even tried one on one training with any of them. It's time to step up as a Bora." Jin began storming out of the room.

Carl wanted to scream. He wanted to tell Jin to watch his mouth. To stay out of his business. To tell him he didn't know what he was talking about. Yet, everything Jin said rang true in his mind. He'd been swallowing so much work that he barely had time to breath. He kept thinking about the past and focused on other people's work to keep those memories away. He completely ignored his obligations as a Bora. As a leader to these kids.

"Jin," he said calmly. Jin turned around, waiting. "You're right. I'm sorry. Sit down." Jin waited a moment before grabbing the chair. He sat down again and waited for Carl to continue. "We gotta figure this out together. So, what do you know about Peter?"

It took a second for Jin to settle down. Once he did he began talking again. "Peter came in with a big mark on his face. Like he was hit. He'd never even been hurt in battle. It was odd." Carl nodded. "I think something's going on at school. It could even be a home issue."

Carl grabbed a piece of paper tightly. Jin saw that and looked back at Carl. "Home abuse? Are you sure?"

"I'm not. It's why I think we should find out. If it is, we can't let it continue."

185

"Not again," he muttered. Jin's face showed confusion but Carl continued. "Well, keep tabs on him. Let me know. Do not do anything yourself. Once we figure this out, we'll handle it together. Got it?"

"Yeah," Jin said unsure. He wasn't sure Carl was in a stable mind to handle domestic abuse. If it was bullying Jin felt he could handle it himself. If it wasn't, he wasn't sure what he would do. Going to Carl, though, didn't seem like a very reliable option.

Christmas day had arrived. Days went by like nothing when the boys rested. Marshall and Nick spent most of their time with their lovers. They walked around the city, explored the parks, hung around the movies. The time together felt great. Where as Fred mostly played video games, catching up on his backlog. Peter kept his rigorous training routine. Not letting even a day pass without him taking advantage of the extra time. He kept his distance from his bloodthirsty father, not sure what his father might do to him in another confrontation. Or, what he would do to his father. He focused on creating elemental gloves repeatedly. He was determined to stick to one type of weapon and master it.

Nick strolled to his father's room to check in on him. Nick watched as his dad put on his tie, shifting his shirt around to get it looking right. "Looking sharp, pops," Nick complimented. His father fixed his shirt straight, picked his tie up and laid it back down over his chest. He turned around from the mirror and pointed to himself, as if to ask Nick once more how he looked. "Yeah pops, you got some style. You're good," Nick said laughing.

"Not too bad yourself," his father said as he started slipping his belt on.

Nick wore a dark blue vest over his button down. He had on nice slacks, with a belt he was given by his mother on his 14th birthday. It was something special to him, even if it was just a normal-looking belt. He also cut his hair, making it a lot shorter. He didn't mind the change, as long as he could still slick it back.

186

Kelly was a huge fan of it. Nick felt that if it pleased Kelly it made him happy as well.

"So, like I said, her family is a bit off. Just her father really. He sees things oddly but her mother is pretty nice." Nick tried to calm his father. His father never really wanted to meet the parents of his son's girlfriend but he didn't have a choice. He promised to show up to the Christmas dinner. Despite arguing about it with Nick for hours.

"I trust you son. I'm still going to worry, though. You know I don't like these types of things."

"I know pops, but it'll go fine. I'm there as well as Kelly. Just talk to us if you get bored. The father will probably talk about weird stuff as always and you can just zone out."

"I won't zone out."

"Trust me pops-" Nick slipped his shoes on. "-you'll zone out. I zone out. Kelly zones out. His own wife zones out. He can talk."

His father slipped his own shoes on. "Great, just what I wanted to hear."

"I like the pun," Nick said laughing.

"Yeah, too bad it wasn't one," his father said, leaving the bedroom.

Fred touched the white walls. He could feel them changing. They were becoming more hollow. He felt like if he put any pressure on a punch he could break it to pieces. He knew the inside room voice didn't like that, though. Just the thought of breaking the walls scared the voice. Fred wanted to see what would happen but he couldn't. He let himself move back from the wall and looked around the empty room.

He always felt lonely growing up. With the exception of being friends with Marshall he never had anyone to count on as a friend. He stayed in the shadows, skating by classes, wondering what his future held. He wasn't sure how to even adjust to unfamiliar situations. He never had a job, he never needed one.

His family was so wealthy he'd be fine for the rest of his life. He wasn't a bad kid, he wasn't a crazy one. He was a blank slate, though. He had no memories from high school that were memorable. He mostly remembered video games he'd played over anything that occurred in school. So, as he stood in the white room, his lonely feelings he had bottled up crept in.

"Why don't you rest?"

"Okay, seriously, you sound like a damn broken record now." He flung his hand in the air and brushed it away. Trying to scare the voice away like a mouse.

"You keep fighting me. Why? When all I'm doing is helping you. No one helps you like I do," the voice sounded deeper this time. Such a slight change but a change none-the-less.

"You really have to leave me alone now." Fred walked over to the wall. He felt like punching it dead center. He felt like breaking down the walls. Breaking down the chains. Breaking it all down to finally burst free from the pain and suffering. Would punching the walls do that? He wasn't sure, but he was will to discover if it would now.

"You must stop." The voice was rising. Every time he went closer to the walls the voice grew louder. He could sense the voice was getting nervous. Was the voice worried it would be unleashed and it couldn't keep him in anymore? That's what Fred had to find out.

"You know what? I need to know what you're all about." Fed drew his fist back.

"DO NOT DO THAT!" It roared. The voice was darker than it had ever been. Its scream was so loud that it made him jump back. "You will not destroy what I have built."

"Sorry, voice in my head, but you don't get a say in this." Fred began walking towards the wall, ready to finally break them down. Before he could reach them though he awoke on his couch to a knocking at the door. He grunted, slamming his fist into the soft pillow. There was another knock and he bit his lip. He was sweating like crazy and in no condition to go out. He slowly got up, feeling the pain sear through him. He tried ignoring the pain and opened the door anyway. Marshall and his lovely girlfriend Lucy were standing there. She waved at him smiling, Marshall looked at him oddly.

"Dude, you run a mile or something?"

"Nah, bad dream." Fred waved them inside. "Sorry let me just change. Take a seat guys. I'll be back out in a minute." Fred jumped up on the steps that lead into the hallway towards his bedroom. "You can have anything in the fridge if you want. Let me just change this shirt." He went into his room and began digging for clothes.

"Sure this was a good idea?" Lucy asked.

"Yeah, he's fine. Just been going through some stuff." Marshall sat down.

"This place is huge," she said looking around the kitchen. The kitchen alone was bigger than either of their rooms at their own homes. The living room was almost the size of their homes in general. She was stunned how big the entire house was, and they were still only downstairs.

"I've been coming here since I was five." He looked around the house quickly. "It's pretty much same old same old to me. He's not lacking money though that's for sure," he said with a dry laugh.

"I never really hung out with him. I guess its weird 'cause we're both loners. You'd figure we'd attract to each other."

"Hey now-" he began as he grabbed her. He pulled her down to him on the couch and kissed her quickly. "-the only one you should be attracted to is me. Don't forget that my sexy dumpling."

"You keep calling me dumpling and you won't have a girl to get jealous of," she replied, giggling. He kissed her again and she returned the favor. Neither questioned yet what their relationship was or how it was going but they enjoyed the ride, none the less.

"So fun to be the third wheel," Fred said. They broke up the kiss, both embarrassed. "Let's go get some food shall we?"

"Sounds good to me," Lucy said getting up from the

couch. "Where do you wanna eat, Fred? Since Marshall is paying, I say we go somewhere expensive."

"Whoa, what?"

"I say like Outback Steakhouse."

"Uhh no..."

"How about like a fish restaurant. I could use some seafood."

"Hello! I said dinner! Not a three hundred dollar meal."

"There's that fancy Italian restaurant. I hear it's only hundred and fifty a plate."

"Okay, enough! You're killing me," Marshall cried out. Lucy and Fred cracked up. Christmas wouldn't be lonely for once, and Fred was glad for that.

Nick sat in the living room with Kelly on his side. His father was sitting in the arm chair watching the TV. Kelly's parents were in the kitchen finishing their dinner. His father relaxed, it had been awhile since he'd been off work. He smiled at his son and continued to watch TV.

"I'm glad your dad came."

"Me too. He's been so busy it feels like I barely see him anymore."

"You've been busy yourself," she added in.

"Baby, we went over this. I go to the gym after school," Nick said with tiredness in his voice. They'd been arguing about the issue of Nick spending an extraordinary amount of time at the gym. Little did she know it wasn't just a simple gym. He couldn't let her know about the Unknowns. There were strict rules in the organization and he didn't want to disrupt that. He wasn't sure if he was loyal or scared what might happen to her.

She grabbed his empty cup. "Its okay babe, you keep lifting weights. I just figured I'm more fun than that." She got up and went towards the kitchen. He let out a sigh, tired of the small bickering they were going through as of late.

"You can't win the argument," his father said without

taking his eyes off the TV.

"Yeah, but I'm not doing anything wrong."

His father chuckled. "That never matters."

"I just want to stay healthy." It was only half of a lie. The staying fit and healthy part was a bonus. He had to train though; death was a close friend to him, as of late. He didn't want to meet it anytime soon.

"That's great. Yet, the girl in there wants you to spend more time with her. In five years from now she'll remember you coming over and spending the night with her instead of going to the gym. That's how they operate. We forget things days later, they remember things years later. So, don't mess it up so soon." His father took a sip of his drink and went back to watching TV.

Kelly came back into the room. She sat down on the couch and smiled, passing Nick's refilled drink. "Why don't we go bowling next week?" he asked.

Her eyebrow raised. "Bowling?"

"Do you not like bowling?"

"I do...just an odd request out of nowhere."

"You're right. We don't spend enough time together as of late. I want to though. I'm sorry for being the boyfriend who's always busy. I want to spend as much time as possible with the girl I love. If that means skipping a day at the gym to have fun with my girlfriend, so be it." She smiled and grabbed his hand. It was just what she wanted to hear.

"Sometimes baby, you're something else." She leaned in and he kissed her. The arguments always were terrible but the makeup made all the stress go away.

"Aw, so sweet!" Kelly's mom announced as she walked in. "Aren't they sweet?"

"Super sweet!" Kelly's father was just as cheerful.

"Sweetest ever!"

"Sweet like cupcakes!"

"Sweet like cheesecake!?"

"Sweet like jelly!"

"Sweetest of them all!"

Nick's father couldn't take his eyes off of them. They were like a singing duet, but scarier. He looked towards Nick who gave him a wide eye glance. Almost as if to say, "I told you so". They stopped speaking about sweetness and looked towards their company. "Who's ready for din din?" the mother asked cheerfully.

"We're all ready, mom," Kelly said, feeling slightly embarrassed. She couldn't control how her parents acted. Yet, being cheerful all the time was always a nice thing. She never disliked that part, just the overexcited yelling.

They all began walking to the kitchen. Nick's father grabbed him and pulled him back for a second. "Are you kidding me? These two are like Mary freaking Poppins! You could of warned me better."

"Oh, just wait. We haven't even gotten to discuss the importance of singing and being in-tuned with nature," Nick chuckled. His father groaned as he followed his son into the kitchen. As Nick turned the corner he felt a sharp pain in his head. He doubled over for a second, not use to getting the calls as of late. His father placed his hand on his back.

"Are you okay, son?" his father asked. He nodded back.

"Now? No way! I can't just leave here." Nick looked around the room. He knew the destination of his new hunt was near. He told his dad to go ahead and he'd meet him. His dad stood there a second, worried, before moving on. He quickly doubled back and made it into the living room where he was just sitting. He saw the rock engraved with an address right below the mounted TV. He walked over to it and looked at the address. "Oh, come on! It's Christmas!"

"This is the best lobster, ever. Thank you so much best buddy!" Fred said happily. Marshall shook his head, Lucy laughed.

They sat in seafood restaurant, appropriately called "Lobster Head". Marshall had ordered some shrimp with pasta. While Fred and Lucy both ordered their lobster. The room they sat in was dimly lit. Paintings of ships, sharks, whales, and other fish were pasted all over the walls. The waiters dressed in orange hats with smiling lobsters on top. Fred found it ironic they were smiling while in this place they get boiled up and eaten. Still, the place gave a happy vibe and cheerfulness, something that Fred and Marshall needed desperately.

"This is a pretty cool place. I've never been," Lucy said. She looked around, wanting to order all the seafood in the tanks.

"It's nice. I've been here a few times with Marshall. We use to go with my parents. When they were home anyway." Fred took another bite of his food.

"Yeah, those were pretty good times. Your parents paid for anything; even then you were pretty loaded."

"Yeah, some good times. We use to eat here, go home, and play some Pokémon. I have to say it was some pretty great times." Fred said laughing. Marshall smiled at the memories.

"We would sneak out of day camp once in a while-" Marshall began. Trying to get Lucy to listen but more so he wanted to egg on Fred. Resurface some old fun memories.

"-Oh my God! You remember? We'd go to McDonalds, buy like twenty one dollar hamburgers-"   Marshall finished. "-and sell them for three dollars apiece. We'd make bank. It was pretty awesome."

Lucy smiled. She liked watching her boyfriend so happy. Watching him re-live memories was nice. He didn't show his softer side much around the guys. Only to her. "That sounds pretty awesome. So you guys hung out a lot, huh?"

"Yeah. We kind of grew up together and were best friends. Things just got weird in high school." Fred commented casually. Marshall stopped eating, feeling the guilt form in his stomach like a sack of bricks.

"Listen Fred, about that-" he began but Fred put his hand up.

"Dude, the past is the past."

"Still, that's no excuse. I should have-"

"Like I said man-" Fred put his food down. "-it's the past. Let's just focus on the now."

Marshall wanted to speak some more but saw Fred grab his head. Marshall knew what was coming next. Fred opened up his squinting eyes and looked around the restaurant. Marshall waited eagerly while Fred searched the area for the tomb.

"Is he okay?" Lucy asked leaning to her side towards Marshall. Whispering very low so nobody could eavesdrop.

"Yeah, it's a mission."

"Now!?"

"Yeah, he's looking for the tomb to tell him where to go."

"No way!" She was far too excited. Marshall had to place his hand on her knee. He looked at her, eyes dead serious. "Sorry..." She looked at Fred then went back to eating.

They had a talk about the situations with the Exterminators. They had to keep it secret. If anyone found out it could put her in danger. He didn't believe his friends would do anything but the higher ups would. This was a delicate situation. Killing wasn't uncommon for them. He wouldn't let them hurt her, so they kept their secret quiet. For now, no one knew that she had the knowledge of the Unknowns.

Fred pushed himself up from the table and walked towards the fish tank closest to them. Inside the tank the rock sat engraved the address. He took a mental note of it then walked back to the table. He let out a breath, long and heavy. "You'd think we'd be off just one day, huh?" He gave a small laugh. "Sorry, Lucy I gotta head out. Thank you guys for the dinner." Fred got up.

"Baby I'll be by later. I'm going to go with Fred. He hasn't been feeling well as of late."

"Nah that's fine..." Fred began but Lucy got up from her chair.

"That's fine babe!" She said cheerfully. "I'll see you at my house," she began and gave Marshall a kiss. Turning to Fred she waved goodbye. "See you later, feel better!"

"Well I didn't expect that. I for sure thought she'd be pissed." Fred said as he watched her walking out the door. Marshall threw his money on the table and grabbed his coat.

"Yeah, she's a cool chick. Let's head out and do this fast."

194

Marshall wanted to spend the rest of the night with Lucy. Not going out on a cold night to fight an Unknown.

Peter sat on his bed exhausted. He'd been able to create over sixteen balls of fire before feeling a massive drain. He was getting stronger and felt amazing every moment. He soon could prove he's unstoppable. Yet, he didn't want to get ahead of himself so he kept level-headed. He focused on training, not proving he was strongest just yet.

A knock at the door made him flinch. He was hoping it wasn't his father. They only passed by each other, most time his father too drunk to move. He'd like it to continue that way. He received a gift from his mother earlier in the day, but that's it. His dad did not wish him Merry Christmas either. He didn't mind though, the less interaction with his father the better.

"Come in," he said in a low voice. His sister walked in holding her new Ipod. It was her brand new gift for Christmas. "Hey, need something Quin?" She shook her head. "What's wrong?"

She walked into the room and shut the door. She came over to him and sat down. "Are you okay? You look upset."

He looked down at his hands, dirty and messy. "Yeah, I'm fine. Why'd you think I was upset? I'm happy, see?" He pointed to his face as he put up his infamous fake smile.

"I know you sneak out at night sometimes. You're hardly home. You don't even say anything to me anymore." The sadness in her voice did nothing for Peter. He tried to understand why she was hurting but couldn't. She never seemed to show much interest in her brother. She kept to herself almost all the time. She never really hung out with him. So why was she concerned now of his activities outside?

"Are you snooping on me?"

"No, I just don't want to see you..." she started. She sat there looking down at the floor. She never really talked to her brother.

195

"I'm sorry," he said. He didn't know much about what she was going through but he tried to make it up to her. She felt sad and he knew he had to fix that. "I'm sorry if I made you worry. I've just been going through a lot. I promise you, though, I'm okay. So don't worry." He patted her on the head. She smiled and nodded.

"Okay!" she said excited and then ran to the door. Before shutting the door she looked once more at him. "Merry Christmas!"

"Merry Christmas," he said smiling back. She left the room. He then heard his phone go off. He picked it up and saw a message. Nick sent it less than a minute ago. The only thing he could ever ask for Christmas.

"Fifth and 60th street. Meet you there. Merry Christmas!"

Chapter 21 – Teamwork

"How do I approach this one?" Nick contemplated, walking into the kitchen. He saw Kelly's mom placing food on the table. His father was speaking to Kelly's father, telling him all about his job. Nick knew his father didn't care about. That didn't stop him from sharing it, though. Kelly looked at him from the table and gave him the "What's wrong?" eye. Nick cocked his head to the side, trying to show he wanted to speak to her in private. She excused herself a second later. He walked back into the living room, she joined him a moment later. *"Tell her you feel sick? Didn't work last time. Tell her you need to run home and get gifts. Then your dad will say something. Come on think, think, faster! Oh, she's here, think!"*

"What's up?" she asked walking right up to him. He could already sense she was antsy. It was as if she knew he was going to say something horrible.

"I have to go," he couldn't even get further before he saw her eye brows fold inward. He could tell she was getting flustered, quick. "I'll be back real soon. Peter got into a fight and he needs me to bring him to the hospital."

She stood there beyond angry, unsure what to say. Then she spoke, soft but upset. "Is he okay?"

"I don't know. He just texted me saying he needed me. I swear I'll be right back. No more than an hour."

"An hour!?" Her voice rose.

"I'm going to run to his house and check if he's okay. If not I'll take him to the hospital. I'll take my dad's car. It should be no more than an hour. I'll try to get back quicker."

"But dinner..." her voice trailed off.

"Baby, I'm sorry, I swear I'll hurry. I want to spend the rest of Christmas with you."

"Okay." She wasn't sure what else to say. Her feelings

blended together from angry to upset.

Opportunity to spend time with his love one was flickering away. Especially since he just told her he wanted to spend more time with her. "I'm really sorry," he muttered but she just kept her eyes on the floor. "Please, don't be angry."

"Just hurry back." She turned and went back towards the kitchen.

"Goddamn it! This thing is so freaking dead!" He gritted his teeth and ran towards the door. He scooped up his jacket and hat as he began walking down the steps. He started to text Marshall and Fred as well to tell them to meet him, not knowing they had a hunt themselves.

They arrived near the docks. Marshall peered down the empty docks, looking for some type of creature. They already jumped the realm and were hoping the creature would show itself quickly. It was freezing out and both wanted to be home next to a warm heater. Fred walked closer to the water, feeling the icy chill of the wind hit his face. "This was a very stupid idea."

"Isn't it always a stupid idea?" Marshall answered. His teeth clicked together fast, he could feel his body getting colder. He began to rub his arms trying to warm himself up. It was always cold around this time in New York, but much colder near the water.

"Where the heck is this thing?" Fred walked to the edge of the huge dock. He peered over to look for the Unknown. Nothing was on the surface of the water. The waves splashed against it, a bit of water hitting his face. "Nothing here. Come on, this is dumb."

A tentacle came flying out of the water and wrapped around Fred. It easily picked him up, making him scream. Marshall's eyes grew wide as he watched his friend suspended in air. "Fred!" He roared but the beast had already flung his friend. Fred slammed twenty feet away, right into the concrete and rolled over, a terrible crunching sound ringing in the silent night. "No!"

Marshall ran towards him.

The tentacle went to the opposite side of the dock and swung. It went swiping right towards Marshall. Marshall at the last second jumped, but the tentacle was fat. It made him drop mid jump. He slammed on his back with a hard "thud" and laid there for a moment gasping for air.

Fred was already pushing himself up. He had his Rod in one hand. His face was badly scratched up from smearing against the ground. "You have no clue how much I hate water," Fred said through his teeth. He spit once fully up and held the Rod tight.

Marshall got up slowly. "Tentacle beast? This is like a bad episode of Japanese anime." He grabbed his Rod and looked towards the water. The Unknown had already retreated himself entirely into the water. "Any idea what we should use to fight this?"

"I got one," Fred said grinning. He concentrated and moments later the elemental blaster formed up his arm. "I feel like blasting this thing to pieces. What's your thoughts on that?"

"My thoughts..." Marshall concentrated on a new weapon. The metallic arm he was so used to using quickly changed from a hand to a claw. Sharp and deadly, the finger tips reached upward to a foot long. Easily able to chop off anything in front of him. "are to either blast him or slice and dice. Let's do this." Both boys began their jog towards the edge of the dock again.

Peter put his hand on the alleyway's wall; his stamina was almost completely drained. *"Why didn't I take a break? I should of known we'd get a call eventually."* He trained so much since he figured the missions wouldn't come during Christmas. Now, he was exhausted and could barely keep himself up. How was he to fight an Unknown in this shape?

He pulled himself away from the wall and walked onward. He'd been so determined to fight as of late he couldn't give up now. *"It could be a Rockus. If so, that's easy enough. I'll set an*

199

explosive fire ball near it. Pops ups and falls on its back. Nick finishes it. Simple. Easy." His breathing became heavier. He grabbed his chest and stood still. "It's the gloves," he gritted the words through his teeth. He formed them back to a Rod and felt a heavy force lift off of him. He looked towards his Rod.

The Rod was very much the perfect weapon. You can create anything you wanted to but it had such a double edge to it. You hold whatever you created too long and it'll eat at you. It feels as if the Rod tries to rip you up from within. It needs an energy supply and if you aren't willing to give it, it has no problem taking it by force. Peter loved to have the power in his hand, yet sometimes he felt a strange feeling towards it. Fear he believed, but he tried to hide those feelings behind him and focus on his missions ahead.

He marched ahead, feeling far lighter. He hoped to make it to the destination in the next ten minutes. He couldn't help but wondered if he'd be any help to Nick in his current condition.

Nick almost slid on the ice patches. He made his way towards the destination as fast as possible. *"You keep messing up. She's going to hate you forever. Pops is going to ground you forever. What the hell are you doing? Just let Peter deal with it."* Nick left his father's car at Kelly's home. Not taking the chance that the Unknown might damage it and he'd get blamed for it. Nick also couldn't let Peter deal with it alone. Nick already felt like the leader of the group. When they fought all together he would almost always lead the attacks. He felt like each one of his friends in the units counted on him to fight. With no text messages back from Fred and Marshall, he felt he had to step up.

He ran past a huge group of people singing Christmas jingles to a home. Nick almost forgot it was Christmas. He was running towards an Unknown to stop him from breaking into his world while people are singing joyful songs. He sometimes wondered how people would react if they knew monsters existed. Fairy tales sound better to the masses, though, he thought.

200

Every house he passed was beautifully lit up. Lights decorated all the houses from the roof to the front door. Even the mail boxes were done up really pretty. The lawns usually had tons of iconic Christmas decorations. On top of that, some even had an electronic Santa singing to people as they passed by. Even though he was invisible, it still went off. He found that funny as he wondered what people would think if they saw it.

He arrived at the place but saw no Unknowns. "Why are you guys always hiding!?" He screamed. The night air echoed his yells. The beast was still in hiding, though, no movements made. He walked near the houses looking for some type of clue. Besides seeing a few Christmas decorations outside and brightly lit houses he saw nothing. He was quickly getting inpatient. Time was wasting. He wanted nothing more but to get back to his girlfriend.

"Hey, sorry I'm late," Peter said arriving from the other direction. He placed both hands on his knees and bent over, breathing heavily. "I was training today. I'm afraid I won't be very useful."

"Why are you training so much?" Nick said, meeting him the rest of the way. "You'll push yourself too far."

"There's no such thing as too far. We can only become stronger based on training. I just have a focused mind. I can't help it." Movement from behind Nick made Peter survey the lawns.

"No, pushing yourself too far will set you back. What if you get injured?"

"Duck!"

"What?"

Peter grabbed Nick and dove for the car. Both hit the concrete hard behind the vehicle "What the hell are you doing?" Nick groaned. Then four large spikes struck the car, one flying right past their feet. "Whoa!" Nick tucked his legs in and looked under the car. He couldn't see the Unknown but it was near. He saw a snowman. There was a reindeer. He saw a scarecrow. Then a Christmas tree. "I don't see anything. What the hell Unknown is it?"

"I don't know if you noticed, but it's December." Nick

looked up at Peter. "Why would a scarecrow still be outside?" Another group of spikes hit the car, one flying through the window, shattering the glass.

Fred pointed the elemental blaster over the dock. "Get out from under there you ugly piece of..." A tentacle flew out of the water, heading right for Fred. He jumped back, aiming his elemental blaster where he stood. The tentacle came up and he fired. The force of the blue electric wave was so big it almost knocked Marshall off the dock. It created a gust of wind as it flew past Marshall and into the tentacle. It blew into chunks everywhere. Green and purple liquid sprayed all over the dock. The beast could be heard underwater, loud and in agony.

"You made it mad," Marshall said, laughing. He readied himself. He was ready to strike the next tentacle to emerge from the darken waters. Slice it into pieces as it tried another attack on the boys. Yet, nothing came. He waited another few moments but still nothing. No sound from the water either. "Maybe it was just a tentacle beast."

Fred rose from the ground. He could feel a good chunk of his energy was eaten away but he was still in the fight. He wasn't about to fall out just because he used his trump card. He figured he had another shot or two before he was counted out. He smiled before speaking up. "I wish it was that easy. He'll be up. Probably really pissed off too. Who can blame him? I just did some serious damage."

Five tentacles flew up from the water and smashed onto the front of the docks. The boys jumped back not expecting so many. The Unknown planted its tentacles into the ground and flew from the water, screeching, as it threw its body onto the concrete. It was a jelly-like monster. Huge fat blobs surrounded its main body, while the tentacles were made of some strong shells mixed with its soft body material. Its green eyes looked menacing but the gigantic body would make it a slow moving Unknown. Especially on the ground. The boys had the advantage now.

Marshall darted to the left while Fred went right. Fred was letting the elemental blaster build up. He could feel the heat growing within.. It was as if the weapon was a part of him. Now he waited for the right moment to strike. The Unknown gave another nasty screech. Fred kept to the side, just out of its field of vision.

Marshall went around the creature then went forward. He lifted his claw hand and swiped down once close to the back right tentacle. With one solid slash the tentacle was severed. It was like cutting butter with the claws. They were as sharp as his imagination can make them. They ate away at his energy the longer he kept them on; however, he could feel the power coursing through them. He let the purple blood paint his face as he relentlessly attacked. He slashed the next tentacle with the same ease, his body was now covered in the Unknown's blood.

Fed aimed his elemental blaster at the creatures head. He was aiming for the soft center, taking steady aim. He let out a soft breath; he could feel something like tension building up inside him. His head began giving a weird ticking sound that he couldn't simply ignore. It was getting louder the longer the fight went on. As if it was a countdown timer.

Marshall slashed a chunk of soft jelly out of the creature's side. Blood was spraying out more. *"This is the most disgusting thing ever."* He thought as he tried to wipe some of the blood off. The Unknown slid his tentacle around him and tightly lifted him in the air. It began squeezing tighter, trying to crush its new prey.

Fred tried to find a spot to strike but was afraid he might hurt Marshall. *"Are you kidding me? How did you get caught?!"* He looked to the back end of the creature. If nothing else he could hurt it enough to make it drop Marshall. He shot the blast near its backside, the creature roared with anger as it almost stumbled forward. However, it refused to let go of Marshall.

Marshall was screaming from the terrible pain. It felt as if he was suffocating. He couldn't feel his arms anymore. He was using all his strength to fight back; making sure the creature didn't snap him in two. He yelled for Fred to help but Fred wasn't sure what he could do.

The jelly-looking creature shot his other free tentacle right into Fred's stomach. Fred flew back and hit his head hard on a pole near the sidewalk. He went unconscious almost immediately. The beast screamed again, this time for victory.

Nick grabbed his Rod. He was trying to figure out what could do to damage a scarecrow. He'd never faced an Unknown like it. It was mostly made of straw, so fire would be his weapon. He hadn't used the elemental weapons enough to really fight well with. He was a more hands-on person. "I need your help."

"What can I do?" Peter asked panting.

"Form those elemental gloves."

"But-"

"I need just two shots. You got that in you?"

Peter looked at the determined Nick. He could feel a sense of conviction in the boy. "Yeah, I think I can manage that."

"All right. Stay here. I'll let you know when I need you." Nick said. He walked from out of the car and faced the Scarecrow.

The face looked so happy it came off as scary. Its eyes and mouth were plastered in an overly cheerful way that made him want to run away. Its body was made of straw, sharp, and mixed with spikes that looked extremely sharp. The right side of it was made of bone. The purple hooks on its hands made it even deadlier up close. It was dressed in reddish-colored clothes that made it stand out in the wintery background. "Man, I hate anything related to Halloween," Nick said forming his Rod into a big wooden bat.

The creature laughed. It was hollow and heavy, as if to provoke him to fight. He laughed back. "I like an Unknown with a sense of humor. You guys are far too serious all the time." Nick pointed the bat at him. "Batters up." Nick strutted towards the creature. It laughed again and then turned around. Spikes lined up, pointing towards him. He flinched as the Scarecrow threw its hands up. A bunch of the straw spikes flew out. He jumped to the side but wasn't fast enough and he was struck with three of the straw spines. They were only a few inches long but they were sharp enough to break through skin. He cursed under his breath as he ripped them out of his arm. One of the longer, deadlier, spikes laid only inches away from him; impaled deep into the car door he leaned against.

"I thought you were supposed to be a funny one." He got up and gritted his teeth. "You're just as nasty as the others. My turn." As the Scarecrow turned around Nick came full swing. The bat connected right where the Unknown's face was. The Scarecrow's whole upper half bent backwards, as if it was about to snap in half. Then it came right back up and unleashed one of its hooks at him. He threw his bat up and the hook grabbed on to it. It yanked it out of his hand and flung it behind itself. With its free hand it tried to swipe at Nick. He rolled to the left, out of reach. He then darted behind the creature trying to recover his weapon.

The Scarecrow laughed and shot out more spikes and pines from behind. Four of the spikes impaled the ground right near his feet, one grazing the side of his leg. He rolled again, forward, snatching his bat in the process. He ran up the stairs and hid behind the porches wall.

The Scarecrow laughed more. An evil, sinister, and loud laugh as if it were toying with its prey. It was amused to watch Nick run around in circles. As if this was all just a big game and the prize was to finally kill the victim.

"Are you okay?" Peter shouted from behind the car.

"Just fine and dandy!" Nick said sarcastically. He touched the wound on his leg. He had been in far worse situations. He wasn't about to give up so easily. "So the bat didn't do a thing. My plan is still in effect, though."

"Yeah, about that plan. You never told me what it is." Peter checked his hands. They were shaking. He could feel the energy slowly leave his body. "I can't keep up these elemental gloves much longer. I need to act."

"Soon. Just listen for my call." Nick tightened his grip on the bat.

The room was flickering. The once brightly lit room was now barely keeping any light on in it. Fred had to wonder what was happening. He'd never seen the room like this. "Hey, other self, you here?" He asked the room. There was no response.

He got up and walked to the walls. He could feel the hollowness. As if he could punch it with only a part of his strength and it would shatter. He wondered if this is what he was supposed to do. Break the walls down and let himself out of this containment.

He heard screams from afar. He shot his head back to where he came from but nothing was there. Yet he could still hear a faint sound from that area. "Hey other self, is that you?" Again there was no response. Despite that the yells kept coming from that direction.

"This is freaking me out," he muttered under his breath. He took a step to the side and for one split second could hear the yell. It was loud, as if it was right in his ear. All he could hear was a scream. So loud, so scared, dying. It was one he had heard before. It was Marshall.

"Marshall!? Where are you?" He looked in every direction but saw nothing. He touched the walls, trying to push them in. They felt like they would give in at any second. "Marshall where are you? Answer me man!" he screamed.

"Do not break the walls!" The room's voice came alive. The room flickered worse than before. It was as if it was giving out.

"Why not!?" he yelled angrily. He wanted so bad to break the walls yet he had no clue what urged him to do so.

"You need to stay here. To rest."

"No! You keep saying I shouldn't break these walls but you never tell me why!" He roared in anger. He could hear his friend's screams. They were getting louder. "Tell me now before I break these damn walls down!"

"If you break them, you are free. Breaking them will make

you understand anger. Will make you feel power like you never felt. It will show you the meaning of fear." The room's voice sounded upset. As if it already knew he made up his mind.

"I don't have a choice. I have to save him," He let his voice lower. "I can't watch my best friend die."

"You might die."

It struck him hard. Up until this point he never thought about death. Every once in a while after a mission he wondered if he made a mistake what would have happen. Him dying, how people would react to that? Yet, up until then, he never sat and really thought about it. What happens if he dies, then what? All this fighting, all this killing, is it all worth the price of death? He never questioned it. Now, he was forced to answer it.

"You said might. There's a chance I won't."

"If you don't die, you will suffer."

"If I watch him die, I'll suffer anyway."

"It is your choice now. I gave you options and you keep dismissing them. I won't hold you back any longer. You can stay here, rest, sleep, let the dangers of life pass you by. Or you can head off and save your friend. Will your friend be grateful though? What if a fate much worse is held for him. Then what?" The voice let the question linger. It was a tough one to handle. He never thought about the what-ifs in situations.

"You probably think I'm crazy but in life we only live "what ifs". What if I did this? What if I did that? What if I never met him? What if I never saw this letter? What if I died against that first Unknown. What if, What if, What if. What if I stand here and wait another few minutes while my friend gets broken into two. What if. Well, I gotta stop worrying about that. I just have to do what I think is right and hope for the best." He looked at the wall, placing his hand on it and felt its coldness. "I have to chance to do something different. To help people that need helping and-" He pulled his hand back. "-I can't ask what if I'm doing the right thing. I have to act on it!" He threw his fist forward. It shattered the wall. He was then thrown into complete darkness.

Nick rolled from one side of the wall to the next on the porch. The second he came out of cover the Scarecrow unleashed a few pines and a spike. All missed, but barely. Its aim was getting too close for his liking. He bit his lip as he leaned against the wall. *"If I make one mistake we're both dead..."* Another three pines came flying overhead. They landed into the side of the house. *"...then again if I sit here we're dead anyway."*

Peter came from behind the car and threw a ball of fire. It was a weak throw, as if it was his first time throwing a baseball. It was so weak it rolled oddly to the side of the Unknown. However, the creature was so focused on Nick he didn't bother to look to the side. Peter opened his palm wide and the ball blew into flames. It caught the Scarecrow on its side. It hollered in anger as it tried to brush off its straw side with the boney hand.

Nick peered out from cover. He saw Peter leaning on the curb. "I told you to stay still!" He roared. He rolled out of cover and on to the lawn. He came from behind the Unknown and gave it a hearty swing. The bat smashed the back of its head hard, yet the creature came right back up from it. It was more worried about putting out the fire.

"I thought you needed some help," Peter muttered as Nick came closer.

"Yeah, but now you can't even stand." Nick watched as the Scarecrow got most of the fire to simmer down.

"Yeah, well looks like this thing is invincible." Peter could barely catch his breath. He was heaving, as if the gloves were killing him.

"Take those off." Nick looked back at the Unknown. It was getting the fire out of its hat now.

"I can't. You need them."

"I need you not to die."

"I'm fi..."

"I said take them off." Nick looked back at the Scarecrow. Just then as the smoke was rising into the air from the creature he figured it out. "Wait. You have one more in you?"

"Yeah, I think I can create one more." Peter gripped tightly to Nick's arm. Nick could feel the sweaty palm as he helped him to his feet. He looked into his friend's eyes. Anger, determination, conviction. All these were burning through Peter. Nick saw what he needed to take down this creature.

"Put the fire on the bat." Peter looked up, puzzled. "I need you to make this bat on fire."

"What? Why?"

"Just do it." Peter placed his hand on the bat. "Hurry!" The Scarecrow turned around. readying itself for another spike launch.

The bat ignited quickly. It started in the middle and as Peter made his way up the bat it followed in a wave. After it was done Peter collapsed to the ground. "Hey, you alright?"

Peter returned the gloves to Rod form. He looked up at his partner, one eye shut. "That's all I got. Your turn."

Nick nodded. He looked forward, his bat lit up the entire dark night. The cold air couldn't even lessen the flames that waved so viciously. "All right funny guy, time to burn you down. Get it? Burn you down." The creature laughed as its spikes and pines readied themselves. "Glad you liked your own death joke."

Nick rushed forward; the pines and spikes came at him. He moved to the side, putting his free hand up to his face. He could feel the pines striking his leg, his stomach, even one in his finger. He pushed forward but then a spike came flying towards his face. He put his palm up and the spike impaled it. He was almost thrown back but he pushed forward. Using one hand he swung with everything he had. It slammed into the creatures face, flames bursting all over. It crumpled to the ground fast, trying to slap away the flames.

Nick knew this was his one chance. He tried to swallow the pain he was suffering in his injured hand. It hurt so much he was beginning to feel dizzy but he lifted his bat high above his head. It came down on the Unknowns stomach. Flames caught on the straw quickly. The beast cried out. Nick continued. He slammed his bat on the creature's leg. It also caught on fire. He slammed it again on the chest. Fire was spreading quickly. He slammed it again on the face, repeatedly. Screaming, cursing, and crying. He wanted nothing left when he stopped hitting. After a minute or so of constant bashing he let up. He looked down to see the creature was entirely on fire. He could hear the fire making a crack and pop sound as the smoke rose into the air. He stepped back, pointing the bat at the blazing creature. "Exterminators one, crazy psycho Scarecrow zero." He smiled. He transformed the flaming bat back to a Rod. He placed it on his belt, hit the beeper, and sat down watching the fire grow bigger.

Marshall was doing everything he could to fight back. However, the tentacle was squeezing tighter the harder he fought back. He could barely breathe now and could feel his back giving out at any moment. He couldn't believe he might die, not like this. He could feel his arms losing their power as he was slowly drifting out of focus.

He remembered his friends. He finally had the connection he did with Fred that he had years ago. Someone he could talk to, count on, be himself around. He finally got that back. Nick and him got along well enough, always fighting over who calls the commands and does what. It was a simple matter of butting heads but he learned to respect his new friend. Then there was Peter, the odd one out. Yet, he couldn't help but feel he could count on him in battle. As he cried out again when the tentacle got tighter he could only think that he was about to lose all of that.

Then as quickly as he was scooped up he was dropped down. He fell on his feet, feeling all the weight of gravity hit hard. He tumbled over and the tentacle let loose. He could feel the blood in his body rushing back. His arms beginning to regain the strength he once had. His feet were beginning to work again.

Though he heard a terrible screech from the beast, he ignored it. He needed to focus on recovering before the beast struck again. He heard another terrible squishing sound. He heard the Unknown howl again in pain. Blood sprayed all over the docks in front of him. He looked to his side to see Fred standing there, in front of the beast.

"Fred?"

No response. Fred was breathing heavily, his whole body rising and falling with each breath he took. "Fred?" Marshall called out again. Fred glanced back. His face was normal. His breathing was heavy; Marshall could see it rise out of his mouth from the cold. His face a little bloody, but mostly filled with the beasts blood. Nothing stood out, except the eyes. Dark red, glowing eyes. Due to the night, they shined. Almost as if they were diamonds.

"Fred..." Marshall began but Fred already had his back to him. He launched himself at the creature.

The Unknown tried another swipe with his last remaining tentacle. Fred jumped over it with such ease it looked impossible. Once back on the ground he dove forward, struck the beast in the soft core and went as deep as possible. Blood came oozing out from where his hands struck.

"Fred... what the hell?" Marshall said in disbelief. He watched his friend move with such swiftness he couldn't believe it. It was as if he was a whole different person. A different creature even. He fought as if he was an animal. Driving his hands into the belly of the beast, as if to show the creature who the alpha male was.

Then blood sprayed all over Fred. All over the docks. It even sprayed all over Marshall who was yards away. It was raining the blood of the Unknown as it howled in agony. The last cry of pain it would ever scream.

Fred had ripped the creature into two. It was a vicious way of exterminating, one the boys had never done before. Usually putting a creature out of its misery was something the boys were accustomed to. Fred had completely and utterly tore the creature up. Marshall watched his friend stand in front of the monster as if he just won a boxing match. He stood over the dead, like he finally won the right as king of the jungle. As if it was beast versus beast instead of extermination.

"Fred..." Marshall let his voice trail off. Not sure how to

contact his friend. Not sure if he wanted to at this point.

Fred turned around. His hands filled with purple blood. Yet what caught Marshall off guard were his nails. They were longer than usual, around five inches long. His eyes still shining red. The rest of the body looked like his friend, yet it didn't feel like his friend.

"I killed it." It was Fred's voice. Yet it wasn't. It sounded like him, yet it didn't feel like him. Marshall was scared of him. Scared of his best friend that he had known for years.

"I saw," Marshall said in a low voice. He wasn't sure how to speak to his best friend. He felt like he was talking to someone else. The eyes scared him most of all.

"I didn't know I had that in me," Fred said. He walked towards Marshall. Marshall backed up. "Hey, you okay?"

Fred looked worried. He must have seen how scared Marshall was. "Listen, you just tore that thing in half." Marshall rose to his feet fast. "I don't know what the hell you are but stay away!"

"What I am? I'm Fred you idiot," Fred said half laughing. Marshall backed up some more. "Dude, what is your problem?"

"You look like a monster!" Marshall shouted.

"What? How do I look like a monster?" Fred was confused. As if he didn't see himself as one. He hadn't notice the change in himself yet.

"Look at your freaking hands dude! You have cat-like long nails or something!"

Fred looked down. He could see his long nails. He himself jumped back. "What the heck!?"

"That's what I've been trying to tell you!" Marshall started walking forward. A moment ago he was scared of his friend, now he was scared for his friend. He could tell it was Fred now, yet Fred didn't know what he was.

"What the hell is this?" Fred studied his hands. He was scared. He'd never seen nails so long on himself. They were sharp. Deadly. He could do a ton of damage with them. Most of all though, they reminded him of the wolf. The creature that almost

212

killed him. He fell to his knees. "What is happening to me?"

Marshall fell to one knee. "Dude, its cool. Hit the button. Get backup to clean this mess up. We'll talk to Carl about this."

"No!"

"No? Dude you're changing into a werewolf or something."

"No, we tell them and they'll take me away." Fred was so scared his voice began to crack. He could feel the pressure building in him.

"This isn't a sci-fi movie man. They won't take you away."

"Why wouldn't they!?"

"Cause you're a human. Not a monster."

"You just said it yourself, I'm becoming one!" Marshall watched as Fred screamed in fear. He just realized how scared Fred really was.

"Calm down. We won't tell them then." Marshall placed his hands on Fred's shoulders. "Just relax, dude." He said soothingly. Fred looked up at him. Marshall noticed the red eyes were gone, now replaced with his normal brown ones. "There ya go. Looking better already."

"Huh?"

Marshall noticed the fingers returning to normal as well. "Look down."

Fred watched his hands returned to the shape he was used to. "Oh thank God!"

"See, nothing to worry about. Call for backup. Let's get this cleaned up."

Fred rose with Marshall. "What do we tell them?" They looked at the jelly-like creature. Its body was ripped wide open. All four tentacles were slashed off. Its blood was sprayed all over the entire dock. It was a massacre-looking scene.

Marshall raised his hand. "I had the claw hands remember. We'll blame it on that. Don't worry." Fred nodded and hit the button. Marshall would never rat out his friend. If he felt that it should be kept a secret it would be kept a secret. Yet he was scared. Not for himself but for his friend. He didn't know what to do. Now with the promise, he had no one to go to.

Nick dropped Peter off at home and made his way back to Kelly's house. It was over an hour and a half. One of the Exterminator's at the cleanup patched him up as best he could. Healing his hand and placing it on himself with a transfer seal of magic. It was dangerous but useful in situations like his own. His hand was sealed and perfectly fine. Yet the pain from the attack was still there. The drain from the Rod left him tired. He had grass and dirt all over his clothes.

He wasn't sure what to say. He wanted to speak to Kelly first before his dad. He knew his dad would be pissed. Probably even ground him forever. Yet, he was more worried about her. What would she think of him now? The second time he left her alone with no reason to back it up. The excuse of Peter in trouble was all fine but not when he was dirty himself. She wouldn't believe him no matter what lie he spun.

He thought about telling her. The secrets of the organization would be between just them two. She was trust worthy. She'd understand why he had to leave so often. Why he'd come home all banged up. Why he would need the training. It would solve all the issues they had while fighting. It would make everything so much easier.

He just couldn't. If she knew it would put her in danger. He wasn't going to allow himself to put someone he loved in danger. He fought too hard to get her; he wouldn't let her go now. He could lift so much weight off his shoulder, if he told her, but he couldn't allow himself too. This was one of the inner struggles of being a leader. Having the responsibility to protect the ones you care about. He knew he couldn't speak about the organization.

He walked up her steps. He still hadn't had a plan on what to tell her. He watched as his cold breath flew up in front of him. It was so cold out, yet he couldn't feel it. He could only feel the knot in his stomach. He didn't want to knock on the door. He wanted to run away. Think of some big excuse and come back the next day.

214

He decided to knock on the door, regardless of what the consequences were going to be.

He heard feet coming towards the door. They were soft and quiet, he knew it was her. He braced himself. He had a feeling he was about to get screamed at. She opened the door. She saw right away the dirty and ripped cloths. She saw the blood on him despite his best efforts to clean it off. She saw his face, a face full of sadness and guilt.

"Baby, I'm so so-" he began but she held her hand up.

"Come in. Let's get you cleaned up."

She moved out of the doorway and waited. He came inside the house and looked at her. He could feel her sadness but more so the worried look on her face concerned him. "I'm sorry," was all he could mutter. She shook her head and kissed him.

"I said its okay. Let's get you cleaned up," she said softly.

Chapter 22 – Those Days

Carl walked down the steps to his home. He thought about the situation at hand. He was dealing with an over abundance of problems on his plate. So much, in fact, that he couldn't even find time to sit with his unit. He hadn't even done any one-on-one training with them. He felt terrible about it, especially since he was their Bora, the one to guide them with their extermination job. Instead, he focused on everyone else's problems instead of his own. He was doing the opposite of what he promised to do.

Today he felt he was going to change that. He called up Fred and told him to meet in his office. It was already February and the boys did enough training by themselves. They rose to fine warriors, handling every mission with swiftness and determination. Questions arose, but no matter what, they did as they were told.

He thought about his own problems. He stopped drinking two weeks ago. He finally let go of the addiction. Every night he felt the tug of the demons ripping at his insides. The alcohol wanted in; he wanted it inside him driving his problems into oblivion. Yet, every night he fought against it holding the addicted self at bay by reading. He let it swim around in his mind but never surface.

He was scared it would happen again. A total shut down in him. He had already lost so much in the past. Made so many mistakes. He blamed himself entirely for a lot of it, despite only being partially to blame. He wasn't sure why he blamed himself for so much. Probably because it was easier that way. He always felt like a leader, ever since he first joined the organization. In his mind leading was everything. So, if someone under his lead made a mistake it was his fault.

He didn't want to push himself back into depression. When he lost his first team completely, he broke. He went into a deep depression and went off the map. No one could find him. He made sure of that. Still, in all his time of hiding, he wanted nothing more than to be found. He was off the charts for years. No one followed him. He felt free from the organization, even if he knew no matter how far he ran the organization would never let the grasp they had on him go.

He made his way past a busy street. He looked at the small kids playing alongside the street. One boy had a penny in his hand which he threw on the ground. It flipped over causing half the kids to howl in excitement. The others yelled in defeat. It always was a competition in life, he felt. No matter how young or old you are you're always betting yourself against or for something. Even watching the kids he could see that.

Carl never failed a mission. Even as an Exterminator he finished every mission to a "T". His whole unit survived growing up together. They all became Protectors or Boras in the long run. Even the most challenging Unknown he went up against was eventually taken down. Yet, something went wrong. When he became a Bora something changed. Missions were mostly eliminating creatures. Raising four young people to eventually become pro executioners of Unknowns was another thing. He somehow slipped there.

He reached the wooden house. Opened the door and made his way towards the elevator. He stood in the elevator for a moment. He wouldn't fail this time. He felt this time he could prove he was worthy of being the leader. He wouldn't let himself slip again.

Kelly laid her head on Nick's chest. They lay down in the field outside the park. In February it was still cold. The wind was at a all time low today, though. They watched as the clouds passed overhead with the sun shining through when it could. "It's beautiful."

He smiled at her. "Yeah, it is," he responded.

"You ever think about how we first met?" She placed her hand on his chest.

"Yeah, I told you that you had a nice pen."

She giggled. "You were so corny. So weird."

"Hey!"

"Still, I wanted to get to know you so bad. You were different." She looked at him. "Something special."

"I'm just me. You're the one who's special." He gave her a small kiss. She lit up. He loved doing things for her and watching her face light up in response.

A small chill went over both of them. They cuddled up tight for a moment till it past. Once it did, they let go and watched the sky. They tried to make out different shapes from the clouds. "A heart, you see it?"

"No. That looks like a guy with one arm," Nick said, pointing.

"What!? How do you see a guy! It's a heart."

"It's a guy."

"Okay, pen expert," she responded, giggling. He tried pushing her off playfully but she grabbed his shirt. He held her tighter afterward. The joy he brought her just being close was enough to make him feel happy. The missions and training began to be tougher than he expected on his time and body but he kept at it. When he saw her though, it all went away. All the pain. The frustration. The missions. Just happiness remained. He sometimes wondered if he was allowed even that in the lifestyle he was chosen for.

"During the summer I think I'm going to try getting a job," Nick said softly. She smiled.

"Sounds good to me. I think I'll try getting one myself. We're just about done with school anyway. No need to wait around."

"Once I get enough money I..." he began, not sure how to finish. He'd been thinking about the future as of late. What moves were the *right* moves? He kept wondering and questioning himself. He decided though he'd never find out unless he asked. "-

218

I'd like to get my own place. I'd like you to move in with me." He held his breath.

She kept viewing the sky, not saying a word. Complete and utter silence took over the air. Then she spoke. "I'd very much like that. To be together with you, more." He let out a heavy breath, one that held the weight of the world. He grabbed her tighter. He felt no other words needed to be said.

"You think I can come with you one time?" Lucy said to Marshall as they walked out of a local restaurant. The cold chill wrapped around their bodies as they began walking against the wind.

He glanced over to her. "I told you before, you can't. These missions are top secret. You wouldn't even be able to see anything."

"I just want to see what you go through."

"That's the thing, you can't see anything. I told you I jump realms."

"Why don't you let me jump with you?"

"You don't have a beeper, first off," he pointed to his beeper. "This thing is what helps me cross over. You don't have it, meaning you can't jump. Listen baby, we went over this before, you can't come along. Not only is it bad for me but it's dangerous for you. What if the monster attacks you? What if you get hurt?"

"You get hurt all the time!" she answered stubbornly.

"Yeah, but that's on me. My mistakes. If you get injured in anyway, I can't handle that. So no, you cannot come along." He looked away, walking just slightly ahead of her. She was agitated and he could feel it. He was a big push over, but not on this perticular subject. The danger was too much for him to ever risk her life.

"You're being unfair," she spoke low and soft. He ignored it for a moment. He knew she was being a baby, not getting her way, but he couldn't help but feel for her. If he looked at her he knew he'd wanna give in, so he kept his eyes glued to the streets.

Watching car drivers yell out their windows at the people slowly crossing the street. He watched the food carts on the streets offering anyone who passed them a free desert. He watched as people gambled at the end of the block, common thing on the street corners of New York City. Little did they know what hid behind all this. What was in the realm right beside them.

"I'm not being unfair. I'm being safe. I told you when we started this secret that we couldn't push it. We're doing something that's against all the rules. If the organization ever found out-" Now he turned to her. She watched his eyes. "-they'd put an end to this. I'm pretty sure they'd shut you up in the worse way possible. Probably send me to execution or something. We can't let that happen baby. We have to stay under cover." He stopped and grabbed her shoulders. "You have to understand that."

"I do," she said smiling. "It's nice to see you care so much."

"Of course I care. I..." he almost let it slip. The amazing feeling he'd been experiencing the last few weeks. He wanted so badly to tell her. He just wanted to scream how much he loved her. He was too scared though. The bravest of all the boys. One of the most outspoken people in the entire school. Yet, he couldn't say three simple words. "...just want to keep us safe. Let's go."

He caught a small sadness in her eyes but once he grabbed her hand she smiled again. He led her towards his house. She smiled even bigger as she tightened her hand around his.

Jin grabbed Peter's hand and twisted it around him. He spun Peter around and held his arm behind him. "Do you quit?"

Peter gritted his teeth. "No."

Jin pushed harder, putting more pressure. "At this rate it'll snap."

"I give," Peter answered quickly. The pain built up too much. He almost tripped once he was let go of. He turned to Jin. "One day, I'll beat you."

"I fully believe you will," Jin told him, smiling. "You're one of the best Exterminators I've fought at such a young age. You haven't even had full training with Carl and you fight like a pro. Well, with your elemental gloves at least. Close combat can use a lot of work." He laughed. Peter waved his hand in a dismissive manner and walked to his bag on the floor.

Peter took a sip of his drink and looked at Jin. "If you master one weapon, you'll never need another."

"If you master all weapons, you'll never have to worry about somebody else mastering just one weapon." Jin laughed again and Peter couldn't help but join in. "Thing is, you're strong-" Jin sat down near his bag. "-you just need to focus on every aspect of fighting. You're quick. You think on your feet and that will help. You can summon more elemental powers then most people in their first year. You have the determination, as well. If you don't want to use other weapons - fine." Jin pointed to the whole gym in front of him. "You just have to be a valuable asset to your unit."

"I am valuable."

"You are, but if you don't want to master another weapon you must master support. You're not a close-range fighter but a far range fighter. If you can master being the best support on the team you'll never need to get into close combat." Jin tapped his own head. "It takes a lot of guts to go in head-to-head with an Unknown. It takes a lot of brain though to stay away and strike from afar. Being safe should always be the first goal."

Jin had come to like Peter as a student of sorts. Carl promised to step up and take care of his own team. Jin felt a odd, maybe special, connection with Peter. In a lot of ways, Peter reminded him of a younger brother. Someone so eager to learn everything he knew. Also eager to prove he was better than him. It was a love and hate relationship that made Jin so intrigued by Peter. His motives weren't unnatural but his mind was. He thought differently. He focused only on training. When other kids thought about girls and school problems, even Exterminators, Peter focused only on training, learning more about Exterminators, and hunting Unknowns. He knew from the very start that Peter would

221

be something different, something unique.

Peter flexed his fingers. He already reversed his Rod back. He felt his energy slowly creep back into him. Far quicker than a few months ago. His stamina and dexterity grew every day. He could feel it, even if he couldn't explain it. His body only grew a little bit but it was everything else that grew exceptionally. He felt he had to prove he was better. He never figured out why he had to, though. It bothered him every day to know he had motives but not sure why or what they even were for at times. He felt he had to prove to someone, but who was that someone. His father? His friends? Carl? Jin? The question kept circulating in his mind for days and still no answer. It became the only problem Peter couldn't master.

"I think we should head out. We trained for almost two hours. Sure you're parents are wondering where you are on a school night." Jin checked the time, it was getting close to nine o'clock.

"Eh, they don't care."

"Of course they do. Every parent cares about their kid, even if they don't always show it."

"No, trust me. Drunken people care about when the next drink is up and that's all."

This got Jin's attention. He remembered he was still keeping tabs on Peter but no evidence had showed up yet. Peter hadn't shown any new scars so he couldn't relate it to a family situation or school. Jin kept a close eye when he could, but if nothing was there he couldn't prove a thing. "Is your father abusive to you in any way?" It was a straight out, blunt question. He figured he had to ask somehow, and this was the best way.

Peter took a second to think about it. The organization didn't need more problems. He wanted to keep his teammates away from his personal life. No need for them to be sucked into a terrible father-son relationship issue.

"No, he's just a bum." Peter laughed. The laugh was fake yet Peter hoped Jin would buy it.

"All right, well then let's get you home."

Peter felt the bluff laugh had worked. Why wouldn't it? No one cared enough to pry into his business. He didn't want anyone to interfere in his personal life anyway. He liked to be alone in this. At least that's what he told himself. "Okay," he said, almost sadly. Real emotion began to spill in but he soon buried it again. He was good at that.

Carl was in his office looking at Fred who was checking out the room. Carl didn't want to train until he had a chance to get used to the kids first. He was a trainer but also a mentor. If his own unit didn't trust him, how could he train them? "You haven't said much about your life. Tell me more about the parents."

"Screw 'em. They never did me any favors." Fred picked up a baseball and threw it in the air, catching it with his left hand. He studied the ball, yet his mind drifted to a different place. "They're never in town. I really just rather not talk about them."

"Fair enough," Carl said sitting down. "How do you feel about the other boys? Are you getting along with them all?"

"Yeah, of course. We've all been through hell together. We're gonna stick together, of course."

"Anyone you don't see yourself getting along with?"

"Is this some type of test? To see if I'm stable?" He could feel himself getting upset. He wondered if Marshall mentioned the incident that happened a month ago. When he began forming into something...something he was scared to talk about. Especially to the organization.

"Not at all. I just want to know more about my students."

"Nick's cool, Marshall is an idiot but my best friend, and Peter is slightly weird yet I feel I can always count on him. I actually can count on all three. So yes, we all get along." Fred tried not to show his fury that was growing. He'd rather not lead Carl on to show him how scared he was.

"I see. Well, I'm very glad you all are getting along so well." He watched as Fred's eyes darted around the room. "What's wrong? You seem nervous."

"I'm not."

"That's what a nervous person would say."

"I'm not nervous. I hate being interviewed."

"This isn't an interview."

"Then stop acting like it's one!" Fred threw the baseball across the room. It flew into the wall directly to the side of Carl's face. The speed was amazing; if a normal person saw it they'd guess he was on the baseball team. The ball would have hurt anyone in its way. Carl didn't move a muscle. Instead, he smiled at his student.

"Something's troubling you. What is it?"

"Nothing. Not a thing in the world!" Fred placed his hands on the desk. "What's troubling you, big boss? Why haven't you've been training us at all?" Fred's voice was getting deeper, angrier, darker. "Why have we done all the damn self-training while you sit here wallowing in your past? You messed up? Oh poor Carl, what will he ever do?" His voice changed, both sinister and playful.

"Fred, watch the next words that come out of your mouth."

"Or what?" Fred leaned closer in on the desk. His teeth showing, a smile that could only be considered wicked. "Are you going to betray me, too?"

"What did you say?"

Fred backed off the desk and looked away. He could feel his body shifting. The anger fighting its way up his body but he forced it to stay at bay. He needed to keep calm. Needed to restrain himself from getting upset. From unleashing whatever has been trying to get out. He could feel it growing the last few weeks but he kept quiet. Not even telling Marshall, his closest friend and the only one who knew about his secret.

"I said..." Fred was spun around by a furious Carl. He had an extremely tight grip on his student as he put his face right in front of Fred's. "What did you say to me?" Fred felt the spit from Carl hit his face. He had never seen the calm and collective teacher so livid. He had never seen someone as angry as Carl was at this point.

"I said...I said..." Fred couldn't find the words. He couldn't remember the words. "I don't know what I said. I'm sorry," he said, fumbling words.

Carl could see the boy was telling the truth. The Fred of a few seconds ago was gone. Replaced now by a frightened child. He let go of his student and backed away. He himself had to calm down. His temper is what got him in trouble before. He didn't want to reveal this side of himself to anyone. Especially to his unit.

"I'm sorry, too." Carl rubbed his head. "I thought I heard something. Brought back memories."

"Why don't you tell me about some of your memories?"

It was a simple enough question. Everyone wants to know about a person they care about. It's only natural to be curious where a person came from and how he came to be. Carl didn't let the question hurt him like it usually does. Instead, he reached back to when he began his Exterminator days. "Well, when I was in my first year, I was grouped with three girls."

"Oh," Fred said, now taking a seat. "Go on. This I wanna hear more of."

"Well, it was three young ladies. All older than me though at that time."

"How old were you?"

"I was fourteen."

"What!?" Fred was in shock. He felt they were too young to be in the organization. Yet, Carl was just starting high school when he joined. "Weren't you afraid? You were just a kid."

Carl laughed and nodded. "I was scared. Not to mention being the only boy on my team as well as the youngest, was scary. I had to be the leader, though."

"You were the leader?"

"Yeah. I couldn't let my team down. They were all great fighters, however, I was the one with the plans. When we worked together with my strategies we almost never lost. My team survived their entire run. Two of them are still alive now." Carl pointed to the picture behind Fred.

Fred took a look to see the smiling faces of four young people. One girl was red haired with a bunch of freckles on her face. She had braces in her mouth and looked to be around sixteen. The other two were hugging each other. One with black hair, one with brown. The black haired one was the oldest-looking one, probably in her late teens with her two fingers up in a peace sign. The brown haired one was waving at the camera. All the way to the left was Carl. He was looking at the girls smiling, as if he was proud. The youngest of them all, yet he still looked like the leader. The way he smiled in the picture, his eyes nearly shut closed, joyful of the company he was with.

"You look so happy." Fred kept his eyes glued to the picture.

"I was. Those people were my family. They still are. The one with red hair," Carl said pointing to the girl with braces. "That's our Gada. She's the boss of this place. Her name is Amanda but everyone calls her by her last name. Ross."

"Whoa, so the one who runs this whole organization is your friend?"

"Yeah, best friend."

"Any perks?"

"Not a single one."

"That sucks," Fred said laughing. He looked back at Carl. Could see him reliving the past. The many years of going on missions as a young Exterminator, killing the Unknowns of those times. He could see how much Carl missed it. "What about the other two?"

Carl looked down at the floor. "Amber, the one with the black hair is still alive. Funny enough, Peter would like her." He walked over to his desk and sat down. "She focuses on magic. She's one of the best in the business and an excellent Protector. She hunts like no other. I've never seen someone so advanced with magic like her."

"And the other...is she gone now?"

Carl nodded. "She is. I..." he began. Memories resurfaced

226

like a wave, hitting hard. He remembered so much good, yet so much bad crept in with it. He tried to separate the two but it was almost impossible. In such a short time everything went terrible. All the good he worked towards was shattered so quickly. "Let's save that discussion for another day. I'm getting a bit tired."

"Yeah, me too," Fred lied. He could see his boss getting tired. Weak from just bringing up the past. He didn't want to push him any further.

"I'm glad you came by today " Carl rested back in his chair. "Sometimes talking things out can help."

"I agree." Fred got up from his chair. He felt calmer, as if he was getting used to Carl. This was the first real conversation he had had with his Bora. It felt like something was building, more so he got to see a little into his teacher's world. It was a damaged place, but an intriguing one, none the less. If Carl wanted to help his student, Fred felt he needed some help from the others. He was willing to try. "I'll head out now. Take care Carl."

"Take care Fred."

Chapter 23 – Company

Fred walked towards Peter. Peter was inside the gym bending back his arms, stretching out his legs. "Hey Pete, how's things hanging?"

Peter's face turned towards Fred. "Hey Fred. I'm fine. How are you doing today?"

Fred shrugged and dropped his bag. He went straight to stretching, too. "Decent, glad it's the weekend." It had only been a week since Fred was in Carl's office, he kept thinking about the incident. The second when he felt so angry he couldn't see clearly. When he wanted to rip off his Bora's face. It stilled remained fuzzy however, as if it was trying to repress the memory quickly.

"I agree. It'll be nice to get a few hours of extra training in."

"I was thinking of extra rest," Fred said, laughing.

"Hey Fred, can I talk to you later on?" Peter wasn't sure what came over him. He felt the need to speak to someone. Fred nodded.

"Everything okay?"

"Yeah, it's just some stuff I want to go over. It won't take long."

"All right man, just remind me..." Fred began but the door opened. Marshall and Nick waltzed inside the gym laughing.

"Whatup, my brothers from another dad."

"It's my brothers from another mother," Fred pointed out.

"I don't think so," Marshall responded.

"Let him have this one. Trust me, it'll be a lot easier that way," Nick said.

"So, anyone know why we're here today? I just got a text from Carl and Jin to meet here." Nick threw his bag to the side and began stretching. Marshall followed his lead.

"No clue, we both got the same text." Fred pointed to Peter

228

and himself.

"Well, more training can never hurt," Peter said getting up.

"Did you take my advice?" Marshall asked.

"What advice?"

"Getting a girlfriend?"

"I told you I'm not attracted to any-" Peter began.

"-girl in class. Yeah I heard you. I'm saying any girl on the street. Dude, you focus so much on training you don't live. Come on!" He slapped Peter hard on the back. "It's time to loosen up and live a little huh?"

"Do not hit me."

"Or what? You gonna punch me, sissy boy?" Marshall chuckled.

Peter got into Marshall's face. "I said, do not touch me."

"Hey bro, get the hell out of my face." Marshall stood over Peter. Peter didn't back down though. He looked up at Marshall, anger flaring in his eyes. The boys were meant to butt heads. Ever since they first met, Marshall thought lowly of Peter. Peter's whole objective with the training was to prove he was strong. Valuable.

"Okay guys, chill out." Nick stepped in between the two separating them with his hands. "We don't need this right now. We're teammates remember?"

"Just tell freak over here not to get all pissy."

"You keep calling me a freak," Peter said plainly.

"That's 'cause you are." Marshall put his hand out. "I mean, look at you."

"Let me ask you a question smart guy," Peter started, walking towards Marshall. Nick tried to step between them but Peter put his hand up. He walked past Nick and back into Marshall's face. "Is it really wise to piss off the freak then?"

Marshall met his gaze. For a moment it looked as if he would punch him. Fred and Nick stayed tense, ready to leap in if it broke out into a fight. Marshall kept his face still, looking into the eyes of his teammate. All he could see was eagerness.

Marshall smiled and placed his hand on his shoulder. "We cool man," he said softly. Peter relaxed. This wasn't a person he had to prove his strength to. They knew he was a powerful ally. He smiled back. "You still a freak but you're *"our"* freak."

The boys conversed a few more minutes. Talking about school, how it was already half way done, what their plans were during the summer and so on. Marshall was heading to Florida for the summer with his brother. They'd stay with their grandparents for two months. Nick knew he'd be going with his father on vacation for a while but not sure for how long. Peter planned on staying in New York City mostly focus on training. Fred wasn't sure what he'd be doing this summer, other than hunting more Unknowns.

As they were talking the doors from the other side of the gym opened up. In strolled Carl, Jin, and four other people. They all looked to be around the same age as the four boys. The group consisted of two girls and two guys. One guy was African American, tall, bulky, and seemed to be leading the group. The other boy was of Indian decent. He was short, bald, and wore business type clothing. The two girls walked side by side. One with dark brown hair, glasses, freckles, and a cute bow on the top of her head. The other had black curly hair, crystal blue eyes, and pale white skin.

"Well, hello ladies!" Marshall greeted the girls. They looked at each other and giggled. "My name is Marshall, this is my crew." He put his thumb up and behind him, pointing to the other three boys.

Nick pushed Marshall out of the way and walked up to the tall African American. He extended his hand. "My name is Nick. Pleasure to meet you."

He met the greeting. "My name is Daryl. Nice to meet you."

Nick let go and nodded. He then pointed to each member of his unit. "The big mouth is Marshall. The serious one over there is Peter. The other one is Fred. This is my team of Exterminators." Nick hadn't ever called his friends his team. Somehow he felt obligated to act as if it was his team. Usually Marshall would be the first to protest in this type of situation, yet he smiled and nodded. All of them nodded, it was as if they accepted Nick as the leader, naturally.

"This is Sam," Daryl began, pointing to the black haired woman. "This is Rachael," placing his hand on the other girl's shoulder. "And the quiet one on our team is called Ali. This is my team of Exterminators." Nick felt the same as Daryl. Proud of his team. Proud to be a leader to them.

The door swung open again and two ladies walked in. One with black hair, one with red. They were much older, around Carl's age. As they walked forward Carl spoke up. "Boys, I'd like to introduce you to your Gada. She is the leader of the organization."

The boys watched in awe as the two ladies approach. A heavy sense of power came from both of them. The red haired fighter was their Gada. Her name was Amanda Ross. Everyone just called her Ross. "Pleasure to meet you boys. I've heard a lot about you four." She then turned to the other group of four Exterminators. "Not to count you out either. Because I've heard quite a bit about you guys, too." She had a bright smile.

"So you're our leader." Marshall stepped up. "I got a few questions for you." Nick placed his hand on his friend's chest to hold him back.

"Marshall, back off."

"Why? I have a few questions is all."

"Be respectful. This isn't just someone you can throw your questions at."

"Hey listen, she's our Guda right?"

"Gada," Fred corrected him.

"All right whatever-" Marshall took a deep breath. "I just want to ask her questions that Carl didn't answer. I'm not going to attack her."

"Let the boy speak," Ross said. Nick looked at her then back to Marshall. He slowly let go and let Marshall proceed on ahead.

Marshall walked a little further and stopped a few feet away. "I'm just curious since you're our leader, is killing the only thing we can do?"

"You're referring to the Unknowns?"

Marshall cocked his head to the right. "I'm just curious why we can't do something other than killing them. It doesn't make sense that we always have to kill."

Ross looked at Marshall and smiled. She remembered reading his file months back. He was rash, outspoken, yet kind-hearted. She always knew someone would speak up in a group. People had questions; she had so many as a young Exterminator. Yet, she never pegged Marshall to be the one to question things. She couldn't help but smile, feeling the slight resemblance to her childhood memories.

"If we leave them in this world it begins to break barriers." All the young Exterminators looked puzzled. "Even having Callers and Healers on our side disrupts the balance. Realms are meant to be set in place, not broken. These creatures come here upset, angry, and want to destroy because of it. Jumping barriers usually disrupts their minds. At least it's what we're told by certain Unknowns who come through and still keep themselves intact. The Callers we pulled through to our world still have trouble adapting to our world. This world isn't meant for them. The barriers aren't meant to be broken."

Everyone listened. It was information they assumed but never knew how serious it was. They knew they had to exterminate. It was who they were. Yet they all questioned it at times, Marshall most of all. They now were accepting the fact that this job was serious so they couldn't slip up.

"Fair enough," Marshall stepped back into his group. "If I figure out one day how to keep peace amongst the Unknowns and us we better do it. I don't want to exterminate them for no reason."

"I like your way of thinking, young one," Ross said cheerfully. She looked at her old friend Carl. "How are you doing?"

"You know, same old. Training these crazy kids. How are you? Also, I don't get a "Hi", Amber?" He looked past Ross to the Protector standing next to her.

She looked to her side at her old teammate. "Sorry, was

just studying the fighters. Hi little one."

"Hey, I'm not little anymore!" Carl yelled loudly, the women both laughed.

"You'll always be my little Carl," she told him happily. She could remember how they trained together when they were kids. The brute force of his power, the magical abilities she had clashing together. They were almost unstoppable.

"So you're a Protector right?" Peter asked Amber. Amber turned to the young Exterminator and nodded.

"What's a Protector?" Fred asked.

"It's the highest status you can go as an Exterminator for hunting. We're just trainees. Beginners. Once we are able to obtain four Rods we can either become a Bora like Carl or a Protector like Amber," Peter informed them, as if it was natural to him.

The Protector and Gada looked at him, slightly surprised. "He reads a lot," Jin pointed out from Carl's side.

"I hope to be the strongest Protector there is," Peter said with conviction. He could feel his body heating up. He wanted to fight to prove how strong he was.

"I don't think so," Ali said loudly. "I plan to be the strongest and become the personal Protector for our Gada."

"I don't think it's wise to try and take my spot," Peter said stepping forward. This was the first time he ever stepped up to the plate. He felt like this was his moment to prove himself. He was standing in the presence of his Gada, the leader of all. If he had to prove to anyone his strength it was her.

"Geez, they act like I'm already dead," Amber said, laughing.

"Peter here is hot headed when it comes to fighting." Marshall stepped in front of Peter. "Yet, I agree. I think we should have a little face off. See how the teams are coming along."

Daryl stepped up. "It's up to your leader. I wouldn't mind a spar."

Marshall looked back to Nick. Nick wasn't planning on fighting today. Just a bit of training, yet he now felt the hunger to battle. He looked at Daryl, could see the same eagerness. He felt

Marshall and Peter's willingness to fight. "I don't see why not," he said stepping forward.

"These young ones," Ross said while walking over to Carl. "You'd think they'd want to conserve energy. All they want to do is fight."

"Can you blame them? It's what we used to do," Carl said with a slight chuckle.

"Yeah, but..." her voice trailed off. "Well, if nothing else I can see how the teams have progressed. Why didn't Gail come for her team today?"

"She's on a hunt. Something big came through today," Jin answered.

"What came through?" Now Amber was interested.

"Nobody knows but it's big. The Callers said the next few weeks are going to be rough. They sense a lot of big signals trying to break though. The Summoners are up to something," Jin whispered in a low voice, not wanting the students to hear as they got ready to fight.

"I've heard about the bigger-than-expected signals popping up, yet I didn't know the forecast was this bad. We should be on high alert. Any news on the hunt for the leader?"

"Nothing," Carl replied, gritting his teeth. He could feel himself getting angrier but he hid it behind his invisible shield he kept from the world. Especially from his friend, who he didn't want to worry.

"Well, best we could do now is wait and attack when the time is right," Ross chipped in, watching the fighters line themselves up for battle. "For now, we watch as our replacements battle it out. In a few years these will be the Exterminators having to deal with these issues."

"Oh God, help us," Jin said, they all laughed.

Nick grabbed his Rod. He looked at his opponent, trying to figure out what they would create. He had to be careful. Making the wrong weapon could result in a lost battle. He turned to whisper into Marshall's ear. "Create that gun."

"Wouldn't that kill them?"

Nick turned around. He gave Marshall a long sharp looking eye. "THE gun. Remember training?"

Marshall already had formed the weapon. "I just like messing with you."

Nick turned around. "How the hell are we a workable team?" he muttered under his breath. He thought about what weapon to use. No one on the other team made a weapon yet, they too waited for Nick to make his. It was a game, something they weren't used to. Unknowns attacked based on instinct. Humans don't operate the same. Nick knew this. Daryl's team knew this.

Fred created the Zoran weapon and darted forward without saying a word. Nick formed his pole-arm and dashed to the left. Marshall already aimed at Ali, ready to fire once he made his move. Peter formed his glove and was already forming a nice sized ball of fire. The girls departed and went separate ways. Nick followed Rachael, watching closely what she made. He already saw the glove. He knew she'd use the same tactics as Peter.

Fred was already in Daryl's face. He swung a punch but Daryl swiftly moved his face to the side, causing Fred to miss. Daryl counter-acted with his own punch, planting it right in Fred's face. Fred's speed made him swing back further then he should have. Daryl still hadn't created a weapon. He was still able to take down Fred without one.

Peter threw the first ball of fire at Sam. She already formed a huge iron shield and placed it in front of her. The ball of fire exploded into tiny flames. It was big enough to hurt anyone on full contact; however, against a shield it did nothing. Peter gritted his teeth. He knew he failed on the first attack so he began looking for a different target. Once he looked to his side it was too late. A ball of water came flying at him. It splashed him hard in the chest and forced him back over twenty feet. He hit hard on the gym floor, feeling a huge amount of pressure on his chest from the water ball. Rachael had gotten him before he even saw her.

Marshall took a shot at Rachael. He saw the opening. She wasn't fully recuperated from her attack. She was hit with a bullet, the second the bullet hit her, it exploded, forcing her back. Impact bullets the boys called them. It was a great weapon in training, helping to improve accuracy without hurting anyone...much.

Sam was running forward towards Marshall. She had her shield below her hips, readying it for an uppercut. "Sorry lady, gonna have to be quicker than that." He raised his gun and aimed at her. Shot. She lifted the shield up and blocked the incoming bullet. The force of the bullet pushed her back some but not enough to stop her movement completely. She lowered the shield and kept charging. Marshall already hoped she'd do that so he shot another bullet towards her leg. She wasn't expecting it and it made her trip forward, slamming her pretty face on the back of the shield. "It's best you stay down," he told her with a grin as he stood above her.

A mechanical hand grabbed his shirt at that moment. He looked at it, seeing it tighten the grip around his shirt. He looked at the line it started from behind the arm. It slithered all the way to Ali who had his arm changed into the new weapon. "Oh...this is gonna hurt..." The hand retracted and dragged Marshall along with it.

Nick watched as his friend was getting dragged across the gym. He was on the attack already though, no time to intervene. Fred was slowly regaining his stance but Daryl stood there waiting, as if he wanted someone to attack him. Nick was glad to oblige.

He ducked to the side of Daryl and brought his pole-arm towards the back of Daryl. Daryl moved in perfect sync with the attack. Dodging just enough to the left, grabbing the pole-arm, and flinging Nick forward. Nick tumbled over but was back on his feet. No pole-arm in hand. Daryl held his weapon.

"Not bad," Nick said.

"Almost had me. You aren't bad yourself. A little more training and you'll be something fierce for sure. Yet, you rely on weapons too much." Daryl threw the pole-arm to the side. "It's time to see how you are in a fist fight." Daryl stepped forward and swung a hard right. If Nick hadn't moved back in time he would have been knocked out.

"Whoa, okay tough guy." Nick put his fists up in fighting stance. He had never boxed in his life and Daryl seemed to be a natural. This disadvantage was huge. Nick had stamina but no experience in a fist fight. The odds were against him.

Three quick jabs towards Nick. Nick couldn't dodge any so he put his hands up in a defensive position. Even taking the jabs to the back of his arms hurt. He could feel the massive amount of strength in each punch. Daryl went for one full swing right into his right arm. Nick was feeling pain but if he dropped his arms he would have taken a hit right in the face. A big slam and Nick couldn't feel his arm anymore. The pain was so horrible it made his arm numb. He trailed backwards, letting his arm hang low. It hurt so much yet he couldn't feel most of it. He let it dangle as he thought of a new plan.

"You're a tough one. Most people wouldn't even have let me jab at them, let alone take a full swing," Daryl said smiling. "Like it kid. Got some real guts."

"Kid?" Nick ran forward. "You're not much older so shut up and-" he ducked under Daryl and drove his left fist up. It made full contact with Daryl's chin. "-let me show you guts!" he roared. The hit was perfect. Daryl grunted as his head flung in the air. It would have been a perfect knock out. Nick wasn't a left handed person, though.

Daryl tipped backwards but kept his balance. "Damn it, I was talking!"

"Never put your guard down. Come on where did they teach you to fight?" Nick held his badly injured arm. The numbness was almost gone, replaced with a sharp pain.

Daryl wiped his mouth where a little blood trickled down. "You've got some balls, I'll give ya that." He put out his hand. Nick shook it. "I'm glad to know other Exterminators out there who are strong willed."

A flaming ball of fire flew past the two boys and towards Rachael. She grabbed the balls of fire with her glove and crushed it. The fight between Nick and Daryl might have ended but Peter and Rachael were still going strong. Nick and Daryl moved out of the way as the two watched each other, waiting for another move.

This time she threw the ball towards Peter. Peter grabbed it and crushed it as well. "Seems we're tied here," she said laughing. Peter wasn't angry. For once he was having fun. As if he met someone who was on his level who can use the same skill set as him. Who actually posed a challenge to him. He had found his rival.

"Al lright kids, it's time to call it quits," the Gada announced. They obeyed without question. They all gathered up near the leaders, shaking hands, commenting on attacks, and laughing about the events that just took place. Then took a seat to rest. The sparing was something they all needed. Both teams seemed to naturally get along with each other. "I'm glad to see how far you guys are coming along. You all have a certain gift, unique to you, specifically. The way you guys flow as a team without any commands is amazing. I'm guessing you practice with each other so much it comes natural now days. I'm very proud as a Gada to see two of my units doing so well." They all cheered in response, feeling amazing about themselves. They were getting graded as powerful allies to the organization. Their first real recognition had finally come.

After the cheers and the pep talk, the kids began to separate. They found out that Daryl and his group were from New Jersey. They took transportation here from the underground only took thirty minutes. Daryl assured Nick he'd come back and hang out sometime. Their respect for each other was too great to ignore.

Fred commented on Ali's hand. The way he was able to grab Marshall and drag him around was both amazing and funny. Marshall didn't find it that funny but Fred did. Ali did as well. While Sam commented on the cheap tactics used during their fight, Marshall informed her there is no such thing as cheap tactics. There are tactics that work and ones that do not. It's up to the person to use the one tactic to win.

Peter tried to hold his excitement in but he couldn't. The way Rachael fought amazed him. He never felt any kind of feelings towards another person, especially female. He worked as

238

a team with Nick and the others. He respected Carl and Jin. Yet he couldn't help but smile at Rachael. He felt something different for her. Not envy, not respect, but something different. He wanted to see her fight more, fight against her more, as long as he was close to her. He was experiencing a strong desire and he didn't even know it. He shouldn't be able to know it as he never felt feelings like this, never even knew they existed or how to react. They were surfacing though, and he didn't really know how to deal with it. Other than smile at her and nod to everything she said.

"So do you think we can work together sometime?" she asked.

"Yes!" He was so happy he couldn't hold it in. He didn't know the feeling of embarrassment or fear of rejection. All he knew was that he felt something, happiness, and he didn't want to let go of it.

"Awesome! I'll give you my number. We can train sometime. Maybe even-" she began, her cheeks turning red. She had never asked anyone out before. She had never been asked out either. She felt her cheeks were so hot they would burn off. She couldn't stop mid-sentence though. She had to tell him how she felt. "-maybe we can go out sometime. Like a date?"

Peter was too busy in this euphoric happiness to notice how important the question was. "Yeah, that sounds fine to me!" He just wanted to be close to her. Not really to date her but to fight her. He felt her power like it was his own.

"Awesome!" she yelped. She was so excited. Peter shared her excitement, though for different reasons.

The Gada, her Protector, and the kids all left. Peter and Fred walked out together as well, saying they felt tired. Jin walked slowly out with Marshall discussing the girls. Despite both having girlfriends it didn't stop them from discussing the other females. Especially ones their girlfriends didn't know about. They were arguing over how hot Sam was.

Nick followed Carl into his office. He was rubbing his arm. The pain was greatly reduced after the fight but it still tingled. He was eager to meet up with Daryl more. He never thought of boxing as an alternative. He was so heavily invested in using his Rod that he never thought about the possibilities of using just his hands. It was better late than never to learn.

"I just wanted to talk to you for a few moments about today," Carl sat at his desk.

"That was fun as heck, I gotta say!" Nick sat down in the chair across. "I can't believe the other Exterminators' strength. Others just like us, some even stronger than us. Makes me eager to meet more in the organization."

"I'm glad today was fun." Carl smiled. He felt the boy was growing to be a fine leader. "You showed great leadership today. The way your team moved, without barely any commands, was exceptionally amazing. You moved for targets based on you seeing an opening. I should be congratulating each and every one of you for today's showcase of fighting skills. I feel you deserve the most praise, though, simply because you made those plans of strategy. You may sit here and not take the credit but you deserve every ounce of it."

Nick felt a certain pride in him. The way he set up so many plans in battle and the way his team moved today was great. All his hard work at home trying to figure out plans of attack. Ways to work with each team member. He felt that it finally all paid off. He was even able to show his Gada, the leader of them all.

"I expect to see you guys grow in ways I could of only hoped to imagine. I talked one-on-one with Fred and he seemed to be going through a lot. I look at you and I feel like I have nothing to really talk about with you. You seem happy enough, you work hard, and you show your emotions while fighting. Did you need to tell me anything?" Carl wasn't going to sugar coat questions anymore. His students might need him and he had to make sure he was clear to them that they could come to him for help.

"I think I'm okay. I also worry about Fred..." he let his voice trail off. "But I also worry about Marshall and Peter. They all make me worry 'cause as close as we all are we all live our own lives. All making either really great choices or really bad ones. We can only do so much to help lead them or help them, right?"

Carl watched as this young man spoke the truth. He nodded.

"So, I am afraid for each and every one of them. Yet they have to live their own life. If they fail or mess up I'll be there for them. Till then, though, I can't help in any other way than that," Nick gleefully said. He felt that his team would come to him if any problems occurred. Till then, he trusted them.

"You know, Nick you were born to be a leader." Carl was beyond proud. He felt Nick would be the leader he hoped to always raise.

"Now, I do have some questions about other things," Nick said.

"Shoot."

"Girl issues."

Carl picked up his baseball and threw it in the air. "This is gonna take a while, isn't it?"

"Maybe...uhh...yeah," Nick laughed.

Peter was walking side by side with Fred. They hadn't said much but he could sense something was off. Fred was outgoing and fun. Yet he kept his mouth completely shut. As if he was afraid of what he might say. Peter waited, and waited, and waited some more. Nothing. Peter looked at him the whole time then spoke up. "Are you doing all right?"

"Yeah, it's just..." Fred let his voice trail off. Only Marshall knew of his problems. He kept quiet about them, despite his temper getting worse. "You've ever seen the Hulk?"

"Like the cartoon?"

"Well, the comic, but yeah."

"I have."

"Well funny thing is..." he began looking around. No one would care what he was saying but he felt like it was a special secret. A heavy burden that he carried. "...I kind of become something like that." He waited for the laugh. Peter just looked at him.

"Huh?" was all Peter muttered after a few moments of silence.

"I become this...this thing. Like a monster of some sort. I don't change form or anything like the Hulk but I become strong. Fast. Different." Fred looked to Peter for help. Peter looked at him in disbelief.

"Are you taking drugs?"

"No, I'm not taking drugs!"

"Have you've been drinking alcohol?"

"NO!"

"You sound a bit crazy. Not to be mean or anything." Peter looked back towards the road. He liked Fred as a person he could depend on in battle. Fred also was very easy to talk to about problems. Yet, now he sounded too crazy for Peter to even take him seriously.

"Dude, listen. I become some crazy beast!" Fred was getting angry. Peter ignored him, focusing on something else. "Hey, listen to me!" Fred grabbed his friend and threw him against the wall of a local bakery. "I'm telling you what's happening to me and you ignore me!? Why!?" Spit flew from his mouth. Peter watched, not sure how to react. He wasn't scared but he was curious of the change. He could see the anger in his eyes. He could see a slight change in color as well. He peered deep into Fred's eyes, to see a tiny hint of red in the center of them.

"Your...your eyes," Peter muttered. Fred let go of his friend and backed off. "What happened to your eyes?" Peter asked. Fred stepped back. "I saw something in them. Is that what you were just talking about?"

"Just forget what I said." Fred waved his hand, covering his face with his free hand. He began to back away. "Just forget it." He began to break out in a jog.

"Wait! Don't run!" But it was too late. Fred was already half way down the block, covering his entire face from the world. Peter stood there, not sure how to react. He never felt this way before either. Anger. Excitement. Happiness. He experienced all of those now multiple times. Yet this was something new. He was feeling worried. Worried about his friend.

Chapter 24 – Secrets

Nick picked up his phone. It was a text from Kelly. *"Hey, cutie. When you coming over?"* Nick smiled. It had been less than a day since they'd been together. Each day they've spent together, the harder it was to be separated from one another.

"I'll be there in less than an hour."

"Okay, hurry! I can't wait to see you. I got a surprise for you ;)"

Nick jumped off his bed. He didn't need to be told twice. He quickly snatched some clothes up and threw them on. He grabbed his beeper and Rod just in case and ran down the steps. His smile was bigger than it should have been, but he didn't really care. His mind was focused on the surprise he was about to get in a few minutes.

"Hey Nick, come here for a second." Nick had his handle on the door. He turned to his father.

"Yeah pops?"

"Come in here."

"I got to go. It's..."

"I said come here now, this is important." Nick lowered his head, said a curse under his breath, and walked towards his father.

"Yeah pops, what's up?"

His father looked at his son while drinking his morning coffee. "How's classes going?" He asked between sips. Nick knew it was coming. It was almost March and school was ending in a few months. Meaning report cards were coming in soon. Which usually meant Nick was in some deep trouble.

"I think I'm doing okay," Nick lied. His grades were barely passing. He knew he wouldn't have good grades in any of his classes but he didn't need his father to know that. Not yet.

His father put his mug down. "You're a terrible liar. I got a call from your math teacher. They said if you don't put in more effort they might fail you. This is your senior year. Do you really want to be left back?" His father wasn't angry. He was disappointed more than anything.

"No pops, I won't fail. I promise I'll get my grades up before the year ends." Nick sounded sincere enough. For a moment or two he actually thought that it was possible, as well. The amount of training him and his team did though made it almost impossible. With the amount of missions given to them, it was getting to the point that to do anything extra you'd have to have almost no sleep. The only free time he got he spent with Kelly. He found her far more important than math or science. His father didn't see it that way.

"Please, I don't want you left back. This is important. I know you think high school isn't important. I've been honest with you most of your life."

"Most?"

"Well, that one time with the hamster..."

"Lucky!?

"Anyway, back to the point. High school is just a small part of the very big scheme in life. It's still very important to get through it. Graduating makes your life a lot less stressful in the long run. Trust me on that." His father was a smart guy. He built his construction business from the ground up. He also never graduated high school. He never even stepped foot in a college. He worked hard to get where he was and he didn't want his son to have to go through the same struggle.

"I got it dad. I promise, I'll try harder." Nick began to walk backwards. "I really got to go."

"Put too much time in with the girl, not enough on the future. Just remember you can't be there for her working at a hamburger shop the rest of your life."

"I understand pops and that won't happen." He opened the door. "I'm going to start working in the summer, after I graduate. You'll see. I'll be home a little later." Nick waved and shut the door. His father rubbed his eyes, feeling weary. All he did was care for his boy. It was only natural to care about your own son's future more so, than for Nick to care about it.

Marshall entered the park. He hit the button on his beeper and went into the other realm. He was told by Carl to meet him at the park, but to jump realms first. It was for a meeting of some sort, a one on one, t talk about issues and get to know each other. Marshall wasn't the biggest fan of talking things out but he didn't mind Carl. He figured he could ask more questions, solve more issues he had on his mind, as of late.

As he walked deeper into the park he imagined how much his life had change. He didn't hang out with anyone at school anymore. Mostly stayed around Fred or Nick. Even sometimes Peter. Though mostly he just talked and Peter sat there. He kept his same terrible grades, dealt with his same annoying brother, and everything else felt the same from last year. What changed in his life was Lucy. Lucy changed a lot for him.

He loved the way she smiled. The way she grabbed his hand. The way she laid her head on him. Even the way she put him in his place. She wasn't afraid to speak her mind. Marshall loved that about her. He'd always be the one to be the most outspoken in a group. He was never afraid to tell them his side of things, no matter the situation. With Lucy, he felt as if it was an even playing field. That she had just as much as opinion on subjects as he did. She wasn't afraid to speak her mind and neither was he.

They also had the secret.

The secret that sometimes haunts him. He could feel a terrible tug at his gut, feeling as if he wasn't supposed to ever tell her. Yet, he had, and he wasn't sure why. He had people in his circle of friends to speak to. He had Carl, as a mentor, in case he needed to let his problems out. Yet, he broke one of the biggest rules and told Lucy the secret. Now, he had the fear in the back of his mind that someone would find out.

He spotted a huge silver beast. He went for his Rod but saw Carl standing next to it. The Unknown was Silver, the pet

246

wolf that Carl had. He must have sensed Marshall because he stood up and turned towards him. "Hey, big fluffy," Marshall called from a few yards away. Silver ran up to him, then once close enough, licked his face. "Ugh, your breath dude!" he yelled, laughing. He pushed the big silver wolf out of the way.

"He missed you," Carl said walking up to him. Silver gave another lick on the side of Marshall's face.

"I missed him too. Big dumb boy," he chuckled and patted the big wolf down, brushing his shaggy fur. He remembered going into a brawl with the beast, Silver easily dispatched all four boys and still stood even when they gave it all they had. Such amazing strength from such a beautiful creature. Marshall loved how kind Silver was to them, but he had no doubt in his mind that Silver could easily kill them if he was ordered to. Which he might be commanded to if they found out Lucy knew their secret. Dark thoughts and what ifs surrounded Marshall's mind.

"So, I figured we could walk around some with Silver. Talk about any issues you were having." Carl looked at Marshall who kept patting Silver. The wildest one of the batch of kids, yet one of the most reliable. Not so much because he would follow commands. If anything he'd disobey them on purpose to prove he could. No, it was because of his kind nature. Something he hid from so many people. A joker amongst the crowd, a loyal friend behind the scenes.

"Yeah, that sounds good to me." Marshall began to walk away from Silver. Silver trailed behind them as they both traveled deeper into the park. Marshall watched the kids playing in the small water park. Jumping into the water sprayers then back out, yelling and screaming, so carefree. "How's the work load going? You've seemed a bit less stressed lately."

Carl laughed. "It never gets easier. You just have to work with it, get better at it, and then it'll get better."

"Sometimes I wonder what would of happened if I never picked that letter up." Marshall glanced one last time at the kids playing in the water. He wanted to be like them for just a moment. Not have a care in the world.

"You can keep wondering that or accept that it was fate."

"Don't believe in fate. We all have choices. I made mine." Marshall looked back towards Carl. "Why didn't you become a Protector instead of a Bora?"

"I wanted to help others." Carl thought about becoming a Protector at one point. Sent out on high signal missions, hunt and kill, it was something he was very good at. He felt the obligation in his mind to help others, though. To raise others to the best of their abilities.

"You haven't been helping us though. We basically built ourselves up to this point." Marshall never held anything back. Carl admired that in a lot of ways.

"I know. I've failed to train you so far. I've been dealing with-" he didn't want anyone to know about his drinking problems. He'd kept it at bay for weeks now. Bringing it up wouldn't help anyone so he kept quiet. "-issues. However, I'm here now and I will be helping. Especially with training as soon as I can. I have to handle a few more cases but I'll start training in terms of fighting with all of you soon enough. I'm evaluating everyone's mind right now. Getting to know you guys is the first step in my training process."

Marshall paused a moment before speaking. "I don't mean to be rude or anything. I'm just stating you should of started sooner. Still better late than never."

"Is there anything bothering you?"

"No." Marshall said shortly.

"Nothing? No issues with teammates, people in the organization? How about any issues outside of your job?"

Marshall thought about it for a moment. "Do you believe people could change?"

"I do."

"I don't."

"Why's that?"

Marshall laughed. "People don't change. They adapt to situations, sure, but they don't change."

"People change all the time. Sometimes people have to

change in order to survive." Carl pointed out the boys. "Without you guys changing, becoming stronger, you'd never been able to survive for so long against the Unknowns."

Marshall shook his head. "We changed our physical bodies. We were able to become faster, stronger, maybe even smarter. Sure. We didn't change us, though. We became what we were meant to become."

"Oh, now who's the one bringing up fate?" Carl asked, grinning.

"No. What I mean is the person we are didn't change. We adapted. We're always had the ability to do what we do every day now. The difference is we adapted and changed our bodies to physically be able to complement our fighting style. The fighting style is made up of the person who is using it. You can follow someone to a "T" while training but in the end you'll always have a slightly different fighting style. Even almost identical fighting style is still "almost" and not completely. 'Cause we are who we are, a person. We are individually different. So I believe we don't change, we change things around us We are who we are, it's impossible to change."

Carl watched his student. He never thought much of Marshall's intelligence. He was always the loud mouth, funny guy. Inside though, it was obvious Marshall thought a lot about social issues and things no one else cared to discuss because they were afraid to speak up about it. Marshall wasn't. "Fair enough. I will take that into consideration."

"I mean the reason I'm stating this is 'cause I think I'm changing sometimes." Marshall studied his hands, as if there was something on them. Something only visible to himself.

"Changing for the better?"

"Changing at all should be impossible. I shouldn't be changing my emotions to something I'm not used to."

"Who's the girl?"

"Girl?" Marshall asked surprised. He never mentioned Lucy to anyone really. He kept his relationship on the down low except for his friends.

"Only a girl can make you feel this way. Especially at your age. Who's the girl who's changing the loud mouth Marshall to the sensitive, thought-provoking kid standing in front of me?" It was Carl's turn to laugh now.

"She's amazing," Marshall said with a distant look. It was always the first thought that popped in his head when he thought of her. "I think she's changing me. I feel different when I'm around her. I feel different just being near her. Like I can achieve more, I can be more. Yet, my beliefs make me believe opposite. So what's the real answer? Em I really changing? Or is this me adapting to who I really em when I'm in this type of situation."

Carl expected to talk about a number of subjects with Marshall today. He knew his student wasn't shy of asking questions. This wasn't one of the questions he foresaw coming. "It's called love." Marshall tried to wave it off. "Yeah, something like this has to be love. You don't feel the change in you unless it's that. You feel obligated to do better for yourself, because you want to do better for her. Right?"

It was as if Carl was reading his mind. He never talked to his parents about this type of thing so this was the closest he was going to get to speaking with someone. An adult. Someone he trusted. "I...I think I love her. I just can't tell her I love her."

"Why not?"

"Because..."

"Because of what?"

"Because what if she doesn't say it back?" Marshall looked up at Carl. Carl nodded.

"The biggest fear in the world. Rejection."

"I don't fear rejection. I fear resentment."

"Why would she resent you?"

"What if I say I love you, she doesn't back. Then she thinks this whole time I was over my head. That I cared too much. What if she never wants to speak to me again? What if she runs away from me? What if..." Marshall would have kept going but Carl put his hand up.

"Stop with the "what ifs" and focus on the now.

Remember? We got this one chance to try things. You'll never know unless you tell her."

"But what if..."

"What did I just say?" Carl asked firmly. Marshall wanted to say more but kept it in. He didn't want to hear that, something he already knew, but he knew that was the only real answer. To try. It wasn't resentment or rejection that scared him. It was the fear of trying and failing.

"I just want to know what to do if I mess up. What can I do to fix it?"

"Sometimes Marshall, questions just can't be answered."

Now Marshall laughed. "That means you haven't asked the right person the question yet." He winked and fell back to Silver. He patted the giant wolf on the neck and the beast returned the favor by licking his face. "Sometimes I wonder what would have happened if I didn't pick up the letter." He looked into Silver's eyes and patted his fur some more. "Now, I don't really care what would have happened. I wouldn't change this for the world." He walked forward and met Carl's gaze. "So old man, what can you tell me about this organization?"

"Things that will turn your head right around."

"Well then, let's get started," Marshall said grinning. Carl couldn't help but grin back.

Fred stood in total darkness. No white room. No voice overhead. Nothing but darkness. He felt alone, trapped, and terrified. The once safe haven area in his mind was shattered. He was the one who broke it, now he wanted nothing more but to repair it.

"Other self, are you here?" he called just loud enough for an echo. Nothing. Again the darkness answered with silence.

He walked forward. He wasn't sure where he was going but he wanted to meet some type of end. He knew he was getting worse, that he was losing himself to something. What was he losing it to though? He couldn't figure that out. They told him the wolf hybrid could not transform him into a beast. Yet, that's exactly what was happening. He was changing into something different, and he had no clue how to stop it.

As he kept walking forward he wondered what he'd do. Who can help him now that the situation was getting worse? Peter thought nothing but terrible things about him now, he figured. Even in the last few weeks in training Peter kept his distance. He kept his eye on Fred, as if he was watching for any slips. It infuriated Fred but he kept his anger down. He couldn't get too upset, otherwise his other self would break though.

"I told you not to break the walls."

The voice boomed loudly and Fred jumped back. He hadn't heard the voice in so long. It sounded distorted. He was just glad to hear the voice again at all. "Other self! You're still alive! I've been wanting to speak with you!" He was so happy he kept yelling. It was as if hope came back into his heart again.

"Why did you break the walls of salvation?" it asked sadly. Fred could even hear the voice breaking down as it asked.

"I broke it 'cause I had to save my friend."

"You broke the one thing that protects you. You unleashed something far worse. And for what? A boy? His fate did not matter." The voice sounded upset now. A slight hint of agitation tossed into it now.

"His fate matter to me." Fred placed his hand on his chest. "That was my duty at the time. To protect a friend. To protect my teammate. I had no other choice."

"You always have a choice."

"Not then, no I didn't. I had to do what had to be done."

"In order to save one you might have killed many. Are you sure it had to be done now?"

"I'll never kill."

"What if that wasn't your choice?" the voice inquired, waiting patiently for Fred to reply. Fred wasn't sure how to. He wasn't sure if he even wanted to at this point. He felt like he was losing the war with his body and needed answers. He didn't want to argue over actions that were in the past.

"Listen, I don't care about that. I'm changing into

252

something different. I need to know why this is happening to me."

"We make choices in life. Those choices will always affect us; what's more curious is how they will affect the ones around us."

"Okay, other self, you're pissing me off again. We go through this every time. Just give me a straight answer. What in the blue hell is happening to me!?" he roared. Anger began filling the whole dark space. The voice didn't return. There was only silence. Seconds flew by. A minute went by. Minutes began to pass. Fred put his face into his hands and began to cry. A cry he had held in for weeks now. He couldn't help it. The feeling of something changing inside him and he had no clue what it was, scared the heck out of him. He wondered if he would change completely one day. He wondered if he'd even live another day at this rate. Something was changing and it was happening quicker than he expected. He wasn't sure what to do.

He lifted his face out of his hands and he was back in his living room. He fell asleep on the couch again. His whole body dripping with sweat. He could feel his heart pounding, as if he was just jogging around the block for hours. "What...is...happening..." he muttered before covering his face once more.

Peter opened the door to his home only to be met by a screaming match. His father was yelling at his mother. Peter wasn't sure how to deal with the situation. He felt like the best option was to move back to where he came from. He didn't want to get involve with the parents fighting. He slowly closed the door back when he heard a crash. He swung the door back open and slammed it closed behind him. He could hear his mom weeping from the other side of the apartment.

His father said something inaudible and stumbled into the hallway. "Go help your mom. Dumb idiot slipped," he slurred drunkenly as he pushed his son out of the way.

Peter ignored him and ran into the living room. He could see his mom on the floor holding her hand, trembling. He could see the deep cut on her hand, blood dripping from her wound. She looked up at her son with blood shot eyes. She was crying for a long time. His father just decided to shut her up quickly by flinging something at her. He saw two broken pots beside her.

Peter turned around towards his father. "Get out of this house." Peter walked forward. His father waved him away, fumbling with his jacket. He was trying to get it on to leave the apartment. Peter walked up to his father. He could smell the terrible breath. "I said, get out of this house." Peter now pointed towards the door. His father looked at him, shocked.

"What did you say you little sh-" Peter didn't even know he had struck him. He let his right fist go and it struck his own father on the top of his head. His father wasn't bracing for it, didn't expect it, so he went down hard. His father laid on the ground for a second, dumbfounded that his own kid just nearly knocked him out.

Peter walked away from the drunk on the floor and towards his sister's room. He opened the door to look inside. He saw his sister under the covers, peering out over them to the doorway. "Hey, you okay?"

She nodded to him quickly.

"Don't worry. Just doing some clean up out here," he said softly. He knew he had to keep his little sister calm. She didn't need to know the whole situation. "I'll tell you when to come out. Don't want to dirty the house." She nodded in agreement. He shut the door and looked back at the hallway. His father was stumbling back to his feet all the while cursing violently under his breath.

"I think it's time you left my house," Peter told his father. He had no emotion in his voice. It wasn't a threat, it was a fact. Peter felt it was time for this drunken fool, who he once called a father, to leave for good. His father, however, had a different plan.

He came charging at Peter. Peter so badly wanted to summon his glove but instead took a side step. He laid his foot out and his father went flying over it. He tripped and smacked his chin hard against the kitchen counter. As his father laid on the floor screaming, holding his chin, Peter went for the house phone. He snatched it up and gave it to his mother. "Call the police," he told her urgently. That's when he felt his father grab him and throw him into the table.

Peter slid across the table and fell on the other side. It was a loud crash but the pain wasn't anything terrible. Peter had felt a lot worse in the last months. He began to regain his stance when his father flipped the table, launching it at his own son. Peter covered his face just in time as the table fell on him.

"You little bastard! You think you can do whatever you want. I don't think so, you piece of crap. Come on get up!" his father screamed. Peter slowly pushed the table off of him. He was getting angrier. He could feel his hatred towards his father building up like a volcano ready to erupt. He could feel his blood pumping. He didn't want to fight. Yet he was itching for a fight with this drunken fool. He flung the table to the side, dishes crashing all over.

Peter rushed his father, pushing him back. Despite Peter's increase in strength and stamina it was hard to fight a drunk still. Especially one that towered over him with at least hundred pounds on him and had years of getting beaten in bars. His father grabbed him by the hair. Peter let out a short yell before his father punched him in the gut. A strong right slam into the upper part of his stomach. Peter spit all over his father's shirt. "You think you can hurt me!? You little piece of waste!" His father slammed him against the counter. Peter felt his side burning as he fell to the ground.

If only he could summon his gloves. He could end this right now. His father wouldn't even stand a chance. He could throw a single fire ball in his dad's face and end his pitiful excuse of a life. He could do it with such ease. No one would even know. No one would even care. It would be the simplest thing in the world to do.

He couldn't do it, even if he wanted. As he laid there on the ground holding his side he still couldn't break the rules. He then felt another punch to the back of head. He let his whole body lay against the cold floor. He could feel himself going in and out.

Black, then the living room. Black, then his father kicking him again in the side. Black, and then his mother screaming for help. He soon slipped into unconsciousness.

Nick sat on the bedside. Kelly slid into her pajamas as he set an alarm clock. They went to school together so they began stay over each other's houses. They were planning on moving in with each other so their parents understood. To a point. They made sure to be very quiet at night. Not making too much sound. The rules of living with parents.

He put the covers over himself and watched as she put cream on her legs. "I put in an application to work at a local game store," he said reading a text from his phone.

She looked up at him. "That's great, hun. I hope they call back."

"Yeah, I figured it be a good place to start my work life. I mean a serious one and not one working under my pops."

"You worked for your dad?"

"Yeah," he began. He put his cell phone down. "I worked on my days off from school. Dad gave me a decent cut and I'd help with the construction of building whatever project they had. It was pretty fun. Least when I was hanging with the guys. My dad made me do double the work for half the pay. He wasn't the easiest to work with."

She placed the bottle of cream on the counter and slipped into bed next to him. "It's just tough love. You know he cared."

"I know. It was a good workout regardless." Nick flexed his muscle. Without a shirt on it was easy to see how much the training helped. His entire body was curved, true definition of a full body work out. His arms were bigger than any kid his age should have been. His chest and abs outlined almost too perfect. He felt amazing.

"You know there are some perks to letting you work out so much after school."

"Yeah, I knew you wanted me for this body," he said,

laughing and winking at her.

She outlined his body with her hand. He watched as she followed his entire chest up to his face. She placed her hand on his cheeks. "I love the person you are though more than any workout can give. I want you."

This was the reason he loved being with her. She wanted him and nothing more. She never asked for anything he couldn't provide. So he kept close to her. Making sure she was always happy.

"I love you so much."

"I know," she said cheerfully.

"Hey!"

"I love you too, babe." Her smile was so big it made him smile again.

"Is it weird, when I think of my future and I can only see it with you there?" he asked thoughtfully. He wasn't sure how to approach a situation such as this. Always wondering how she would react. Yet, he felt safe enough around her now to ask plainly.

"I think the same. Every move I make in my mind, you're there." She leaned over to him, placing her head on his chest. "I think of where I'll live, where I'll work, what college I'll go too. It makes me worry about the future. Then I think of you. It all seems okay then. Like there's nothing we can't do together." She used one finger to outline the tip of his chest down to his stomach.

"I don't ever want to be without you." He held her head. He began brushing his fingers through her hair. He could feel how soft it was. "Will you stay with me no matter how bad things get?"

"What's going to get bad?"

"I'm just saying in the future. No matter the struggle, we'll fight through it. Figure out a solution to all our problems. Not just give up so easy." His voice sounded strain. The horrible outcomes have been floating around his mind but he tried his best to push them away.

"I'll never give up on you..." she let the words linger in the air. They sat there in silence for a few minutes longer. "Never."

Jin came into Carl's office. It was late, way past midnight. As far as Carl knew Jin didn't have any missions on-going. He wondered why the young man needed to speak to him so late. He told him to sit and began drinking another cup of coffee. Coffee was the first thing he replaced his drinking with. It wasn't the best substitute but it was a substitute none the less.

"Is everything okay, Jin?"

"Yeah, just doing a follow-up." Jin sat down. He looked tired. Worn out from all the things going on in his life as of late. He couldn't cover it up very well.

"You look exhausted. Are you sure you're doing okay? I told you not to overexert yourself." Carl placed his mug down and walked around the desk. He placed his hand on Jin. "Speak to me. What's wrong?"

Jin didn't want to go over his personal issues. He knew Carl cared, though. So he let a little of it slip in the conversation. "Emily, it's been rough."

"Is everyone having girl problems as of late?" Carl laughed. "First Nick, then Marshall, and now you? I'm so glad I'm not dating at the moment."

"It's just that we don't see each other much. I've been so busy with training, missions, helping the kids..." he began but Carl stopped him.

"I told you to leave the kids to me. I started the one-on-one training. I'll help them out from now on. Please, do not overburden yourself with even more than you already have on your plate."

"I know, but I feel some sort of obligation," Jin said sitting back in his seat. "These kids...they feel like my friends now. I can't just walk away. I want to see them get better."

"You can, but worry about your personal problems first. Emily is a great person. Don't let her slip away from you." He waited as Jin thought about the issue at hand. He agreed with Carl, even if he wouldn't admit it straight out.

"I know. It's just...I don't know, just problems." Jin waved his hand. "Let's get back to the subject at hand. I've been trying to keep tabs on Peter."

This intrigued Carl. He was worried about his student. "Anything? Is it family problems? Bullies at school?"

"I haven't seen him in any fights at school. Nor did I see him come in with any new scars and bruises on his face. Either it was a one-time thing or he's the best cover up kid I've ever seen."

"So nothing then?"

"Something is odd, though."

"Well, let me hear it. So far, all I'm hearing is we're back at square one. Nothing has changed." He sat back in his chair looking at the ceiling. He never wanted to see his unit suffer. Yet, if he didn't know the problems, how could he fix them?

"Peter has problems relating to regular humans."

"I read the reports. Sociopath tendencies. I know all about them."

"And yet, he's been showing emotions as of late."

"I've noticed that, too. I figured it's the difference of human interaction. He'd never been with a group of people as much as now. He's experiencing emotions based off the fact of being outside his norm. It's only natural emotions would spark up," Carl finished. He grabbed his baseball and threw it into the air.

"I understand that, sir. Saying that, he keeps his anger in check. We don't know when he's angry or upset. When he's happy or faking it. It's odd we can't pick that up yet, and we've known him for like half a year." Jin was trying desperately to plead his case. Everything he said, though, was already on Carl's mind and answered too.

"I can sense when he shows true emotions. When he is Peter and not just following other peoples' ways of interaction. Maybe not all the time but I can sense a good portion of it." Carl flung the ball as high as the ceiling went. As it fell he looked towards Jin. "He'll come around to us, don't worry." He caught the ball without looking.

That's when a huge thud hit the door. Jin jumped out of his chair and turned towards the door. Carl dropped the ball and went towards the door placing his hand on it. "You have your Rods on you?"

"Got my gloves already on." Jin put his hands in front of him.

Carl nodded and held his hand on his hip near his Rod. It had been weeks now since he'd had to use his weapon for fighting. He felt his heart thumping hard in his chest. He hadn't been in danger in so long he almost forgot the feeling. The feeling of being alive again.

He slid his hand in a downward motion, the door swung open. Carl was ready to strike but froze in his steps.

Blood dripped down from Peter's forehead. His face was badly banged up and looked to beaten to a pulp. He held on for dear life on the hallway wall. He looked up at both Jin and Carl, who were in complete and utter shock.

"I have a secret..." he gasped through his bloody teeth. He stepped forward, tripping, and falling straight to the ground.

Carl moved quickly and snatched him midair before he could fall on his face. He held him in his arms and turned him over quickly. He could see his student was badly beaten, nearly to the point of death. He could see his nose was badly bashed in, where most of the blood on his face was coming from. There was also a bad gash on his forehead from a boot of some sort. The teeth were filled with blood. A solid punch to the mouth would do that.

Peter looked up at his mentor, seeing only a bright light shining on him. He wasn't sure how he made it here. He heard his father slam the door in his house as he awoke. He felt far worse than he could have ever imagined. He'd never been beaten this bad in a fight, let alone by his own abusive, drunken father. He heard the police sirens and moved quickly. He knew if they found him they would ask him a hundred questions on what happen. He couldn't let that happen. He wanted no one to know about his personal life. Especially his Exterminator co-fighters.

So he stumbled his way out of his apartment. He saw his sister watching, scared, as he made his way out. He had to get to the Station. He had to make sure they kept their attention on something important. A diversion.

Jin took off his shirt and bent down. He tried wiping away some of the blood on his face. Peter tried to focus. He needed to tell them before it was too late.

"Get some healers. We have to get him patched up quickly before there is any permanent damage. Go!" Carl ordered. Jin got up, about to leave the room.

"Wait-" Peter used whatever little strength he had left to yell. Jin turned around looking at the injured boy. Carl waited as well, scared and nervous for his recruit. "-there's danger..."

"Who did this to you?" Carl demanded.

"Fred..." Peter said before gulping. Carl looked at Jin. Jin stared back in shock. They didn't expect to hear that.

"Fred did this?" Jin asked, confused.

"No," Peter closed his eyes and bit his lip. He had to tell them. "Fred is becoming something. He's becoming an Unknown. I saw it...stop him." Peter let the shining light take over. He closed his eyes. He could feel them watching him as he drifted off. He just hoped the warning was enough to have their attention turn towards it. Not towards his personal problems at home. His last emotion before drifting off was guilt. He betrayed his friend's trust. He had never betrayed someone before. He never had a friend before to betray. He wasn't too sure he'd have a friend after that. He slipped away into total darkness.

Chapter 25 – Run

Nick walked with Kelly to school. It was Friday, the day before the weekend. He was so excited to have the next two days off. He wanted to train tomorrow and then take Sunday off to go into the city with Kelly. He had the perfect plan on Sunday to take her out to dinner. She didn't have a clue. Which made it that much more exciting.

"It's such a beautiful day out," she commented, looking at the trees. She put her hand in the air and let the cold breeze surround her. It was getting warmer but sweaters were still needed. The weather felt amazing today. The sun was shining brightly on them. Not a cloud in sight. The wind was a bit chilly but not consistent. It was the perfect day to take a long walk.

He watched her. He loved just looking at her, happy. He kept thinking about when they moved in together next year. He tried calculating how much money he'd need for an apartment. The prices were outrageous here. Even for a good job. He was thinking of moving. Then he wondered how that would interfere with his Exterminator job. He had a lot to discuss with Carl. For now though, he watched her smile and felt everything was just right.

They reached the school. Kids crowded around the front screaming at each other to be heard. It was getting close to the end and everyone was on edge. They wanted to move on with their life. The seniors were now deciding what college to go to or what job to get. It was a rush of excitement and being scared that filled the entire front of the school.

Nick grabbed Kelly's hand and they pushed their way through. He held her hand tight while shoving his way through the huge crowd. He politely tried to ask people to move. Most people didn't even hear him, to into their own conversations. So, he took it upon himself to move them by shoving them just slightly. He kept a low profile at school just because he wanted to get by in it. With his grades he didn't know if he'd be able to. He figured maybe taking a short break on training to catch up. He didn't want to repeat his senior year.

They finally got through the front and into the school. "People are crazy," Nick said walking forward. She trailed right behind him.

"They're just excited about graduating. Aren't you?"

"Yeah, if I graduate."

"I told you to come over and we'll finish up the homework you missed. Together." She strained the word together. He seemed to want to fight her whenever it came to the school situation. She was a serious student, after all.

"I know. I've just been busy."

"Yeah, I know, the gym."

"And fighting crazy monsters on the verge of invading our world and killing us all." He laughed. "Yeah the gym but also other stuff. I also got my dad breathing down my neck about school. So, don't worry, I'll get on it."

"You better. Otherwise I'm going to find the first college guy who says my pens are nice and take him on a date," she winked at him giggling.

"No matter what-" he said turning around and looking at her very seriously. "-he could never judge a pen the way I can. I am the pen master."

She laughed and pushed him away. "You're so weird!" She laughed more.

"Ah, but you're dating the weirdo. So, what's that make you?"

"Oh, whatever!"

"I'm just saying, baby. It takes a weirdo to love a weirdo."

"Yeah, I'm starting to see that." She walked ahead of him smiling. He trailed behind her, smiling back.

"Got a cute butt by the way."

"Stop looking at my butt." She covered her bottom with both hands.

"Butt's so big, I can see it even now." She shrieked and slapped him on the shoulder.

"Don't talk to me. Ever!" She walked away quickly.

He ran behind her. "Hey, let me finish! I was gonna say I like big butts and I cannot lie!" he laughed. They ran all the way to class.

Back in the darkness, Fred felt alone once again. He hadn't shown up for training in over a week. Claiming he had a stomach virus. It was better that way. He felt terrible, his body aching every single day. He hated how weak he had become. Especially after all the training he went through. He was feeling great. Yet now, ever since he broke down the wall, he felt terrible.

The wall.

He still wasn't sure what the wall was. He broke it down to save Marshall. Weeks later he still had no idea what it did. He remembers flashes of when he changed. Breaking down the wall let out another side of him. He felt like himself, yet, it felt as if something else was inside him. How can there be another person inside one body? He was Fred. There is only one Fred.

Then what the hell saved Marshall?

He felt alone. Scared. Weak. He tried to call Marshall but he was usually busy with Lucy. He wanted to go to Nick, his leader, but he was always busy with Kelly. He tried talking to Peter but was blown off the last time. He couldn't go back to him, especially since he ran away from him last time.

So the black room was where he ended up.

That's where he was now. This is where he spends his alone time. Every time he shuts his eyes he awakens in it. The room filled with nothing but black walls, black skies, black everything. It was a morbid feeling. Something he was disgusted by, even though at times, it felt like a home. The other home he resided in whenever he fell into a deep sleep.

"Other self I know you're here. I know you've warned me. I messed up. I broke the walls. Now I'm changing and I need help.

Is there anything you can tell me?" he asked the nothingness. The voice usually returned after a short while so he sat. He sat wondering how little hope he had left. He was only seventeen. Almost eighteen. Yet, he was on the verge of losing himself. The scariest thought was he wouldn't see his twenties. He pushed those thoughts away as much as possible.

He thought about his past. What mistakes he had made that got him to this point. Why did he go out that night? Why didn't he just ignore the rock? What made him so determined to find out if these monsters were real? He couldn't find a justifiable answer. Which made him feel even worse about himself.

He hated the fact he felt alone. The dark room made it worse. Almost as if it was saying "this is now your future" and he had to deal with that. He had to deal with the pain that grew in his chest every time he opened his eyes again. He wondered when that pain would subside...forever.

"Just rest..." The voice was soft. Fred could barely hear it as he stood back up.

"I can't rest though. If I rest, I end up here."

"Things are only going to get worse."

"I know! Tell me how to fix that!" he screamed in frustration. He could feel fear biting on the back of his neck.

"You cannot. Only accept fate. Run. Do not let them catch you!"

"Catch me!?"

"Do not let them have their way. You are you. Run! Run till you can't run anymore!" The voice gave a huge booming effect. Almost as if it was its final hurrah. The room soon went perfectly silent again. Fred was once again lost in the darkness only this time not waking up right away.

Marshall was sitting at the table trying to open the milk. He flipped the tip but the top still wouldn't open in a perfect triangle. He tried to rip it open but that only made part of the cardboard fall into the milk. "Goddamn! You'd think after years of advancement

265

in technology they'd make it easier to open milk cartons!"

Lucy was sitting across the table. She got a good laugh out of her struggling boyfriend. "Really? The mighty Exterminator Marshall defeated by milk!" she said in a funny cartoony voice. She laughed even harder. He just looked at her, annoyed.

"Ya know what? Why don't you hush up and help me." He slammed the carton of milk down. "I can't deal with this stuff. You're a woman after-all. You guys do well with this type of kitchen stuff."

She stopped laughing and snatched the milk. "First off, this isn't kitchen stuff. It's opening a carton of milk. A monkey can do that. Next, if you ever gender identify me I'll leave your ass at school." He grinned. Despite her joking he could sense some seriousness in her voice. She slammed the open milk carton down, some of it spilling on him.

"Geez lady, just a joke," he waved his hand in a funny fashion. "No need to get all bent out of shape."

"Just shut up and drink."

Nick sat down near Lucy. He was confused and worried and it must have showed because Marshall looked at him. "Yo dawg, you okay?"

"Yeah, fine. Hi Lucy." She smiled back in acknowledgment. "Hey Marshall, can I talk to you in private?"

"Uhh I'm drinking here," he took a sip of his milk. "Just tell me what's up."

"It's about stuff..." Nick looked at Lucy. "Sorry, no offense Lucy, just man stuff. I'm sure you don't want to hear it."

Marshall gave her a quick look. As if to say "it's Exterminator business". She nodded to him and worked her way out of the table. "I'll go take a trip to the ladies room. You boys try not to get too...rowdy."

"We will try baby. No promises though!" Marshall yelled loudly as she walked away. He turned back to Nick who still looked worried. "All right man, what's wrong? You look like you're about to throw up."

"It's Peter. He wasn't in class today."

"This is what's getting you sick? Come on man." Marshall rolled his eyes and began drinking more of his milk.

"Have you ever seen Peter miss a class?" Marshall looked at him now, thinking about it. "Like ever?" Now Marshall felt a bit weary.

"Now that you mention it...Fred isn't here either."

"Are you serious?"

"No, I'm joking."

"Dude!"

"Yes, I'm serious!" Marshall looked around the lunch room, as if to look for anyone listening in on them. "Do you think a mission went bad?"

"I didn't get a text message or anything. I'd figure Carl would have called us if something bad went down." Nick could feel his head spinning. He was thinking of every possibility. He worried both were hurt, or even worse. This was the exact situation that he didn't want to be put into. As a self-entitled leader he felt the pressure none the less.

"Alright let's just chill. I'm sure both are fine. Just a weird coincidence they are absent." Marshall said trying to sound confident. Nick knew he was trying to keep calm cause the situation wasn't normal. It wasn't normal for both boys to be absent on the same day. Especially Peter, who almost never missed a class. It was just too important.

"I say we go to the Station after school."

"I say we go right now," Marshall said determinedly while getting up. "Screw school. We need to check up on our unit."

Nick knew he couldn't leave. He was already struggling with grades. If he left now it would end badly. He needed so desperately to catch up on grades, otherwise he might have to repeat his senior year. That was the last thing he wanted to do. "I don't know if I can leave."

"Hey man, our friends are in trouble. We can't just sit here and wait till this crap gets out." Marshall was waiting for his friend to get up. To just march out of the school and rescue their friends, if they needed it.

Nick was about to argue. He could feel the need to finish school. Yet he had a small flashback of Fred in danger. The way his face was in horror as he was being bitten. He could remember the feeling of failure as he almost watched his new friend dying. Now he had a choice to check up or hope for the best. He wasn't about to sit this one out.

"Let's go."

Both the boys headed towards the doors and began making their way towards the Station to check up on their unit.

A knock came from the front door. Fred jumped to life. He was in the deep, dark room he had been living in the last few hours. He could feel his mind slipping more and more into it, losing touch with reality. His heart was pounding so hard it felt as if it was about to break through his chest. He was sweating like a mad man. He wiped his head and shifted his feet off the couch. He leaned forward, taking long, deep breaths.

He heard another knock. Then there was a call at the door. It sounded like Carl. His heart began to speed up. *"It's fine. He's coming to check up on you. Just get up and answer the door. Stop acting like a freak,"* he thought as he lifted himself off the couch. He could feel every ache in his body spring to life once he was fully up. He groaned and walked forward. Each step he took, he felt less of the pain. He told himself it would be fine as he could feel his heart rate returning to normal.

"Who's there?"

"It's Carl. Please open the door."

"Be right there," he called weakly, walking closer to the door. He didn't like the sound of Carl's voice. It sounded even more formal than usual, which was pretty hard to imagine.

"I'm here too, Fred. We're just checking up on you." It was Jin's voice. He trusted Jin. He felt that Jin looked out for them when Carl didn't. He knew he didn't need to worry now. He gladly opened the door, smiling.

Carl stood there with Jin. Both looked very serious. Behind

them was another girl dressed in a business-like suit. Fred wasn't sure what to make of the visit. It seemed innocent enough, yet he still had something in the back of his head telling him to run.

"Hi," he said cautiously, making sure not to show that he was nervous.

"Hi, Fred, how are you feeling?" Carl asked.

Fred shrugged. "Decent I guess. Feeling like I got a bad cold or flu or something." He tried to play it off cool.

"That sucks. Mind if we come in?" Jin asked. Fred moved out of the doorway and let them in. The girl in the business suit came in last. He slowly shut the door behind him and looked back towards the group.

"Sorry, I look like a bum. I've been trying to sleep a lot. Sweat this thing out ya know?" he said moving to the side of the doorway. "Sorry I made you guys worry. Who's this, by the way?" He looked towards the business-looking lady.

"My name is Maria. I'm here to find out more about the situation you're having," she responded. It caught him off guard. He guessed that she wasn't supposed to say it like that either since Jin and Carl looked shocked when she said it so easily.

"Maria!" Carl shouted, annoyed.

"Situation? I don't have a situation."

"It's not what we've got in our report. They say you are changing."

"Maria!" Now both Jin and Carl yelled at the same time. She seemed unchanged by the yells. She focused only on Fred.

"I don't know why you guys are here but-" Fred moved to the door, hand on the handle. "-I think it's time you leave. Before I call the cops on you all. Especially you, crazy lady." Fred tried to keep calm yet he could feel his heart racing. He felt his temper rising, even though he didn't feel angry. He felt something far worse than anger. *"Run,"* a voice said urgently in his head. He pushed the thought away and watched for someone to make a move.

"We aren't here for that Fred. We simply came here to check up on you. To make sure all is well," Carl said smiling.

269

Usually Fred trusted him but right now he felt something was off. Carl was acting friendly but his face showed concern. What type of concern though? For himself or for Fred?

"I really need you guys to leave...now." Fred could feel his body booming. Something wanted to be free. As if it wanted them to stay. Stay so that he could get frustrated beyond control and it could show its true self. Fred felt less and less like himself as of late.

"Listen man we're just gonna..." Jin started walking forward.

"No more talking. You're coming in with us to the Station. You need to be put on trial." She didn't have a problem speaking freely. Fred could feel his heart speed up.

"What the hell!?" Jin said angrily.

"Maria, wait outside," Carl said softly. She shook her head.

"He is to come in with us. Do not forget your place. This is a matter we can't simply ignore."

"He isn't doing anything wrong, so back the hell off." Jin now stepped between Carl and her. "He hasn't even been asked. You can't force him to just go."

"As a Protector I can force whatever I want." She pointed her finger to his chest. "You better back off before you say the wrong thing and end up in trouble."

"I'm not going anywhere." Fred flung the door open. "Everybody just leave me alone!" he screamed as he ran outside.

"Great job, Maria!" Jin yelled as he ran after him. She also ran into a sprint. Carl looked around the house. So quiet, so gloomy, so depressing. This was not a house you wanted to live in, especially alone. He looked towards the door. His student was on the run. Scared out of his mind. It was his fault. He hadn't been paying attention. He could fix it, though. He had to try. If he didn't try, he'd hate himself more. He ran outside the door a moment later, leaving the depressing house behind in silence.

Kelly walked outside the school building. Once again she was left wondering where her lover had gone off to. So much hidden from her, yet she somehow still trusted him. Did it make sense? Was she being dumb? Child-like? She felt that way a lot of the time. She loved him though, that made her trust him. It's what she felt in her heart.

She sat on the edge of the school letting the cold air touch her. She was freaking out about school ending. She watched as the kids all laughed and walked home. She wondered if any of them cared about their future. She did. Every day she thought of the different possibilities of where she'll end up in a few years. Wondered what career she would have, what school she'd graduate from, what kind of life she would have. All these questions, she kept juggling around in her mind. She hated it, but that's the way she worked. She couldn't change.

"Need a buddy to walk home with you?" Kelly looked up to see Lucy standing next to her. "Boyfriend left you here?"

"Yeah," she said sadly.

"Yeah, mine left too. Aren't we super lucky?" Lucy giggled. Kelly couldn't help but go along with her laugh. "Come on, let's get out of here. I really don't want to be around school when I don't need to be."

They began making their way towards home. Kelly lived only ten minutes away from Lucy but they never hung out. They've gone to the same schools for years. Been in some classes together. Even had some projects to work on together. Yet neither of them ever really hung together outside of school. Never really wanted to get to know each other. It was odd.

"I have so much homework today. What about you?" Lucy asked cheerfully. Kelly snapped out of her deep thinking and nodded. "Hey, you okay?"

"Yeah..."

"Thinking about Nick?"

"Uh huh," she said softly. She felt bummed about it. Like he didn't even say goodbye to her today. What a silly thing to get upset over she told herself. She couldn't help it, though. This was the first love she ever had.

271

"Don't worry. He'll be back before you know it."

"Yeah I know. It just feels different when he's not around."

"Yep! I feel the same. I get scared and worried about Marshall. One, cause he's Marshall. Two, cause I feel he might get hurt."

"Exactly! I know it's just the gym yet I get this weird feeling that he's in danger. Is that weird?" Kelly tried to smile but couldn't. She wanted to know why she always had to feel upset when Nick wasn't around. She wanted to know if Lucy was the same or not. Only Lucy could understand where she was coming from.

"They do what they have to for good reason." Lucy knew she couldn't tell Kelly. Things were to be kept secretive. She wouldn't betray Marshall's trust. "Our men have to do what they have to do. We just have to support them."

"I know. It's just hard."

"It is."

"I just miss him."

"I miss him, too."

They walked in silence, both reflecting on the past memories of their dating life. They felt a strong gaping hole when the guys were gone. Kelly worried but wasn't sure why. Lucy worried *because* she knew. Dangers always lurked and anyone can die from a number of things. Every time they went on the missions the percentage of death rose exceptionally. They kept the silence up the whole way home while trying to figure out how to cope with their missing beau's.

Fred jumped over the garbage can on the street. He ran into the middle alleyway. He could feel the burn in his chest. The voice in his head was telling him to "run", it was like a repetitious slogan. He was dripping in sweat but still felt the air biting at him as he ran, almost as if it was attacking him. He didn't know what to do. They mentioned a word trial. What was that? What did they want to do to him once he was captured? He knew only one thing. Run.

He shot out of the alleyway and onto the street. He hit the beeper button and jumped realms. He dashed between two people on the street. They could feel his presence but couldn't see him. They both turned to their sides, trying to locate what hit them. They didn't see a thing. He was already down the block when they gave up their search.

He stopped at the street light, trying to decide which way to go. Where wouldn't they look to find him? He had to think fast. He quickly took a glance behind him. He saw Jin and the woman, Maria, turning out of the alleyway where he just came from. He didn't have time to decide where to hide. He ran to his right and was nearly hit by a car as it drove right past him. He darted through traffic as best as he could. They kept their normal pace due to not seeing him, so it was his turn to be quick on his feet to not be hit. Jin spotted him once he reached the end of the street. He yelled as both he and Maria ran towards him.

Fred kept running. He could feel his lungs burning. He needed to hide somewhere safe. *"Do not stop. Run!"* the voice roared in the back of his head. "Shut up!" he screamed, running down the street. The voice told him to run again. That's all it said. Run. How long could he run for, though?

"Fred!" He heard the scream as he darted to his left. He ran half way down the block and dove into the middle alleyway. He slowly walked to the middle of it and hid behind the trash can. He could feel his heart pounding hard on his chest. *"Do not stop! RUN!"* The voice was getting louder. It wouldn't stop repeating the words. He ignored it, listening for footsteps.

Jin and Maria stopped at the end of the block. Jin looked down the block Fred went down. "You go that way, I'm going to go across the street and check down that block. If you see anything let me know. Do not approach him."

"It's our job. I will arrest him if I see fit." She sounded annoyed.

"We don't know what's wrong with him. Scaring him won't help our situation."

"Our situation is blown if you haven't noticed. He knows

he's done wrong. He also knows we're on to him. I will capture him or you will. Simple as that. Now go." She ended the conversation before Jin could say another word.

Fred could hear her walking down the block slowly. How could he hear so well from here? He didn't care at the moment. They knew he couldn't be far. That he must be in hiding. He slid a little bit more to his left side, trying to conceal his entire body. He didn't know what they'd do if they found him. He wasn't even sure what he did wrong. Yet, he felt if they caught him, he'd be finished. They'd exterminate him. He found it ironic. He couldn't help but give a small chuckle. *"Run,"* the voice in his head said again. He sat still trying to keep silent.

Nick stepped off the elevator. Once he stepped out he grabbed on to the wall. He still hated the rides down. They gave him a terrible curl in his stomach that took a while to go away. He shook his head trying to wave away the terrible feeling.

"You okay?" Marshall asked. Nick nodded.

"Let's go see our friends."

They both made their way towards the rooms. They checked Carl's office but it would not open. They tried knocking, no answer. So they kept on walking. Next they checked the healing spots, nothing in the entire room. They felt a little better not seeing their friends lying on the tables, badly injured. They kept walking forward. "There's only one place left to check in here."

"You think they skipped school for training?" Nick asked.

"Peter might. I can't imagine Fred would."

"Well there's only one way to find out." Nick walked a bit quicker, wanting to get the anticipation out of the way. They walked to the gym door. Nick placed both his hands on the door. He felt the pressure. If they weren't here, where could they be? Dead? That was the last thing Nick wanted to think about. He pushed open the door.

Peter threw another fire ball against the gym wall. It

274

exploded into a dozen small balls and hit the floor. A bunch of little pops and the fires went out. Peter looked to see his teammates entering the gym. He returned his gloves back to a Rod and attached it to his belt. "Hey," he said. He wasn't sure what else to say.

The boys walked up to him and stopped. Both saw the bad bruises on his body. The left side of his neck was dark purple. His face was badly beaten. Purple covered the majority of his face. His lip was badly cut as well. He looked at them without showing much emotion. He didn't feel any emotion but they didn't know that. They weren't sure how to approach the situation.

"Dude, what the heck happen to your face?" Marshall finally said.

"I fell," Peter answered flatly.

"All right that worked last time. This time it looks like you got into a fight with a bear." Marshall pointed to his neck. "The bear won. You look terrible."

"Thanks," Peter said and sat down.

"We were worried. What happened?" Nick asked as he sat down across from Peter.

"If you say stairs one more time I'm going to give you another black and blue." Marshall sat next to Nick.

"I don't want to talk about it." Peter kept to himself this long. Why did he need to tell anyone about his personal problems? He could deal with it. He failed to fight against his father once. It won't happen again though.

"Listen man, we're here to help." Marshall wanted him to know. Despite them butting heads Marshall cared about his teammates.

"I don't need help."

"Your face says otherwise."

Peter shook his head and looked away. Nick watched him closely. "Please-" Nick started. Peter didn't look back. "-I need to know. We are in this together. Who hit you?"

Peter wanted someone else to rely on. His whole life he'd been told to do things himself. To not bother his father or his mother. To just focus on helping himself. So, till this point, he felt he didn't need help. Even then he felt an urge. An urge to spill all the information about what happened the night before. How his father beat him brutally. To the point he was almost killed.

"I said...It was nothing." Peter couldn't say the truth no matter how much his mind told him to do so.

Silence swept the gym. It was as if nothing else needed to be said. "You're a coward." Both Peter and Nick looked towards Marshall. "Stop being such a coward. You've never been. It doesn't suit you well."

Peter looked at Marshall. He never knew how to gauge his teammate. He felt Fred and Nick were far more reliable in terms of friendship. Marshall, however, was always the one to call him out. To say what he thought. In a way, Peter respected that. At this point though it made him hate him. "I'm no coward. I just don't need other people invading my personal life."

"Your personal life is a part of ours. We are a team."

"Just a team."

"No. We are family."

"We are not..." Even as Peter said it he didn't believe it. He didn't believe his own words. He never doubted things he said. If anything was wrong with Peter it was that he was always too sure of himself. This was the first moment when he said something, yet didn't feel it was right. Did that mean they were his family? He never thought of it like that.

Marshall looked angry. He was about to say something when Nick put his hand up. Nick looked at Peter, sadness in his eyes. "When you hurt, we hurt. When you don't trust us, we can't trust you. If you don't want to be a part of this team, tell me right now. I've been thinking a lot about my responsibilities as a leader. I am here to help in any way I can. If you can't even talk to us about a personal problem how are we supposed to work as a team? We are a team. We are family."

Again silence swept the gym.

Peter never had a family. At least, that's how he always felt. He cared for his mom in a way a kid does for their mother.

Yet he never felt a close attachment to her. He cared for his sister but only to protect her. Just like Kelly. He cared about so little and wanted to protect even fewer. Yet now he had two people in front of him telling him that they are his family. That they wanted to help him. How should he react, he asked himself. Something he finally couldn't answer himself.

"My dad..." he began. They both looked up at him. He could feel his eyes getting watery. *"Crying? You don't cry."* The tear began to trickle down his face. He felt such a heavy pressure, as if this was building for years. "He beat me. I tried to stop him but he beat me down. I had a chance to stop him and I failed. I have all this power-" he looked at his hand and curled it. Feeling the power he holds once he has on the elemental glove. "-yet I couldn't do a thing without my Rod. Without it, I'm still a weak little kid. He's the one who owns me. How do I break that? How the hell do I stop that!?" He was yelling now with tears flowing out freely. "How do I stop this monster? I can shoot an Unknown point blank in the head. I feel nothing. I feel like I killed something terrible in the world. Then my dad beats me. Beats me till I'm almost freaking dead!" He's screaming so loud. He's on his feet throwing his hands up in the air. "I can kill monsters so easily! Yet, I can't kill the monster that hurts the most!" He looks at the boys. They stare, horrified in some ways, but they seem more worried than anything. He can see it. He can sense it. He lowers his voice. Almost to a whisper "Why can't I stop him? Why can't I kill him?" He fell back to his knees and let the tears drop from his face. The pain was terrible. He couldn't stop thinking about how much hatred he had for his father.

Nick got up and walked over. He placed his hand on his shoulder. "We will help you. You'll never have to deal with this alone again," Nick said calmly as if he were already formulating a plan to stop the terrorizing father.

Marshall stood and walked to the gym's wall. He formed his Rod into his famous metallic arm, which now reached up to his shoulder. He drew it back and smashed it again the wall. Hard. A huge crack formed on the wall. He smashed his fist again. Then again four more times. Then once more before he stopped. He looked at Peter who watched with confusion on his face. "If he ever touches you again..." Marshall looked at the wall then back at Peter. "Let's just say, he ain't no wall."

Peter never felt support in his life. As he watched both friends come over to comfort him, he felt something new. A feeling he never had in all his years of living. He felt cared for. That these boys cared more about his life than his own family did. They were willing to fight for him. Die for him. Now, he felt the same way about them.

The steps began to approach from the opening in the alleyway. Fred felt himself tensing even more. His heart was pounding so hard he couldn't hear anything else too well. He bit his lip. He could feel his body heating up as if he was...changing. He felt himself getting angrier.

He grabbed a garbage can and began crushing the side of it with his hand. All the feelings in the black room were rushing back to him. The feeling of being alone. The morbid feeling. The feeling of death gloating over him. Most of all, he felt betrayal. Who would tell them about his change? It must have been Marshall or Peter. They told them he's becoming a monster. Now he had to escape his fate. A fate he knew wouldn't be peaceful.

"Fred. Step out from behind there." He heard the stern voice of Maria. She was standing only a few feet away. He could smell her. It was a mix of perfume and sweat. She was scared as well. Not knowing what he was capable of. He found it funny. He wasn't sure what he was capable of. "Fred, please. You must come in with us. We have to figure this out."

"So you can put me on trial? Send me to my death!?" His voice was angrier than he intended it to be. He could feel his breathing getting heavier. "Just leave me alone!"

"I can't do that." She took another step closer. He could hear her breathing now. The sound of each step she made. Her heart pounding. He could hear it all.

"Please, get back!" he warned her. Despite everything in his body hurting and his mind ringing, he needed to warn her. He wasn't able to control his body. He wasn't sure what was happening.

"Just come out and we can discuss this."

Fred grabbed his chest. He felt a burning pain in itt as if it was about to rip right through. *You didn't run. Now you must rest.* The voice sounded so soothing. Fred let his fear wipe away. He closed his eyes. He didn't want to be here anymore. He didn't want to suffer anymore. He didn't want to be on the run anymore. He wanted to be left alone. So, if he couldn't be left alone, he decided to leave everyone else alone. He let himself drift back to the black room.

Maria slowly moved forward. She took a glance back, wondering if she should grab Jin. She felt the backup would be very beneficial. Yet she didn't want her chance to slip away. This was her one chance to capture Fred. He may run again if she went to get backup. She wasn't going to take that chance.

She made her way around the garbage cans and looked at Fred. He was cowering near the wall. He was shaking, giving soft moaning sounds. "Are you hurt, Fred?" she asked softly. She felt her voice might have cracked if she said anymore. She was getting scared. She also felt pity watching him crying in the corner.

"I thought I told you..." his voice was deeper than she remembered. It had a certain thickness to it now. Old, ancient, slightly...evil. "To leave me alone." He turned, eyes bright red. He launched at her, she tried backing away, but he caught her on the left side of her face. He dug his claws into her cheek then swiped, blood spraying all over the alleyway walls. He went sideways upward, and ripped right through the skin. Blood was already running down the walls as she let out awful scream.

"Why do they never listen?" Fred asked, his voice sounding more sinister.

She yelled so loud that Jin heard her from half a block away. He darted towards the position the scream came from. She held her face tightly but she felt blood pouring through her hands.

The wound was bad. She couldn't see out of her left eye. She already figured she lost it. She backed into the wall crying. Fred looked at her wondering what she was thinking as she lay there holding her face, sobbing.

"Why did you not listen?" he asked. She just cried more. "I asked you, why you still came? Even after ample warning you still proceeded forward. Did it not occur to you I might be dangerous?" His voice switched from playful to sinister. "I feel like you hunters never learn. You foolishly go in, head first without thinking of the consequences. Well, now you see. Well, I guess not fully see." He let out a horrible laugh. One that made her cry even more.

Jin turned into the alleyway. He saw the scene but wasn't sure what to make of it. He saw Fred towering over Maria speaking to her. He saw Maria leaning against the wall holding her face. He slowly made his way forward, trying to make his footsteps unheard.

"You're...a monster!" she spat out, blood hitting the ground. She was angry but more so scared. She'd never been so scared in her life.

"A monster is created." He pointed to her. "Just remember that when they ask you why I attacked you."

Jin formed a gun and pointed it at Fred. "Stand down."

Fred looked towards his friend. He laughed. "You are something else."

"Stand down or I will shoot." He had his aim directly at Fred's head.

"I swear you Exterminators have no clue what you're doing." He laughed again. The laugh filled the entire alleyway.

"I won't ask again. I will shoot you if you don't get on your knees and-"

"Shut the hell up!" he roared at Jin. Jin backed up a few feet but kept his aim on Fred. Fred smiled at him. "Do you really think you can shoot me? I am your friend, no?"

"You aren't Fred. I don't know what you are," Jin answered darkly. "So, I have no problem shooting you in the damn head. Now get the hell down."

"I've had enough of these games." His eyes shined so brightly in the dark alleyway. "Let the fight begin!" he roared and charged forward.

Jin shot but it missed, he wasn't expecting Fred's speed. Fred moved so quickly, he was already in Jin's face. He grabbed Jin and threw him into the wall. "Do not interfere with me again!" he thundered in his face. Jin gritted his teeth as Fred's hand held him into place. He tried pointing the gun back towards Fred without drawing attention but Fred grabbed his hand. He did a quick snap to his hand, making him drop the gun. Once it hit the floor it turned back to a Rod.

"Fred, wake up!" Jin pleaded through his teeth.

"Fred is no more. You can call me Riven." He smiled. A smile so big it made his eyes light up even more. "I have returned!" He let Jin go but not without slamming his fist into his stomach. Jin buckled over right away. Riven slammed both his fists into his back. Jin could sense the loss of feeling as he collapsed. He was going in and out of consciousness.

"This is getting ridiculous. You damn Exterminators need to learn your place." He began walking towards the exit. Riven touched his new body. He felt it was perfect. So young, so fresh. It felt great. He smiled as he studied his hands. His claws already extended. Soon he can transform to his full form.

"That's far enough." Riven looked up. Carl was standing at the end of the alleyway. Riven expected the master to be surprised but instead he kept perfectly calm. As if he expected Riven to have taken over the body.

"You really shouldn't stand in my way," Riven said laughing. He pointed back towards Jin and Maria. "Your little followers didn't have much luck there. So, think twice before you give orders."

Carl grabbed two Rods. Forming one into a metallic hand, the other into an elemental glove. "It's been a very long time since I've been in combat like this."

Riven stretched out his fingers. "You really think you can stop me, old man? I'm a creature of ancient times. You can never stop me."

"How did you take over his body?"

"Oh, so you didn't know? Yet you act so calm. Why?"

"I picked up on it when you came out in the conference at my office. I figured something was wrong but I wasn't sure what. Now I can see. You're transforming to one of those wolf hybrids. I can't figure out why though. As far as I knew you can't transfer genes." Carl studied Fred...Riven. Looking at his body. No scars or face tissue was missing. It was different than the last wolf hybrid.

"They don't. You are born a wolf. However, I am no wolf." Riven spoke slowly almost as if to draw out the conversation. He liked to converse. Play around with his prey.

"Then what are you?"

"Do you believe in God?"

"What does that matter?" Carl began to form an element in his hand; something invisible to the eyes of Riven.

"It means everything. Because I am what you call...well, that would spoil the surprise wouldn't it?"

"You're an Unknown."

"To simplify it, yes."

"Then my religion has nothing to do with you. Just like any Unknown I've ever met, I can kill you.

"Are you really willing to kill me? In this body?" Riven looked down. He put his hands on the body, smiling.

"You aren't Fred anymore." Carl stepped forward getting ready to strike.

"True. Then again you have no problem killing off your students. Isn't that right?"

Carl launched without another word. He dashed forward and threw his right hand. The fist made contact on Riven, slamming right into his face. Riven fell back but grabbed the ground, breaking his fall. He got back up, growling in Carl's face. Carl threw his palm outward. A strong force hit Riven throwing him back several yards, slamming right into the garbage cans Fred was once hiding behind.

"You really talk too much. Did anyone ever tell you that?" Carl let his guard down. He watched as his student, the boy he took under his wing, rose from the ground. It wasn't the Fred he knew though. Wasn't the once chubby scared boy he took care of. It was now something different. An Unknown. Yet he had no clue how it was even possible.

Riven dug his claws into the concrete wall aside of him. "You think you're so perfect. You've done more harm than good and you know it," he spat.

"I'm not really sure what you're referring too but I'm sick and tired of hearing you speak. Your little mind games won't work on me. So..." Carl dashed forward. He laid his palm out again, a mere foot away from Riven. Before Riven could even try to swipe his claws he was thrown back again. He went flying up then back down in a hard crash, slamming his back hard enough to create a cracking sound. Carl began his walk towards the creature.

Jin began to crawl back up. "Carl," he began, trying to regain his posture.

"Stay here. I have to finish this." Carl walked forward, holding his metal hand tightly together. He was ready to finish the job. He had no choice. Fred... Riven, had done too much damage. Trying to kill two Exterminators was a serious crime. It was easier to end his life now then put him through a trial. In which case they would find him guilty.

"Carl, don't kill him."

"Jin, stay out of this."

"Carl! He's still Fred. He hasn't completely changed," Jin pleaded. Carl felt the words hit him. He wanted nothing more than to see Fred again yet, as a Bora, as an Exterminator, he couldn't let him live. He knew better than that.

Riven was back on his feet shaking his head violently. He was getting annoyed. "If only I was at my full form you wouldn't be able to do this," he roared. "I will kill you."

Carl went quickly up to Riven. Riven tried to swipe forward in a stabbing fashion. Carl grabbed his hand with his elemental glove pulling him forward with a fierce tug. Then he

283

landed a perfect face shot with his metallic hand. There was a terrible-sounding crush as Riven was lifted off the ground and fell backwards. He laid there motionless.

"Carl! Do not kill him!" Jin was limping towards Carl. He could still feel the pain in his gut from Riven's attack. He couldn't watch Carl kill his own student.

"Jin. I won't tell you again. Stand down. This is not your decision. It is my student. He broke the laws." Carl stood there glaring at his broken student. He didn't know what to do. He knew what his job entailed but he couldn't just kill his student.

"You can't just kill him, we can help him! If anything he can be put on trial."

"I can't take that chance!"

"He isn't David! Stop focusing on the past!"

Carl turned around, his face red. "You don't know anything about that. You shouldn't talk about things you have no freaking clue about!" Carl was losing his composure. Jin did the opposite of what he set out to do. Instead of calming him down, he ignited him further into anger.

Back in the black room, Fred felt at peace. As if he didn't have to worry about the problems he currently had. All the lonely issues, all the hatred he'd been building up, was now gone. He lived peacefully. Something he had wanted so badly.

He couldn't stay here, though. Something felt off about it. He would love to let it all drift away into the darkness. Let himself finally rest, but he had things to do. Friends who counted on him. He couldn't just lie around.

"Other self?" He began to push himself up. He felt no pain. No anger. Just the feeling of needing to fight. To get out of the room.

"Rest now young one."

"I have to go." He was back on his feet.

"Rest. No need to fight anymore." The voice was very soothing.

"Yeah, can't do that. I have to get back to my friends."

"They betrayed you. They led you to more pain. You were hunted. Now, let me handle it while you rest."

"Sorry other self but that's just not how it works." He laughed. "I need to get back and help."

"Last time you helped, it led to, what? Do not fight. Do not push. Just rest."

"No more resting. I need to get up and do something. There's no walls to break, I need to wake up now." He could hear voices now. A voice he was somewhat familiar with.

"If you don't rest you'll bring more pain. You cannot live how you want to live. Peacefully. Is that not what you want?" The voice was losing its power. Fred could hear the other voice louder now. It sounded like Jin.

"I'm glad you're looking out for me other self but I got obligations. My friends need me on the team. I can't just lay around and wait for them to do all the work. Now let me out!" He was yelling now. The voice tried to respond but lost itself. He could hear Jin and now Carl speaking. They were arguing about something but he couldn't make it out.

"Let me out other self. Right the hell now!" he roared. Moments later the blackness disappeared as he was thrown back into the real world.

Pain shot through his entire face. So much pain suddenly on his entire body. He cried out in anguish like never before. "What the hell!" he roared as he grabbed his bloody face. He could feel a terrible pain in his chest and stomach as if a two pound cement block slammed into him. All the attacks he was hit with when he was Riven came rushing back. He never experienced so much misery before. It was almost unbearable for him.

"Fred?" Jin asked cautiously.

"Why do I feel like a truck just slammed into me?" Fred asked still moaning. The pain was terrible.

"See! He's still him. That Unknown hasn't taken over!" Jin yelled. Carl watched Fred carefully.

"Unknown? What are you talking about?" Fred sat up. He let go of his face. He could still feel hurt but he was able to put it aside and let it subside.

"He doesn't remember..." Carl sounded upset.

"That's good!" Jin told him loudly. "Means it wasn't his fault."

"Doesn't change what he did." Carl looked back at Maria. She was leaning against the wall, holding her face, while looking away from the entire situation. She lost an eye and was badly mutilated. She didn't want anyone to see. A once simple, yet pretty face was now completely destroyed.

"What did I do?" Fred asked, trembling.

"You..." Jin began but wasn't sure how to finish. How do you tell someone they turned into a monster and almost killed someone?

"We have to get him to the Station," Carl stated.

"A trial!?" Jin said shocked and scared.

"Do we have a choice?" Carl asked.

"No, you do not." It was a tall framed, muscular, ill-tempered looking man. He walked forward, two other people followed behind him.

"Aric?" Carl asked, surprised.

"Maria called. Told me what happened." He stopped a few feet away from them.

"When did she call?" Jin asked surprised. He'd been so busy arguing with Carl he hadn't been listening to Maria.

"Doesn't matter, she filled me in. This boy must come with us."

"I will be taking him in," Carl replied firmly.

"I think not. This boy is heading straight to trial. He is already considered a dangerous killer." Aric's voice was monotone. Not even a slight sense of emotion as he spoke. This scared Fred more than anything. He got up and began backing towards Jin and Carl.

"Listen I don't know what I did. I'm sorry for whatever it was. I just don't want to go with this guy." Fred began sweating more than usual. He could feel the pain coming back.

"I will take him in. He will be put on trial. There's no need to scare him more." Carl said with a stern voice. He wasn't about to back down and let someone take his student away. It was his responsibility.

"We will follow then."

"Fair enough. Help Maria up. We will walk ahead and meet you at the house." Carl grabbed Fred's arm and nudged him forward. Fred excused himself and moved forward. The three Protectors went to help Maria. Fred walked forward, with Jin and Carl trailing behind.

"What happened?"

"Terrible things," Carl answered grimly, glancing behind him. He saw Maria back on her feet, crying.

"I don't remember it. I don't remember what I did." Fred wanted to cry. He did something and he didn't remember a thing about it. How could that be? The question rang in his head.

"We'll figure this out. Don't worry," Jin tried to reassure him. Yet Fred felt a terrible outcome was coming.

"If I fail this...trial...will they put me to death?" Fred didn't hear a word. That was the only answer he needed.

Nick returned his spear to its Rod form. "I say we get out of here. Had enough training today." His shirt was soaked. The amount of training was double of what he expected. Whenever he worried, he had to get the anxiety out some way. Training was the best outlet he could think of.

"I thought we were waiting for Carl? Ask him if he heard anything about Fred." Marshall stopped running laps and caught his breath. "I mean, we can't leave. We have no clue where Fred is."

Peter felt a knot in his stomach. Was this guilt? It must have been. He didn't want to tell the boys what he told the others. He was afraid they wouldn't trust him. "I'm sure he's fine. Probably just home sick again."

"I think Pete might be right. Why don't we stop by his house and check?" Nick asked while grabbing his backpack.

"All right, sounds good to me." Marshall snatched his book bag up too.

Peter walked behind them. He wasn't sure how to approach them. To tell them what he saw in Fred. That he was too worried about his own problems at home so he diverted the attention of the Exterminators on his teammate. On his friend. He didn't know how to say a word. He was scared of losing the one thing he had gained. Trust.

They pushed through the gym doors. Marshall shoved Nick in playful manner. They laughed as they compared muscles. That's when they caught sight of Fred walking towards them. He was beaten badly in the face. They could see Jin and Carl walking behind him. Then four others were following behind them.

Marshall ran up to his friend. "Fred!" Jin went in front of Fred and stopped Marshall. "Hey, move out of the way. I want to see my friend."

"You can't right now." Jin held Marshall back. Nick moved closer, confused at the situation.

"What's going on?" he asked calmly.

"Don't worry about it guys. It'll be fine," Fred said smiling. They could hear the fakeness in his voice.

"What did they do to you!?" Marshall was shouting now.

"Marshall calm down," Carl said quietly.

"No! Why is his face so messed up? Who are those guys!?"

Aric moved up to the front of the group. He nodded to Jin, who let go of Marshall. "This business is none of your concern. You can step aside right now." Again the monotone voice. It was as if he was reading words off a piece of paper.

"That's my best friend! You're damn right it's my business." Marshall stepped closer. Aric began to get tense.

"Marshall! Stand down. I will explain it all to you soon." Carl was now the one getting upset. He didn't need another student to go on trial. "I promise, Fred will be fine."

Marshall stood face to face with Fred for a moment. He

288

could see the pain in his eyes. The pain of giving up. He wasn't afraid anymore. He accepted whatever judgment they gave him. Marshall didn't like that.

"I want to know what's happening. Not later. Now!" Marshall demanded.

"You are to remove yourself right now," Aric said, his voice loud like thunder.

"Move out of my way," Marshall said trying to push Aric out of the way. Aric grabbed his hand and spun him around. He slammed him against the wall.

Nick already had his spear formed in a second and placed it right at Aric's head. The other Protectors moved with the same swiftness. "Peter!" Peter already had his glove formed and had a flame in his hand ready to throw. "You two move any closer and he's dead!" Nick roared. Aric watched the tip of the spear at his throat. Marshall grunting as he was pushed against the wall.

"Nick, stand down," Carl said very calmly. The situation escalated far past what he had expected. It was spinning out of control.

"Stand this, son of a bitch!" Marshall cried from the wall. He was pushed up against it so hard his words came out jumbled.

"I will kill you. Back off of Marshall right now." It was as if Nick only focused on his friend. He saw one friend being taking away from him. Another being hurt. "I am their leader. They will not be harmed." All three boys could feel it. They felt they were the strongest team out there. Peter kept his guard, flame ball in hand. Both Protectors were ready to strike but staying perfectly still.

Aric loosen his grip and threw Marshall to the side. Marshall held his arm, hurt from being held so tightly from behind. Nick dropped his spear and backed up a few feet. Carl felt the situation getting a little better. Even so he knew the kids would not back down.

"I did terrible things," Fred said. Everyone looked at him. "I need to be held accountable for them."

"What are you talking about?" Marshall asked. He was

getting annoyed.

"I've done terrible things. Maria is badly hurt. I almost killed Jin. I attacked Carl. I need to be answer for those crimes." He held his head down. He didn't want to see the confused and hurt eyes of his teammates. "I need you guys to stand down. I will handle this."

"You didn't do any of that. It's all bull!" Marshall shouted. This time Nick held him back. "I know you! I know you'd never hurt anyone!"

Aric grabbed Fred and pushed him forward. They began to walk past the boys. Nick held Marshall back despite Marshall not fighting much. He watched as his best friend passed him by. Besides the slight glance he gave before walking by, Fred kept his head down. He felt ashamed.

As they walked into the gym Marshall fell to his knees. "He didn't do it."

The boys looked at him. Not sure how to respond. None of them understood what was happening. In a matter of minutes, one of their teammates was dragged away, set up to possibly die. They stood there wanting answers, yet too confused to even ask them.

"He didn't do it..." Marshall's voice dragged on. None of them knew what to do. A part of them was gone. Their team was broken.

Chapter 26 – Trial

Marshall pushed himself out of bed. He felt terrible. His best friend was convicted of multiple offenses. Maria, one of the Protectors that chased after him, lost an eye. She was badly injured and was making sure she held his actions against her accountable. Jin recanted his attack, saying it wasn't the real Fred. Even so Fred had to go on trial.

Jin explained to them that a trial is when they bring an Exterminator panel made up of about six judges and they decide if the accused will be sentenced and then convicted. In serious crimes, such as hurting innocents or attacking fellow Exterminators, the penalty is usually death. If it came to that they would execute him a day after the sentence was announced.

Marshall got dressed. It was a Saturday and he had the whole day free. He told Lucy he had problems at the Station and would be there all day. She didn't ask any questions, just told him to be safe. He wanted nothing more but to spend his day with her. Now he had to go to a trial in which his best friend could be sentenced to death. He was scared out of his mind for Fred.

He slipped on his shoes while thinking about all the times he had spent with Fred. He remembered when they would cut eighth grade classes and head to the movies. They were still best friends then. The year after that it all changed. They would skip every Friday and check out whatever latest movie came out. It went on for over four months before the school finally called up their parents. Fred's parents didn't even bother to come home from their trip. Marshall's parents yelled at him but that was about it. So they continued to do it till school was let out.

He walked outside, bundling his jacket up some. There was a cold chill in the air today. Gloomy and dark. He looked up at the sky. Grey. It was as if to show how empty and shallow this world could be at times. He focused on the road ahead and made his way towards the Station.

He remembered times when Fred would sleep over at his house when they were kids. They would build forts in his room by placing pillows on top of each other to play king. They would make believe his little brother, Matt, would be the main big bad guy. He would roar and come towards the fort. Then Fred and Marshall would jump out and attack. The fort always got destroyed, even if Matt never reached it, which then it would be their fault. They didn't care, it was to much fun to care.

Marshall didn't want to think about the past. It was hard to imagine it was so long ago. Everything changed during high school. Once it came along, Marshall began hanging out with the football team because of class. Fred moved to the quiet side, never making any other friends. Marshall left him there. He wanted to become popular and Fred didn't. So he simply focused on himself trying to fit in with people who never wanted to be real friends with him. He only realized it at the end of high school. Was it too late? He thought so. He thought how lonely it must have been for Fred. With the weight issues, Fred never went on dates. With his boring style, none of the kids really wanted to hang out with him. His main friends were online. He played video games with people more than ever hanging out with anyone in person. Was that his best friend's life? Being alone, all the time? Not even having his parents around to comfort their own child?

Marshall hated himself at that moment. He clinched his fists. He could feel himself wanting to cry but he kept his composure. He couldn't let himself fall, not yet. He had to be strong. Had to be strong for his best friend. It was him on trial, it was Fred. If he faltered now, he'd be no better than when he left his best friend to hang out with the popular kids. No, this time he was going to be there for support.

As Peter was walking towards the Station he still felt that awful knot. *"Why didn't I tell them about me? Why did I tell them about Fred? Why? Why did you do that?"* He spoke to himself but came up with no answer. He felt terrible for what he had done.

When he came home later that night his mom hugged him like never before. His father was in jail at the moment. No one had the money to bail him out, nor did anyone want to. Peter was okay with that. If he saw his dad he wasn't sure what he'd do. His mom told the police what happened to him but without any proof they couldn't press those charges. Peter liked it that way. He'd rather not be in the local newspaper stating how he was beaten by his drunken father.

He made sure his sister was okay from the whole altercation. She assured him that she was fine. She looked more worried about his face than anything else. He laughed and told her it was just a scrap. He'd be fine. Little did she know that their father almost killed his own son. Peter thought it was best she didn't know that.

Peter rested longer than usual. His normal six hours of sleeping became over ten. He felt tired. Not physically tired either. It was the first time he felt guilt. He betrayed one of his only friends and couldn't own up to it. He didn't know how to fix this problem. He tried to formulate a solution but nothing sprang to mind. All the power in the world was in his Rod, yet nothing could change his friend's fate. Fred might die tomorrow and he felt he was to blame.

Peter watched as two friends played catch across the street. The one friend had great aim while the other barely could throw. The perfect shot waved it off and told him he'd get better. The other seemed so angry even though it was just a game. Peter felt the kid's pain. Others saw things as no big deal, when he felt it meant the world to him. This kid who couldn't aim was trying to prove he was good. Why didn't anyone else see that?

Peter still didn't know who he was trying to prove anything to. As he walked against the cold, he tried to figure it out. Every time he went to training, he felt he was reaching a new goal. A goal that felt untouchable. It couldn't be reached because there was no answer to it all. He trained and trained for something, but he couldn't figure out what that something was.

He tried to wipe his mind clean. He knew he could do it. He didn't think about anything. Lack all emotions. He was good at that. He kept walking, letting the wind touch his face. He let everything in his mind fly away. No matter what the strong knot in his feeling remained. A reminder of what he did wrong.

Nick sat on the steps of the Station waiting. His two teammates should arrive any minute now. He could only focus on one teammate though. The one he failed. It crushed him. Fred could very well die today and he couldn't do a thing about it. He couldn't save his friend, despite being their leader. This was his job and he failed at it. He had one more ace up his sleeve but if it didn't work out. Then all of this would have been a waste.

Nick always tried to help people out. It was just who he was. Yet, when it came to helping out a friend, one who desperately needed it, he was failing. He tried to stop them by force yesterday, but it would have made the situation worse. They probably would have condemned all of them if he pressed the assault.

He told Kelly he might be busy the next few days. She would usually argue but she must have heard the strain in his voice. She simply told him that she loved him and to take care of himself. Call her if he needed to talk. He kept that in the back of his mind. If the trials went wrong today, he wasn't sure who he could turn to.

He watched the cars passing him on the streets. It was a slow day with very little traffic, which was basically unheard of in New York City. The gloomy skies did this, though. People didn't like to go out when there was a dreadful aura surrounding the city. The skies as plain as possible, as dull as possible, the morbid feeling taking over the city kept many off the streets. It was as if it was a true representation of what was happening on this day, yet no one out on the streets knew about what was happening underground.

He saw Peter walking down the block now. Nick smiled

and got up. He didn't want to be alone anymore. When he was, the thoughts of failure crept into his mind. Little did he know all three boys were having similar thoughts.

"Hey Pete, how ya doing?" he asked as his friend approached. As usual Peter kept up a blank appearance not showing any emotions. Nick confused it sometimes as a cover or wondered if that was how he actually operated.

"I'm fine. Any word from Carl?"

"Nada. I heard to meet here from Jin and that's all. I hope Fred's doing okay."

"I doubt they would mistreat him."

"Yeah...I can't believe it. Why did they go after him? Did he really flip out or something?" Nick couldn't understand it. Fred was the most stable in the group. He was a happy-go-lucky person who just liked to have fun. To imagine him attacking his fellow Exterminators, almost killing her, just didn't seem logical to Nick. He couldn't comprehend it.

Peter could answer the first question. He knew why they went after him. Did he really change into a monster though? Peter saw a slight hint of something hidden beneath but was too preoccupied by other things to really take notice. Now he wanted to know more. "I-" he began when Marshall came up from behind.

"Hey," he said. He looked whiter than usual. The cold air mixed with the gut wrenching knot in his stomach.

"Hey. Are you doing okay man?" Nick asked.

"I'm fine. Any word from Fred?"

"No," they both answered. Marshall nodded.

"Peter, did you read anything about these trials?" Marshall asked. Peter turned to him, surprised he actually asked him a question.

"I don't know much. I've read a little and Jin mentioned how they are run, but that's about it. A few judges on the bench while he pleads his case. The majority of votes wins. There'll be stands for us to watch so we can see the trial." Peter placed hand on the bottom of his chin, rubbing it while thinking of the what was to come. "I don't know who the judges are. They may be random for all I know."

"They are," Jin said from the doorway. They looked up at him. "It's time to go. We gotta get to the trial sector. Let's go." Jin turned around and the boys followed. They could feel the pressure more now than ever.

They made their way through the Station, going through the gym and passing the double doors on the other side. The boys had never been to this area. When they entered, they were amazed. The room was huge. Blue in design with two huge computers on both sides of the room. They lit up like a Christmas tree. Green, yellow, and red lights going off on them. In the center of the room were ten pods. They had an oval shape, all linking up to dark tunnels in front of them. "These are transporters. They take us to other Stations and sectors," Jin announced. They looked on in amazement.

Marshall went up to one and touched it. A cold chill from the machinery greeted his touch. It was massive. Able to easily fit him and give him enough wiggle room. "We ride this thing?"

"Yep," Jin said happily.

"Man, I thought the horror ended with the elevators," Nick said laughing. The boys all had a good laugh then. The tension in the room lifted some.

"Need me to ride with you?" Marshall grinned.

"Uhh no, I think I'll survive."

"If you're scared though I can be there for you," Marshall said in a high pitch voiced. "Don't ever be scared, sweetie."

"I will punch you if you keep talking," Nick said with a dry smile. He touched the pod's glass. It slid open quickly. "Do we really just hop in?"

"That's right," Jin opened his own and jumped in. "Once in hit the blue button. That will close the top. Hit 331. That's the trial area. It's a fifteen minute commute. So just stay calm and relax, it'll be over before you know it.

All three boys got in their own pods. They did as they were instructed. The pods closed and they began moving forward slowly. Nick grabbed tightly on the sides of the pod. He was worried how fast they would go. Surely not much faster than the elevators. He bit his lip. The pod shot forward. He was pushed back with such force he could feel his upper lip lift. He already hated the trip.

A screen projected on the pod's glass. It was Jin who looked very comfortable sitting in his seat opposite of Nick. "This is the fastest way of transportation. You could get to another state in less than thirty minutes. I prefer it to cars."

"Yeah, this is pretty fly!" Marshall said excitedly. He was projected on another screen, looking around his pod enjoying watching all the lights blinking around him.

"I'll take my chances with my test in the summer. I want a car. This is horrible," Nick said gritting his teeth. The pressure on his body was more annoying than anything else.

"Oh you big old baby. This is awesome!"

"Shut up, Marshall!"

"No, you shut up!"

"Both of you shut up!" Peter now screamed as he was also brought up on the screen. They both went silent. Then all three broke out into a laugh. Jin watched them laughing for a moment and joined in. With all the tension there had to be something to break it. Acting like kids wasn't a bad idea.

They arrived a few minutes later at a new Station. As they got up they looked around the room they had just arrived in. It was very similar to the pod room at their base. "Did we just travel back in time?" Marshall asked.

"Why would we travel back in time?" Nick shook himself. He still felt some effects from the pod trip.

"This room looks the same as the one we left from."

"It's the pod Station. They won't be vastly different," Peter informed them. Jin nodded to show he was right.

"That's stupid," Marshall said waving his hand. "They could have at least put a new coating of paint or something. People will get confused," he said as he walked towards the doors.

The boys followed. Jin looked back at the pods watching them close automatically. They had finally arrived, yet none of them wanted to be here.

As they walked through the doors they could hear the chatter grow ten times louder. There were easily over fifty people in the room all talking at once. The stands were set up like a gym stadium with eight rows going up. A bunch of people, who the boys assumed were Exterminators, sat on the benches talking. Some people stopped to look at the boys then pointed and began talking again. "Seems we're popular here," Marshall whispered to his friends.

"This trial must be big news. This is a lot of people," Nick said, both worried and sad. If the story spread this quick through the organization it meant bad news for Fred. He must have broken the rules so bad people had to see the outcome.

"Let's find seats." Jin walked forward and the boys followed.

The room was brightly lit. It was as clean as it could possibly be. As the boys shifted and began to climb the steps Nick took a look around the room. In the center were three chairs. A few feet in front of that was a huge table which contained six chairs. "That's where the judges sit?" he asked Jin. Jin looked and nodded. "So why are there three seats in front of the table?"

"It's for Fred," Jin answered.

"Why are there three though?" he asked. The doors opened and Fred walked in. Nick and Marshall stood up. They could see his face looked a bit better from yesterday but he kept his head lowered. The blabbing dropped to a very low volume yet everyone kept talking. Nick could feel his heart pounding as he watched his friend walking towards his seat. Carl walked right behind him.

"We're right here man! Don't worry!" Marshall yelled from the seats. Everyone looked at him, pointing and talking. "What the hell are you all looking at!?" he yelled. They all kept talking about him, now looking the other way. He sat back down, pissed off. "These people act like he's an animal or something, getting ready to put on a show."

"Just ignore them and keep calm," Nick said sitting back down. He felt nervous. He was watching one of his own being put on a trial for something he knew he couldn't have done. He had a lot to learn about his teammates, his friends, but they were not betrayers. They wouldn't hurt their own unit. That's what he kept reassuring himself with.

Carl let Fred sit down. He put his hand on his shoulder and pressed in. He bent down and whispered, "It'll be okay. Keep calm. I will vouch for you here." Carl then went around and took a seat himself.

The room was still chattering, though a lot lower. "It's like a sport to these idiots!" Marshall roared. "They're being disrespectful. That's one of their own up there!"

"They are curious Marshall. No need to get upset," Jin said calmly.

"That's a human being!" he yelled.

"That's your best friend," Nick said softly. They looked at him. "So, it means a lot to you. You want nothing more than to run down there and take him out of here. Save him from all this. You still sit here, though. Upset you can't do just that. Isn't that right, Marshall?" Nick now looked at his friend. Marshall felt a tear forming. He looked away and rubbed his eyes.

"I just want to get this over with."

As if it was on command the doors on the far side opened. Everyone went silent as the judges walked in. In the lead was the Gada, Ross. She led the group, closely followed by her Protector. Three older men followed and one young girl coming up last. They all sat in their respected seats and began shifting themselves to get comfortable. Fred looked up from his chair, his stomach feeling empty despite eating less than an hour ago. He could feel a ringing in his ears from his heart pounding so hard making it so he couldn't hear.

"Today we are here to place judgment on a fellow Exterminator. Fred Sinco, please stand," the Gada ordered. Fred got up slowly. He felt as if his insides we're going to come out of his mouth. He looked up at the judges, scanning each one.

"My name is Fred. I am an Exterminator under my Bora, Carl. I am-" he lost his train of thought. He wasn't sure where he was going with it. He looked around the gym to see dozens and dozens of faces looking at him. He felt he was about to throw up. He sat down, his legs shaking violently. "-I...I..." He didn't know how to continue. He sat there looking at his Gada wondering if she took pity or was disgraced. Yet she sat there with no emotion on her face.

Carl stood up. "He's only a boy. I will continue for him, if that pleases you Ross," he said firmly. Ross nodded, Carl continued. "Yesterday, we were to bring Fred in for questioning. Some questionable events have been happening as of late. We figured going to him and talking would help us to determine what to do. When we got there Fred got nervous and ran. Only natural for a boy to be scared when he is told he was being taking into custody."

"Why did you run?" she asked. Fred could feel all the eyes in the place on him now. He looked back up at her.

"I...was scared," he said in a low voice.

"You thought you're own Bora would hurt you?"

"No."

"Then why did you run?"

"I was afraid I'd hurt him." The gyms chattering exploded as everyone began whispering. The Gada watched Fred flicking his fingers back and forth.

"Did you know at that point that you were dangerous?"

"I didn't know what I was capable of," he said sadly. It was true. At that point he didn't know what was happening to him. Just something was changing and not for the better.

"So you ran and Maria was able to catch you."

"I hid out of sight. So they split up. She came my way. She heard me behind the garbage can. I told her to stay back. I told her to stay away from me! I could feel it! I could feel whatever it was wanting out! Why didn't she listen!? Why...Why?" He began crying. He hadn't cried at all the night before. The whole time before the trial he felt his body was in a shocked state. As if he didn't know how to deal with the situation he was dealt with. Now, as he told his story, he felt the events happening again in his mind. The terrible feeling of anger. The feeling of clawing someone's face and tearing it apart. He wanted to vomit right there.

"You gave her warning and she still continued?" the Gada asked. She hadn't heard this part.

"What does that matter?" Now Aric walked into the room from the pod section. He made his way towards the final free chair. The voices grew in volume as he made his way forward. Nick watched him. He wanted nothing more but to jump off the stadium and attack. He felt nothing but hatred towards him.

"This man attacked a fellow Exterminator. He dug his claws into her face and swiped. She didn't even have time to react. She could feel her face getting torn apart, losing complete sight in her right eye." He looked around the room. "We made rules. If you attack an innocent or a fellow Exterminator you are guilty. You must be held accountable for your actions. We cannot let him go simply because he says he doesn't remember."

"He wasn't himself. It's different than claiming he doesn't remember." Carl now stood up.

"You believe he's some kind of Unknown then? Isn't that even more reason to put him down?"

"We don't put down our own. We don't know what happened to him but we're gonna figure it out."

"We figured it out already. He attacked a fellow Exterminator. Judgment is plain as day now." Aric sounded smug while saying it. He felt like he was in the total right. He wouldn't even listen to what Carl was saying.

"It isn't your decision. It is the judges," Carl said firmly. He turned back towards the Gada.

The Gada looked at the judges who sat by her. She could feel the sudden pain of placing judgment soon. As a Gada, it was always her obligation to see things fairly. She looked at Fred. "Please continue, young man. After you gave her warning, she still came towards you."

Fred took a moment to remember. The part after that

301

became a blur. Flashes of what happened came up yet he couldn't see them clearly. As if it was watching a fuzzy old movie. "I...I think I turned to her. Struck forward. She tried backing away. I was far too fast for her. There were claws digging into the side of her face," he said. He felt he would throw up at any moment. He could remember her eyes widening right before he swiped. "I swiped....I...I cut...I cut her face right across...I..." He got up and vomited in front of him. He stumbled backwards as he heard the crowd giving disgusting grunts. He was beginning to feel dizzy. Carl grabbed him by the shoulders.

"Are you okay?" he whispered.

"I remember...I remember it...it was horrible," there was pain in Fred's voice. Carl heard it as well. It pained him to see his student like this.

"He's not doing too well. I think we need to rest."

"What? Rest!? This is a trial. He doesn't need rest he needs to be convicted!" Aric stepped to the side of the vomit and faced the crowd. "Do you believe one should be set free for his actions? He remembers the events clearly! If it truly wasn't him, how could he remember!?" The crowd roared in agreement. Only a few shook their heads. The boys sat there, stunned.

"We must place judgment on the ones who do wrong. It's that simple." Aric faced the Gada. She was displeased by his performance, but the crowd wasn't. They agreed with him. How was she to pass judgment against her own people? She looked at Carl, she could see the sadness engulf his face.

"We will decide that together. It is not your choice Aric. Now sit down before I have you removed." The Gada wasn't playing favorites. She simply didn't like people rallying up everyone and getting them into screaming matches.

"Oh, I will stay quiet." Aric sat down. "I have already shown that everyone thinks this man deserves death. He has done wrong. He now must be held liable for it." The crowd nodded in agreement.

"This is an organization!?" Marshall rose from his seat. "We're supposed to work together. Fight together. Stop the

Unknowns from coming into our world. We stand here now convicting someone who didn't do anything." He put out his hand. "He said multiple times it wasn't him. Don't you understand that?"

"If I kill someone, boy, can I say it was me sleep-walking? I wasn't aware I stabbed something? I mean honestly, if we believed everyone's murder stories there would be no judgment to pass," Aric said smugly from his seat. He laughed. Some of the people in the crowd followed his example.

Marshall felt so angry. So upset. Yet he didn't know what to say. He wanted to yell at them all. Tell them how stupid they were being. He instead sat back down looking at his friend watching him. He could feel tears falling down his cheeks but didn't make a move to wipe them away. He could feel the sense of loss.

"I am the leader." Nick stood up. He began walking down the steps. People moved out of the way so he could make it to the base floor. Everyone in the gym kept quiet. Not a word was spoken. They were all focused on Nick.

"Young man, please remain in your seat," one of the old judges ordered. Nick ignored him completely and walked over to Aric. Aric sat there staring up at the young Exterminator.

"Do you lead anyone Aric?"

"As one of the head Protectors, I lead over thirty people."

"And when one of them is out of place, do you yell at them?"

Aric shrugged. "Of course I do. It's my job. What are you getting at?"

Nick walked over to Fred. He lifted his head and looked at him dead in the eye. "Did you intend on hurting Maria?"

"What?" Fred didn't know how to answer.

"I said. Did you intend on hurting Maria?"

"No..." he whimpered.

"This thing inside of you. What is it?"

"I don't know."

"It changes you, yeah?" Fred nodded. "Into what? You get claws. That much we figured out. Your eyes are red. What else?"

"Oh this is horse s-" Aric began but Nick talked over him.

"You change into something far stronger. Evil maybe? You aren't yourself." Fred nodded. "Gada. Judges. This is Fred." He pointed towards his friend. "This is the Fred I know who I fought with. This is the Fred, I know, who saved my life before. This is the Fred I know who I go to school with. This is the Fred I know who is my brother." He placed his hand on Fred's shoulder. "The Fred that attacked Maria was not this Fred. It wasn't Fred at all. It was something else. A demon."

"A demon? Oh, come on now!" Aric screamed in disbelief.

"Riven," Carl said. The Gada looked at him. "He called himself Riven."

"Riven?" She questioned the name. It sounded so familiar.

"You can't be buying this! Demons do not exist!" Aric was on his feet now.

"We fight monsters that are made of rock. Wolves ten times the sizes they should be. Even dragons from what I've heard. And you question demons, of all things?" Nick got a few laughs out of that one from the crowd.

"Sorry, if I'm not religious boy. I just find it absurd and convenient that you thought of a demon right now," Aric grinned menacingly. "Do not believe this, judges. Demons do not exist. I've been hunting over twenty years. If there were demons out there, I'd know of it."

Nick watched the man fighting against every word he said. He wanted to transform his Rod and stick his spear through his head. Such violent thoughts were passing through his mind but he shook them off. "I'm not sure, but I've been studying up on it. Carl let me know about the name Riven last night. I looked back and there are stories of this thing. This creature that attaches itself to peoples bodies and lives in them till they decay like a parasite."

"And it just happened to fall on your friend?" Aric spat.

"The wolf hybrid in the first hunt we ever went on. It attacked Fred, actually in a way it was almost playing games with him. It wanted to see how he reacted."

"So? Unknowns like to hunt. We've known that for years."

304

"What if it was checking to see if Fred was a suitable body for it? He or it, whatever you wanna call Riven, needed a new body. It's face was degenerating. The body was getting old." Aric just shook his head and looked away. "This demon Riven from old stories is a terrible demon. It feeds off the body till the body gives out."

"So you're saying this demon is inside your friend right now?" Aric asked. "Well, then let's bring it out and see it."

"No," Carl stepped in front of Fred. "Trust me that's a very bad idea. It's pure evil whatever it is. I hadn't had a chance to look up the name so I sent Nick to do it. I figured he might figure out a clue. This is the clue we needed. He is innocent."

"Gada, please tell me you don't believe this." She looked at Aric. He was angry. Angry because he was proven wrong or angry because Fred might be set free, she couldn't tell.

"I'm interested to hear more of this Riven demon. What else was said about it?"

"I couldn't find a lot of information. It seems to cover its tracks quite well but it's quite possible this demon has lived hundreds of years. The thing that made me think, for sure it was a demon was the fact the Callers that night picked up a small signal. They even told Carl that. Yet, that wolf hybrid would not have given off a small signal. It's a heavy signal, that would require better trained Exterminators than us. So how come the Callers didn't pick it up?"

"Are you saying..."she began.

"It was already here," he finished.

"A trap?" she questioned.

"I believe so. Peter has a theory that it might have to do with the Summoners." The room erupted in chatter. The Summoners were a big subject around the Exterminators lately. Their actions were quiet, as of late, even though something was always brewing.

Even Aric was listening to Nick now. Things have shifted and the threat was bigger than a simple betrayal. The Gada placed her back to her seat and rubbed her temple. The judges looked at her then back at the crowd. How to address the current situation was impossible with all the new information coming in.

"We need Fred. He's the link to finding out exactly what the Summoners are up to. This demon that invaded him seems to be sleeping for now. I believe as long as Fred is out of danger we can keep it that way." Nick wasn't really sure if any of that was true. He was just giving his best efforts to keep his friend alive.

"Fair enough," the Gada said looking side to side. "I think we can agree for now to keep Fred in containment until we figure out what's going on. There's no need to execute anyone if they are innocent. We will figure this out and we will pass judgment after all the new information has been processed fully. Lead Protector Aric, I'd like to see you in chambers." Ross got up and the judges followed her lead as she left the way she came.

Aric got up and looked at the Exterminators. "Figure this out. Get that demon out of the boy. 'Cause if this is a plot on the Summoners part we're in for something nasty," Aric said fiercely. Carl nodded and Aric took his leave.

"That was quick thinking, boy," Carl noted.

"I watch a lot of "Law and Order"," he smiled.

"Thanks man," Fred said softly. He felt a sense of relief he had missed for so long.

"Any time. Let's get out of here. I got some things to tell you, Carl."

"I'll meet you in my office. I have to take Fred and lock him up for now. He'll be safe, just away from everyone else for a while." Fred nodded and Carl helped him up. Jin, Marshall, and Peter ran down from the steps towards them.

"Dude, you were like one of those badass lawyers on a TV show. Nice job!" Marshall was beyond excited. He punched Fred softly on the arm. "Had me scared for a moment. Thought they were going to chop your head off."

"Not funny man."

"I'm glad it turned out this way," Peter smiled. "I'm also sorry Fred."

Fred looked at him puzzled. "For what?"

"For-" None of them knew he sold out Fred for his own gain. "-not being there when I should have been."

"You were here now. That's what matters." Fred waved and went along with Carl.

"Seriously dude, that was awesome." Marshall was still super excited. Nick nodded and thanked him. "Also...thank you. What you did was something I can never thank you enough for. You saved my best friends life. I..." Marshall tried to find the words. Something stronger than a thank you.

"You're welcome." Nick smiled. Marshall laughed and placed his arm around his friend.

"Let's get back on the pods!" Nick grunted. They all laughed.

Marshall dropped on to his bed. He could feel all the stress he was holding onto slip away. Lucy crawled onto the bed next to him and began rubbing his back. For a few minutes they laid there in silence. She could sense he was tired, exhausted, and wanted to be left alone. The peacefulness that filled the room was nice. It had been a while since he had that. He absorbed it as much as possible, letting the stress disappear.

"You okay, hun?" she asked softly. He shifted to his side and looked at her.

"Was a rough day."

"What happened?" She laid her hand on his knee and rubbed, trying to relax him as best she could. Sensing he was beyond tired; mostly mentally.

"It was Fred. He was put on trial."

"For what!?" Her voice was loud. It shocked him a bit. He sometimes forgot how much she knew about the Exterminator life. How serious and violent it could get.

"Basically, he hurt someone. It wasn't really him, though. It was some type of demon. At least that's what we've gathered so far." Marshall laid his hand on her cheek, rubbing it softly. "Nick was able to convince them of that. Meaning he was spared."

"Spared? As in if Nick didn't have anything to say he'd be-" she began but couldn't finish.

"They probably would of killed him." She gasped. She knew of the dangers but not how serious they could be.

"But...he's one of them."

"Not when he almost killed one."

"Then they really will execute you if you go against their laws?" She sounded scared. He knew what she was thinking.

"They'll never find out about us."

"But if they do."

"They won't."

"But what if they do?!" She slammed her hands down. "Then what? What are we going to do!?" She sounded almost hysterical. He had never seen her flip out so bad over anything. They discussed it before and he went over it a lot.

"Baby, we're fine. They won't find out. Even if they do I won't let them hurt you. Stop worrying and calm down." He placed his hand on her stomach and rubbed. "Let's get some sleep. No need to worry. We are fine. Trust me." She trusted him. She wanted to trust him. The Shadow that hovered over her was still glaring, wanting more.

Peter walked home with Jin. They kept quiet most of the way home. It was hard to discuss the events. Peter loved the fact he didn't feel the emotions others did. It was easier to cope with situations like the one he just did. He simply kept a blank slate and nodded and agreed with people. The whole time he sat there he felt like he was going to burst out of his seat. He didn't want to see one of the only people he ever called a friend be sentenced to death. If they did convict him he was pretty sure he'd jump from the seat and try to stop it. Luckily, it didn't come to that. He even got some of his guilt off his chest with an apology. Fred understood. That's what true friends do. They forgive. At least that's what he was told. Now, he believed it.

"That was a close one huh?" Peter snapped back to the

current setting. He looked over to Jin who was watching him.

"Yeah, it was scary," Peter tried to sound spooked. His emotions were completely empty at the moment. After his last one, happiness, subsided he felt nothing. He was eager to gain another, back yet nothing crawled back into him.

"Nick has a sharp mind, that was perfect timing. I can't believe he kept that one hidden. If we didn't have that...Fred would have been found guilty." Jin sounded sad when he spoke. "You guys are going through more then I'd imagine. I never thought it would get this messed up."

"Life gives us obstacles. It's our choice whether to beat them or fall to them. Today, we beat them." Peter smiled. It seemed like the appropriate attitude to give. He wasn't really sure how to feel about it though. Did they really win? It didn't feel like it.

"That we did. Now we just have to worry about Summoners."

"Do you think it's a new plan?"

"It's something bad. That much we can gather. We just have to figure out what it is. As always the good guys are a step behind." He laughed. "Together, though, we always come out on top. We are the good guys."

"I think you've watched too many movies," Peter said dryly.

"Always the downer, aren't you?" Jin shoved him playfully. "Sometimes being the happy one can get you further."

"I get pretty far just fine now. Thank you very much." Peter winked.

"Pete," Peter now looked at him. "I think it's time we step the training up. Soon they'll reward you with two Rods. When you get them it's time to train with double gloves." Peter got excited. He'd been waiting for more training. especially from someone experienced.

"I like the sound of that!" he said happily. He could feel being happy, it was always strange yet rewarding.

"Good. Because what's coming is going to be tough. I don't

want any of you to be unprepared," Jin said placing his cold hands into his pockets. "All right let's get home. It's freezing out." They began picking up the pace. As they walked Peter imagined having the second Rod. Imagined what kind of elemental creations he could make. It made his blood run hot despite it being freezing cold out.

Nick entered the office. Carl looked up, waved him in, and went back to writing his report. Nick closed the door and sat down. He gave a quick look around the room then back at Carl. "Today was...it was really, really close," Nick said. He felt far less tense then before. He gave it his best shot and it came through pretty well.

"Yeah, you did amazingly. I can't commend you enough."

"I did it 'cause I had too. No need to thank me. This is my team. I don't plan on losing any of them. That's a promise." Nick put his thumbs up.

"Most kids would be too afraid to even talk to the judges. You stepped right up to the plate. You stopped a judgment that could have ended a life. For that you should be very proud. As your Bora, I couldn't be prouder" Carl smiled as he looked at his student. Growing so quick. A little goatee forming on his chin. His eyes were weary, yet determined. His face worn, yet ready to fight at any given moment. This was the true look of a leader.

"Thank you." It was nice to get noticed for his work for once.

"Of course. Now you said you wanted to talk about this Riven."

Nick sat down. He rubbed his hands together as he held on to a terrible secret. "We have a problem."

"Seems we always do." Carl sat back in his seat.

"This demon, Riven, isn't just any Unknown. I don't even know if it's an Unknown."

"Not the most religious person right now. Are you saying it's from our world and not a different realm?"

"I honestly don't know. Like Aric was saying, He'd never fought one of them in all his years of hunting. Did you ever hunt one?"

"No." Carl placed his hands on the desk and fumbled with the baseball. He could feel this was about to get worse. "So let me hear it. What are we dealing with here?"

"Through research I found that this demon has been around awhile. Hunting humans, possessing them. Usually it's quicker than it was for Fred. Usually friends of the host would document the changes. Soon after they would disappear or worse, ended up dead." Nick let out a sigh. "Making researching this thing really annoying. Even online."

"So, we know it's a hunter. It kills without mercy, either. It's also pretty smart if it covers its tracks. It knows there are hunters out there like us. My bet would be it's an Unknown. A unique one though. I have never hunted a demon. Do we throw holy water at it or something?" Nick got a small laugh out of Carl's joke.

"Well, that's the thing. From research I see only one way of stopping it."

"Well, let's hear it."

"Death."

"Death? Do you mean-"

"We have to kill Fred...before he fully becomes Riven." The room was complete silence. Nick had been holding the secret to himself the whole day. He finally let it out and his leader knew. He still didn't feel better about it. The end result would still be the same. He had to kill his friend in order to save him.

Chapter 27 – Signals

Marshall walked off the elevator towards the containment room. He was up early, way before he usually wakes up. He could barely sleep the night before. He needed to see his best friend. Make sure he was doing well. So he woke up around six, got ready, and was in the Station by seven. He wanted to make sure he could talk to Fred in case anything else went wrong.

 The Station was dark. Carl hadn't even gotten to his office yet. No one was in the gym either. He heard weird sounds from one room. He knew right away it was the Callers. They were searching to see if anything crossed over as of late. Luckily it had been quiet.

 He reached the room, placed his hand on the door and it slid open. He entered in. Inside were three separate rooms with huge glass shields in front of them. On the side was another sliding door which only opened from Marshall's side. It was to keep the prisoners in. The rest of the room had the same white painting as the entire Station.

 Marshall walked to the glass and placed his hands on it. He saw Fred sleeping on the bed inside the room. He knocked lightly to try to get his friends attention. Fred just groaned and turned to his side. Marshall knocked again, louder. Fred cocked his head towards the glass, only one eye open. "Hey dummy, wake up!" Marshall yelled.

 Fred yawned and got himself up. He felt terrible. All his worrying the night before took a heavy toll on him. He felt as if he had a hangover. "What are you doing here?" Fred wobbled his way towards the glass. He leaned against it, yawning.

 "How ya doing?"

 "Wonderful. I feel like I'm in prison."

 "You kind of are."

 "Thanks for the update."

"I'm sorry," Marshall said looking down. Fred looked at him confused.

"What's wrong?"

"I should have stood up yesterday. I should have said something. Not just sit and wait. I'm. ." Marshall felt his eyes getting watery. He couldn't even look at Fred since he felt so ashamed.

"You did what you should have done," Fred said lightly. "I didn't expect you to go all pro lawyer on me."

"Nick did what I should have done."

"Nick did it 'cause he's our leader. You don't have to put that responsibility on your back too. You already did enough."

"I should have done something..." he let his voice trail off. Fred shook his head.

"You didn't have to do anything more then you did."

"Yes I did! I'm supposed to be your best friend! I should of protected you!" The tears were now flowing freely but he didn't care. "I couldn't even stand up against them. They had you pinned. What if Nick didn't have that information? You would have been sentenced to death. Then what? I watch my best friend die!?" He slammed his fist on the glass window. "I should have done something."

Fred placed his hand on the window where Marshall was standing. "You were there for support. That's the only thing a friend can ask for," Fred said softly. Marshall was sobbing openly now. Putting all the blame on himself. "If you did something crazy yesterday you could have been put on trial, too. Then what? We'd both be sitting on death's door right now. What's that solve? Not a damn thing. You did just fine yesterday. I'm actually proud you didn't do anything stupid." Fred smiled.

Marshall wiped his tears. His cry turned into occasional sobs. Fred let him compose himself some. He felt like he failed his best friend. All he wanted to do was protect his friends. "I just can't lose you man. You've been there since I was a little kid. Been there when I was dumb or in trouble. If I lost you I...I don't know..." He gave up trying to create a sentence. He just placed his head against the glass window.

"Thank you," Fred said quietly.

"For what?" Marshall asked without looking up.

"For being my best friend."

Nick woke up next to a sleeping Kelly. She was in a deep sleep. He placed his hand on her hair and stroked it. He loved her so much. It made him wanna keep fighting. If these Unknowns ever crossed over they'd hurt someone like Kelly with ease. He wasn't going to let that happen. He was her protector.

He didn't sleep well. His eyes wanted to stay shut as he sat up in the bed. He thought about the talk with Carl. They agreed not to tell anyone the secret. The secret that Fred had to be killed. There was no way to extract the demon from him. Had that really been the only answer they could come up with? From past experiences of people posting in logs and journals it seemed to be. It was only internet searching, though. Nick planned on going into a deeper search. He had to find more answers. He couldn't just kill one of his own. Not after he spent so much effort trying to save him.

He looked back down at her. She slept so peacefully. He smiled and slowly inched off the bed placing her head on the pillow as he did. He made his way to the bathroom and shut the door. He washed his face off, trying to catch some type of relief. Everything was coming apart so fast and he had nothing to hold it together.

His dad texted him to call but he didn't feel like it. He knew his father would have tons of questions about school. It was getting closer to being over and Nick was barely making it. Chances are he'd fail and have to redo his senior year. If that happened his father might go crazy and kill him. The irony.

He stepped out of the bathroom and put on his jeans. He figured he go get some coffee for Kelly and himself. It seemed like a good way to start the day. He wasn't about to catch anymore sleep anyway.

Yet the trial kept flashing in his mind. He couldn't get it out of his head. He never felt so nervous in his entire life. He had the information from the night before but didn't know if it was going to work. He put all his bets on the information he gained in a single night. He put someone's life in his hands. What if it all went wrong? What if it didn't work? Would he have felt even more guilt? Felt it was his fault then? He wasn't sure. It played in his mind like it was on a treadmill, taunting him to get to the end results. It was better not to think about what ifs.

He grabbed his cell phone, threw on his shirt, and snapped on his Rod and beeper. He began to walk out the door when Kelly woke up. "Where ya going?" she asked, yawning.

"I'm going to go grab some coffee. I'll be back in a little while." He didn't look back. He didn t want to miss her. He always did but when he looked at her it hurt more. He'd rather just lay by her at all times but this was life. It's not so simple.

"Okay. Hurry back." She fell back onto her pillow, rubbed her face into it and drifted back into a light sleep. He left the room.

Once outside he began walking to a local coffee shop. He was nervous. Everything in life was happening so fast. School was almost done, talks about moving in with Kelly, still no job, his dad down his throat. Not to mention he had a secret; killing creatures called Unknowns. Life couldn't get much more complicated.

His phone rang and he pulled it out from his pocket. He picked it up. "Hello?"

"Nick?" It was Carl's voice.

"Yeah, what's up?"

"Get to the Station, now!"

"I just woke up. I was going to get coff-"

"Now!" Carl's voice commanded sharply. Nick pulled away from the phone for a moment.

"All right man, no need to shout. Are you okay?"

"The Callers. They've picked up on a lot of huge signals. Something isn't right. Hurry!" Carl hung up the phone. Nick turned around and ran towards the Station.

Peter got off the elevator. Someone ran right past him. He moved out of the way at the last second. The guy said sorry and jumped into the elevator he just came from. It shot up. Peter had never seen the Station so busy. It was almost always quiet. He made his way towards the gym.

He got a text message from Carl telling him to meet him here. That something big was happening and that every Exterminator needed to get here as soon as possible. Peter wasn't sure what it could have been but he didn't want to miss it. Most people would panic, yet it made him excited. It was time to get back into action.

He opened the gym doors and saw his group there. Also Ram and two ladies standing next to him, one being Emily the other being a short, orange haired fighter. She had huge bug-like eyes and a scar on her left cheek. He quickly walked over to them to see what they were chatting about. He reached for his Rod for reinsurance.

"Pete," Nick said as he came into the group.

"I'm glad you can join us, Peter. We've got huge problems." Carl looked to Ram. They nodded at each other.

Ram looked at the boys. "The Callers have picked up on huge signals. These are deadly Unknowns, capable of killing you pretty easily. I need you to understand that." The boys and girls nodded. "Good, 'cause we have to send you guys out to hunt them. There are over thirty signals throughout the northern border. We've dispatched as many groups as we can. However, Carl and I are going to deal with two of them. They aren't far from each other and in Jersey. Emily and Gina here are going to handle another signal. That leaves you three to take down one, too."

"Us, alone?" Marshall asked surprised.

"Yes. I know it's scary but together you should be able to do it."

"I called Jin and told him to meet you at the location. No call back yet but he'll make his way there for sure when he can. Till then, you have to get there as soon as possible. Unlike smaller signal Unknowns, this size signal can break through the realm. They can even break into our realm, completely. Meaning regular civilians can see them. We can't let that happen." Carl looked at his students. "I believe each and every one of you has the ability to stop these things. Don't look at it like you only had one year of experience, think of it as you almost have a whole year of experience. You will be fine if you fight together."

"All right then. Marshall. Peter. This is it." Nick stood up. "It'd be great to have a fourth teammate but let's just say he's taking a break." They nodded. "We do this one for him." Marshall nodded again, with a thumbs up.

"Plus, we can tell him he missed out on killing a big ass Unknown." They all laughed at Marshall's joke.

"Then let's get going. Where is this signal?" Peter asked. Carl gave them the directions. It was upstate New York. Right in the middle of nowhere.

"What the hell is this address? It's not even a real address." Marshall looked at it.

"Head there and look at the map at the local Station. It'll pin point the position. Please, all of you be careful. If it gets to rough you retreat. Do not put your life in danger. Be safe." Carl had enough pressure almost losing Fred. He wasn't about to lose anyone else.

Ram and the girls left first. They took the pods all the way to the right. Carl wished them good luck once more before jumping into his own pod. The boys watched as he went then looked to each other.

"Little bit scary, huh?" Nick said to them.

"It sucks Fred isn't here," Marshall said sadly.

"A fourth person would definitely help," Peter pointed out.

"We can't free him. He's already in enough trouble." Nick turned to the two boys. "I know it'd be easier but is it worth getting him in more trouble?"

They both thought about it for a minute. They all agreed it was best they left him here. They didn't need another trial to occur. There was already enough pressure from the current situation.

"All right, you guys ready?" Nick asked. They nodded. All three jumped in their pods. Nick held his breath for a moment and hit the blue button. Everything shut. He put in the numbers of the Station he was told to punch in. A moment of a silence and then he heard the pod start up. Then it shot out, taking them towards the huge signal.

Kelly sat up in her bed. She looked at her phone. No text or call. It had been over an hour and Nick never came back.
"Again...disappearing." She hated it. She loved him though. She didn't understand why he just left at times. Why he didn't come back for hours. Why he came back with bruises and sometimes even bleeding. Was this the life she would live with him?

She threw her bed cover to the side and got up. She grabbed a shirt from her draw and threw it on, then slipped on pants and made her way out of her room. Her mom was making breakfast. "Good morning honey!"

"Morning mom," she replied miserably as she sat down at the table. She leaned her head against her arm. *I get to sit here and worry for the next few hours. How is this fair at all?"*

"Are you okay, honey?" her mom asked.

"Yeah, just thinking."

"About?"

"How dumb guys are."

"Oh, that's my favorite subject." Kelly laughed.

"Mom, is it weird when guys disappear?"

"Yes."

"Well, awesome then..."

"Do you trust him?" her mom asked. She looked at her mom and nodded. "Do you think he's cheating?"

"How would I know?"

"You'd have a pretty good idea. He'd act distant. His attention wouldn't be towards you. Calling another person a lot. Texting these days I guess. If he was cheating you'd have a pretty good idea he was." Her mom lifted the pancakes and placed them on a big empty plate.

"I don't think he is. I think he's keeping secrets though." She played with the fake flower on the table. Twirling it and picking it apart. She tried not to think about it, yet it was all she her thoughts were focused on.

"A secret, huh?" Her mom said, loading another batch of pancakes on the plate. "Well, everyone needs secrets. Exposing yourself to the world about everything is never the smart thing to do. Secrets make us unique. They make us special. If the secret were to hurt you it's best kept a secret. If you don't believe he's cheating, I wouldn't push it," her mom said happily.

She didn't feel the same though. She wanted to know why he couldn't tell her. It wasn't as simple as her mom explained. She felt there was something bigger behind it all. She got up from the table and went to the door. "I'll be back!"

"I just cooked!"

"I'll be right back. Going outside to make a call." She left before her mom could respond. She pulled her phone out and called Lucy.

"Hello?" Lucy said on the other end. She sounded tired. Kelly thought she sounded worried as well.

"Hey, this is Kelly!" She tried to sound cheerful as possible.

"Hey! How are you?" Lucy cheered up a bit when she heard it was Kelly.

"I'm good just hanging out. I have a weird question."

"Uh oh."

"Well it's not weird it's just...is Marshall there?"

"No, he left early today. Actually, I must have been still sleeping." She sounded okay with that. Why was she okay with it and Kelly wasn't? Did she know Marshall's secrets? She needed to know the secrets, too.

"Nick left, too. He was going for coffee and never came back. He seems to do that a lot."

"I'm sure he's fine. Probably got a call from Marshall to hit the gym." She sounded so sure. So carefree.

"Yeah… about that. What gym do they go to?" A pause. She knew more than she was letting on. Kelly was getting curious.

"I think it's the World Gym."

"I guess I'll ask Nick about it when I see him again. Whenever that is." She tried to sound playful. She was getting annoyed. Lucy knew something but wouldn't tell her. Now she knew she was alone, surrounded by these secrets.

"Yeah, good idea."

"Well I'm going to go eat some breakfast. Just checking up to see if you heard anything."

"Nope. It'll be okay though. They're tough boys," Lucy said happily.

"Tough boys? Why would that matter?" Again a pause.

"I just mean they can take care of themselves! Anyway, I got to head out too. I'll talk to you later. Goodbye!" Lucy hung up. Kelly slowly put the phone back into her pocket. She felt something was funny. Nothing seemed to fit right. She leaned against her front door, wondering why secrets kept piling up. What was so important that no one would let her know?

Fred sat in the room. Alone and cold once again. He hated it. Yet he kept calm. His friends were working on a way to help him. As long as he waited, he would be free. The voice reminded him to run and get out at times but he ignored it. This time he kept a focused mindset of getting out of here and being free.

He knew the voice was now a demon. It was Riven. The demon that possessed him after being bitten, trying to take over his mind. Riven almost accomplished it the other day. Fred was so afraid he might transform back to that terrible creature that he almost wanted to stay in the cell forever. It was easier this way.

He heard the door open and stood up. "Hello?" he asked but no one answered. He walked over to the glass window but saw nothing. "What the heck?" He walked to the edge of the glass window to see if anyone walked in. Nothing.

He backed off the glass window and looked around. He

began to worry again. Was something trying to harm him? He went to grab his Rod. Nothing was there. *"They took it away idiot! Just be calm. No one is there.'* He slowly backed to the wall and watched. Nobody came in.

He let out a sigh. Just a malfunction. Why was he so worried? No one wanted to even come in the room. They were too scared of him. He was scared of himself.

The door to his cell flew open. He jumped again. He stood waiting for someone to walk through. Yet again, no one came in. "Hello?" he called again. No one answered. He saw a piece of paper outside the doorway. He tip toed towards it. He kept his guard up every step he took, glancing back and forth to see if someone set a trap.

He leaned down to grab the paper, lifted it up and looked around again. Still no one was there. He looked back at the letter and read it.

Upstate New York Station. Head there right now. Your friends are in danger. They will die without you. Good luck.

He looked back up after reading. He tried to find who dropped it off but no one was there. He stepped out of his cell and ran to the doorway. Even the hallways in the station were completely isolated. Not a single person was here at the moment.

He looked back at the piece of paper in his hand then towards the gym. If he left they'd put him back on trial. If his friends were in danger, he could be their only hopes for survival. He didn't even know if they were in danger. What if they were, though? He pushed the piece of paper into his pocket and looked back towards the gym. *"Damn it!"* he thought.

Chapter 28 – Choice

Nick pushed himself out of the pod. He felt groggy. The trip was worse than he anticipated. It took almost forty minutes and his head was throbbing. He went over to the wall and leaned against it for a moment. He kept breathing nice and slow, trying to sooth the headache.

"You okay man?" Marshall asked once getting out of the pod.

"Yeah. That trip was long. I hate that thing."

Peter now rose from the pod wiping himself off. "Hurry and regain your posture. We have a mission to do."

"Okay Mr. Serious, calm down. He needs a few minutes." Marshall began stretching. Getting ready for the fight that awaited them.

"I don't mean to sound rash. It's just that this is our first major mission. I don't want to mess it up," he said without emotion. It made it sound more like a command rather than a statement. The boys looked at him.

"I got it, man. Let's do this," Nick said pushing himself off the wall. He stretched a little bit then began heading towards the doors with the other two boys following his lead. They all felt the tense moment in their stomach. This was what they were training for. Fighting the creatures that held the biggest threat to humanity.

They marched through the doors. This Station was colored blue instead of white like their own Station back home. "Now see, this is color!" Marshall proclaimed.

They quickly made their way to the elevators and took the trip up. It was set up the exact same way as their own Station. The ride felt longer then it usually did, however. It just added to their anxiety of not being sure what awaited them above ground. All they knew is they couldn't let whatever it was stop them. This was the first big threat they had.

They all got off the elevator. Peter walked over to the map pasted on the empty cabin wall. Marshall went over to the table and sat on it. He looked around the ugly small brown cabin. Nothing special about it. It lacked any design. It only had a map, two chairs, and a table. "Well, isn't this the prettiest cabin ever?"

"It's pretty plain." Nick looked around himself.

"That's my point. Sarcasm man!"

"I got it. I just wanted to piss you off." Nick walked over to Peter. Peter kept his finger on the map. Guiding it across the forest area. "You see anything?"

Peter nodded. "Should be less than a mile out. It's in the middle of the forest based on the points Carl gave me."

"Sounds fun!" Marshall exclaimed, trying to lighten the mood.

"This is serious! This is the most important mission we've ever had," Peter said quickly. It was sharp like a school teacher. Marshall looked at him then laughed. Peter shook his head and looked to Nick.

Nick placed his hand on Peter's shoulder. "Stop worrying. We are in this together."

Marshall slapped both of his friends on the back. "Guys, this is it. We've been training so hard to fight the big baddies. We're about to go head-to-head with it right? So stop worrying and let's go kick this damn thing's ass! If we sit here we won't get anything done!" Marshall headed towards the door. He hit the beeper and entered the other realm. The boys followed.

"Shouldn't we discuss a plan of attack," Peter asked.

"Nah, we'll discuss it on the way to the place," Marshall responded nonchalantly, opening the door.

They walked outside. The woods were right in front of them. It was still cold out so most of the leaves were blown off. The forest looked almost dead in a way, grim and dark. Similar to the situation they were put in. "Oh, how fitting. This looks like a perfectly fine forest to walk through " Marshall said gleefully, walking forward.

Then the ground shook. It was a heavy shake, one that

made all three boys jump. Then another boom. They moved back a step. Another ground shuddering boom. "Okay, now that sounds bad," Marshall said in a low voice. They heard something crashing, closer this time.

"It's coming towards us?" Peter asked.

"It seems that way. Get ready. Form the Rod based on attack. Plan A or B depending on what we are up against," Nick commanded. The boys nodded and snatched their Rods. Nick grabbed his own and stepped forward. He would be leading the attack either way. He felt the sweat trickle down his neck as another boom hit the ground. The footsteps were only moments away.

Marshall saw a shadow. It was too dark in the forest to see the shape but it was big; at least thirty feet tall. Marshall looked at his teammates. "This thing is huge guys! It's coming from the right!" They all looked to where Marshall indicated the beast was. They heard another footstep, thundering nearby, and then they saw a hand grip a tree from the darkness.

"Everyone step to the left. Be ready to form the weapons." Nick could feel his gut twisting as the creature grunted from the darkness. Then it poked its head out. The Unknown had a huge eye in the middle of its forehead, looking down towards the boys. Two large tusks were coming from the bottom of its chin. It walked out some more. It had huge green cloth pants covering its lower half. Its torso was completely naked and covered with thick hair. It held a club in one hand, colorful ribbons dangling at the end of it.

"Holy freaking sh-" Marshall began, but the beast roared so loudly the boys all jumped back even further. It towered above them with its massive body.

"It's a Cyclops!" Peter yelled.

"Plan B!" No one moved except for Nick. "I said Plan B! Nothing changes!" Nick roared. The boys snapped back to reality and formed their weapons. Nick created his spear, Marshall created an elemental blaster, and Peter finished it up with his elemental gloves. "Strike formation. Marshall, keep it off the EB, distract it then hit it. Go!" Nick moved into action. The plans were set. So much training, it all lead up to this moment. The moment to see if it worked in a real fight.

The Cyclops roared again and swung down the club. It wanted the fight as much as they did. It stepped forward and lifted the club to swing again at the incoming Nick. He stopped and ran to the left. The beast growled as it followed him.

Marshall ran all the way to the right, trying to position himself. He needed time to charge the elemental blaster. He also needed to get out of sight of the Cyclops.

Peter formed a ball of fire in his hand. He dug his fingers into it and began massaging it. He darted forward towards the side of the Cyclops. It was busy trying to chase Nick. Peter threw the ball above the Cyclops. Once it reached just over the head, he closed his palm. The ball reacted and blew up. A bunch of small flames landed on top of the Cyclops. It roared in pain as two of the small flames hit its eye. It swung backwards violently, trying to attack whatever just hit him. Peter was yards away, at safe distance.

Nick took the opportunity and ran forward. He stabbed the Cyclops in the lower backside then quickly withdrew as the brute cried out. It turned back around and slammed the club down blindly. Nick was safely out of reach by the time the club struck. The wind and force of the club striking the ground, however, hit Nick strong enough to make Nick fall backwards. He almost lost his balance but managed to grab onto a nearby tree with his free arm.

The Cyclops lifted its gaze to the sky and roared. Nick watched as this mighty beast showed its dominance, trying to show it was the strongest of all. As Nick watched he thought how proud this Unknown was for being so powerful. He quickly shuffled out of the way and into the safety of the trees.

Peter already had a new elemental ball in his hand. This time it was ice cold. He held tightly to it waiting for the right moment. The Cyclops looked at the retreating Nick and grunted as if it had already won the fight. Peter slowly moved his arm back, setting up for a good aim at the Unknowns club arm. He had to make sure he hit it dead on. He swerved the ball in his hand and then launched it forward with everything he had. The ball went flying. The Cyclops turned just in time to swat the ball with its club before it hit. The entire club began to freeze over. The creature watched, confused as it did. The ice stopped covering the club at its tip. The Cyclops tapped it with its free hand. It showed disgust for the ice cold and quickly pulled away its hand grunting. It threw the club to the ground angrily and slammed its fist to its chest. It looked at Peter with revenge in its eye.

"Not so fast!" Nick yelled from behind it. Nick stabbed the bottom of its leg, right above the foot. It bellowed in pain as Nick drove the spear in as deep as he could. Then Nick quickly pulled it out and retreated back into the forest. The Cyclops glanced behind itself. Its eye trying to find the new prey.

That's when the electric blue wave of energy struck its left shoulder. The Cyclops didn't even have time to fully turn its head back around before it blew up. There was an awful scream, a blue flash, and then electricity spitting out from the impact. The Cyclops collapsed to its knees placing its right hand hard on the ground and looking at its left shoulder. A huge chunk of flesh was now missing. Blood was flowing down its shoulder. Even a direct blast only took off part of its shoulder. It still could operate its left hand.

"Are you kidding me?" Marshall said in disbelief as he looked from afar. He looked in amazement as the mighty beast began to stand again. "This thing just took my best shot. I've been charging that for like two minutes!" In most cases a fully charged blast could kill just about any Unknown they've fought so far. The Cyclops was in another league.

"Do it again!" Peter already formed a new ball. This one was glowing with silver lighting. "We can't let up!" Peter moved in closer to the beast, still keeping a safe distance.

Nick traveled around the forest looking for an opening. The Cyclops was already on its feet trying to pick the next target. Nick knew not to get close unless it was distracted. It would be certain death to go head to head with such a mighty creature.

Peter threw the silver ball. The Cyclops charged forward, its left hand covering its face. The silver ball erupted into a terrible guest of wind, slicing up its arm. It wasn't forceful enough to stop the Unknown. It charged straight for Peter. Peter turned and ran towards the house. It wasn't a safe haven but at least it was something he could hide behind. Every six steps Peter took was one step for the Cyclops. It was running at full speed and would catch up to him in no time.

Marshall fired another shot from his blaster. It didn't charge for nearly as long as the last, so it wasn't as powerful as the last one. The Cyclops saw this one coming and moved out of the way. Such ease for such a big creature. The blue electricity blast flew past it and hit a tree, ripping it to pieces upon impact. As the tree came crashing down, the Cyclops decided it wanted a new target. It began to walk towards Marshall slowly.

Marshall was panting, exhausted after two shots in a row. He chuckled. "Damn, not smart planning on my part."

Nick came running out of the forest towards the Cyclops. He had to play it perfectly. "Pete, wind up!" he yelled. Peter watched him going towards the Cyclops then nodded. He formed another silver ball, a lot smaller. He launched it towards the Unknown's foot. The ball bounced a few times then rolled up against the Cyclops' feet. It looked back as it turned around. Nick was only a few feet away.

"Now!" he roared.

Peter crushed one hand against another.

The silver ball blew up.

Nick was tossed upwards into the sky. The Cyclops watched in anger as he saw the boy fly up. "Whoa," Marshall gasped from the side.

Nick came flying back down with spear in hand. He drove it right into the right side of the beast's chest. Its eye blinked and opened even wider as it cried out. Nick let go of the spear and hoisted himself off the beast. He fell on his back and rolled away. He scrambled away to get a safe distance from the beast.

The Cyclops grabbed the spear and tore it out of its chest. It looked at it briefly before throwing it to the side. It screamed in aggravation. It was getting stabbed, shot at, and electrocuted. Now it was beyond angry. It wanted its prey to die.

"Okay, so I'ma take a guess that this thing is now really pissed off." Marshall had regained his strength and began running. He wanted to get as much distance as he could.

"Keep your distance. We keep hitting him with whatever we got! Don't back down. We got this!" Nick yelled as he made his way in a circle around the beast. He was going for his spear on the ground a few yards away. The Cyclops caught sight of him though, and ran towards the spear. Nick wasn't keeping an eye on the creature but towards his weapon.

"Nick! Watch out!" Peter flung another ball. This one was green. It flew past the Cyclops and onto the grass. Peter tensed his fingers and dug them into the dirt. The ball went into the ground and out shot vines. They slithered around the monster and attached to its legs. The beast almost ripped them apart but too many attached themselves at once, making it fall to his knees. It screamed in anger as it tried ripping off the vines.

Nick rolled forward, grabbed his spear, and came back up running. He had his weapon of offense again. It was now time to strike. The beast had its head turned towards the veins, still trying to rip off them off, they were keeping him in a vulnerable place. He went forward, stabbing the creature in the left shoulder. This time the Cyclops flung its fist away from ripping the vines out to hit Nick dead in the center. He went flying and came down hard on the ground a few yards away, lying motionless.

"Nick!" both the boys yelled. Marshall was working on another attack while Peter was trying to think of what else to throw at the beast.

Nick laid there feeling nothing. The pain was so bad he felt numb. He couldn't hear anything, he couldn't breathe. He felt like this might have been it. That he tried his best but slipped up and got caught by one of them. This Unknown would be able to kill him. This was all part of the game, right? Someone is always the prey. Sometimes the predator becomes the prey.

Then he coughed a loud, heavy cough. He could finally breathe again. With the breathing came the terrible, sharp pain in his chest. He grabbed his chest and cried out. It was the worst pain he'd ever felt. It was as if a truck just hit him head on. He let out another breath. It hurt just as much. He took a deep breath. That also hurt. He moved his body and that hurt the most. He opened his eyes to see the Cyclops ripping the last of the vines off his feet. *"Get up quick. This thing is gonna tear you into two!"* he told himself, yet his body was in too much pain to move.

Marshall was getting ready to fire another blast. He knew he only had another shot or two in him. He was using up his energy fast with each shot. That meant he couldn't miss again. He took steady aim as the Cyclops began to lift itself up from the ground. He had a perfect shot of its back.

"Wait! Not yet!" Peter shouted.

It was too late. This time a red fire wave shot from the blaster. It flew towards the Cyclops at amazing speed. The force behind it ignited the grass as it slid above the ground. It was going to hit the beast right in the back. Marshall tightened his grip as he fell to the grass, feeling the little energy he had left keeping him up slowly slipping away.

The blast was nearly to its target when the Cyclops turned. It lifted its right hand and brought it down. The blast was caught under the beast's mighty hand, slamming into the ground it turned to smoke. Besides some blood dripping from the creatures palm it wasn't hurt at all. It roared, this time in victory. It had stopped the best sneak attack they had.

Marshall laid his free hand on the ground watching as the Cyclops slammed his fist on its chest. "It's too strong..." he muttered under his breath. The Cyclops wasn't even fazed by it.

Peter threw an ice ball at the creature's leg. It quickly froze all the way up to its groin area. The beast roared as it turned its head towards Peter. He threw another ball, this time at the creatures other leg, freezing that one too. It tried to move but without luck. Another ball came flying at him. It hit its chest freezing almost its entire torso. Another one hit its back, freezing up just about everything else. There were two more for the arms. The creature reached out towards Peter but was too slow. The ice stopped all movements in place. Peter threw one last blast at its eye, freezing the entire head of the Cyclops. The Cyclops stood there, reaching out towards Peter only a few feet away, frozen solid.

"No way..." Marshall took a deep breath, watching in amazement.

Peter fell to his knees. The energy consumption was huge. He never threw that many elemental balls so quickly. Two or three at a time was one thing. The amount he just used nearly made him faint on the spot. He tightly grabbed the grass below his hands and pulled it free. "Yes!" he exclaimed so loudly, it made both Marshall and Nick look at him. "I did it! Damn it, I freaking did it!" he screamed in victory.

Marshall threw his non-blaster hand up in the air. "Hell to the yeah! You go man! That was freaking awesome!"

Nick was slowly getting back to his feet. He still felt a terrible pain thrumming in his chest. He, however, felt a relief. The beast was down. "That was sick!" He tried shouting but even that hurt. He laughed and held his chest. Happiness couldn't be stopped no matter how much the pain.

Peter got back to his feet and began walking towards Marshall. Nick grabbed his Rod and did the same. Marshall sat on his behind, looking up at the sky. "I can't believe we did it. That thing was so damn huge. I swore we were all gonna die today," he said laughing.

Peter sat down next to him. "That was amazing. The thing nearly killed us all. At thirty feet tall, it easily had unstoppable strength. Yet we did it. We stopped it. Just us kids. We were able to stop it." Peter smiled. He felt the power in him. He never felt so happy in his life. If it was as if he had just completed one of the major goals in his life.

Nick sat down and rubbed his chest. He was beginning to feel slightly better. "Damn thing knocked the crap out of me. I feel like I've been hit with a really big car." He winced in pain.

"That was amazing, Pete. I can't believe you did it." Marshall smiled at his friend.

"Yeah, Pete, that was amazing. Great job," Nick added in.

Peter shook his head. He loved the feeling of being complimented on his strength. He was a true person, though. "Nah, it was us. All of us defeated this thing. Without you guys it would of never fell. Without hurting it that bad, it could never have worked. It only worked 'cause we beat it together. As a team." Peter looked up the sky. "We are the Exterminators."

"That we are," Nick said falling back into the grass.

The door burst opened from the cabin. All three boys looked towards it. They saw Fred step out of the cabin, looking amazed at the Cyclops in front of him, frozen. "Over here, bro!" Marshall called loudly. Fred was startled then made his way towards them. The whole time walking over he kept his eyes on the Cyclops, amazed at its size.

"Guess I missed the party," he said wryly, now facing the boys.

"Yeah, that thing wasn't a party. More like the swat unit who shuts down the party," Marshall said chuckling.

"Why are you out of the containment?" Peter asked.

"Yeah about that..." Fred started.

"Dude, we saved your ass yesterday. Now you broke out? You know they're gonna have your neck for this one." Nick shook his head.

"I know. I was released suddenly though. I don't know what happened. One second I'm standing in the room doing nothing and the next the door opens. They gave me this." He passed the note to Nick to let him read. "I couldn't just ignore it. What if you guys were in trouble?"

"We had it handled," Peter answered, slightly annoyed.

"I couldn't take that chance."

"You really should have stayed in that room," Nick said looking up from the note.

Marshall stood up. He had his blaster back into Rod form.

331

He put the Rod on his hip and looked at his friends still on the ground. "Hey, this is our teammate here. He came to help us out. We can't get mad at him for that."

"What if they put him back on trial?" Peter asked. "Then that whole thing yesterday was all for nothing."

"So, let's get him back to the Station. Back into the room. They'll never know," Marshall said happily.

Nick rubbed his chest some more before he stood up. He let out a tired sigh. "Let's hurry. Hopefully, no one got back yet." He began walking towards the house. Peter got up and followed closely behind.

Fred turned to Marshall. "Are they really pissed at me?"

"Who cares? Big babies. You'll be fine. Let's get you back, man. I'll tell ya all about one eye ugly over there."

Crack

Nick turned his head to the side. He looked at the frozen beast. Its ugly face was looking at him. Its big eye moving around beneath the ice. "Oh...no..." he said. He side stepped and grabbed Peter. "Get back!" he roared. Marshall and Fred looked up. The ice shattered suddenly into a dozen pieces followed by a roar so loud and frightening that everyone cowered.

"No way," Peter said in disbelief. He was sure that would have killed it.

"How the hell?!" Marshall said, wide-eyed watching the creature shake itself off.

It looked at each boy before grunting and then it turned to walk away. It began walking towards where it had come from. The boys looked at it, confused and scared.

"Is it running away?" Marshall asked.

"Not a chance. This thing is a brute force," Nick responded.

"Where the heck is it going, then?" Marshall watched as the beast stopped near the forest.

"The club," Peter said simply. The Cyclops bent down and grabbed his weapon. He studied it then slammed it on the ground. The ice cracked and began sliding off the club. It slammed the weapon again on the ground, causing the rest of the ice to slide off easily.

"Awesome. Not only is it pissed but now it has a car-sized weapon to kill us. Wonderful." Marshall formed his hand back into the elemental blaster. He was in a weakened state with only one more shot at best.

The Cyclops looked at the boys. Its breathing was slow and heavy. They could see its breath in the cold, rising to the sky. It was angry yet it didn't charge this time. Instead it was studying its prey, acknowledging them as a formidable opposing force. It stepped to the side and watched them closely waiting for them to strike.

"Okay, so it's ready for round two," Marshall sighed. He was panting. "Yet, I don't even think I can make it half way through this round. I'm exhausted. So I'm open to any plans. Preferably ones where we don't die."

"We have a fourth player now," Peter said looking at Fred.

"Yeah, just tell me what to do, Nick." Fred looked down to grab his Rod, only just then realizing he didn't have one. "Oh crap..."

"Just stay back! We can't afford you to get hurt. Riven might take over again." Nick was angry. He didn't know why or how Fred got out but it ruined everything. He couldn't put his friend at risk.

"I could distract him!" Fred pleaded.

"I said stay the hell back!" Nick was screaming now. "You have no Rod. You're basically useless right now. So shut up and stay back!" Nick commanded. Fred wanted to argue but saw his face. His mind was made up.

"All right..." Fred walked up the stairs to the cabin. He watched closely as the boys began to shift to the left, trying to figure out a plan of attack.

"So leader," Marshall said looking at the gigantic beast waiting for them. "What's the plan? Down a man, we're all damaged or weak, and this thing still looks at full strength."

"The odds are against us." Peter flexed his fingers. He

could feel his energy fading quickly.

"Same plan as before. This time don't miss Marshall. Peter distracts it for just long enough. No more games, I'm going for its eye."

"Eye? Dude that's like right in its face. He's gonna kill you!" Marshall was surprised at Nick. Nick always wanted a safe plan, but this was the most dangerous so far.

"I agree with Marshall. You get that close you take a very big risk of dying. You sure that's our best plan?"

"Get this damn thing on its knees. It's time to finish this," Nick said plainly. He had enough of this Unknown beating them down. He stepped forward. The beast shifted, getting ready for attack. Nick walked slowly towards it.

"This damn plan is horrible. Leader my ass!" Marshall jetted to the right. He had to get far enough to be safe but close enough to make sure he didn't miss. This was his final shot; he could feel it in his body. He wouldn't have another chance.

Peter formed a yellow ball. The one he hadn't had much practice with. It was his final trump card. He was hoping that it would work. If not they were in big trouble, their plans were coming to a full stop soon enough.

Nick broke into a sprint, screaming at the top of his lungs while charging. He could feel the sharp pain in his chest but he ignored it as best he could, with the spear tucked to his side. He couldn't be afraid anymore. He had to be reckless if he wanted to kill this Unknown. It was too powerful to hit and nip.

"Nick, eyes shut!" Peter screamed. He threw the yellow ball as far in the air as he could. Nick looked up at it, seeing it shine in the sky as it came falling down a few yards ahead of him. He covered his face. The ball dropped near the Cyclops' feet. It roared and went to step on the ball. Peter closed his fist, and the ball exploded. A bright light went off and the Cyclops yelled as he became temporarily blinded. The explosion caused such a bright light that it made even Nick stop fully for a moment. He hid behind his arms, waiting for the light to die down.

Marshall uncovered his eyes and aimed at the beast. He

needed to take the beast down so he aimed low. He shot the half charged blast right at the Cyclops, hitting it on the right knee cap, and exploding on impact. The Cyclops cried out so loudly it made Fred jump back. As it collapsed to the ground it dropped the club.

Nick pulled the spear back and drove it into the eyelid of the Cyclops. It cried the loudest cry, so far. Nick dug it in further, pushing it in with all his body weight. He went deeper, blood spurting out. He pushed even deeper, the Cyclops continuing to bellow in pain as it slammed its hands on the ground. Nick gave one final push, blood splashing all over him.

The Cyclops was shuffling around his hand along the grass. It grabbed the club and swept his whole front. Nick wasn't prepared and was hit by it with full force. It made him slam into the ground and roll all the way to a nearby tree which he slammed up against. He groaned, feeling the original pain now amplified. Yet, it wasn't a full strength sweep. The beast wasn't fully ready to strike. It was still crying, trying to rip the spear out of its eye.

"Nick!" Fred screamed from the cabin. He ignored his leader's instructions and ran towards him. Marshall was on the ground breathing heavily. He had used about all the energy he had left. He let his elemental blaster turn back to a Rod and attached it back to his belt. He watched as Fred ran across the field to Nick. "Careful! Thing is still active!" he screamed. Yet he couldn't stand up to follow Fred in pursuit. He was just too tired from the last shot.

Peter watched closely as the Cyclops swung widely. It was angry. He curled his fist up, knowing he had almost no energy left. He'd used his best attacks and the thing was still standing. *I need more power. I need more damn power!"* He was getting angry. He kept concentrating, trying to think of another attack. He needed stop this beast. He just couldn't figure out a way to do that.

Fred reached Nick and turned him sideways. Nick shut his eyes tightly, trying to fight away the pain. "Hey man, you okay?!" Fred watched as he saw blood trickling out of his friend's mouth. Nick opened his eyes and grabbed his friend's shirt tightly.

"I told you to stay back!" he gritted through his teeth and

then coughed, blood coating the grass next to him.

"Man, screw that. You're like dying here," Fred said holding his friend back as he coughed some more. "That thing hit you dead on. How you're still alive is beyond me but I'm not leaving you here. Let's get you back to the cabin." Fred grabbed his friends arm and put it over his head. Then he began to lift him up. He used all the strength he had to push him up. Nick was injured to the point he was almost completely dead weight. Yet Fred didn't leave him there. He pushed him up, leaning on the tree for a moment before he began walking towards the cabin. Nick wobbled and hopped with him.

"Guys, get out of there!" Marshall roared. He saw the beast violently smashing the ground randomly. He was getting closer to Nick and Fred even though it couldn't see. It slammed its huge fist down as much as it could while also swinging its other hand with the club violently. It was hoping to strike one of its attackers in the process. "Hurry!"

Peter summoned another ball of fire. He didn't have much strength left. He knew it couldn't do much. He knew he couldn't watch his friends get crushed, though. He did a full 360 degrees, gathering as much momentum as he could before he launched the ball. It flew directly at the beast's face, blowing up on impact. The Cyclops roared as it tipped over and slammed face-first onto the ground. The fall was tremendously big, it almost knocked everyone off their feet.

Peter fell to the ground, almost completely blacking out. He'd used far more energy than he anticipated. He transformed his glove back to his Rod and dropped it. He had no energy left to fight. Sweat was dripping from his head. He'd given it his all. He just hoped it was enough to stop the creature. His hope was crushed, however, as the beast rose yet again.

It lifted its body with such ease. It was almost as if it wasn't damaged at all. It stood again, blind as a bat. It roared, but the roar was mixed with a cry. It wobbled for a moment, almost falling again. It was hurt badly, yet it still had too much pride to accept defeat just yet. It then broke into a full charge, going right for Nick and Fred.

Nick looked back. "Move!" he screamed but Fred saw it was too late. No way to move them both out of the way. So he shoved Nick to the side hard, getting him as far as he could. Nick fell hard on the ground but in a safe distance. Fred was slammed hard by the Cyclops and went flying. The Cyclops grabbed him midair and began to squeeze him. Fred cried out in pain. He could feel his bones slowly being crushed. "NO!" Nick cried out as he watched his friend getting crushed.

No one could help him though. Everyone was defeated. Nick laid on the ground, not able to get up by himself. Marshall was stuck on his knees as he watched his best friend getting crushed. Peter was blanking out, not able to even lift his head off the ground.

Marshall watched in horror. Again, he had no power to save his friend. He grabbed his Rod and tried to concentrate. He needed just one more blast to win. He needed that one more attack to save his friend. He focused hard. *"Body please, just need one more go. He needs me!"* He tried but couldn't. He couldn't summon anything. He had no strength left. He laid his head onto the ground. "Not again..." he muttered. He wasn't able to save his best friend again.

Nick began to get back on his feet. He didn't have much left. His body ached everywhere. He was the leader, though. He couldn't just give up. He was back on his feet. No movements made. He didn't know how to approach the situation. How to stop a Cyclops without any power? He stepped forward, and collapsed. He couldn't do anything. *"No, get up! You are their leader. They count on you! Get up!"* But no matter how much he wanted to he couldn't. His body couldn't move. He sat there, his fingers gripping the grass in anger.

Fred was losing consciousness. He felt his arms snap. He would have let out a cry but he was already fading out. He couldn't comprehend what was happening. Again he was on the verge of dying. His life was slipping away from him. *"I don't want to die,"* he thought. He was scared.

337

"Let me in. Give up."

He heard the voice. The voice that once talked to him. The only voice that helped him before. His friends on the ground were not able to do anything. He liked the soothing feeling. He could feel the pain slip away.

"Let it go. You've been through too much. I will take care of you." The voice was filled with kindness. It only wanted to help.

"Will you save them?"

"Save who?"

"My Friends." Fred heard no response. He couldn't hear anything. He looked to his side and saw his friends trying their best to rise but no luck. Nick was pushing himself up despite being badly injured. He couldn't risk his friends getting hurt any worse. *"I will let you in, just promise to save them,"* Fred pleaded.

After a moment of silence the voice spoke up. *"I promise,"* it responded.

Fred smiled. Up until now he didn't have a choice. Things got so bad yet everyone always chose for him. Nick saved him multiple times. Marshall always tried. Even Peter helped him before. Yet, he never made a choice. This was his one choice. He had a choice to save his friends. He smiled as he let himself drift away. He could feel everything floating away. Everything slowly becoming dark. He couldn't hear his friends cry for him but he saw a glimpse of Marshall on the field, his hand reaching out for him. *"It's okay Marshall, it's my turn to save you..."* he thought. It was his last thought before slipping away.

The Cyclops began to tighten his grip. It was ready to finally break its prey. It had finally won. It could feel it. The prey was in his hand with the heartbeat slowing. It had won the hunt.

"Someone help him!" Marshall screamed. Everyone wanted to, but no one could.

Fred slithered his arms free of the grip and struck downward. The claws, already inches long, dug into the Cyclops' fingers. He slashed across, leaving a huge claw mark across its hand. Blood instantly starting flying everywhere. The Cyclops yelped and let go of Fred. Fred landed on his feet in a heavy way, his body trembling from the change.

Nick looked up at his friend, seeing his face changing. It became more elongated. His skin began ripping off, pieces falling to the ground. His teeth become sharp and long. His nose was longer than any others. His ears perked up, with hair forming on them. His entire chest ripped out of his shirt, hair growing in pitch black in color. He grew in height to almost nine feet tall before he stopped. The beast howled in victory. Nick saw the first Unknown he had fought in front of him. Riven. "Fred...no..." he muttered looking horrified at his friend's change.

The Cyclops roared back. It couldn't see but he wasn't ready give up. It swung its fist violently forward. Riven jumped, using the fist to launch himself at its head. It began slashing at the already injured eye. Ripping away at it quickly, slashing over and over again while blood and tissue went flying from the claws. The Cyclops toppled over and fell on its back, crying out.

The boys watched in horror. Peter was back to being conscious, watching as his friend fully became a wolf hybrid. It was no simple tale, his friend was truly changing. Now it was too late to help. He'd fully become what they had feared. Peter looked at him. An emotion he never felt before began to swirl in his stomach. Fear.

Marshall watched in disbelief. His best friend was a creature now, not the boy he'd been friends with for years. Not the boy who he told his secrets to. Not the boy he went to school with. He was fully changed into an Unknown. The very thing they are meant to hunt.

Riven flung his arm forward. It ripped through the beast's eye, plunging deeper. Riven tore out a ton of the eye tissue. Blood was everywhere on Riven, but also flowing down from the Cyclops eye like tears. The Cyclops could barely keep its fist raised anymore. It tried to pull Riven away but the mighty creature slashed the arm away, cutting off a finger. The Cyclops finally stopped moving after a few more moments of brutality from Riven. After a minute, Riven stopped attacking the lifeless creature and moved to stand on its chest. It looked up the sky, hands by its side as it howled. It had won the battle.

The boys didn't know how to react. They knew it wasn't Fred anymore. That didn't mean they accepted it. It didn't make sense. Fred was standing there one second, the next Riven stood there - fully transformed. The body barely resembled anything of Fred now. They saw an Unknown standing there, not their friend.

Riven looked around at the boys. He saw Nick was the closest and went forward. Hopping off his fallen prey he walked towards the Exterminator. "Hello boy," it said as it stood over him. It could strike at any moment, finishing off the helpless boy.

"Riven?" Nick said unsure.

"Good guess. We meet again don't we?" It laughed. "You were pretty good the last time. I don't remember quite well but I think you might have killed me."

"How are you still alive?" Nick didn't even need an answer. A demon couldn't simply die like an Unknown normally does. That much he gathered.

"I passed my spirit on to Fred when I bit him. It was a seal. It's why I was in a weakened state when we fought. Did you actually believe you could kill me so easily?" The creature laughed. Nick looked disgusted. He was too late to save his friend after all. All the work since then mattered not.

"Actually..." Peter was now standing on his feet. "I was the one that killed you." He looked into Riven's eyes. He could feel the beasts power. He wanted that power. He wanted it so he could crush him. Anger filled his body.

"Lucky then, boy," Riven laughed.

"Let's see if I can get lucky twice." Peter had no energy left. He knew the bluff was fake. Yet, his emotions overran him. He was simply pissed off. His friend was gone and now an Unknown stood in front of him.

"Give him back..." Now Marshall was dragging himself towards the group.

"No can do. He gave himself to me. He's gone now." Riven touched his chest. "It's quite a great body. Full of youth. It's been awhile."

"Give him back..." Marshall demanded again, only a few feet away now from Riven.

Riven watched as his host's friend pushed himself forward. He liked his spirit. "Like I said boy, it's simply impossible."

Marshall grabbed Riven's fur. He pulled himself up and looked into the beast's eyes. "Give me my best friend back. Right now!" he yelled. Tears were flowing down his cheeks. "Give him back, you son of a bitch!" He hammered one hand on Riven's chest, crying out in pain. "Give him back! Give him back! Give him back!" he repeated over and over again. Tears were falling to the ground.

Nick watched, no feeling in him. He felt numb. He failed. He couldn't save his friend after-all. It was his responsibility and he had messed it up. He wasn't sure what to say or do at this point. He just watched as Marshall begged.

Riven grabbed Marshall and flung him to the side. Marshall lay on the ground, beaten and battered. He tried to pull himself back up but couldn't move. Riven watched the boy try. He felt pity, in a way, for the boy. "His sacrifice was to save you. Without me, you'd all be dead. He gave himself to me. You Exterminators need to learn to respect that. He made a choice. Now you must deal with the consequences." Riven looked to Nick. "Tell Carl the day will come. We will rise. No more hiding. No more running. It's time to end this war. It's time to bring it all together." Riven began walking away towards the forest.

"I will-" Marshall said through his teeth. He had his face in the ground. His pain was too much to bare. He couldn't stand thinking about it. So he turned to anger. He looked up at Riven. "-kill you. I will find you. I will corner you. Then I will kill you. You took away my friend. I promise you I'll take away your goddamn life in return," he said, spitting with anger.

"I look forward to that," Riven smiled. He turned back towards the forest and headed off. The boys sat there. The Cyclops was dead yet they felt they had still lost. They lost their friend. The once four man team was now reduced to three.

Chapter 29 – Gone

The boys sat in the gym. They weren't allowed to leave so they sat next to each other not saying a word. Nothing needed to be said. They had killed the Cyclops. It was a fearsome monster that nearly killed them all. Somehow though, their teammate, their friend, saved them all. He gave himself up and a demon took his place. Riven was its name and it was able to easily dispose of the Cyclops. It warned them something else was coming. The boys simply did not care. They were still in shock over having their friend there one moment and gone the next.

In the gym, stood Carl and Ram. Joined by them were a couple of Protectors and Aric. He was terribly upset. He wouldn't let anyone leave till he figured out how Fred had escaped in the first place. The boys were wondering that, too. They remembered seeing the note but that's all they saw. The note could have been from anyone.

"So, let's go over this one more time," Aric said walking over to the boys. Carl walked near them, guarding them in case Aric flipped out. "You say Fred just showed up at the field? Despite no one being here to set him free?"

"Yes," Nick answered.

"No one set him free? Not one of you let him out of here?" he asked again, the exasperation evident in his voice. He had already convicted the boys for doing the deed despite having no proof.

"No," Peter answered.

"And he just transformed into this creature? He transformed and walked off? Not walked off 'cause he was going to be convicted for escaping?"

"No," Marshall answered.

"I find it very convenient that he transformed on the field and walked away, yet no one besides you three saw this. He

342

somehow escaped despite being in top security. I mean, honestly boys, is this the best you can do?" Aric laughed.

Marshall looked up at Aric. "Shut up."

Aric looked back at him. "I don't know how you boys freed him. I really don't. Those codes are impossible to know unless you have high security. Just so you know though, when I find out how you did it, I won't let any punishment go undone. You will all suffer for disobeying a direct order. To leave your teammate to his fate!" Now he was yelling. The boys didn't move, didn't even flinch.

"We didn't do anything. He somehow escaped and got to us. Then he..." Marshall wanted to continue. When he thought about the events, things just got worse. He wanted to forget about all of it. All the problems that circled around him. No one felt as horrible, about the fact his best friend was gone, as he did. He still couldn't fully grasp that.

"Then he transformed into a wolf hybrid. I saw it with my own eyes," Peter spoke up. All attention went to him. "He became a beast. It was a wolf body and face. It tore the Cyclops' eyes to pieces. If you go look at the scene, you'll see that. After Riven killed the Cyclops it walked into the forest, giving us a warning that they are coming. That "they" will unite. That is all we know. That's all we saw."

The silence swept the room. Aric half believed it. The boys were badly hurt and tired. They used everything they had on the field yet the beast was clawed to death. By very long claws. The only thing he could think to do that damage was another monster, yet his Exterminating years were reminding him demons just weren't real.

"I still don't fully believe it. I will look more into it. Something is fishy and I'll find out what it is," Aric spoke loudly. He wanted to make sure the boys understood.

"I think that's enough questions for today," Carl said tersely. "Let them rest. We'll go into a full blown investigation down the line."

Aric nodded and walked away. Most of the Protectors

followed him. Carl watched as he walked away and then looked back to his students.

"Are you guys okay?" he asked worriedly. He could see each and every one of them giving a blank stare, their minds were far away from here.

"They're hurting. Both mentally and physically. I think its best they get home," Ram said quietly, walking near his friend.

"I think you're right. Boys, go home and get some rest. I'll be in contact with you soon. If anyone wants to stay and talk I'm available." Carl tried his best to show he cared. The boys had just lost their friend. He lost another of his students. He felt like he wanted to slam walls and break tables yet he stood there with his best poker face, trying to support the remainder of his unit.

The boys all got up and began walking out of the gym. No one said a word. Just complete silence, no one wanted to talk.

"Ram, let me talk to you in my office." Carl trailed behind the boys while Ram followed closely.

Kelly waited on her steps. It was raining now, nothing too heavy, just a light drizzle. The air felt heavy, as the humidity was high. No one was out on the street. Everyone was in their homes nice and cozy. Kelly couldn't stay inside though. She waited on the steps for Nick. He had promised her he'd be back hours ago. She knew it was best to just go inside and expect to speak to him tomorrow. She didn't want to let go of the hope that maybe her boyfriend, her lover, would show up again though.

She had never dated because she was afraid. Strong fears of being left by someone she trusted were proven by little dates she had been on before. They just wanted her body, not who she was. So she stuck to the non-dating rule. It worked for the most part. That is until Nick came along. *"Stupid pen expert..."*

She loved him very much. He was kind-hearted, brave, and always caring man. She couldn't imagine finding a better person to love. He had secrets, though. She wasn't sure if they were bad but they were certainly breaking up the relationship. He would leave for hours without telling her anything. He'd come up hurt and again not tell her anything. These things had to stop. Either that or she had to know what it was. Because if she couldn't figure it out, she was going to give up. As much as it pained her to do so, it hurt more to continue going on this way.

She looked down the side of the street. She saw someone walking towards her. She knew before he even lifted his head, it was Nick. She rose from her seat unsure if she was angry or happy anymore. She wanted to go hug him, kiss him, to bring him as close as possible. At the same time she wanted to slap him and ask him for the last time where he was.

He took another step and stood waiting on the bottom of the stairs. The rain was hitting the top of his head. His beard was dripping water. It was a mix of tears and the walk in the rain that had his face soaked. He looked up at her. He didn't know what to say.

"Where were you?" she asked. Not harshly. Not mean. Just worried.

"I-" he didn't know where to begin. He didn't know what to tell her. He didn't even register the events fully in his mind. "-I've lost..."

"Lost what?"

"Everything..."

"What are you saying?" She stepped down to another level. The rain teasing her as it hit her shoe. She was still under the cover of her house, but barely.

"I can't tell you."

"Why the hell not!?" she yelled, her voice almost breaking up. "Why do you hide everything from me?"

"'Cause I have to."

"Why do you "HAVE" to?!"

"I just do..."

"Not good enough! Tell me why right now!" She stepped hard on the next staircase level, yelling with everything she had.

"It's to keep you safe! I have to keep you safe! I do this to keep you safe! Goddamn it, Kelly!" he was screaming, waving his

345

arms in the air. "I need to keep you safe 'cause I won't let them hurt you! I won't let anyone hurt you!" People began to peer outside their windows. "You think I like this!? This goddamn life I now live?!"

"Your life with me?" she asked sadly.

"No, damn it!" he yelled, but lower this time. "I love you. I want to stay with you. To do, that I must protect you."

"From what?" She wanted to know so badly.

"I can't tell you that." He walked up a stair, reaching out and touching her cheek. His cold wet hand against her dry soft skin. "I can't tell you 'cause it'll put you in harm's way. Do you understand? I want to but I can't. It's to protect you. I swear."

She looked at him. She wasn't sure what the secret was. She knew that he was fighting himself internally, trying to decide what to do. She loved him too much to make him suffer between choosing. "It's okay. I trust you." She stepped down and put her arms around his wet clothes. She pulled him closer, holding him tightly.

He began to cry. She had never heard him cry like that. It was loud, so loudly it was the only thing she could hear even with cars passing. He was crying hysterically. He held her tightly, pulling her tightly to him. She held tightly back. She didn't want to let him go. He needed her more than anything. She cried with him.

"I lost him," he muttered between the sobbing. She tried to understand but didn't. So, she did what she could and held him, rubbing his back, and telling him it would be okay. All he could say for the next twenty minutes were the same repeating words: "I lost him."

Carl sat down in the chair. Ram looked at him oddly. "Why aren't you sitting at his desk?" Carl just looked down at the floor. He let out a huge sigh. "Hey, are you okay?" Ram bent down and could see his friends' eyes were closed. A tear began to roll over his cheek and fall to the floor.

"I failed again," Carl said softly. He felt the pain from

years ago return.

"You didn't fail." His friend placed his hand on Carl's shoulder. "You had no way of knowing what would happen if Fred went out there."

Carl looked to his side, eyes teary. "It was my fault he even went out there. He should have been locked in here. What the hell happened?!" He wanted to cry more but his tears didn't come. It came from too many years of losing people to cry like he used to. He wasn't sure if that made him feel even worse. That he couldn't cry for the fallen ones anymore.

"We'll figure out what happened. You can't just sit here though and blame yourself. Never again, remember?" Ram watched as his friend nodded. "Come on, we will get through this. We always do, right?"

"Yeah..." Carl let his voice drift. He wasn't sure how to react anymore to situations like this. He stayed distant for this fact alone. The loss. It's harder than anything.

"You changed that boy's life."

"Yeah, by ending it," Carl laughed an empty laugh.

"You gave him a life he never had. His mom and dad don't even know their own kid's age. You cared for him. You introduced him three other boys who loved and cared for him. He, for once, fit in with people. You told me he was an outsider. Then he met these boys and reunited a friendship and made new ones. You changed his life forever. Don't ever let anyone tell you different. We all pass away one day, it's the memories and experiences we have during life that make us truly live."

Carl looked up at his friend. He knew he could count on support. He had it last time, but the betrayal was far worse then. He knew he could bounce back from this. He knew he could help the others live on and not give up. "You're right. I have to be strong for the others."

"That's right. They are young. They haven't been through anything like this before. We won't let them do this alone."

"It's a terrible life to live at times. Losing so many." Carl looked towards his friend for a response.

"In life, we always lose the ones we love. Exterminators or not. It's the way it goes. We have to live for the ones who aren't living anymore." Carl nodded to that and got up. "What do you wanna do now?"

"Find out who would free Fred."

"And then what?"

"Kill the son of a bitch."

Peter was soaked. He walked into his home and went right straight to the bathroom. He threw his clothes off and into the basket on the floor. Placing his hands on the counter, he looked into the mirror at himself. He had gained so much muscle. He felt amazing in terms of body strength. He came so far in a few months it would be impossible not to feel this way. Eeven with all these new improvements, he still failed to save his friend.

He slammed his hand down hard on the counter. He could feel the sharp pain instantly shoot up his arm from his hand. He bit his lip as he slammed his hand again. The pain soared again through his entire arm now. He did it again, this time yelling. He did again, yelling louder. He did it again, screaming. He did it again, this time feeling his face getting wet. It wasn't the rain. It was tears.

He never cried. He looked into the mirror and saw them flowing down his face. They came without him noticing. Was it the anger? He sometimes cried when he was angry. Short little tears though, not like this. He could feel emptiness in his chest. He had lost something important. It was like having your favorite toy stolen from you.

This was losing someone.

Peter never had before. He wished death upon his father at times, but his father was still walking around drunk every night. Now, he never had to see him, thanks to the police, but he still wasn't dead. Fred was dead though.

"That doesn't make sense. Why is my dad still alive and breathing and my friend is dead? Someone who helps the world is

348

dead and someone who wastes his way in the world is alive? This doesn't make sense." For all his book smarts, Peter couldn't understand it. Life was the hardest problem in the world. He felt the balance was so shifted. It made no sense why the good leave and the bad stay. It doesn't make any sense at all.

Peter turned on the shower. He let it run hot so the steam would build. He wanted to wipe away everything. Usually the shower helped with that. To clear his mind of everything. He was able to do it a lot easier than others anyway.

He stepped into the very hot shower and let the water splash on him. He could feel the steam building up. He laid his head on his arms while leaning on the shower wall. He let go of everything, trying to free up his mind. It was a simple way of having a completely empty slate.

No matter how hard he tried though he kept picturing Fred. He saw Fred when they trained together and when they fought together. He even saw flashes of Fred in his final moments when he was getting crushed be the Cyclops. *"Why didn't we stop him?"* Peter questioned himself. At the time of fighting he thought having backup would be great. Now, all he could think about is if Fred never came then he might have been saved. He might still be with them. Instead, he was gone and replaced by a demon called Riven. Everything went wrong.

Peter didn't want to blame himself but he still felt the guilt. He felt the sadness building. Most of all, he felt the emptiness, the missing feeling, tugged at his heart. He never felt it before. That just made it far worse to experience.

Marshall opened the door to his room. Lucy sat on his bed, looking up at him. He pulled his shirt off and threw it to the floor. He unbuckled his wet pants and kicked them into the corner. He grabbed an old shirt to dry his wet hair and flung it to the side afterward. He lay down on the bed, putting his face on her lap.

"Baby..." he said softly, his voice cracking slightly.
"Yes, babe?"

"I.."

She put her hands through his hair while looking at him, feeling sad.

"I lost...I lost..." he began to cry. It was just a small sob.

"You lost what, babe? Tell me." She stopped going through his hair and laid her hand on his back. He rolled over and looked up at her.

"Fred's gone."

"Gone?"

"He's dead." Marshall hadn't said it till that point. He hadn't even told himself that. He kept the words out of his mind and mouth. Now that he said it everything hit him at once. He felt such a heavy pain it made him cry instantly. He rolled back over and buried his face in her legs. He grabbed her shirt and pulled strongly on it. So much pain. He couldn't breathe. He gasped for air between the sobs.

"Babe...I'm so sorry," she said softly, holding his head while putting her head on his back as he cried. "I'm sorry," she repeated.

He remembered meeting Fred for the first time, just as little kids playing around on the playground. He saw Fred had a Godzilla comic. He went over to him and asked if he could read it. Fred said no. Then he let him read it, but only together. Marshall let him borrow one of his Godzilla tapes. Ever since then they've been best friends.

He cried harder.

He remembered third grade with Fred. Marshall was getting yelled at by a teacher. Marshall said a curse word at the teacher. Back when you were that young you weren't allowed to say that. He was about to be sent to the principal's office when Fred cursed too. They both got detention for a week, but together.

He cried even harder feeling the tears coming out like a river. He couldn't stop thinking about the past.

She let him cry for several minutes. After a while he slowed down. The amount of sobs decreased, his tears didn't come out as quick, and his face returned to his regular color instead of

350

bright red. He let out all the pain that was going through him.

"Baby..." he muttered, his voice still sounding high-pitched.

"Yes, babe?"

"I love you," he said without any regret. He wasn't going to wait anymore.

She was shocked by the words as she looked at him. He rolled over again and looked back up. She didn't know how she would handle her future with him but she did know one thing.

"I love you too."

Jin pushed open the door. It a two story apartment building. He folded up the umbrella and placed it on the floor before he ran up the stairs. He could feel his cold hands heating up. He was angry. Upset. He needed to figure out what happened.

He opened the door to the apartment. The main door opened to the living room. The lights were off, pitch black. He looked to where the light came from; the dining room. He walked into it. At the large table was a man with blond hair, spiky on the tips, but pushed down. He had his glasses on like usual. A huge scar ran from the bottom of his eye down to his neck. He smiled at Jin.

"Come in!" he announced happily.

"You promised!" Jin roared.

"I promised what? I promise a lot of things. You have to be a little more specific," he said, laughing.

"You swore none of them would get hurt!"

"None of them did."

"Fred is dead!"

"Where did you hear that?"

"Riven took over his body."

"It was his choice," The blond hair man said leaning back in his chair. "He wanted to save his friends."

"What the hell are you talking about?!" Jin asked, yelling.

"They would all be dead. He let me take his body in order

to save his friends-" Riven stepped out from behind the wall. He was in full form now. His teeth were razor sharp when he spoke. The skin was completely intact. Nothing decaying, as of yet, like when the boys first fought him. He was in good health with his new body. "-I did not force him. I gave him a choice, he made one."

"You lied! You promised me the boys would be safe."

"I said I'd try to keep them out of harms ways. This is war." The blond haired man stood up.

"You said this war needed to end. You said we were to unite, yet now you go after kids! You lied!"

"Riven is the one who saved you all those years ago, or did you forget?" The blond haired man gave Jin a grin. "He saved you from certain death. We need him in our ranks. He was going to die in that old body."

"You didn't have to take Fred!" Jin said. He could feel tears wanting to come out. He remembered all the times he was with Fred. All the times he hung out with him, trained with him. He felt terrible now that his friend was gone.

"You got too close. Do we need to pull you out already?" The blond man asked, his voice not changing at all. It was a playful tone.

"You promised me you wouldn't hurt those kids. You said you needed to stop Carl. That he would be the main problem. Now you attack others? What aren't you telling me?"

"Carl is the problem." The blond man's voice changed. He sounded annoyed now. "We must extract revenge on him in subliminal ways. We want to change this world for the better, right? We need to get rid of the ones who will oppose us. I have no problem letting the innocents free. However, Carl is not innocent. Far from it! He is also training these kids to be something far worse. Exterminators just like him. I can't allow that."

"Are you saying you'll try to kill them all?!" Jin could feel an awful, sinking feeling in his gut.

"No. The boys, as of now, hold no interest to me. Riven will try to change them, make them join our cause. This is why I needed him back. Once they are all on our side you'll see my reasoning for taking Fred first." The blond man walked around the table and stood in front of Jin. "Don't worry, all of it will come together. Fred didn't want to fight anymore. He let Riven take him so he could save his friends. Riven did just that. He saved them. So you can see it was the right thing to do. Right?"

Jin looked at the blond man. This was his true first friend. The one who molded him into the person he was. He felt like he could believe in him. "Yes, you are correct. I just...didn't understand."

"That's okay. Sometimes being mixed up with Exterminators can do that." The blond man laughed loudly.

"No need to worry. Soon we Summoners will get our chance to strike."

Chapter 30 – Surprise

Three weeks had passed. The outside investigation for the missing boy, Fred, had made a huge buzz in the community. Police interrogated Nick, Peter, and Marshall various times, trying to get as much information as they could possibly get. The full search went out four days after Fred was missing. His own parents didn't even get home until two days after it had happened. Only then did they call the police. The search was insanely thorough, but no results came from it.

    The boys kept to themselves. Marshall took a few days off from school. His parents didn't like it but they'd never seen him so down. The result of losing his friend crushed him. He wasn't sure how he was going to operate. It especially hurt when on the news they would say there was still a very good chance he'd be alive upon finding him. Marshall knew that would never happen. He knew instead that a demon had taken over and his friend was gone forever. This was the hardest thing to accept. That his friend would never speak to him again.

    Peter kept his training up. It was the only way to keep his mind off of what happened. Staying home, watching TV, even reading did not distract him enough. He went back to training. He needed to be stronger, faster, better. He needed to be. He never wanted to lose another friend again. He swore his life on it, that it wouldn't happen again.

    Nick stayed with Kelly every day. They went to school together and returned home together. Instead of going to training Nick focused on filling out work applications. He wasn't sure if he'd be going to college but he knew he needed a job. So while Kelly eagerly chose colleges, he focused on getting a job to support them both. He soon planned on moving out and for that he needed money. He also pushed hard on his school work. If he could graduate and be done with school he'd be happy. His father would be happy. Kelly would be happy. The world would keep turning. Everyone would be happy.

Carl began making a sheet of training schedules. It was time to train with the boys and he wasn't going to let them slip up. He needed them to focus, in order to do so he had to push himself. The boys could easily die in battle, but with training, that can change the outcome completely. He took it upon himself to finally step up as a Bora. He almost went back to drinking, especially after Fred died, but who would he be saving then? Save him a few minutes of grief? Wasn't worth it.

Jin kept his routine up. He worked out by himself, sometimes sparing with Peter, but mostly hunting down Unknowns as he was told to. He could feel the war, the one only the Summoners seemed to be aware of, building up. They were becoming restless, especially his master. He wasn't sure how it would end but he knew which side he was fighting for. The Exterminators based their whole lives on killing off the Unknowns. Summoners just wanted to unite everyone. The choice was clear to him. He chose the Summoner's side but remained undercover with the Exterminators.

Nick walked into the gym a week later. He finally felt it was time to get back into training. He put all his paperwork in for several jobs. He also brought up his grades in school. He felt he could finally get back into his Exterminating job. He saw Jin standing in the gym talking to Emily.

Nick made his way over, waving as he approached.

"Hey man, haven't seen you in here in like forever," Jin smiled at him.

"I'm sorry about your loss," Emily said.

"Thank you," he responded. He could still feel the pain within.

"I was just telling Emily about the investigation. The outsiders aren't gonna be a problem. Fortunately, the Exterminators have got some pull within the government, so they will try to push the case quickly through. Still, police will probably keep harassing us for a while." Jin glanced at Nick who was still looking at the floor.

"I'll keep telling them the same thing. I don't know what happened but I want to know. That's all I'm supposed to say right?" Nick began moving past the two. He grabbed his Rod and began concentrating.

"Yeah..." Jin watched Nick. He was just a shell of his former self. He still hadn't fully recuperated.

"Nick, maybe it's best you still take some time off," Emily suggested.

"I've rested enough," Nick said forcefully. He formed a sword with blunt edges. He faced both Jin and Emily. "You two, come at me."

"Nick, come on," Jin protested.

"I said come at me!" Nick cried angrily.

"Nick, this won't solve anything," Emily said, her voice sounding strained.

"Fine, if you won't attack, I will!" Nick blasted forward. Both Exterminators went for their Rods. Just in time they formed their own blunt swords. Nick went to slash Jin but it was a fake move. He came swinging at Emily, instead. Emily already had her sword midair ready to strike instead of just defending herself. She was hit right in her side. She gasped as her eyes bulged and she grasped her side. It was a strong, heavy hit.

"Nick!" Jin yelled, going into attacking position. He went to strike but Nick already had his sword back up in defense. They clashed, a loud echo filling the entire gym. Nick twirled around and came with another swing. Jin easily dismissed that with an upper slash. Jin then moved in closer and shoulder rushed Nick. Nick went tumbling back and fell on his bottom, his free hand breaking his fall.

"Damn it!" Nick yelled hurriedly getting back to his feet.

"You hit her hard, Nick. What the hell?!" Jin was bending down to aid Emily. She held her side, her face filled with discomfort.

356

"I didn't mean to hurt her-" he started with a loud voice. Then he looked at her. She winced in pain as Jin touched her side. "-Emily I'm sorry," he finished, his tone a lot softer.

"Hey, it's okay!" she said giggling. "I've been hit with way worse."

"You sure you're okay?" Jin asked.

"I'm sure, hun, thank you." She smiled up at him. He helped her back up on her feet.

Nick looked down at his sword. He felt he had so much power when he held his weapon. It was like he could do anything. *"Yeah anything, except save your friend."* He hated his mind process. Everything related back to Fred eventually. He tried to forget but he couldn't.

"Nick, do not push yourself," Jin said, staring at him with serious eyes. "You push yourself and you'll just overdo it. You just lost a friend. You have to accept that. You also take the burden of being the leader. So you blame yourself. Stop, it's silly. Everyone fights for their own lives; everyone knows that coming in here."

"Yeah but..."

"No buts. He came in here knowing the risk. He fought his best every time he stepped out there. You keep blaming yourself and it'll solve nothing. You have to be a leader to everyone else still around. That is a real leader!" Jin raised his voice. He needed Nick to see that a leader must continue to lead even after his soldiers have fallen.

"I know...it's just that it's hard. I can't stop thinking if I had more power. If I was a little stronger..." Nick let his voice disappear into the vast gym.

"Anything could of happened out there. Hell, all of you might be dead right now if it wasn't for Fred. Fred died sacrificing himself for you."

Nick felt a sharp pain in his chest. He had the same statement in his mind the last few days.

"What gave him the right?"

"What?"

"What gave him the right to do that? To let himself die for

357

us!?" Nick could feel his eyes wanting to cry, yet he had no more tears to release. He cried himself dry over the past few weeks of blaming himself.

"Every man gets to choose."

"He didn't let me choose!"

"Every man gets to choose when he feels it's appropriate. He died knowing you three would be safe."

"I didn't get a say in that!"

"You are a leader, not a slave owner, Nick. You can't just tell others what to do. You lead people and they follow. You do not command people to the point where they have no self-conscious choice to do what they do." Jin watched Nick. He could see how angry he was. How upset he was. He wanted to stop but he knew Nick needed this.

"I never said he could run in there and save me. He should of freaking stayed near the house! Why did he run towards me? After I told him not to!?"

"He made a choice."

"I didn't accept that choice!"

"Well, that's just too damn bad!" Now Jin was shouting back. Nick curled his fist. He wanted to punch something. Anything.

"Why did he die!? I was the leader. I watch over them. So why didn't I die?"

Jin stopped for a moment. He finally saw it...the pain on Nick's face. It wasn't a simple case of grief. It wasn't guilt. It wasn't even the fact he was really angry. He saw what Nick's true pain finally was. "You're scared aren't you?"

"What!?" Nick said, sounding offended.

"You're scared of the choice. You thought, this whole time that he's been gone, that if you could make that choice yourself, you wonder if you would have been brave enough to sacrifice yourself in that position." Jin lowered his voice to a calm tone. Emily looked at him then Nick, sadness written all over her face.

Nick wanted to yell back. Tell him he didn't know what he was talking about. Yet, he just stood there. Someone finally knew what he was thinking. "I just don't know..." he said.

"See Nick that's the thing." Jin walked up to Nick and placed his hand on his shoulder. "I believe the only reason he did what he did was because he had a leader, someone to follow. He died knowing he'd protect his friends. He did it 'cause he knew you'd do the same. That might be one of the only reasons he did it." Jin tightened his grip on his shoulder. "You're a damn fine leader. Don't ever doubt your motives or what you stand for again."

Nick looked into Jin's eyes. He could see everything he was thinking spilling out from him. All the hatred he built up for himself leaving. He questioned his abilities as a leader and always doubted it. Now he had reassurance. That he would of have done the same thing in that position. "Thank you," Nick said quietly. Tears finally came.

Peter stepped in to Carl's apartment. He had never been in it but he was surprised by how small it was. With such a high position in the organization he expected a bigger home. Instead it was a tiny single bedroom studio. The room was a mess with clothes and beer bottles on the table stands. Peter walked around the tables and sat down on the empty chair across from the bed. Carl sat there just staring outside the window.

"Sir?" Peter looked to the window but he saw nothing. He turned back to Carl. "You needed to talk to me?"

"Did you free Fred?" Carl's voice was so low Peter barely caught it.

"What?"

"Did you free Fred? The day of the hunt against the Cyclops."

"No. I told you I didn't. I was fighting the Unknown at the time."

"I find it odd." Carl took a heavy breath.

"What do you find odd?"

"That a few days prior you told me Fred was changing, yet

359

on that day you were the one who came in with a bunch of bruises with blood coming out of your mouth." Now Carl turned to him.

"I..." Peter forgot about his father. He didn't want to mention anything about him to anyone.

"You never explained why you were nearly dead. You just put out the fact Fred was changing. All the attention turns to him. We hunt him. Put him on trial. He somehow gets free. He becomes Riven. And we've lost an Exterminator."

"What are you getting at?" Peter asked plainly. He felt no emotion. He looked at Carl with an unreadable face.

"Sounds like good motives for a Summoner." Carl stood up quickly and formed a sword. He put it to Peter's neck before the boy could react. Peter sat there, not moving a muscle. "Are you one, Peter?" he asked quietly.

"No."

"Then what the hell happened to you that day?"

"I don't want to speak about it."

"Guess what? You're going to otherwise I bring you in for trial. Then everyone will hear about it. Is that what you want instead?" Carl held the sword only inches away from Peter's neck. Peter still did not move, did not show emotion, he just looked up at his Bora.

"Do you not trust me?"

"You have to gain my trust. Right now it doesn't look very good for you," he gritted through his teeth. "I won't be betrayed again."

"I did not free Fred." Peter closed his eyes. He looked to the floor, ignoring the sword next to his throat.

"Then what happened to you?"

"My father beat me till I couldn't stand. He probably would of killed me if he wasn't so thirsty for more alcohol. He tackled me to the ground, punched me, kicked me, nearly killed me. I didn't want anyone to know. I wanted to keep my personal life out of my job. So, I focused the attention on Fred to get away from that. I didn't know it would lead to his death. I didn't know anything like this would happen. For that, I am sorry." Peter looked back up. He pushed the sword out of his way. "I am not a Summoner, though. My loyalty will be proven in time if you don't believe me now. Just know, though, I fight for the Exterminators and that is all. If you don't want to believe me that is your choice. I can't change that for you, you'll have to do that all by yourself." He stood up. "I'll take my leave now." He began walking towards the door.

Carl put his sword back to Rod form. "I'm sorry, I didn't know."

"That's 'cause I didn't want you to." He stated as he continued walking towards the door.

"I will take care of your father."

Peter put his hand on the doorknob. He waited a moment before looking back. "He's in jail now. Once he is out he is gone. If he dares put his hands on me again I'll make sure he won't live to drink another drink again." Peter opened the door.

"Peter...I'm sorry," Carl said as his voice decreased in volume.

"Goodbye." Peter closed the door.

Carl stood there, ashamed; blaming his own people for his past mistakes. His own students who looked up to him. He had been betrayed before but it was no excuse to blame everyone for the past experiences. He had to fight the demons yet no matter how hard he did they always returned; sprinting around in his mind like the devil on your shoulder.

Marshall walked up to his door. He had just come from a run, drenched in sweat from the now warm weather. He walked into his home and threw his shirt into the laundry right away. He went into his room and kicked off his shoes. Lucy was sitting on the bed, looking at her nails. "Hey babe, whatsup?" he asked rubbing some deodorant on.

"Yeah, we have to talk." She was still looking at her hands.

He sat down next to her. "What's wrong?" he asked. He felt something terrible in his stomach.

"It's about us."

He felt his stomach turn. "What's wrong? Did I do something? I know I've been training as of late but it's just been helping me deal with the probe-"

She put her hand up and looked at him. "It's not that. I need to know how serious you are about us."

He looked at her confused. "What are you talking about? I told you I loved you. You know how much I care about you."

"I know...I just need to know that you'll always be there."

"Of course I will." He put his hand on her cheek and rubbed. "Why would you think I wouldn't be?"

"I just need to know you'll always be by me."

"Always."

"When I'm hurt or sick."

"I will."

"If I ever got fired from a job or failed school."

"Yes baby, of course!" he laughed.

"If I was pregnant?"

"I'd be here for you. No matter what," he said smiling.

"Good, 'cause I'm pregnant."

"What?" he said, his voice cracking half way through the word.

"I just took two tests."

"What?"

"I didn't want to tell you right away."

"What?"

"I've been trying to gather money to take another test, just in case."

"What?"

She slammed her hands down on his legs. He jumped up. "Stop saying what! This is important! Talk to me!"

"I..." He didn't know what to say. The jokester was out of jokes. The fast talker couldn't even speak. "I got nothing."

"What?"

"I don't know what to say, baby," he said truthfully. His heart was pounding faster than it ever had before. "I'm trying to grasp the situation here."

"I know it's scary, but I'm scared too. Please talk to me. And don't just ask me what over and over again." She was on the verge of crying.

"We'll figure this out. I'm not going anywhere. Like I said, I'm here for you." He gave her a kiss. It was a long and strong kiss. He could taste the salty tears falling in-between their lips. They separated and looked at each other in silence. They now had to work together as things were about to get a lot more complicated from here on out.

"And you thought dealing with Unknowns was going to be tough," she giggled.

"Not funny."

"Too soon?"

"Yeah," he said smiling. He put his forehead against hers, feeling her warmth, trying to figure out their future.

Chapter 31 – Moving On

End of May finally came. Graduation had passed three days ago. All three boys were completely done with school. They all passed. Peter scored mostly A's and was guaranteed to be accepted into just about any college. Nick got his grades up quite a bit, snagging a few B's along the way. Marshall did just enough to pass. He was focusing on other ventures besides college.

They had posters all over the school for the missing boy, Fred. The boys knew what had happened to their friend, but no one else did. They brought him up at the acceptance speech. Congratulating him and hoping he'd return home soon. Many of the students even cried some. Fred wasn't well known but due to disappearing out of nowhere people still seemed to care. Either that or they worried it might happen to them, too.

Marshall spent his time filling out job applications and running around town trying to find work. He had to prepare for the baby in a few months. She'd been pregnant since March, meaning the baby would be coming around in November. He wasn't ready, but he forced himself to be. He went on a major job search, hoping to obtained one. In the mean time he set up to go to Florida in a few weeks with his brother. Lucy was now tagging along on the fun, little get-away.

Nick was getting ready for the two month vacation with his father. They would head to Pennsylvania for a few weeks and have some time to themselves. Carl warned him if signals were close he would still have to do his job. Nick didn't mind. The hunts became a part of his life recently. He didn't even need to be told to do them. He felt obligated to.

Peter still focused heavily on training. He wanted to become the strongest; it was his determination that pushed him. Yet, he began building other parts of his body. Running more than he had before. Push-ups and pull ups to strengthen his body. He needed to be ready for whatever circumstances he was put under. Due to his ability of not having too many emotions, he was able to handle losing Fred faster than the others. It gave him a slight edge in enhancing himself even more.

Carl focused on getting better himself. He cleaned up his entire apartment, threw away all his bottles and made sure to focus on the boys. He began to get back into training himself as well. His famous fist and push fighting style never failed him. He was powerful with just about any weapon he used, yet he wanted to get back to his original state as being one of the only unbeatable Exterminators to ever live.

Jin. Jin still wasn't sure what he was doing.

Jin sat at the end of the table looking at his master. The blond man was writing down something quickly, eager to finish like he was racing an invisible clock. Jin knew this man as the one who had saved him years ago. He wondered if it was the same man sitting before him now. The blond man seemed intent on revenge; on destroying the boys with whom Jin had become friends with. This wasn't the same person that rescued him years ago.

A sharp slap on Jin's back startled him as another guy walked into the room. He sat down next to him, took a sip of his drink, and laughed. "Haven't seen you around lately. You turning Exterminator on us?" He was a bit older than Jin, in his mid-twenties, spiky dyed red hair, and green eyes. Quite an odd looking man, even goofy, but he was anything but that when it came to business.

"No, just been busy doing my job. How have you've been Cole?" Jin looked his old friend in the eyes. Cole had been one of Jin's sparing partners before he went undercover in the Exterminator base. He taught Jin a lot of the beginners stuff. How to use a Rod, the power is possess', when to call your limits and so on. He was a great trainer but also a crazy man at heart. He never really put limits on himself.

"Wonderful! I went out last night, got messed up, took a girl back, then left before she woke up. So I'm doing A-Okay. Just another wonderful day. How about you, boy?" he asked while chugging more of his drink.

"Good. Keeping to myself yet getting as close as I can."

"Ah the trickster you are. I always thought you'd do great undercover. Still with that chick, what's her name?"

"Emily," he quickly said.

"Yeah. Cute ass on that broad. Bet you show her a good time, you trickster you!" Cole slapped him on the back, laughing harder than before.

"Will you kindly shut up?" the blond man said, annoyed.

"Sorry boss man." Cole looked back towards Jin. "So how's everything else? Anyone bother you at all? Remember if you get too close just pull out. We'll handle the rest." Cole spoke in a much softer voice. Trying his best to not annoy the boss.

"I'm fine. I know my mission, don't worry."

"Hey, I'm not worried. I know you could handle it, kid. You are like my prodigy after all," Cole grinned.

"I think I far surpassed you by now. Thank you very much." Jin let a smile sneak out.

"Oh boy. I'd love to test that theory one day," Cole laughed. He got up from his seat and looked towards the blond man. "All right boss I'm out. Gotta grab a few hours more sleep. I'll be back tonight to discuss more of the plan." He looked down at Jin. "You owe me that fight too. Don't forget." He walked out the room and down the stairs.

Jin looked back towards the blond man. "The Boss" they called him. Yet, Jin preferred real names. "David, I've come to talk," he announced, just loud enough to be heard from the other end of the room.

David, the boss, looked up. "Calling me by my first name. This must be important. What's wrong, Jin?"

"Nothing is wrong. I just...I need you to agree not to hurt these kids."

"I already said I wouldn't, didn't I?"

"Yeah, but you said that before. Then Riven came into the picture."

David put his pen down and wiped his face with his hand. He made a moaning sound, as if to say he was bored. "You asked me not to hurt the kids. Months later the kids are fine and dandy. Did I not keep my promise?"

"Down the line though," Jin pushed. He had to make sure his new friends weren't in any type of danger.

"If it comes to the War, then it's up to them. If they side with the Exterminators, despite how foolish it would be, that is their choice. I made mine. You made yours. They will make theirs. Simple as that." David smiled at Jin. A soft yet sinister type of smile. "You worry too much. Anyone ever tell you that?"

"All the time."

"You should listen to them." David dropped the smile and picked up his pen. "Do yourself a favor and take a break. You'll need one. Soon you won't ever see one." He went back to writing. Jin sat there, satisfied some, yet still worried.

Marshall walked into the gym. He saw Peter and Nick sitting down. Next to them were Daryl and his group. *"Today you tell them. These are your friends. They deserve to know you're gonna be a daddy. A daddy. That's so weird."* Marshall smiled without realizing it. "Hey creepy smile, how's it hanging?" Nick asked, everyone laughed.

"First off it's not creepy, it's sexy. Second off, I'm fine. Thank you very much. Hey Daryl, Sam, Rachael, weird other guy."

"My name is Ali."

"Yeah, like I said. Weird other guy." Marshall sat down next to Nick.

Peter sat next to Rachael. They were talking about different elements. How to use them in different ways. He was especially excited to tell her about the grass vine one, in which he could create vines from the ground to grab on to things. She never thought of it, so she was very grateful for the information. He wasn't really getting the concept that she was interested in him. He didn't get that even though he felt the same for her. He wanted to know so much about her, not fully understanding that he already liked her.

Nick talked to Daryl more about the fighting styles. Nick had been watching some videos on boxing. Trying some daily training routines that boxers do. He also began hitting the punching bag more as of late instead of relying on the Rod alone. To be stronger and better with a weapon means you must become strong with your own fist. That was what Daryl told him.

Sam looked at Marshall. He looked at her, then away. He felt bad whenever he was checking out another girl. Especially knowing he had Lucy at home. Even more so, now that she was pregnant. "I'm sorry," she said to him. He looked back to her, confused. "About Fred. He seemed really nice." He felt a sharp pain in his chest. It wasn't as if he forgot, he just learned to accept the passing. It still hurt when someone brought up his name though.

"Thank you," he said.

"Welcome," she looked away.

The doors opened. Carl and another person walked in. Next to him stood a tall bald person with an ugly robe-type uniform on. Marshall stood up and laughed. "Look, it's the guy from Star Trek!" He pointed at the bald person next to Carl.

Nick grabbed his friend. "Sit the hell down moron, and shut up!"

Marshall sat down but pushed Nick off. "I'm just saying. It looks like him."

"Kind of does," Sam said laughing.

"Please, Star Trek people are much better dressed," Ali said waving his hand.

"That's our Bora. His name is Scott. Be respectful," Daryl said loud enough for everyone to hear.

"Sorry. Gee, always so serious." Marshall sat back, arms

crossed.

"Hello Carl's unit. Nice to meet you." Scott gave a short wave. "I've come here today, with Carl, to announce your ascension." The boys broke into a mutter. The girls gave each other a high five.

"What's an ascension?"

"What do we get?"

"What's that?"

Carl put his hands up. "Everyone listen up. You will be getting your second Rod today." Everyone muttering broke into a cheer. They all began shouting in excitement.

"Now the reasons behind you getting these second Rods are because of the way you dealt with those large signals. Cyclops and Dire Wolves are nothing to take lightly. Both are very dangerous Unknowns. You did very well under very tough circumstances." Scott tried to simmer down the shouting but everyone was too excited. They all knew they would eventually get a second Rod, they just never knew when.

Peter was the first to walk forward. This is what he'd been waiting for. He'd been trying new strategies with his elemental glove. He was fully prepared to use two Rods now. He walked up to Carl, with his hand out. "I'm ready," he said. Voice as plain as day.

Carl nodded and grabbed a small case. It had a big silver P on it. He handed it to Peter and smiled. "You are ascended. Use the Rod wisely; it is now a part of you." Peter nodded and walked away. He felt himself disconnected from the world more as of late. Except when he was around Rachael and Jin. Even Nick and Marshall, he seemed to have drifted away from. Training lessened with them. He avoided Carl at all cost. He felt they blamed him. He decided to stay away until he was powerful enough to prove he was a worthy part of them. Or even above them.

Everyone follow Peter's lead. They each went up and grabbed their case. They studied the second Rod. Feeling the raw power just like they did when they held the first one. All of them were thinking of different ways they could use the second weapon.

They were chatting about their previous experiences with just one Rod and talking about plans on how to use the second, to incorporate it into their fighting style.

After a while Scott took his unit back to the pods. They had to head home before it got too late. Everyone said their goodbyes and left. The boys were left in the gym talking to each other. Carl looked around the gym then grabbed the last suitcase. He walked over to Marshall and gave it to him. Marshall looked at him confused. The case had a silver letter on it. F.

"What is-" Marshall began.

"It's for Fred," Nick said.

Marshall took the case and looked at it. He nodded and tucked it under his arm. "Thanks. I got it."

"I'm very proud of you. All of you. You've come a long way. I know I've been ignoring my duties as a Bora. I promise you I will change that," Carl announced. They all nodded in agreement. "Okay, go home. I'll see you guys soon." Carl turned away. The boys did the same, heading towards the elevators.

Once back outside they began walking down the block together. Marshall turned to both of them smiling. "So I got some news!"

"We know, you somehow passed school," Nick said quickly.

"I've been meaning to ask how you did that," Peter said. Nick laughed.

"Nice!"

"Okay enough of the let's-jump-in-and-make-fun-of-Marshall time. I'm serious." Marshall wiped his forehead. The heat was finally building up in the city. It was already becoming hot and humid again. Just like when they had first met.

"All right, what is it?" Nick asked.

"Well...you know I'm dating Lucy right?"

"Yeah dude, I saw her at the dance."

"Right, she's amazing."

"Okay..." Nick said looking at him strangely.

"Well, we would, ya know, have fun when we were by

ourselves."

"If you are trying to tell us about your sex life I'm not really interested," Peter said looking away.

"First off, it would be very interesting, seeing as you don't even have one. But no, it's something else." Marshall looked away. He watched little kids playing hide and seek in a yard across the street.

"Dude, what is it?" Nick asked impatiently.

"Well, you'll be the first ones to know...I'm-" he held it back for a second. No one else knew. Only him and Lucy. He was now about to tell his best friends. His only true friends. "-going to be a father!" Then it was complete silence. No one spoke. Peter look at him in shock, Nick had his mouth wide open. Marshall looked at them, waiting, sweating, needing some kind of a response. He could feel his heart pounding and his stomach turning all at once. "Guys! I said I'm going to be a father!"

"Are you sure?"

"Did you take a test?"

"How do you know?"

"Why?"

The questions came in waves. Marshall put his hands up in a stop motion. "Wait! Listen! I just found out a couple of weeks ago. The baby is coming in November. It just happened. We didn't plan for it."

Nick was in total shock. Peter shook his head. "This isn't good. What about your Exterminator duties?" Peter asked.

"I'll still do them," Marshall answered.

"Do you even have the slightest clue on how to raise a kid?" Nick asked, skeptically.

"Lucy and I will figure it out!" Marshall responded.

"You don't even have a job," Peter pointed out.

"You're eighteen man. She's seventeen. You guys just started your life together," Nick added.

"I get it. We are stupid. We should have been more careful. It's too late now though. We are having this baby." The boys watched as Marshall defended himself. "I expected you guys to be a bit more happy for me or something. Maybe more supportive."

"It's not that," Peter began saying. He wasn't really sure how to finish it.

"It's that...we're worried. I think you'd be a great father. You're so young, though. It's not the most ideal time to have a kid either. With these crazy ass Summoners popping up." Nick put his hand on Marshall's shoulder. "But, you are my friend. I will be supportive one hundred percent. You can count on me to help you out the best I could. Not as a leader, but as a friend." He smiled at Marshall. Marshall nodded happily.

Peter walked next to Marshall. "I think it's a very dumb idea. However, it wasn't my idea so that's just my two cents. I will also try to help out in any way I can. Just note, I do not change diapers. I did that with my little sister. I will not do it again." Marshall laughed at Peter.

"Thank you. Both of you." They walked together for a while longer before going their separate ways.

Nick walked into his house. His father was bringing down a suitcase from upstairs. "Hey son!" he shouted as he stepped off the last step. Nick went over and grabbed the suitcase. It must have weighed over fifty pounds. For anyone else it'd be heavy but for Nick it was simply another bag to carry over his back. He placed it near the doorway and looked back at his father. He remembered a similar feeling of bringing these boxes in when he first moved into town, wondering how so much changed in such a short time period. It was almost scary to think that almost a whole year had already passed.

"Thanks," his father said wiping off sweat on his forehead.

"No problem, pops."

"Forgot how old I'm getting. Thing is a heavy bastard," his father chuckled.

Nick went into the kitchen and grabbed a drink. Taking a sip of it as he sat down. "So, we leave in two days?"

"Yep! Are you excited?"

"I am. It'll be nice to get away for a bit."

"Be nice to get away from work for a while. The damn guys are driving me crazy!" He laughed as he sat down next to his son. He placed his hand on his son's shoulder. "I'm really proud of you. You got used to the move quick. You passed school. You even met a wonderful lady. I'd say you adjusted pretty well here."

"I also hunt down monsters and kill them." Nick smiled at his own thoughts. "Yeah pops, it's been a crazy good year."

"Well let's have a relaxing time out there then, huh? Get away from all the stress. I know I sure as hell need it!"

"Yeah, me too!" Nick said cheerfully. He could use the vacation; to get away from all the stress and pain that happened this year.

"Start packing then. We leave in two days. I'm heading to work to finish up some paper work. I'll be back tonight."

"I'm probably going to spend the night at Kelly's house. Want to spend a little bit more time before saying goodbye."

"Even respectful of women. You sure are a great son." He smiled at Nick and rubbed his head. Nick pushed away his hand, laughing. "I'll see you tomorrow," his father said and he walked back up the stairs. Nick watched and then looked towards the window imagining how much his life had changed in only a couple of months. Wondering what else was in store for him.

Peter walked into his house. He could feel a different aura around the house as of late. It was less stressful due to no drunken father being around. His mom was in the kitchen cooking. "Hello honey!" she called loudly. "Dinner will be ready in an hour."

"Sounds good," he said smiling. He began walking to his room when he spotted his sister in the living room watching TV. "Whatcha doing?"

"Watching TV." She kept her eyes on the TV the entire time.

"You want to go to the park tomorrow?"

She turned away from the TV and to her brother.

"Umm...yes?"

"Are you asking me or telling me?" he asked laughing.

"I do!" she screamed in excitement.

He laughed. He wasn't really sure why he laughed but he did. He felt her excitement. A child's happiness just to hang out with her older brother? Perhaps it was the fact she was going to the park that made her that happy. He wasn't really sure but it made him happy as well. "Okay, we'll go tomorrow afternoon. Be ready or I leave you home."

"I'll be ready! Thanks, Pete!!!" she shouted really loud as she ran to tell their mom. He continued to his room and shut the door. He sat at his computer counter and began typing away on the computer unsure of what came over him, but resolving that he didn't want to live so enclosed anymore.

He grabbed his cell phone and went through his contacts. He only had around twelve. He only needed one though. The blue bar on the phone highlighted Rachael's name. He left his finger hovering above the send button for a moment, wondering what to actually do. *"I like her. Do I "like" her though? You respect her power. Yes. You also think she's pretty. Yes. Do you like her though? I believe I do. Do you like her enough to want to spend time with her? Yes. You want to train with her though. Well, yes. I also want to know her. Do you? Yes."* He fought with his mind for a while, trying to figure out the right answer. Then he heard a voice from his cell phone.

"Uhhh hello?"

He put his ear to the phone. "Hi!" he said louder then he wanted.

"Umm is this Peter?" she asked, unsure.

"This is I. Peter."

She giggled. "Hey! How's everything?"

"Good. I was wondering if you wanted to come to the park tomorrow? The one near my house? I'm taking my little sister."

"That sounds awesome!" she said happily.

He could feel his heart speed up a bit. "Really? I was hoping you'd say yes. I really want to get to know you."

"Awww that's very sweet." She wasn't mocking him, but even if she was he wouldn't have gotten it. He was excited that she had said yes.

"I don't want to come off weird," he told her quickly.

"You aren't weird. Not to me. I thought it was very sweet that you called me like this. Most boys would just text me or something. You did a very brave thing."

"Well, my friends tell me I'm pretty brave."

She giggled again. He wondered why she laughed so much. Was it because he was making a joke? Did she naturally like to giggle? He couldn't figure it out. Yet he liked when she did it. It made him smile every time she did.

"Well, come by around one. We'll be there."

"Okay, just text me the directions. I'll meet you there."

"Okay sounds good!"

"See you tomorrow, goodbye Pete!" she said cheerfully.

He smiled. "Goodbye Rachael, see you tomorrow!" After hanging up, he just sat there with a wide smile.

Marshall walked into a small playground to the side of the park. He watched as kids jumped off the top of the obstacles all the way near the monkey bars. He smiled, remembering when he used to do that as a little kid. The youngest kids playing in the sandbox in the middle of the playground were building huge sand castles, only for one of the boys to trample through it and destroy it. The mom's on the bench were chatting away the gossip of their lives. He smiled at it all, as it brought back so many memories.

He walked to the end of the park, ducking under a small tree, and looked at the small underground hut. It was an underground passage he and Fred had made years ago. He remembered they took weeks to build it, putting a little cardboard door on it. The rain and winds had since destroyed the door but the hole still remained. Once you crawled inside the hole it was like a mini cave. He smiled as he peered inside, wishing he was still small enough to fit in it.

375

He sat down outside of it instead and placed the case near the hole. "Hey, Fred. This is for you. I know you aren't here but if you were you'd want this. It's the second Rod. Man, we'd be such a badass team together right now." Marshall could feel his eyes getting watery.

"Is it weird I still sometimes wonder how life would have been without these Exterminator missions. Without the Rods? Without meeting Carl? I wonder where I'd be. I think, maybe you'd be alive. Then again if nothing changed, we'd never have been friends again. It was thanks to these missions we even became friends again..." He looked at the hole. "It's thanks to these missions you aren't here anymore though."

He leaned back and tilted his head to the sky, wondering just what would have happened. "Sometimes I sit wondering what if it was me who Riven took over instead. You would probably go to the ends of the earth to get me back, wouldn't you?" He could feel the tears forming now. "Yet I'm sitting here talking to a hole. What kind of friend em I?"

He closed his eyes as one of the tear drops fell down. He could feel the moisture of it on his face still. "I'm sorry I let you down man. I'm so sorry." He could feel a few more tears falling from his eyes.

After a few moments he wiped his face. "I can't be like that anymore though." He looked at the hole. "I gotta think positive. I cried enough. You wouldn't want me to be a little baby for the rest of my life would ya?" He laughed. "Plus I'm going to be a father. I know. You'd probably say I'm an idiot. It's crazy! Yet, I feel this sense of relief. Like everything is going to be okay. Ya know?"

The wind blew hard for just a moment. He could feel the air blowing through his shirt, wiping away the tears that were left on his face. He let it embrace him while feeling the nice heat from the sun rain down on him as the wind gave him a sense of peace. He loved it.

"I don't know if I believe in all that afterlife stuff. It's scary to think about what happens when we die. I should probably just follow the advice you told me. Stop thinking about when we die

and start thinking about the life we are living before getting there."
He smiled at the hole. "I'm thinking you were pretty much right.
Stop worrying and live a little. Right?" he chuckled.

He twisted around to place the case inside the hole,
pushing it in as deep as he could and then stood back up. He
smiled as he kicked some dirt in to block the holes opening.
"That's for you buddy. You would have been the best Exterminator
on our entire team." He wiped his watery eyes once more before
he turned away.

In front of him appeared a rock. On it was the address he
needed to get to by this evening. The sun was beginning to set so
it was already getting close to that time. He checked the address.
Once taking a mental note he smiled and grabbed his cell phone
placing a three way call.

"Hello?" both Peter and Nicked answered.

"Boys. We got a mission. Meet me in fifteen minutes at the
park." All three hung up, getting ready for another hunt against the
Unknowns.

Chapter 32 – Shadows

"Wes," the youngest of the two men whispered. Wes, a tall young man with brown eyes, turned around. He kept his hood on as they approached the apartment building. "You said four were up there, right?"

"Yes, James. For the fifth time we have estimated that there will be four targets. Our mission is to eliminate all four and gather the crystals. Just follow my lead." James nodded. He was bald, shaved it by himself, with blue eyes. He also had his hoodie up.

They both slipped into the apartment door and slowly made their way up the steps. They made sure not to make any sound as they slowly crept up the stairs. They could hear loud music on the second floor. They chose to ignore it as they traveled up the next flight of stairs. Upon approaching the third floor they stopped. "This is it," Wes said, pointing to the door.

James went ahead and put his hand to the door. He had his pressure glove on as he put his ear to the door to listen in. He only heard faint voices deep inside the apartment. "I hear a few voices but they aren't close. I'd assume it's safe in the front."

"You assume? Just use the ear modifier."

"I can't. I already made a pressure glove and a dagger. I don't want to use the third crystal yet. What about if we get into a fight?"

Wes pushed James lightly out of the way. "I mean really. How the hell are you even one of us?" Wes pulled a crystal from his pocket and held it tightly. It formed into an ear piece with blue and red lines going throughout. He put it on his ear and listened at the door for the voices. He could hear them perfectly now.

"I don't know why we gotta be here this late."

"It's to keep guard of the crystals. They said they'll come by in a few hours to pick 'em up."

"Yeah but why us? We can be doing important stuff."

"This is important."

One of the other men laughed. "This isn't important. It's babysitting. We are being treated like teenagers!"

The arguing continued. Wes pulled away from the door. "Four of them for sure. I could hear the breathing. They seem pretty stupid."

"Perfect. So Neil should take care of them if we mess up. No problems!" James said happily, almost too loud. Wes smacked him in the back of the head.

"You seriously are an idiot sometimes. Listen, we get in there and dispatch as many as we can. Only call for his assistance if we need too. I've had enough of having to rely on our leader."

"All right. Alright," James rubbed the back of his head. "No need to be violent."

"No, there's going to be violence," James grinned at that.

Wes grabbed another crystal out of his hoodie. He formed a dagger and held it in his left hand. He grabbed another crystal and formed a glove. He placed it on the door. After a few seconds of keeping it there the lock snapped off the front. He caught it and laid it on the floor. He then put his finger inside the door lock and held it there. After a moment it came lose and the door slowly opened.

"You ready?" Wes asked. James nodded and they entered the apartment.

Quickly, Wes made his way to the left, sneaking into the dark kitchen. James slid to the right, hugging his back to the wall. He slowly made his way towards the open bathroom door. While he did that, Wes walked through the kitchen. He was used to darkness, so he could see objects in the dark, and he easily made his way to the other side of it. He could hear chatter through the door. He held his ear close and listened. One of the people in the room was leaning on the door he was listening from. Two others were on the edge, near the window. The forth in the center of the room.

James went slowly into the bathroom and ducked under the

379

sink. He placed his hand on his ear and spoke softly. "Positions?"

Wes moved his face away from the door and responded in the same soft tone. "One on the door, one in the middle, two by the window."

"Mark one is yours. I'll get mark two. We both charge mark three and four?" James held his dagger tightly.

"It seems our best option. Keep mark three or four alive."

"Do I have too?"

"James..."

"All right, gee, joking." James looked outside the bathroom door. He could see a straight line into the living room where his target, mark two, was standing. He could see the feet of mark one but no one else. He needed not worry, he would charge in and strike mark two before he could even react.

"On my count. One. Two-" Wes put the long daggers tip on the door. Right where the man's back would be. Right above the stomach. He needed a clean slice. "Three!" He dug the dagger in. He heard a horrible "UGH!" and could feel the pressure of his dagger. The man was already falling to the ground. He quickly withdrew the dagger from the door.

James rushed in the second he heard the dagger entering the first target. He dashed into the room and mark two turned around just in time to receive a slash from the dagger at the neckline. It went in quickly and out just as fast. Before mark two could even raise his Rod he fell to the ground, blood spilling out of his throat.

Mark three and four formed swords and were already in defensive position before Wes broke through the door. Mark one's lifeless body falling to the side. Now stood mark three and four ready to fight James and Wes.

"Who the hell are you guys!?" mark three said. He was a young black man trying to hold the sword straight.

The other was an older lady. She kept her calm, sword held tightly in her hand. She pointed it at Wes. "You dare attack us? Do you know who we are?"

"Summoners?" James said playfully.

The two Summoners looked at each other, confused. "If you know wh-who we are. Why are you at-attacking us?" the younger Summoner stuttered.

"Well, 'cause we could for one," James said laughing. "For two, we need what you got."

"Who are you?!" the lady repeated, this time louder. She was about to strike at any moment.

Wes looked down at her belt, seeing three other Rods. "She's experienced. Be very careful of that one."

"You worry too much man. We got this." James whispered back. James gave a high pitched whistle. Neil, the third of the group, slammed through the window As he swooped in, he grabbed the older woman's head and smashed it into the ground. She cried out in pain as her nose broke instantly. The younger Summoner jumped to the side and backed into a wall. Wes grabbed the woman's head and quickly snapped it sideways. She laid there dead.

"See? No matter how experienced you are a sneak attack is gonna kill ya!" James said gleefully.

"We weren't supposed to call our master, remember?"

"Oh yeah...damn." James looked at Neil. "Sorry."

Neil stood up and looked at the two students, then back at the scared Summoner. "It's fine. The mission will still be accomplished. He's still alive. We can use him for information." He began walking towards the scared Summoner.

The Summoner fell to his knees and began to beg. "Please! I don't want to die! I don't know who you are but I'll give you anything. Just let me live!"

"What are the Summoners plans?" Wes asked.

"I don't know!" the Summoner screamed.

"Where is the Holder of Realms?" Neil asked.

"I don't know!" he yelled again.

"Oh this one is filled with tons of information," James sarcastically said.

"If you don't know anything we won't find you useful at all. We will dispose of you then. Is that what you want?" Neil asked, no emotion in his voice.

"No, no, no!" the Summoner cried. "All I know is that they are getting ready for something big. We gather the crystals to open something. A big something. I guess it's a realm. I dunno! I don't know anything! I swear! All I know is they want blood. The Holder of Realms wants blood. That's all I know, I swear!" He began to cry hysterically.

"I think he's telling the truth," James said.

Neil looked at the young Summoner. He lifted his head. The boy had red eyes, mucus coming out of his nose, tears were flowing down his cheeks. "Is that all you know?"

He nodded. "Yes...please Exterminator, sir. Do not kill me."

Neil looked at his two students. "Exterminators? Isn't that cute," James said.

Neil turned back to the Summoner. "We are no Exterminators. We are no Summoners. We are Shadows." Neil drove his dagger into the boys chin. He watched as the boy gasped for his last breath, blood forming in his mouth. After a moment more he pulled the dagger out. The boy dropped dead to the side of him. Neil stood up and pointed to the middle of the room. Four crystals were on the floor "Gather them and let's go. We got work to do."

The two students did as they were told. The four Summoners lay on the floor dead as the Shadows left silently.

Acknowledgment

Who do I even start with? I wanna thank Emily Suzzane Vinyard for the vast amount of time and effort she put into editing my work. Without her I honestly don't know if I would have even tried to publish it. She's been a big help (and the first to get to read the full novel) so a huge thanks to her! I want to thank the artist who has contributed to the work as well as the main cover artist Tavasai Kong. Now, my personal thanks go out to my family and friends for so much support. Nick and Crystin for having me, 'cause if they didn't I wouldn't be here giving you this book! Thank you, Aunt Cindy, for always forcing me to read more when I was younger. I doubt I'd come up with this story without the mass amount of books I've read. I'm so glad to have an amazing amount of support from family and friends. Thank you all. A special thanks to my love, Kelly Lyrn Simms. She's been nothing but supportive and I couldn't have asked for anything more. Anyone I missed, I'm sorry! I still love you! Thank you and I hope you enjoyed the book!

Exterminators: Shadows

The Exterminators Series continues in 2014! The Shadows are coming, while the true game is about to begin. Who will survive?

Make sure to follow on both Twitter and Facebooks for the newest updates!

Twitter –
www.twitter.com/exterminatorJ

Facebook -
https://www.facebook.com/ExterminatorsSeries

All characters are made up and used for purposes of the story in the Exterminators series. No one is allowed to use these characters unless given the rights to, which is owned by James DeSantis. The author.